# Morag

## By Roy Baldwin

*Creative Gateway*

Paperback Edition: ISBN: 978-1-908636-37-9
Also available in eBook

Typeset in Minion Pro Medium 11/14
Cover and Interior Design: Creative Gateway
Published in Great Britain by Creative Gateway
Norfolk, UK

# Acknowledgement

Morag emerged after following numerous reader requests to continue the Mauveine ghost story series, which I first wrote for the annual NaNoWriMo writing competition in 2013. NaNoWriMo is a fantastic opportunity for all writers, new and experienced, to create a fifty thousand word novel within a disciplined timeframe of the thirty days of November, supported and encouraged online by a vast community of other local and international writers. In its eighteenth year, NaNoWriMo anticipates at least half a million people again to join the largest writing event in the world, from across seven continents including Antarctica. Through its Young Writers Programme, NaNoWriMo also globally provides free resources and a curriculum to over eighty thousand students and educators in two thousand classrooms. In addition, a host of volunteers provide write-ins and events in five hundred regions, including my own in the UK city of Norwich. NaNoWriMo is an awesome writer movement which I am proud to support and encourage.

On this occasion, I decided that I wanted to embark on a new mystery with the cast of McKenzie family characters and the ghostly Mauveine. A riddle was left in the novel Prism of Purpurine, which Victoria McKenzie and her family hadn't resolved. Although the terror was over, what had happened to the family records in their Orsbrick Hall library between the late 1700s and 1860 and why had they all disappeared?

I quickly realised that this new adventure, taking the timeline back to the early nineteenth century when England was buzzing with incredible ferment and innovation in science and technology alongside massive social and economic change, would necessitate a large amount of reading of original texts. Effectively my NaNoWriMo period of November 2015 was therefore taken up by intensive research, and not a single quill hit the inkpot in that period. The challenge was daunting but one benefit, now realisable, of the scanning of hundreds of thousands of old books by Google, is to release an immense amount of original writings, biographies and novels of amazing writers from the nineteenth century, long forgotten and way out of copyright, into the hands of the online researcher in readable digital formats. This is not to decry the many benefits and pleasures of scouring original printed and handwritten text in the likes of the Bodleian or British Libraries. However, the job of the historic fiction writer is to create and weave exciting and realistic stories around past activity and is not the same as the academic historian who needs rigorous precision for their enumeration and interpretation of facts and events.

Morag, like predecessors Mauveine and Prism of Purpurine, once more defies simple categorisation. I would describe the novel as a mystery and suspense mashup of fantasy, history, science, art, romance and adventure. This time, the unravelling of another challenging McKenzie family secret takes our four main female protagonists, Victoria, her daughters Maddie and Belle and her best friend Abby onto a traumatic journey with others not of their time, where they are forced to question their ambition, lifestyle and morals, which are no longer guaranteed in their fight to ensure their existence remains intact.

This book has benefitted hugely from the inspiration and support of people who I would like to take this opportunity to thank profusely:

§: My family, friends and writer network for the ongoing encouragement and forgiveness when I was so immersed in nineteenth century historic research that I completely forgot about living in the twenty-first century and act like a normal human being.

§: Rowena Beighton-Dykes for her excellent knowledge of historic fashion and nineteenth century art and culture to inspire me in the right direction and ensure I know my bustle from my chemise.

§: And finally, Aliyah Marr, who through her uniquely talented and artistic creativity, always succeeds in being a personal source and inspiration for the necessary strength and innovation to see the wood for the trees.

So, dear reader … enjoy

Roy Baldwin, June 2016

# Chapter One

Early February 1841 - at Orsbrick Hall:

The heavy oak front door creaked open inch by inch and a bright and frosty morning revealed a harsh and unforgiving cold as two young women, dressed warmly in thick woollen coats, hats and scarves, emerged carrying a pair of wooden ice skates. A deep layer of hard snow still lay on the ground. It had been an exceptionally harsh winter exactly like the previous two. Such low temperatures had been unknown for a very long time, indeed not experienced since thirty years before in 1812, when the River Mersey froze over and they held amazing frost fairs up and down Liverpool. That was before either of them was born. They giggled, throwing snowballs playfully at one another, whilst waiting for their children. Twenty-five year old Morag McKenzie, mistress of Orsbrick Hall and her twenty-seven year old friend, Medora Leigh, were becoming impatient. Morag looked up at the forlorn expression of her nine-year-old daughter, her tiny face pressed miserably against the glass of the draughty window pane, desperately wishing she could stay behind in front of the roaring coal fire which had just been lit.

"Ellen, for goodness sake, will you come outside please," Morag shouted, waving her arms madly. "The fresh air will do you good—you've been cooped up reading for far too long in that nursery all week."

After half a minute, the door creaked open again and Marie, Medora's daughter, bounded out first, tall for her age at seven, laughing and shrieking with the sharp chill in her face, despite being well wrapped up in her hat and scarf. She ran headlong into the arms of her mother, who twirled her around in the air.

Medora turned to Morag. "Marie takes after my mother, always inquisitive and seeking fresh challenges. Mind you, the way I feel about my life right now, a Napoleonic revolution along the way would be somewhat welcome, don't you agree?"

Morag smiled. She understood only too well. Life for both of them had become hard. Her predicament as a wealthy widow was increasingly precarious with horrendous vultures and speculating predators constantly turning up at the door, brandishing threats, and occasionally weapons, all claiming to be owed various sums of money by her late husband. Fortunately her head butler, Nathaniel Williamson, had recently replaced the nauseating and creepy Ezekiel Rimmer, a serial leerer at all females under thirty, but long-time favourite servant of her deceased husband. Williamson was a burly and aggressive ex-veteran soldier of the Battle of Waterloo, a formidable decorated sergeant who had served right through the Peninsular campaign. The sight of him appearing at the door, armed with a pistol or holding a sabre, replete in his smart, starched uniform, was sufficient to scare off the most persistent and unsavoury chancers and callers. She turned a deaf ear to whatever he said to them, but fortuitously it had the desired effect; they certainly never returned. Recommended for employment personally by the Duke of Wellington himself, through her dear friend Lord Palmerston, there was no way she could turn down such an opportunity, especially when the chance to finally sack Rimmer, the first important task inside Orsbrick Hall she had personally undertaken, arose after the

2

death of her husband. Rimmer had reputedly returned to the canal boats where he should have stayed from the beginning with the rest of his despicable family and was now living with a prostitute in Wigan. She never did ascertain why Rimmer and his even ghastlier father, who lived and died as a recluse in the cellar, had such a persistent hold and influence on her husband and the running of Orsbrick Hall over all those years.

Ellen was now alongside her mother, somewhat cheered up by the promise that she would receive extra lessons in science and mathematics after lunch by her Aunt Ada, who wasn't her real aunt but she had to call her that. Her brother, twelve year old James, dressed in breeches and a brown cap, slowly sauntered over, carrying a bag with the children's skates inside. He was taking his time to hold everyone up and made a fuss of the family dog, Irish, a large wolfhound that bounded out to meet him from a kennel inside the barn.

Morag gazed at her son with deep concern. Surly and unruly, he had displayed a wayward streak since a baby, always wanting to contradict and fight anything she needed him to do. He had, however, been very close to his father who had spoilt and indulged him. It was evident from the moment it happened that James blamed her for his father's death two years before, overtly displaying alternating hate, disdain and arrogance. She was at her wit's end what to do with him. His grievances seemed unbridgeable.

"Mother, may I be permitted to ride with Smithson the groom this morning and exercise my horse?" he suddenly demanded, his squeaky voice already breaking, throwing the bag of skates on the ground. Medora picked it up carefully.

"No James you may not be permitted," Morag replied forcefully. Another battle of wills loomed but she was determined to win. "Our agreement this morning was for you to help Ellen and Marie to skate better, as we have the first opportunity with the pond freezing over fully. Now, can you get a move on please?"

He glowered before replying "Why can't you both teach your fu …" then suddenly he stopped. Medora had caught him with an equal stare of displeasure, quite amazed to hear a child answer back so. Such riposte was not done. His cunning mind quickly reassessed the dynamics of the situation that if he cooperated then he would be allowed out later instead.

"I'm sorry Mother," he grunted. "I had a bit of a stomach ache earlier but I think it's going now."

Ellen ran up and grabbed his hand, pulling him playfully down the slope in the direction of the large pond near the woods where they always messed about, summer and winter, and where James used to fish with his father on Sundays after church. "Come on Jamie, Marie and I will race you to the bridge." They ran off screaming and shrieking whilst Morag and Medora walked slowly behind.

"I just can't afford to stay here, but I'm so eternally grateful for the financial support you and Ada have provided," Medora said carefully, a tear rolling down her cheek. "I don't know what I would have done in France after those last two miscarriages, I was so desperately ill. But it breaks my heart, Morag. The convent was good to Marie and me. I want to return and enter orders, spend the rest of my life in piety and penance for the desperate hurt I've caused my family. I should do good, help the poor and serve God. I converted then, I'm a Catholic now. My sister, my mother, neither of them know I'm here, they must not know. Promise me."

Morag patted her hand. "Listen, I can tell you in confidence that Georgiana bears you no grudges, but she will never forgive her husband for seducing you. Maybe you should write to her whilst you are here?"

"I can't. I can never face her or our mother and the truth is I love that fool Henry Trevanion, and always will. I loved him ever since I was a teenager and we ran off together. Now all he does is spend his time in Brittany shooting and praying. How he survives I don't know. The trouble with aristocrats is we don't know how to work even when we have to, do we? I hope cousin Ada is feeling better today and perhaps she will rise from her bed later. Like me she has not fared well with all the childbirths … But you look so good, Morag. How are you coping?"

"I knocked on Ada's door before we left and Lucy had bathed and dressed her. She was very cheerful of spirit, eating breakfast at last and of course writing up complex mathematics and scribbling another long letter to send to that strange man, Charles Babbage."

Medora smiled … she felt suddenly cheered again. Ada's health was such a worry and that infernal obsession with Babbage and his calculating machines. "Do you think they're having an affair?"

Watching James demonstrate to the girls how to strap up their skate bottoms to their boots, they both smiled, but Morag refused to either confirm or deny the rumours swirling in parts of her London society network. "Well, he is a widower but is supposedly intensely, even malodorously pious. Goodness, sorry Medora, so are you. I didn't mean …"

Medora laughed. "Yes, but that doesn't always stop us does it? Look at me!"

They sat on a log and tied on their skates as the children chased each other around the pond, Ellen demonstrating amazing speed and poise for her tender age. Ellen could easily become a future ballerina, Morag thought, she was so graceful.

"So?"

"So what?" Morag replied coyly.

"How is *your* love life progressing? Managing this huge estate on your own must be hugely difficult and you're so beautiful, Morag," she whispered back mischievously. "You must have lots of suitors … and lovers too. Do I know any of them?"

Morag laughed. Medora was sounding her old self again. "I remember your partiality to juicy scandal, Medora, it runs in the family after your uncle, the dashing Lord Byron. Ada too is not averse to dabbling in some mischief making either, but I have to disappoint both of you and confess firmly. None is the true answer. I have neither the time nor the inclination. Actually, I do need a land manager, that's true; I'm way behind collecting the rents. In any case, I've decided to devote the rest of my life to science and discovery of the natural world and continue the legacy which Malcolm has left … I want him to look down and feel proud of me."

"I believe you, but thousands wouldn't … You and Ada are like peas in a pod," Medora replied with a smirk. "Let's walk onto that ice, I'm raring to go all of a sudden, but I do hope the ice is thick enough. I can't swim."

"Don't worry. Williamson tested the thickness first thing and my outside thermometer said minus seven degrees so it won't be melting just yet."

Soon, the two families were having fun and even James was cheery but studiously avoided contact with his mother, preferring instead to chase Aunt Medora under the bridge and into the smaller adjoining pond. Morag watched them both. James was growing up fast, already tall like his father and broad, thirteen in a month but it was evident to her, the way he was confidently showing off his charms to Medora and making her egg him on that he had inherited the same traits too, another McKenzie womaniser. She would be glad when he goes to the Bluecoats Boarding School in Liverpool next year. She had already agreed arrangements with Headmaster William Forster, without doubt a formidable educationalist who would engender some strict discipline and rigorous education into James's wayward mind. My God, she pondered, he was easily bright enough to attain Cambridge by merit alone if she could only change his stubborn attitude to both her and learning. Perhaps she did need a man, but it would have to be a learned man of science and he would have to be someone very special to replace her deep love for Malcolm. Her emotions remained raw and her reply to Medora was truthful.

"Mama, why are you sat down? I think Papa would have enjoyed skating today too … I do miss him."

Ellen sat down next to her on the log. Morag needed to catch her breath and think. She had felt some flashes of fancy and inspiration about her new indigo dye experiments she was conducting in her tiny laboratory, next door to her study, after something Ada had said first thing.

"Yes, I miss him too, chicken, every day," Morag replied, kissing her daughter on the cheek. Marie had shuddered to a halt on the ice in front of them.

"Ellen let's go and tease Jamie about Kate, then he'll try and chase us and we're much faster."

Ellen laughed. "Definitely, we're off again Mama …"

Morag looked up. "Who's Kate?"

Ellen puckered her lips, making a series of kissing noises, and then both girls flew off laughing, down towards the bridge.

Morag scowled as she remembered that Jake Edwards, the rough landlord of the George, had a fourteen year old daughter called Kate. At his age, James's behaviour was unacceptable given his position. But then she thought back in a flash. How old was she when she married Malcolm and gave birth to James?

Medora had returned and sat down beside her, exhausted. "I can see you've been reflecting on something bothering you, and I'm so used to Ada's foibles so I know it's not science. My dearest friend, I think you should share your troubles. Many will believe you can't possibly have any woes. You have wealth and financial security, two wonderful children, status, a beautiful house and a long life ahead of you. You're only twenty five with plenty of childbearing left. So what is it?"

"I don't want any more children. After Ellen, I lost two sets of twins, both just before term, five years ago. No more ... it's a miracle I'm alive, let alone in good health."

"I'm so sorry Morag, I had no idea ..."

"It was never broadcast, you were in France then and I kept indoors the whole time. My staff were discrete, although I'm sure folk in Burscough town suspected. But it's not that, I just need to talk ... of James and his father. Something about today has brought many memories back."

*

And so, whilst the children continued on the ice, Morag poured out her heart to Medora, who simply sat and listened, mesmerised. It was the first time Morag had confided her deepest personal thoughts and fears to anyone since Malcolm had died. And despite his affairs, she never stopped loving him.

She was only thirteen when she gave birth to James and then married. Marriage from the age of twelve had been legally possible by Act of Parliament since 1823, although heaven only knew how long that would last in the age of the prim and proper Queen Victoria. Admittedly she was old for her years, but quickly fell under the mesmeric spell of Lord Malcolm McKenzie, the forty-three year old bachelor and master of the vast Orsbrick estate, who it was well known had always encouraged a constant string of young, pretty girls to his home. But she was different from the others. Because like her friend Ada she had grown up, thanks to her devoted mother, with a thorough and tough education regime from the age of three, tutored rigorously in both the arts and the sciences. Showing a penchant for logical thought early, she had been taught by the famous mathematician Mary Somerville and astronomer Caroline Hershel, the latter such a tiny, strange woman but so warm, innovative and practical. Those two fiercely independent intellectual women provided her, when impressionable, with the most wonderful and timely role models for how she should lead her own life. Despite the immense changes in society, clever women still struggled to fight paternalism, have a voice and be formally educated. Being taken seriously as worthy scientists was being hindered by Queen Victoria's moralistic push for female-centred families to be at the heart of society, displacing the carefree attitude and laxity of the earlier part of the century amongst the upper classes. Without doubt, the death of Queen Victoria's Uncle William had finally ended the gaiety and sexual latitude of the joyful Regency era.

"My goodness," she lamented to Medora. "Do you realise King William IV had eleven illegitimate children but none who were actually legitimate, which is precisely why his dour, pious niece Victoria inherited the crown."

She continued to explain exactly why there had been such a strong and unique bond between her and Malcolm despite the huge age gap.

"Lord Malcolm McKenzie, like his forebears, had been Cambridge University educated, expected, as always, at Trinity College. By then he had become the head of a long established aristocratic family. The McKenzie's were first ennobled by Henry VIII as hereditary peers, the Earls of Burscough, until the progenitor earldom died out early in the eighteenth century, with the birth and survival of only daughters and no male succession to the then Lady Katherine McKenzie, who like me, became widowed from her husband, Lord Robert McKenzie and took over the Orsbrick estate in the same way. Malcolm McKenzie inherited Orsbrick Hall when he was only twenty and still at Cambridge after his father fell under the wheel of a crashing waste disposal cart in the middle of the night, departing from his aristocratic mistress's Camden town house in London. A sad state of affairs but it caused much cynical merriment in the society newspapers, as his body was buried under two tons of human shit and he actually drowned in it. Malcolm was a serious and studious man who suddenly inherited huge wealth and wherewithal to pursue his dreams. Euphoric and enthusiastic about the immense engineering and industrial changes taking place at the beginning of the century, he would devote himself to his childhood and Cambridge obsession. His life's work would be to replace men and horses by machines and seek to discover and invent new ways to change society and the pattern of work and manufacture using steam power. So he worked his way into the highest echelons of the Royal Society, making academic friends, collaborations and finding sponsors, including King George IV who ultimately made him a life peer for his engineering achievements. His greatest success came from his pioneering development on steam locomotives, designing and collaborating with Robert Stevenson to produce the Stevenson Rocket, which of course won the Rainhill Trials in 1829 and triggered the emergence of the Liverpool and Manchester Railway. Robert Stevenson, his lifelong friend, was a rival in that competition because Malcolm, by then, had designed his own steam locomotive but couldn't get the specific machinery engineered in time. The special alloys he formulated for the wheels and bearings in his new configuration couldn't be sourced in sufficient quantity. He always knew his locomotive would have beaten the Rocket but he took his friend's success in good grace and contemplated what to do next. But 1829 was a special year for a second reason. It was the year he met and married a beguiling thirteen-year-old girl, mature and clever way beyond her years, who fully understood the science and mathematics behind his engineering and with whom he could discuss technical problems for hour after hour. I persuaded him that he should put his research money into railways rather than textiles and manufacture his Galaxy Locomotive ... which he did but which, paradoxically, in the end killed him."

Morag stopped to draw breath and nibble at a giant apple from her basket; she really needed to get that back molar seen to. The Orsbrick cellar had a previous summer windfall of red costards, carefully stored since the autumn pickings. She continued slowly, her voice quiet and mournful as she revealed Malcolm's death.

"Whilst the story was reported and printed as a tragic accident at Manchester Piccadilly Station, the real truth of the matter was disturbingly different. Returning home from visiting one of his many mistresses, Malcolm ran headlong into the station and flung himself under the wheels of one of his own trains, dying like his father ... but why he would take his own life one could only speculate. No notes were left, no indicators apparent, he had left Orsbrick Hall brimming with enthusiasm about his next project. The incident remains an unsolved mystery forever."

Medora flung her comforting arms around her friend, realising that this moment of truth-telling had been a long time in the making. "Now I understand why you're so sad. No amount of wealth can ever make up for the loss of a soulmate. I never realised that you and Lord McKenzie had so very much in common."

"Yes, I helped him daily with his ideas and his business. He relied on me. We spent and enjoyed much time together. I turned a blind eye to his affairs.

"But why?"

"Because I knew he never visited prostitutes and he was extremely fastidious and risk averse about his health and mine. I accepted his long-established bachelor habit of visiting bored aristocratic young women, always of course virgins. He knew I would never leave him. Let us be honest dearest Medora, we women always have to compromise in our hearts and our heads. But now I'm a widow, that gaping hole in my heart has reopened. I have borne a wayward son who despises everything about me. Heaven help me when I have to tell the wretch that he will not inherit the title from his father."

Medora was contemplating many things, but decided she would say absolutely nothing. She indeed knew of Malcolm McKenzie's last mistress, the gorgeous Lady Lucinda Lowe, nineteen-year-old wife of the gout ridden Lord Lowe, Earl of Dukinfield, an ageing landowner, immensely rich from the industrial exploitation of coal and iron ore mining. Lucinda was a known, despicable and loose harlot, especially active with rich army officers. Sadly, the clandestine rumour, not long before he died, was that Lord McKenzie had fallen desperately in love with Lucinda and challenged one of her suitors to a duel

… perchance it was this and the catching of the pox which drove him to that final suicidal despair.

"I think your underlying problem is that young James is confused," Medora said, cautiously changing the subject. "Because he can't reconcile that his mother bore him when she was only a year older than he is now … I do confess he was trying to flirt with me on the pond. Obviously his adolescent desires are welling up, but who does he keep company with to know such tricks? James McKenzie seems to have learned a lot of sophisticated charm and guile already for one so young. And so he looks at you, the mere age of a sister, not his mother and tears himself into knots. He doesn't know how to handle or relate to you. Perhaps the discipline of science is the answer, something that permeates and binds you, him and the memory of his father into a non-threatening alliance."

Morag thought and smiled, "Mmm … very interesting, I hadn't thought of that possibility. Ada isn't the only one with logical thinking is she, Medora. I must confess that James does spend much time with the town blacksmith and his sons who live on my estate, a widower by the name of Fazackerley, who I suspect may not be the best influence on him. There is likely an understandable father-figure feeling for Mr Fazackerley within my son, especially at such a vulnerable age."

Morag giggled stupidly. The relief of some woman to woman confession of the soul at last made her much improved in spirit. "Actually you should meet him Medora … He has, so I am told, a certain and rather quaint masculine charm and an amazing knowledge of practical things and possesses an unusual attribute for one of artisan status. He seems to be well educated and can read and write beautifully … I think a man of secrets. Perhaps he is not all he appears."

13

"I can hear a little canary singing a warbling love song in his gilded cage. Your description of Mr Fazackerley has all the hallmarks of a hint of amicability, perchance by my good friend Lady McKenzie? Well? And you're blushing so admit all!"

Morag could feel her face damnably reddening. The so called handsome Mr Fazackerley had undoubtedly made her think of things she sorely missed in a man. But she would not be tempted further. An impermeable social divide as distant as the moon stood between her and any artisan blacksmith and that was that. Besides she hadn't even met him.

A sound of clumping through the snow provided a welcome diversion as they looked around. Esther, her chambermaid was approaching quickly, panting with exertion.

"Pardon my intrusion milady, but we have an unexpected visitor. Lady Annabella Byron is in the drawing room and requests the company of Miss Leigh urgently to join her and the Countess of Lovelace."

Medora grimaced and turned to Morag. "What on earth is my aunt doing here? Presumably she is on one of her health spa excursions, her latest obsession, but will never miss an opportunity to check up on Ada and instruct her on what to do, despite Ada being married with three children."

"Where are Ada's children?" Morag replied. "She never mentioned them and I didn't ask. She was so preoccupied on arrival and babbling on about Babbage's latest problem to solve before retiring to her room unwell."

Morag looked up at her maid impatiently and waved her on. "Thank you Esther. Please inform Lady Byron that her niece will be on her way back very shortly."

"Yes, milady. Shall I stay and supervise the children?"

"No, I'll continue with them and shall return later."

Medora started to untie her skating straps. "They're with Ada's husband down in their London townhouse. She's quite happy to be away from them for long periods and they are very young and burdensome, unlike mine and I presume yours."

"Yes, I understand. Anyway your aunt isn't all bad. I rather like her apart from the cloying religious zeal, which is, I presume, why Lord Byron eventually left England and never returned. Ada insists her mother is a mathematical genius which is where she inherited her talents from, although I've never seen any manifestation … a real shame that Lady Byron continues instead to be in constant dispute with your mother, Augusta. My goodness, I've just realised. How does Lady Byron know you're here, let alone in England?"

"I don't know which worries me. I sincerely hope that she hasn't told Mother … I'm quite at a loss to even guess what this is all about. Aunt Annabella is complicated to say the least and a law unto her, with the wealth and connections of course to do whatever she likes. Will you be alright with the children?"

"Yes of course, I'll see you later. Go on and face your summons! I assume she will want to stay for dinner too."

*

The unexpected sight of head butler, Williamson, at the front door, silent, arms folded and sporting a very serious expression, set off Morag's alarm bells. Standing outside in the cold and peering through the drawing room window, the unexpected shrieking and shouting, which they all heard from way back was enough of a shock. Quivering with fear, poor little Marie held tightly onto Morag's hand with Ellen hiding behind Morag's bulky coat. James of course, inherently bored with three women whipped into an unbecoming frenzy indoors and squabbling over whatever, gazed at the ground. Slouching against the wall, he brought up and spat out a great gob of

15

phlegm with a disgusting sound and idly kicked at a few stones. However his disquieting nonchalance was suddenly disrupted by a smashing of furniture and Morag's favourite Chinese vase, followed by a silver plate, hurled through the window, missing his head by inches.

He scowled and kicked it to one side. "What the fuck?" he muttered, "I'm off to the blacksmith and congenial company," and ran off in the direction of the distant worker cottages.

"Mama, where is Jamie going?" Ellen wailed, now as frightened as Marie.

"Never mind him, inside all of us," she yelled, with the girls tentatively following in tow, determined to sort this unseemly fracas out inside her own house. Immediately a whirlwind of billowing dresses flew past them as Medora, crying loudly ran off hysterically into the woods.

"Medora, what on earth is the matter?" Morag shouted, distressed to see her best friend so upset, when a second person stormed out of the room, grabbing her sable coat handed by a trembling maid-servant.

"I'm sorry, Lady McKenzie, for this disgraceful altercation," Lady Byron thundered. "My daughter will recompense you for the unfortunate damage caused … I bid you goodbye, I must be urgently elsewhere." Whereupon she flew through the front door, jumped into her luxurious four-horse coach and departed in a great cloud of mud and snow.

Esther the chambermaid surreptitiously led the girls off towards the nursery for a bun and a drink. Morag watched them ruefully and decided immediately. She must find a new governess without delay, someone talented who could educate both children thoroughly in the same way she had been tutored, and in particular prepare James intensively for imminent boarding school. The useless former male incumbent had been sacked some months before. She marched into the drawing room where Williamson and Lucy, the scullery maid, were clearing up the mess. Ada was huddled, her knees drawn up, pale and shaking, in one of the armchairs near the fire trying to get warm. A bitterly cold draught had started blowing through the room.

"I'll ask that blacksmith fellow to put a piece of wood over the hole and repair the glass as quickly as possible Lady McKenzie. May I suggest that perhaps you and the Countess retire to the comfort of your study? I've already lit a good fire and will make some strong coffee."

"An excellent suggestion Williamson, can you also please find Medora too. Here Ada, let me help you up," Morag replied smiling, grabbing a bottle of whisky. There was much less damage than she thought except for her crimson Ming vase on the carpet, broken in two, which did annoy her. Perhaps the blacksmith could repair it. But most importantly Ada wasn't hurt.

*

Sitting peacefully in her large, deep-blue velvet armchairs, nibbling slabs of fruit cake, Morag tipped more whisky into Ada's second large cup of dark coffee. The study fire crackled with a pleasing shower of sparks as the birch logs, which Williamson had piled on top, gradually caught fully alight. Ada had finally warmed up and was looking around the small but very cosy study with deep interest. Two impressively carved mahogany bookshelves, filled from floor to ceiling with a range of brown and red leather bound books, occupied the long back wall and the lovely off-white marble Adam fireplace was topped with a series of small Chinese figurines. The high ceiling had an unusual decoration of geometric circular shapes, intricately patterned in dark crème and green, like offset cogs on a machine and the rich-red striped Regency wallpaper was nicely set off with a series of paintings. Peering closely, Ada realised all of the pictures were of famous scientists and mathematicians, including a large portrait of Isaac Newton over the fireplace. On the other wall she spotted mathematicians Euler and Fourier and indicated towards the second bookshelf. "May I please, Morag?"

"Yes of course. I thought this room would cheer you up a bit. Now, just look on the third shelf near the end and tell me you are wildly jealous."

Ada laughed. "This cheery whisky is playing its part too. Oh my God, Morag, how can this be possible? You have an original, personally signed set of his five volumes … Mécanique Céleste. How on earth did you get hold of such a treasure?"

"They were given to Malcolm after an arduous personal correspondence on various problems he was trying to solve."

"And I bet you two guineas that I know what he was corresponding about. Well?"

"Okay, go on then clever clogs."

"It would have to be that amazing discovery of his, the Laplace transforms," Ada replied triumphantly. "Because of Malcolm's engineering predilections … ahh … Pierre Simon was such a genius and a lovely man. I'm working on the transforms now in relation to a particular set of difference equations, much better tools than Fourier, which I shall present to Charles shortly. He will be impressed I just know he will."

She sat down, contented at last and feeling so much better after the last three days of severe gastritis which had finally stopped.

"So Ada," Morag said, her eyes flashing. "As well as Monsieur Laplace being a lovely man of genius, would you not equally apply the same description to Mr Babbage?"

Ada looked up coyly and tipped further whisky into their coffees as Williamson brought in extra, freshly made. "I know your dubious tone of old Morag McKenzie, and I shall not give you the slightest pleasure of an answer, nor will I confirm nor deny anything whatsoever," she replied with a smile.

Morag laughed, her suspicions well satiated. It was time to change the subject. "So, are you ready now to tell me what that entire fracas was about?"

Ada frowned. "I'm so sorry, I must apologise deeply for the behaviour of my mother who is normally so devoutly calm and composed as of course is my ... err cousin. A bit of a family bombshell, well for Medora especially, who became hugely agitated, accusing my mother of gross deceit. I insist on paying for the breakages and repairs no matter what you say. I know your vase is irreplaceable but I have a similar coloured Ming at my Ockham Park residence and you shall have it forthwith."

"I'm going to ask Fazackerley if he can repair it ... he's a bit of a restoring genius with his hands."

"Fazackerley? I'm not acquainted with this man. Is he a famous London artisan?"

"No Ada, he's my local blacksmith and ..."

"Moreish *is*, I believe, what you were going to say, weren't you?" Ada replied with a coquettish wave of her hand.

Morag laughed. "Touché, my dearest Ada but I'm not confirming or denying either. Now where has Medora got to?"

A loud knock on the door was followed by Williamson, appearing concerned once more. "Milady, Butterworth the stableman and his lads have been searching high and low for Miss Leigh ... They fear she has likely run into the maze but none of them dare go inside without permission and it is becoming far too cold out there with no coat on."

"Thank you Williamson, Please bring me our coats plus a spare one. Lady Lovelace and I will go in and find her. I fear she needs some private comforting. Come Ada, some fresh air now will also be good for you."

"Yes, I agree—we should hurry. Can we take some hot coffee?" Ada replied concerned, as they put on their coats helped by her personal maid, Joanna.

"I shall just fetch you a small flask, Countess," Williamson replied, returning with a leather bottle and some cups in a wicker basket.

*

Outside, they hurried towards the maze whilst Ada expounded on her theories of solving maze problems using geometry and decision making.

Morag interjected. "Never mind the mathematics for once, I can tell you it's a Cretan Labyrinth, which I know off by heart. Wherever she is then we'll soon find her. But, I think you'd better tell me the gist of your family disagreement first."

Striding briskly through the snow, Ada sighed, her colour now returned to normal in the bracing cold. "It's simple actually … Medora is not my cousin, she's my half sister. Mother blurted the whole business out, in her usual detached, unemotional manner, almost gleefully I would add. Obviously Mother's been storing that juicy nugget up for a long time and this is all at the heart of the long-running dispute with my Aunt Augusta, Medora's mother."

Morag frowned for a moment before her quick brain worked out the implication. "My goodness, you mean her father is Lord Byron, her mother's brother and not Colonel Leigh? She's the result of an incestuous relationship? Gosh is this public knowledge, I had no idea?"

"Society rumours apparently have been doing the rounds for years, scurrilous whispering at dinner parties and so forth, and I had picked up some of this tittle-tattle but of course chose to ignore it with the appropriate disdain warranted. There was no direct evidence, but my mother, who has been obsessing and chasing about this for years, claims to have irrefutable proof and that she deemed it now right to ensure Medora and I know the truth first, before she makes some sort of public statement. Of course I was not surprised but have never said anything. You only have to look at the picture of my father and Medora, they look so alike and her unusual name features in one of his poems. Medora went into shock. She plainly had no idea and accused my mother of wanton and evil allegations ... hence the anger on both sides. I tried to intervene with some logic but ... well you saw the result. It really doesn't matter to me. I love Medora and have no problem with it. I believe we both need to reassure her. I think my mother actually feels sorry for her and will likely contribute to an allowance, and I certainly will. Medora will not go without again, believe me."

"I do Ada, you have a kind and sensible heart. Look there's the entrance. Follow me, she's probably ended up at the centre. We must reassure her, she'll be freezing in there."

"I don't need to follow you. I have a Cretan solution already, all worked out in my head!"

They giggled loudly and headed into the dense and thick dwarf box hedging. Soon they found the centre and sure enough, Medora was huddled on a small bench, still sobbing and shaking with the cold. Ada rushed up and wrapped the thick woollen coat around her sister, hugging her hard and stroking her long hair. Morag poured out a large cup of hot coffee which Medora gratefully took and gulped down noisily and then Morag, in turn, hugged her friend and handed her a handkerchief to wipe her eyes. Eventually Medora spoke.

"Thank you both so much. I tried to get out, got lost and ended up back here three times and gave up … deciding to freeze to death in despair."

Ada rubbed Medora's hands and found a spare pair of gloves in the basket. "Here, my dearest sister, I know it's been a terrible shock but you and I are now closer than ever before. And you have to admit, you do now have an amazing father, we both do, so it's not all bad news is it? And I will never, ever, let you come close to become starving and destitute again, I truly promise, wherever you are."

"Really Ada, you're not angry? Aunt Annabella was so forceful and negative; she made me feel like I was a freak. I honestly had no idea, I never did. I must have been living in some kind of make-believe bubble all that time in France."

Ada hugged her again. "You are a very beautiful, talented sister with a lovely daughter, who also has much of her true grandfather in her. Just look at those eyes of Marie. So we'll hear no more about the issue. It's a fact, I'm afraid, my mother has a growing array of peculiar eccentricities, which I have to indulge to keep my sanity prevailing. Apart from the continuing and tedious religious piety, she never wanted me to know about my father either, the negativity drummed into me from a tiny child. She even forbade me to see his picture until I was twenty-one when the heavy cloth over his portrait in the dining room was ceremoniously removed for the first time. We have a genius father both of us can be proud of dearest Medora, and I am sure he loved us deeply all of his short life, as his poems attest, including your name of course."

Morag sat up close and also hugged Medora. "And you will forever be my best friend, no matter what. We will remain as three female musketeers, bound to each other with our shared secrets and will pledge to uphold the virtues of science and mathematics until we die."

They laughed and giggled. Medora was already coming to terms with her new found ancestry. Morag indicated it was time to return as they had a wonderful dinner being prepared which would include all the children. But walking back, Morag quietly reflected on her own family secret, which thus far she had shared with nobody, not even Medora ... that she too was born out of wedlock. Her father was a famous English scientist and her mother had actually been an aristocratic friend of Lord Byron, a musician and writer herself and one of George IV's many mistresses. So it had been little wonder that she too always had a gift and thirst for science since being a small child.

## Chapter Two

**Morning of Christmas Eve, Ormskirk, Lancashire 2025:**

Standing defiantly on its metal stands, the long, dirty hulk of the narrow boat had become a sorry state. The once gaily painted sides were now rotted, covered in ivy-strewn moss and brown sludge. Remnants of grass, weeds and nettles stealthily rose over the sides. Waking from a deep sleep and weird dreams, Maddie quickly showered and pulled on her skinny jeans and a woolly jumper. From her tiny attic window of the Red Lion, she stared out, rubbing her eyes and trying to imagine the boat when it stood proud in its berthing bay on the canal behind. Her father's forebears had once alighted there for food and drink after a hard day pulling coal from Wigan, the shire horses finally rested to graze on bales of hay thrown over the tow path, swathes of steam pouring from their mouths. She pondered over the large painted lettering, J.C. Fazackerley, still visible in dull yellow on the side of the front cabin. The soot-covered metal funnel poked mischievously out of the middle, one sign of a former life huddled from the cold, one hundred and fifty years previously. Three or more generations had lived on those boats although where they fitted only heaven above knew; there was certainly no privacy, young or old, male or female. Many babies were unceremoniously born year after year to illiterate itinerants inside those tiny living areas. Boat people died the same way, unglamorous and old before their time, or they ended blind drunk and drowned in the cold, dirty water, plying their daily hard trade as goods hauliers from Leeds to the once thriving port of Liverpool. Maddie had seen old sepia photos of this particular boat in its heyday, three young men stood on deck amongst a clutter of working implements, dressed in sturdy overalls, braces and caps, one holding the tiller, now vanished, whilst all looked forlornly at the camera as a fourth played a fiddle sombrely in a top hat. Where were the wives and daughters? Such a bygone hard life.

Her father and Lynton had discovered this amazing boat find, lying in the water beside a decrepit barn near Parbold, following a tip-off from an old man drinking in the George pub one night. They had discovered the place where local repairs had been done many years ago and traced the ownership to her father's Fazackerley family, who for generations before and after were boat people to a man and woman, with one exception, the only man who broke away, defied convention and became a stable manager. He bought a house in Burscough and was ultimately shunned and violently ostracised henceforth by the rest of his family. That was Isaac Fazackerley, who eventually married Mauveine McKenzie of Orsbrick Hall in the 1860s, her great, great aunt.

With Lynton's help, her father had begun renovating the boat back to its full glory but neither had sufficient time to make much progress. The boat was rotting quicker than they were restoring. It was such a shame for this rare family heritage to disintegrate into mouldy compost, and, of course, neither of her twin brothers, Ned or Zac were the slightest bit interested in helping out, despite their constant loud protestations that they loved doing practical things. In Ned's case he preferred the inside of the Red Lion rather than the outside, preferably with a sneaky beer glass in his hand and other arm wrapped around girl friend Nancy. Brother Zac usually shut out the rest of the world unless it contained a computer chip, his girl friend Dottie being the only exception to prove the rule. Maddie decided with the help of her twin sister Belle she would persuade her father to bring in boat conservation experts and stop deluding himself that he had the time and energy to do what he used to do thirty years ago before his writing career took off. Julian certainly had the money to buy help, and the local vicar's father ran a club of historic canal boat enthusiasts who would happily set to work on the task if they got paid. Maddie sighed warily. She still hadn't told her mother despite promising herself last night she would. Finding a form of words for her predicament was proving difficult.

A loud rat-a-tat on the door instantly shook Maddie out of her dreamy reverie of Victorian boat people. The handle slowly turned.

"Hey, sis what on earth are you doing staring into space? We're all waiting downstairs, time for the final fitting. Do you realise the time is eight-thirty? You really don't look part of this world today," Belle shouted gleefully, rushing in. She grabbed Maddie by the arm, pulling her gaze reluctantly away from the window.

"This was Dad's room apparently when he and Mum first met," Maddie exclaimed, "and they stayed here with Abby and Lynton who had just bought the pub. He actually started his first blockbuster novel right at that desk, tapping a keyboard into the dead of night." She pointed to an old antique Victorian desk fronting the other window. "Well, so Abby said. Mum used to sleep in the room below listening to him writing away."

"Really? Gosh, I never knew that," Belle exclaimed, her mouth widening to a broad smile. "You mean they never actually slept together when they first dated?"

Maddie grinned. "Shush, don't say that in front of Mum, you know how straight-laced and guarded she gets, especially about her past and Dad. Has Judy arrived yet?"

"Yes, downstairs, trying to prise herself into her wedding dress and working up into a state as usual. Anyway, Abby's gone to Southport to chase up the lost wedding cake and you're the chief bridesmaid so you'll have to sort her out."

Maddie enjoyed being in charge and this day was likely to be a huge challenge, but at least her relationship with Judy had significantly improved since the Orsbrick priory experience. Or should she describe it as a 'happening'? "I'll just find my list," she said. "I spent last night in bed carefully writing out a project plan exactly as Mum had suggested and a speech in case the best man doesn't turn up."

Belle grimaced. "Who is the best man actually? I couldn't work it out this morning from Judy's ramblings ... sounds like someone she once worked with."

"It took me ages to get the gist as she's been so secretive, but eventually Abby gave me a quiet warning the other day. Despite all the years that Abby has taken special care of Judy whenever she was in danger of going off the rails, it took even her some time to work this one out. Quentin was a close friend of Jarvis who Judy's marrying. That's how they met apparently, but last year Quentin went all transgender and had a sex change operation, so Quentin is now Korrin but still insisted that she would be best man—all of it an added complication. On top of that, but keep this strictly between us, not a mention to Ned and Zac and especially not Mum, but Abby is certain that Quentin is actually Caroline's father. They really do look alike, same eyes and nose."

Belle laughed loudly. "Gosh, typical Judy. Korrin is a strange name. I hope your project management skills are good. You might need me as the backup if everything gets out of hand!"

"No problem, contingencies are in place, I've learned a lot from Abby she is so amazingly organised with her life. Anyway, I can always rely on Ned who is dying to practise his boxing skills and thump anyone who gets stroppy—hopefully, it's not Lynton though!"

"Have you met him, the bridegroom I mean? Jarvis Cockle?" Belle asked curious. "Talk about a sudden romance and marriage proposal. I've only seen his picture in the local newspaper but I suppose as Mayor of Southport, Judy is going to have to get used to being in the limelight for a change. He looks very young for a widower with five daughters."

"Only the other day for the first time," Maddie replied quietly. "Abby introduced me when we went to the town hall. He has a chain of health nutrition shops and is very well off. And before you ask, I can see your face a mile off, a mutual love of local history over the summer and Judy's archiving skills is what brought them together, two lonely souls in the night, and sparked off an unexpected romance. His wife died in a car accident two years ago, all very tragic. Actually, he seems a really nice guy, a littler younger than her, very good looking and his daughters who were all with him are gorgeous."

"Mmm ... fascinating. Mind you, it's time Judy found some genuine happiness after those dark years locked inside her own head. He's quite besotted with her so I hear and she's great with his children and they'll have a huge Edwardian town house on the Southport seafront to move into with Caroline and Toby. They're having a live-in nanny to look after the seven kids, now she's just got that mega-job running cultural services in Liverpool."

"I tell you, Judy's welcome to all those children, I would never want that. Come on let's go and find her. I'm looking forward to wearing my new dress, I reckon it must have cost a fortune. Dad insisted on paying for all the dresses so Mum confided."

"Yeah, me too," Belle replied, as they clattered down the wooden stairs towards Abby's sitting room.

*

Inside Starling's cafeteria a much-needed calm and quiet pervaded as Abby, supping a hot cappuccino looked out across the road towards the shoreline. A few windsurfers were taking advantage of the stiff breeze to fly briskly over the frothing waves of the Irish Sea. She was desperate for a breather in her favourite coffee shop after an altercation in the baker's over the missing wedding cake. Thank goodness the manager walked in and sorted out the mess ... and a special baking would be done and delivered late afternoon at the Red Lion for when they returned from the church. Abby had been quite willing to make the cake herself, but whenever Judy had her mind fixated on anything there was no budging her, and the more cajoling, the more her obsessive focus would deepen. Fortunately, Abby knew from many years of painful experience what to expect from her step-daughter especially when stressed, and today would be another of those days without any doubt. Although remarkably, since the shock announcement of her engagement at the last Orsbrick Hall family dinner evening, Judy had transformed into near normality, despite Abby scraping Lynton off the wall as neither of them had any idea she was in a relationship never mind planning to get married. Without a doubt the prospective and desirable son-in-law, Jarvis Cockle major of Southport, had done a power of good already.

Abby looked at her watch as she needed to get back to Orsbrick Hall, where new outfits for her and Victoria were waiting to be put on.

"I'll have one of those only a large one please."

Abby jumped, startled. The sight of Victoria grinning broadly loomed out of the dark interior of the cafe. "Gosh Vikki, what are you doing here? I thought you were with Julian doing a last minute check of the church arrangements?"

"I did," Victoria replied, briskly plonking herself into the plush red seat as Abby waved over the waitress. "At least we went as far as inside the nave with Barbara, the temporary vicar. I must admit I really like the look of her, very forthright and organised. Shame, that the one and only ex-Reverend Welly decided to finally do his long desired hippy trail through Kurdistan and pack in preaching just when we needed him. I miss him actually."

"Yes, me too, he never did officiate another fun double wedding like ours did he?" Abby replied grinning as they broke into a giggle reflecting back to 2010 when she married Lynton and Victoria married Julian together on Christmas Day and half the town turned up, followed by a wonderful foursome honeymoon in the Caribbean.

"So what happened?" Abby queried.

"Lynton phoned Julian in a huge panic as his wedding suit doesn't fit properly. So they've hot-footed it straight down to Liverpool and a special tailor, Jacob Abramovic in Rodney Street that Julian regularly uses, has promised to do an instant alteration. Also, the flowers in the church didn't look the way I wanted them. You know how fussy I am, a legacy I'm sure of living all those years in Holland. So, knowing you were coming here to sort out the baker, I decided to sort out the florist. The manager is personally driving the correct order over now. Their apprentice had got in a muddle with the colour scheme. I knew you would end up in here. By the look of that red face, just had a blazing row have we?"

"Yes, bad even for me," Abby replied still annoyed. "I became somewhat over-assertive and came close to thumping the idiot over the counter. What is it these days about getting a decent personal service from high street shops? I'm sure it's because they've become so used to dealing with online purchases that the few face-to-face customers actually coming in through the door now faze them out. Not like the old days, chuck is it."

"I more than most know too well that your over-assertiveness is never for the fainthearted," Victoria teased, supping her hot drink. "Mmm ... this cappuccino is very nice, hot for a change. Now I know why this is your favourite resting hole in Southport. It's a funny thing though isn't it, that any arrangements involving Judy always have a high probability of becoming seriously complicated for some unfathomable reason. Although I think between you, me and Maddie, we should have the lot sorted for today."

"Hope so. Equally, you can guarantee Lynton will be getting in a state by leaving things to the last minute. I told him endless times last week to check his suit fitting. He seems to believe he has the same lithe figure of twenty years ago and that middle-aged spread is a figment of my imagination to be brushed aside as usual, not worthy of his attention. He's already stressed out simply with the concept of Judy marrying, with added fuel to the flames having to give her away in church and make a speech at the reception. I'll be glad when robots do all these jobs for us. Hey, how about a robot vicar? That could be fun especially if they sing like Welly."

"Now you know how I feel about robots and artificial intelligence," Victoria replied brusquely, quickly moving into her usual scientific thought mode. "They'll never replace humans, despite all the technological hype and over-expectancy circulating for years, and certainly not in our lifetime for anything highly cognitive other than repetitive tasks."

Abby laughed. "Hey, once Maddie gets her teeth into the topic, she'll be changing the world … especially yours."

But instantly she caught a flash of Victoria's bemused expression, realised and moved on immediately. "Before we forget, whilst you're here, let's go and take a peek into that new shoe shop over the road. I think we should arrive later in full preening glory don't you? I'll just pay the bill," she said, waving at the waitress.

But Victoria had gone deathly quiet, immersed in that internal reflective and analytical thought process which Abby dreaded as it always led to an inquisition.

"Out with it Abby, I've known you far too long. I've never minded the way Maddie always confides in you these days being her favourite aunt, it's good and has helped her enormously to mature, but you know something I don't and I suspect I should do. I'm right aren't I? Why should Maddie get her teeth into robotics? Her heart is set on biophysics at Cambridge or, at least, I thought it was."

"Shit, Vikki."

"Well?"

Abby drew breath. She needed a moment to gather her thoughts, once again putting her foot in it. Maddie had assured her she would quietly tell her mother a few days ago about winning a competitive scholarship to Harvard to study biomathematics and artificial intelligence. But where should she begin, including the tricky issue of Janine, her close friend over there? Maybe Janine should be the starting point.

"Okay, as you are now plainly aware I've spoken out of place and will be breaking a confidence with Maddie, which I hope you're going to respect, but I honestly thought you knew by now. One tiny, innocent sentence and you home in like a giant microscope. Don't you ever have a spell of brain death like the rest of us and miss things?"

"Obviously not, so what's going on? Yet more secrets? Start from the beginning, logical and linear just the way I like it."

Abby laughed. The rational, scientific Victoria of old never mellows with age, so she ordered another two cappuccinos. "Maddie has a special friend, the daughter of a senator in the US. She's nineteen and they converse daily and have done for the last eighteen months. Last October, Janine encouraged Maddie to enter an international competition at Harvard to solve an artificial intelligence problem, something to do with aliens and asteroids, don't ask me the details. There was a prize for winners. A generous scholarship to start one of their most prestigious degree courses in biomathematics and robotics this January. Janine is on the course, she's prodigiously clever, a former scholarship winner and lives in Boston. There were three winners and Maddie got top marks. I'm sure the only reason she's not told you is that the course start has been delayed until May and she's been frightened you'll be very anti the whole thing—she is desperate to go. It's time for her to fly her wings."

Victoria stared ahead quietly, shaken by the revelation but remaining passive and unemotional; that was her way of dealing with the news whilst she quickly rationalised the consequences. "I'll be the arbiter of wing-flying. I'm her mother and this is a family decision," she uttered in a firm, deep voice. "And just like I always suspected, she's a fucking lesbian too."

Abby felt her hackles rise and her face redden, the anger was building up instantaneously. "I'm not taking this stupid shit from you, Vikki," she hissed. "You owe Maddie much more than that crass response. Have you conveniently forgotten another former sixteen-year old's burning science ambitions, her unannounced escape from home with her own special friend … going, as I recall, by the name of Eva who she fell deeply in love with and her first genuine emotional connection with another person?"

Victoria remained silent and impassive as she thought of Eva, her chemistry teacher, and holding her close when she died in her arms of a brain tumour after so much suffering, alone at home. A kaleidoscope of warm, vital and fun images flashed sequentially across her mind and their first, gloriously happy ten years together in Amsterdam before they parted, going their own ways. And then she found Julian and fell in love with him. A tear rolled down her cheek. Filled with remorse, she looked directly into Abby's eyes. "I'm so sorry, it was totally wrong of me to react like that."

Victoria's brain was already digesting the entire Maddie scenario. She always made fast decisions in her life. "You know, Eva was the only person I ever felt was cleverer than me at chemistry. She was always one step ahead with a solution to a problem or an angle I hadn't thought about, even when I did my Ph.D. at Leiden University. In those early days, we were totally compatible in every way, academically and emotionally. She was the best thing that could have happened to me when I ran away from home."

"And, you never stayed a lesbian, but so what anyway. Sexuality is a fluid thing for many people in their lives."

"Not for you, though, Abby, you've always been dead straight, albeit displaying a strange taste in men sometimes!"

They laughed, each instinctively knowing the tension had been deflated. They had been best friends for far too long to fall out and certainly not on Judy's wedding day of all days.

"Actually, you don't know everything about me, Vikki," Abby replied coyly, having a quick reminiscence of her own Liverpool art college period which was also very fluid in those days. And she did go to a girls' boarding school.

Victoria looked up startled. But those dark secrets could be teased out another time, preferably after a number of Abby's favourite Singapore Slings. "I've already decided," she whispered slowly, forking enthusiastically at the chocolate cake. "I'm not angry at all. In fact the opportunity is fantastic for Maddie and she will get my full support. I'm very proud of her achievement although I will insist she takes her Cambridge entry exams in February. She should still have a credible backup, just in case."

Victoria took a long sip of coffee before continuing. "And it's good she will have a friend and mentor there already, just like I did in Holland. Maddie is so like me at that age, self-sufficient, mature and organised. I've not given her the same attention as the others like I should have done, she never seemed to need it, well it's now time to change all that. I'm assuming that this was the news she was going to tell everyone at dinner last month, before Judy upset the apple cart by suddenly announcing she was engaged to an Egyptologist mayor with five kids ... I shall never forget Lynton's face."

Abby smiled. "Me, neither. I'm glad you understand what Maddie wants to do. I could never have believed you wouldn't anyway and I did promise her that, she knows it's a big step but

35

I believe she's ready for it … I think you should let me tell Maddie first that I've accidentally let the cat out of the bag."

"I agree," Victoria replied, "And I want to tell Julian now, so I'm going into the yard quickly and ring him—you can do the same with Maddie," immediately heading to the door.

Abby pulled out a twenty-pound note and placed it onto the bill dish. Coffee was so expensive. They simply were not growing organic quickly enough to meet demand, especially as the genetically modified version remained unpopular. She dialled Maddie and the call was answered immediately. "Hey, how's it going in there? Is Judy behaving with her new dress?"

"Hi, Abby," Maddie replied, pleased to hear a voice of sanity. "Belle and I are just going to get her sorted out properly and then we put our bridesmaid outfits on. Her dress has arrived but she's fussing again with Caroline and Toby insisting on making them lunch herself and sorting out their toys. Don't worry, everything will be fine, I promise, for when Lynton and Dad pick her up."

"Good, I have every confidence in you. Now, quickly, I must apologise. Your mother is here in the café. Inadvertently, I let slip a tiny nugget about your Harvard course. I assumed Vikki knew but you know what she's like with the whiff of a conspiracy. I got the third degree to confess all. I'm sorry, but she's fine with everything, very pleased and supportive. She's just talking to Julian outside. Do you want to speak to her?"

"Gosh … I should be the one apologising, Abby. I know I said I would tell her last night but it slipped somehow with everything going on …"

"Hang on," Abby replied. "I'm just passing my phone to your mother."

Victoria grinned. "Maddie, congratulations, such fantastic news, I'm so pleased for you. Don't worry, I understand why you were reticent and I've just spoken to your father who is over the moon and already insisting that he will buy you an apartment on the river as he loves Harvard, and with a spare bedroom so we can visit."

"Oh Mum, thanks, I'm so relieved and excited. It's been hanging over me for ages never finding the right moment or words to tell you … but I did tell Belle and the boys. They are all cool about it. Now I can get on with sorting Judy out. We'll see you later then."

"I reckon Abby has done us all a favour today. No more secrets, so we can relax and enjoy the day too. Okay, see you in church." She handed back the phone to Abby who stuffed it into her bag. "We'd better get going."

Abby was relieved but still felt a deep twinge of inner guilt. There were other secrets as yet unrevealed; very difficult secrets which she again shared with Maddie. How was she ever going to tell Vikki about the near prism of purpurine catastrophe at the former Orsbrick priory, the final dissolution of the lingering Rimmer curse on the McKenzie family, the warping once more of psychic space-time and McKenzie history and the hideous wolves of Hades? And even worse, that she is part of the family? She and Vikki were related. The artistic Warren's and the scientific McKenzie's were all one intermixed clan since the 1660s.

Abby sighed. "I suppose I'd better bite the bullet. I don't have much of an excuse now do I … I'm assuming your driverless BMW is sitting outside? I've left my Mercedes at the gallery."

"Of course, feel the fear Abby you'll love it and these cars are so much safer. You know how much I enjoy being at the vanguard of technology. It's a privilege being selected as one of the trial on-road volunteers, Julian actually knows the CEO who is a great fan of his novels. Who would have thought five years ago that Apple would have bought BMW, merged and jointly created this amazing ..."

"Robotic vehicle is I think what you meant to say?" Abby purred with a coquettish flourish.

"Okay, know-it-all," Victoria replied, pulling a mild grimace. "Point taken," waving her Blackberry phone over the bill and stuffing Abby's note back into her pocket. "Coffee's on me. Anyway, we can relax in comfort and catch up with some belated gossip on the way back to Orsbrick, and I must tell you about my newest dye discovery. Mauveine will be extra-pleased as I've finally completed the work of her last collaboration with her father before he became disabled with a stroke, written as a student paper in 1866. It was very challenging to guess where she was taking her thoughts, which had been a half-finished experiment but chemically absolutely correct, an amazing and innovative discovery before it's time. Xanthene, the first azo dye, heralding the great flurry thereafter of exotic colours. Come and meet son of Beast ... he's a jet black SUV too."

"Xanthene? That one passed me by, even during my textile Ph.D. Who on earth dreams up these strange names? Okay, deep breath, take me to Beast two. I'll try and stay calm. Is there a steering wheel I can grab?"

*

Chaos with kids running around everywhere was building up fast inside the Red Lion as Maddie fought to take charge. As usual Judy remained at the wrong time in another world.

"Listen, Judy, you can let Alicia take over their lunches now," Maddie wailed in calm despair as Belle herded off Judy's children, Caroline and Toby, to another room to try on their outfits. "Now, are you going to introduce me to Jarvis's daughters first before I get you into your dress and paraphernalia?"

Judy looked up and finally realised that she was going over the top, stopped and took a deep breath. "I'm so sorry Maddie, I just didn't realise. Everything going on continuously makes me a bit panicky." She put her hand gently and proudly on the tallest girl, all of them petite with long, brown hair, and reeled off the five names. "First we have Debbie, ten, then Peggy, nine, Maggie, eight, next is Gillian, seven and finally last but not least Angie."

"Who, I assume by the arithmetic progression is six?"

"Of course," Judy replied frowning, puzzled that it could conceivably be anything else.

Alicia, Abby's front of house manager for the Red Lion, immediately took the girls into the dining room as Maddie gently led Judy upstairs towards the main bedroom which Abby had turned into a bridal boudoir. Entering, they both drew breath at the finished white dress carefully placed over a life-sized dummy in the middle of the room.

Judy uncharacteristically threw her hands up in the air, squealed and ran straight to it, carefully feeling over the intricate skirt lace brocade and veil. Maddie stood open-mouthed. The wedding dress was a beautiful creation which Abby had personally designed and supervised, following Judy's exact historic wishes. Abby was so amazingly skilled with textiles. Maddie wished she had one percent of those skills and capabilities, being useless with a needle and thread.

"This is the first time I've seen my dress after the basic fitting and measurements. I couldn't have asked for more, Abby has been a wonderful stepmother to me, Maddie. Without her ongoing care and attention, they would have locked me up ages ago. I love my father, but I owe Abby everything. Do you know how that feels?"

Maddie nodded quietly. She also felt the same about Abby and was still so elated that her very distant forbear and Abby's forbear had been half-sisters all those four hundred years before. But she had to keep Judy on-track, who was now excitedly undressing, completely unembarrassed, which was much more than Maddie felt. She didn't know where to look but eventually glanced shyly at Judy's lithe, and very attractive naked figure, as she picked up the new silk, matching underclothes which Abby had left on the chair.

"When Victoria and Abby got married," Judy continued, "it was a splendid, sunny Christmas Day and they both looked so beautiful, your mother in Mauveine's original 1860's wedding dress and Abby in Lydia's, Mauveine's arty sister. It was then I decided that if I ever got married I would go back a little further in time, right to the start of the period I always enjoyed most when I studied history at Oxford, the time of the young Queen Victoria. Abby has modelled the dress on an exact copy of Queen Victoria's when she and Prince Albert married, even down to the Honiton lace which Abby commissioned and had specially made by a lace craft group in Nottingham. Oh gosh, Abby's even had the wreath done the same in orange blossom and myrtle. White was rare in those days because the dye was so expensive and Queen Victoria set a fashion trend in both colour and lace, admittedly machine made later on in the nineteenth century."

By then Judy had already slipped on a low neck chemise and stepped into the knee-length, baggy drawers with lace decoration and picked up a corset which she was attempting to put on. "Can you lace this up at the back please Maddie? My goodness, these drawers are strange. Designed for the easy use of a discrete chamberpot, hopefully I won't be given one any time soon," Judy continued, breezily picking up two additional petticoats. "Not bad for sex too, don't you reckon? Dress raised and a quick fuck behind the door before anyone realises."

Maddie laughed, tightening up the corset until Judy let out a cry, before she loosened it off. "Overtight corsets were bad for the liver so they reckoned. I'm sure you won't find Abby handing out chamber pots today! You're so slim Judy you wouldn't have needed one of these corsets. Abby warned me that she was fashioning your dress Victorian style but refused to mention specifics, so I pulled out my old history books and checked quickly for the whole era. I think I'm pretty au-fait now with what ladies of wealth and fashion wore then including Mauveine. Those petticoats really do look like horsehair crinoline ... you need to put them on next to keep the dress in place, let me help you. Crikey it's nearly noon, we need to get a move on. Dad and Lynton will be here to pick you up soon and I have to get into my bridesmaid dress yet with Belle. With a bit of luck, she and Alicia will have dressed up the children by now," hearing shrieks of laughter from downstairs.

Finally buttoning up the dress, Maddie stood back in admiration and watched Judy loosen and brush out her light brown hair from her usual ponytail. "You look gorgeous Judy, absolutely perfect for your wedding day."

"When are you and Abby going to tell everyone what happened? Can you put my makeup on please? I've never been very good with mascara."

Maddie stared back, unsure but uneasy. "Sorry, tell them what? Yeh sure, I'll just grab that bag. Do you want pale green eyeliner and a little of the pink lipstick?"

"I found an interesting document whilst you guys were busy fighting the wolves, cleverly hidden inside a hollow book in the

Orsbrick library archives, never been seen since being deposited in 1697. Robert McKenzie had a second younger sister, Rosemary McKenzie, born in the priory to an unknown female and tended in secret by the monks. As a teenager, she fled to Liverpool and ended up sailing to America with an Irish captain and living in Salem. It appears she was a clever and feisty troublemaker, upset a large number of people, especially the Puritans and was accused as a witch in 1693 to be brought to trial. But pregnant she daringly escaped with an Indian slave girl, Mohita. It was assumed she lived out her days with the Wampanoag Indians but Robert McKenzie never knew what happened to her and neither did Lady Katherine Warren who of course he did eventually marry when she returned from America. Abby has quite a blue blood connection to the McKenzie family."

Maddie stopped. "You know all this? I mean you've worked it out? How? I don't understand Judy."

"Listen, Maddie, I'm an experienced historian and archivist. Making the connections and drawing the conclusions were easy once I read all the letters too. I'm also confident that Rosemary's mother was likely to have been Zelda and was fathered by Cameron McKenzie, Robert's father, before the whole priory episode blew up. There may be something left in the psychic miasma which hasn't been fully tied up."

"Zelda? You know about Zelda? You know what went on at the priory?"

"Of course, I was there, why shouldn't I know? You and I joined psychic forces remember at the end, so everything you and Abby saw and remember throughout, so do I. Although I wasn't physically present, I was actually locked up in the library in Orsbrick frantically searching for clues and weaving my knowledge of ancient mysticism into a solution, whilst

Victoria, from her hospital bed, battled her way into the space-time with Mauveine's help to counter the Wolves of Hades with their only nemesis, the ghostly wolfhounds. Zelda was by then a manifest, looking like me but powerless … only Rimmer had the real evil power which you finally overcame Maddie. You were incredible. I have the same psychic gifts as you but your capabilities are far greater than anyone else's, even Abby's. You are the lead carrier of the McKenzie gift on to the next generation."

Maddie was entirely lost for words as she quietly pencilled in the final touches of mascara. Her mind was racing. Judy was so erratic, simplistic and unpredictable and could quite easily blurt all this out in an unguarded moment and cause havoc.

"Oh, something else," Judy continued. "Whilst I was digging through the archives, something struck me as very odd. Between the end of the 1700s and around 1860 there is nothing about the McKenzie family. No papers, books, memorabilia, letters, it's as if a period of history had been deliberately destroyed by someone. It may of course be mislaid elsewhere but I did search hard."

Maddie felt immediate concern. She desperately needed to talk to Abby and her head was pounding away again. But Judy held her hand gently and smiled. Abby stared, this was so out of character, Judy never did touching. But immediately her head cleared and she felt free and light, somehow liberated from worry. At least ten seconds or more passed as reassurance filled her brain. Nothing needed saying.

Judy finally spoke in a whisper. "The mystery is that Victoria still knows nothing, despite her obvious psychic capabilities. I think that's because her time is yet to come. Goodness, what's that noise? The children must be racing up the stairs."

The door burst open and six little girls, including seven-year old Caroline, made up and dressed in light-blue, flowing long dresses ran in shrieking with excitement. Belle was behind, looking terrific in her tailored matching bridesmaid outfit, her hair up and her new contact lenses in. Alicia followed carrying a grinning two-year-old Toby with his striped trousers and jacket, looking a real, tiny Lord Fauntleroy complete with a miniature top hat. Thank goodness he was walking properly.

"Maddie, how are you doing?" Belle cried anxiously and then drew breath uttering a hearty wow, gazing at Judy who blushed, looking so uncharacteristically stunning it almost defied belief. "Lynton is outside with Dad and a couple of horse-drawn nineteenth century broughams for everyone. We're certainly going to the church in style today. Where on earth Dad found those carriages I can only remotely guess. They're ready and waiting, so I told them to go to the bar, find Ned and Zac and all have a quick beer."

"We'll only be one minute, finishing touches now—okay I reckon you're done, Judy."

"Mommy, you look really very nice," Caroline whispered and hugged her mother gently, as the other five girls nodded and they all clustered around Judy, chattering loudly to one another with Toby, red in the face, trying hard to push his way between their legs.

"I'll help you with your dress next door Maddie," Belle cried above the noise, both sidling quickly out of the door as Alicia went back downstairs to tell the waiting males everyone would be ready in fifteen minutes, knowing they would be happy, in their smart top hats, morning suits and tails to down another bottle of pale ale.

\*

Clip-clopping steadily into the driveway, the six horses and three brightly painted, red and yellow broughams with huge wheels drew up gently outside the church door. A large crowd was already gathered outside as Judy and Lynton alighted first to a roaring cheer, her long wedding train, which she was having difficulty managing, swishing to and fro. They were followed by the bridesmaids with Maddie leading. It was evident from the hard worked, red faces of Lynton's colleagues acting as ushers that the church was already full with a number of well-wishers standing at the back. Word had circulated around the community there would be another lavish McKenzie period wedding, the first since the double wedding seventeen years previously. Suddenly Victoria and Abby emerged smiling from the entrance in long bell dresses, bunched out with crinolines and gorgeous matching hats, like Mauveine's guests would have worn in the 1860s, which Abby had also specially designed and made herself.

Abby ran forward and carefully hugged and reassured Judy, who she sensed was becoming flustered and overwhelmed. Judy turned back to Maddie, took a deep breath, smiled and mouthed a large thank you. Gathering her husband and sons, Victoria hurried inside to their seats at the front as Abby took Toby's hand to lead him scampering into the church behind.

She turned to Lynton, taking him to one side as Maddie and Belle arranged the girls in rows, taking one piece of Judy's train each and whispered, "When I said I'd marry you, it was on one condition, remember? I must say, you look impeccably smart for a change."

"Thanks. You know Abby, I genuinely feel good today. It's time Judy flew the nest. Yes, love you and love all your psychic foibles, if I recall correctly. And I still do, darling." He pecked her approvingly on the cheek.

"Lynton, Judy is thirty-eight. She flew the nest a long time ago!" Abby replied, smirking. "Sometimes you can be so facile. Listen … you haven't met the best man yet have you?"

"No, only heard a few days ago. Quentin isn't it? … Actor chap, long time friend of Jarvis. Hey, he has turned up hasn't he with the ring?" Lynton replied, his brow furrowing.

"Yes, except … well he isn't Quentin anymore, he's now Korrin and she's turned up in a dress of course and standing next to Jarvis who is even more nervous than you. I had her period dress made along with ours. She's very tall … so don't turn peculiar when you walk in and go mad. Daughter's foibles today, Judy insisted."

"Fuck me. She certainly has plenty … oops, apologies God." He tipped his hat towards the church steeple making Abby laugh. "But Judy looks so stunning today, even Korrin is forgiven. I promise not to look perplexed. We old dogs of the bucolic punk eighties you know are not quite as staid as we look … even Julian."

"Who has always been far more broadminded than you, lest we old timers forget? Off you go. Mendelssohn's Wedding March has just started."

Abby dashed in as Judy and her entourage of bridesmaids waited for Lynton to sidle over and kiss his daughter proudly on the cheek. She linked his arm and smiled. "This is the most special day I've ever had in my life … Thank you so much for all your understanding, Dad, time to give me away please."

*

Outside, as the crowds cheered and groups of well-wishers gathered around, the McKenzie and Warren families took turns for the myriad of photographs. The local press suddenly turned up, adding to the crush, and requested a few interviews which Abby and Victoria happily provided. Maddie, keen to try the new camera complete with tripod her father had bought her on his last US trip, struggled to marshall everyone together in a fabulous group setting of Victorian period dress. Patiently, she fiddled with the various settings until she could take a series of panoramic shots in three dimensions. The brougham horses, breathing copious steam in the chilling air, were ready again to take everyone back to the Red Lion for the reception and cake cutting. Two old double-decker London buses suddenly turned up, as Lynton announced to the crowds that everyone who had come were also welcome to the reception. There would be plenty of free food and drink laid on in the pub.

As a surge of congregation guests ran to scramble onto the buses, Maddie, gazing at her newly processed photos on her phone, squealed with delight and grabbed Abby's arm.

"Just look, there near the back, standing next to Ned. Who do you see has sneaked in at the end?"

"Oh my goodness," Abby cried. "I can't believe it … Is it really Mauveine and Isi? Don't they look happy and of course fit in perfectly with the all the Victorian fashion and dress."

"They're only on this photo—no others and nobody else's either, I checked," Maddie replied, making sure nobody around was watching. "I'll show these quietly to the family when everyone has gone. But I never actually saw them when I took the picture, did you?"

"No … nor in the church, which surprised me," Abby whispered, puzzled for a moment, wondering whether all was okay. "But they appear contented and certainly wanted us to know they are still around."

"Let's talk later," Maddie replied. "There's something I need to tell you once Judy sets off on her honeymoon. She and Jarvis are going off with all seven children and a Hungarian nanny on the trans-Siberian railway for two weeks. Did you know?"

Abby smiled. She had no idea, another well-kept secret. But she immediately realised that Judy and Maddie had been sharing confidences earlier. They definitely needed to talk, sooner rather than later. Victoria had also said something out of the blue, which was rather disturbing.

# Chapter Three

January 3rd 2026: Special occasion at Orsbrick Hall

Did those giant prawns have a malevolent look or was the McKenzie mood music subtly changing? A pan of chopped and lightly sautéed cod, smoked haddock and a pike caught from the canal, plus secret herbs from her over-thumbed recipe, were mixed together in a giant porcelain bowl. The mashed potato with leeks and other vegetables from her well tended patch at the rear of the pub were added and the final mix placed carefully into two massive cooking dishes. Enough fish pie for twenty people and she had already made an additional dish, if required, now in the freezer.

Let loose in Victoria's magnificent kitchen, Abby was diligently preparing a special meal from her early nineteenth-century Orsbrick recipe book, one of the few handwritten ledgers of that period which she had salvaged from Victoria's library when they rummaged for anything interesting. Personal favourites, put together towards the end of a long tenure by the then head cook, a Mrs Margaret Copperfield, had been developed for the ancestral McKenzie household. Abby had decided that celebrating Maddie and Belle's seventeenth birthday with a genuine family concoction for dinner would be appropriate. She stared at the dates of the entries. The ledger had commenced life in 1815 with an unusual walnut and fruit cake, decorated by a military theme to celebrate the Battle of Waterloo. From the notes, someone by the name of Hamish in the family had fought there and come back at least alive, but by the end of the thick book, complex and innovative main meals had been laid out in meticulous detail. Abby wondered what happened after the last entry in 1839, a spiced venison pie, made from local deer on the Orsbrick estate. She presumed Mrs Copperfield had sadly passed on and another cook taken over. It was a pity she couldn't have detailed conversations with the ghostly Mauveine who appeared only in times of crisis or change. But sadly, as Victoria had ruminated, the physics whatever it was of the space-time division between their different periods simply wouldn't allow it.

The earlier nineteenth century would have been the time of Mauveine's grandparents, maybe even of her father, but so little was known of what happened then at Orsbrick Hall. Abby pondered over the huge gap in the McKenzie records between the late 1790s and 1860. All they knew was the McKenzie family must have significantly grown their wealth in that period from the developing industrial revolution, the activities of which influenced the coal distillation and dye manufacturing factory built by her father which Mauveine herself pioneered. Abby decided that once Judy returned from honeymoon, then she, Maddie and Victoria, using Judy's expertise, would crack this last mystery once and for all.

But the changing mood music still preoccupied her. Too many puzzles remained. She was feeling inwardly depressed about keeping so much from Victoria and was beginning to question whether this really was the best way forward. But now one less secret remained. Victoria had reacted well to Maddie winning a place to study at Harvard and insisted this would be discussed with all the family during the evening. For Abby that was a positive start. She decided the next secret, her concealed heritage, should also go at the same time. No longer would she harbour this knowledge alone having hidden the letters. She would come clean, with Maddie backing her, about the evidence they both found which proved that the aristocratic Warrens were an integral part of the early McKenzie family ancestry, or should they now say the McKenzie-Warren dynasty. This was potential dynamite and her emotions were on fire but the time had come. She had to finally take the plunge and the risk, and rely on Victoria's innate logical and scientific thought processes to accept the inescapable conclusion.

A loud male voice disturbed her train of thought as she was about to put the fish pies in the oven. "Hey Abby how's it all going … wow that food smells good, I just love anything with garlic, well maybe not cornflakes."

Ned walked breezily into the kitchen and headed as usual for the fridge, but immediately his face dropped with the internal contents, or lack of them.

"The smell's not garlic Ned, it's leek," Abby replied, shutting the oven door carefully and setting the timer. "I'm afraid you won't find anything you're looking for in there … Lynton and your father finished the last lot on New Year's Eve."

"Garlic, leeks, all the same to real men. I like my food strong and spicy … like me." He grinned, sticking out his formidable chest, toned from the constant gym and weights he was doing, and gave her another of his cheeky up and down leers, reserved specially for his favourite super-cool aunt … well not really aunt but who was bothered. "I'd better go out and get some bottles from the off-licence. Don't tell Dad will you Abby, he's gone into another ape-shit phase again with me drinking, especially after Judy's wedding."

Abby happily ignored his flirting and laughed loudly. "You were a bit pissed. Aren't you supposed to be eighteen anyway to buy beer?"

"I'm sixteen next month. Me and bro Zac are getting real oldies. Actually Abby, Ade got us all some fake age ID cards printed up by his brother. They're brilliant if anyone does ask, but they never do, Jesus … you definitely won't tell Dad will you?"

"No," she said laughing, handing him a fifty pound note. "Can you get a couple of bottles of Martini, some lemonade and a bottle of lime for Maddie, Belle and me. Your sisters like a little tipple too, especially on their birthday."

"Crikey, I had no idea they were into cocktails and sophisticated stuff … but my sisters are always dark horses. Okay, I'll just get Zac and the dogs, all of them need some exercise especially my little brother."

"So you were the first one out then?"

"Of course. That's why I'm the leader and one inch taller and he always follows, engrained since birth."

Abby laughed again, "Go on, get out of here," she cried, shoving him through the door as Maddie walked up the path.

"Where's he off to looking guilty? The pub, I bet," Maddie chuntered, throwing her bag onto a chair.

"Almost … the off-licence, but he will be bringing back us ladies some suitable refreshment for before and after dinner. Maddie? Whilst you're here?" Abby continued quietly and shut the kitchen door. "Vikki is going to talk over dinner about her time in Holland, properly I think, to the whole family … her idea, not mine. Somehow, your departure to Harvard has prompted her to want to be more open with everyone and let go of some of the old demons. It's taken long enough."

"That's good actually," Maddie said smiling, "although Belle and I probably know more than she realises ... but we won't let on. But that's not all is it, I can tell by your expression. So?"

"I've decided that tonight is a good moment for me to come clean too, about our Lady Bella and Lady Katherine discovery. Will you back me up?" Abby whispered anxiously.

"Yes, of course. It's about time that was out in the open once and for all, one less secretive notch off the bedpost ... not that I have any notches ... yet! And you can then be inducted as one of the family. A done deal, sister," Maddie replied, picking up her bag again. "Like I said before, Dad and Lynton will think the news is fantastic, Ned and Zac will merely grunt, but I feel confident that Mum will be pleased and dead chuffed, as they say around here. Anyway, I'd better get changed. What time will dinner be ready?"

"Around seven. I just need to make a quick starter, my special minestrone soup, I think, that everyone loves with some garlic mushrooms on ciabatta. Now where's that pan?"

Rustling around the utensils, Abby heard the kitchen door behind her open and Maddie depart, as she was handed a copper pan from behind. Lynton had come in. About time wherever he had been all afternoon, hopefully carrying that John Ruskin painting she had desperately wanted him to bid for at the auction. But then she saw the black glove and slender hand holding the handle and turned around slowly, stumbling back with the unexpected surprise.

"Mauveine?" she whispered, snatching the pan quickly, her eyes wide as she watched the door gradually creak shut by itself and the bolt move across. Mauveine was alone, no Isi in sight, and was standing all in black, wearing a long dress, coat, boots and a matching bonnet, like she had just been to a funeral. Her expression displayed a severe look, like the typical Victorian photograph where a long wait to capture the image removed any ability of the subjects to smile. Abby felt an immediate unease.

"Is Isi not with you today?" Abby said in a hushed voice, desperately hoping nobody would try and come in.

Mauveine shook her head, and then spoke in her deep Lancashire accent but with a lilt of an echo, the words slightly tremulous as she struggled to produce the sounds. "I have not got long Abby, but I must insist. You must not tell about the Orsbrick Priory, ever, even though your step-daughter Judy has admitted recollection."

"But Mauveine, I thought you said Maddie and I must tell the others in due course? What has happened? Is something wrong?"

But Mauveine didn't or couldn't answer. She simply stood there immobile and stern, staring back at Abby, a tear trickling down her cheek. Abby wanted to hug Mauveine but knew it was pointless and was about to reassure her completely when the row of utensils behind came into view, as Mauveine gradually grew fainter and disappeared completely.

Abby ran to the door and quietly slid the bolt back expecting to have to open the windows and purge the usual awful smell of aniline or whatever it was left behind, but only a faint and pleasant smell of perfume lingered, like the infused scent of roses.

Abby made up her mind quickly. She should keep this to herself but it made sense to at least confide in Maddie. Once the soup was simmering nicely and some spring rolls were placed in the oven, she went quietly upstairs with two Martini and limes, surveyed the bedroom doors and saw Maddie sitting cross-legged on her bed, hunched over a new virtual reality tablet, her birthday present from her parents. She was wearing a pair of special tinted goggles that made her appear like she was ready for a welding session.

"Maddie," Abby whispered sharply but then realised she couldn't hear and tapped her on the leg.

Maddie's goggles turned green and she took them off, smiling. "Abby, you made me jump, is dinner ready? Mmm... that drink looks nice and timely, yes please."

"In fifteen minutes, I've only got a second. I've just seen Mauveine."

"Me too. She came into my VR screen a few minutes ago when I was trying to create a red and rocky Martian landscape to walk around on. To be honest the scene looked quite incongruous. Ghosts on planets? And she didn't look happy, dressed in some dour black outfit, although I suppose that was fairly normal then. But then she disappeared, nothing. I was just trying to recreate her."

"Mmm ... she spoke," Abby replied.

"Spoke?" Maddie took a deep gulp of her drink. "I think I'm going to need this."

"All she said was that nobody must be told about the priory happening and indicated that Judy knowing didn't matter, and that was it ... then disappeared. Same outfit too as if she had been to a funeral and she looked very sad. Something isn't right ... I wish I knew what. But I suggest we keep this between ourselves. Let's not spoil your birthdays today, especially as I've made a great meal!"

Maddie smiled. "I agree. Whatever it is, we can only wait, but I don't psychically feel anything is amiss. Do you? Judy worries me the most. I still don't understand exactly how much she's aware of. And we both know her thought processes are not always logical or straightforward. We'll have to try and talk to her the moment she's back. I hope she doesn't say anything to Jarvis or the kids."

"No, Judy won't, I'm sure of that but she is a worry. I don't feel anything amiss either, but Mauveine was alone, no Isi to be seen and that bothers me."

Abby threw back a large swig of her Martini then laughed. "Better top this up and get the meal out. I can hear a hungry horde mooching about the dining room and Vikki is probably checking the kitchen to see all is in methodical order ... as if I would upset her meticulously arranged utensils, set out like her laboratory. I shall go and prise those lazy males down there away from the television football to lay the table. See you and Belle shortly."

*

Further helpings of Abby's delicious treacle sponge pudding were being quickly devoured and the chatter grew louder. Julian was generously topping up Lynton's glass from another bottle of a gorgeously exquisite three year Dessimis Pinot Grigio, a case of which had been specially imported direct from the Vie de Romans estate in the north east corner of Italy. Nancy and Dottie were conversing happily about the latest midi-dress craze, sharing their favourite brands with Belle, whose boyfriend Ade was busy in the kitchen preparing a cheese board for the final course. Ned, Zac and best friend Ade had become the star turns at the beginning of the evening, when they first emerged from the kitchen carrying Abby's carefully prepared starters, all dressed in full Victorian servant regalia, with Ned and Ade wearing topical moustaches whilst Zac sported a full beard. Much laughter had peeled around the house as Jeb and Kai, their two wolfhounds, joined in the fun with deafening, deep barks.

A loud ringing of Victoria's spoon against an empty wine bottle drew the chatter and clatter immediately to a halt and the boys returned from the kitchen.

"Now everyone, can I have your attention. Having finally told you all about how I became a research chemist by running away from home to Holland, and the enormous debt I owe to my sadly departed friend and fellow scientist, Eva, I would like to announce my latest surprise discovery. The background research for this owes much to a hand of influence closer to home. Eva taught me how to think, act and become disciplined as a scientist, but being truly innovative in your field requires something more than knowledge and an enquiring mind, vital though those requirements are. This is what distinguishes the genius from the rest of us."

The room had gone completely silent as everyone focussed on Victoria, outwardly very relaxed, her body language overtly displaying a rare enjoyment of after-dinner speech making, something she did infrequently because Julian or Lynton always took centre-stage at events. Julian was bemused watching her for the first time in an expressive mode he was unfamiliar with. Abby was pleased that after a very long time Victoria seemed to be finally coming out of that hardened, unbreakable shell around her, and Maddie and Belle sensed something far deeper about their mother than they had appreciated before. Ned quietly disappeared and returned with a large flagon of best French champagne, whilst Zac and Ade placed glasses for everyone.

"Sounds to me like a toast and celebration will be forthcoming from Lady Victoria McKenzie, well as good as and should be. Dad is this bottle okay?"

"Absolutely Ned," Julian replied, beaming. "Reserved for a very special occasion and today warrants that completely. Go for it when your mother's finished."

Victoria reached for a small wooden box on the Georgian sideboard behind. She opened the box and pulled out two large test rubes, one containing a bright yellow liquid and the other a peculiar greenish-yellow counterpart, which fluoresced vividly as she held it up to the spotlights. Lumpy brown, orange and red flecks swirled and twisted into strange, amorphous shapes, like coloured clouds in a strong wind.

"A while ago, I was emptying a few old drawers at the back of the cellar laboratory. One had been jammed up and never opened but after a struggle and some judicious application of one of Julian's wrecking bars, I managed to prise it free. To my surprise, I found a collection of Mauveine's earliest papers, dated 1864, when she was only just fifteen, describing a number of new theories and experiments she had performed on coal tar derivatives, whilst searching for new artificial dyes. Already at that tender age, she had decided that dyes would have the potential to make her father and her, and the McKenzie family, very rich. Unfortunately, parts of her papers had rotted over time, but I stitched together all I could and then endeavoured to follow what she had done. I can't tell you how difficult replicating scientific processes of that period can be, but painstakingly, over months, which is why I was buried down there all day long, apologies for the hermit like behaviour, I worked her methodologies through … and these two beauties are the result. Belle, do you recognise anything about the second one?"

Belle had already gone through her usual deep thought process, some recent biology recall was sufficient. "It looks like fluorescein stain used to search for foreign bodies in the eye?"

"Hey, I get that," Ned cried, "like in the hospital after I had that punch up with … sorry, I'd better shut up," as Zac nudged him hard. Not a good idea to bring that incident up when Nancy was there, especially as their parents had no idea. Abby smiled, she knew of course.

"Correct, Belle, well done. This is a crude precursor to the modern fluorescein reagent which was initially discovered by a famous German chemist called Bayer in 1872. And in my other hand is the base of emanation, the stunning yellow xanthene dye itself. Except both of these were actually made eight years previously, by an unknown female dye chemist in some obscure laboratory which nobody had heard of called Orsbrick Hall. This, everyone, was Mauveine's chemistry genius. Her most original and far-reaching discovery, using unique and daring methods of oxidation and distillation, not used or understood again until after World War One. Sadly the papers were never published and the commercialisation she planned realised, but the impact remains huge to this day for the dye, paint and drugs sectors, which effectively still use her method. So I would like to propose a toast to my great-great aunt, Mauveine. She had something I certainly haven't got … true genius."

Everyone clapped and shouted. "Right on Mum. Mauveine was definitely cool, even though I'm the only one who hasn't seen her!" Ned cried, unwinding the cork.

Suddenly Abby stood up and raised her hand. "Just hang onto that cork one second, Ned. There's something I want to say as well."

Lynton took her arm playfully. "Darling, I can avert that celebration statement. Yes, I did buy a genuine Ruskin engraving today in a junk shop for a song … now let's get that champagne drunk."

Abby glared and shook off his hand. Sometimes Lynton was always way ahead at missing the point. "No. And this is for your ears too … Victoria, may I?"

Victoria, now seated, looked at the earnest and nervous face of her best friend and knew immediately that whatever Abby wanted to say, it must be significant, especially when she received her full title. She smiled. Abby never could hide secrets for long, even when they shared her luxury flat in Rotterdam in the carefree days of kebabs and men. "Of course, the floor is yours," she said, smirking.

Abby glanced at Maddie to her left. Victoria stared at both intensely, remaining very curious as to what would be revealed. Belle was equally bewildered, realising that her sister was privy to something special nobody else shared. Quickly, Abby outlined the identity and the contents of the explosive seventeenth century library letters she and Maddie had found, which proved that Abby was a descendent of Lady Katherine Warren, James McKenzie's second wife and half-sister of his first wife, Lady Bella. Both women had been illegitimate but well-loved offspring of King Charles the Second. Maddie then took over and went on to explain her own research which finally provided an explanation of the two lines of the family; the scientists like Victoria and the artists like Abby.

"So," Maddie added, her face beaming with satisfaction that at last their secret was shared. "Abby really is part of our family in every way, continuing the artistic talent along the lines of Mauveine's sister, Lydia, and of course Great-Aunt Eveline."

There was a stunned silence for half a minute before Ned chimed up. "Wow, I've gotta say, not one but three super-cool dudes to celebrate—Mum, Mauveine and Abby," undoing the final wire around the cork that flew off immediately with a loud bang, setting off Jeb and Kai again. He filled the glasses quickly.

Lynton immediately stood up and gave Abby a giant kiss whilst Julian, stunned but ecstatic, ran around the table to hug her hard. Belle was very pleased as she chatted with Dottie and Nancy excitedly and then to Maddie congratulating her on the detective work. Abby glanced at Victoria who did not appear unhappy but decidedly subdued, pondering silently on her own until Zac and Ade brought her out of her deep thoughts with big hugs and more words of congratulation.

Julian called for attention. "Grab your glasses and let's toast three beautiful, successful and talented family pioneers and welcome Lady Abigail Warren formally into the fold at the same time. Me? I'm just the lowly jack of all trades and master of none, a Fazackerley turned Endersby-Finnis to the core."

They laughed and toasted again. Finally, the teenagers began to disperse to watch an art-house film which Lynton had brought in. Abby glanced over, pleased to see Victoria's eyes were now brighter, but knowing that she needed to reconcile this bombshell information carefully. Something was happening inside Victoria's head that even Abby was finding hard to read ... a process of thought which only Eva ever really had owned the keys to. Abby wandered over to interrupt Victoria's discussion with Julian.

"I hope, Vikki, you're not angry are you?" Abby ventured, deciding to be direct straight away.

Victoria turned. "The evidence you and my daughter have painstakingly assembled seems irrefutable so I wouldn't venture to dispute the hypothesis," Victoria replied in her usual convoluted science-speak, which sounded cold and callous, but Abby was familiar with the pattern. This was how Victoria came to terms with something challenging but inevitable. "Of course, I'm not angry, how could I be? The whole thing just takes a little getting used to ... but it's a very nice feeling, the same as finding a long lost relative. Remember the unforgettable day you and I first met Aunt Eveline down at the Lodge in Parbold? It feels as mind-blowing as that, but a lovely surprise, Abby." Victoria put her arms around her best friend and hugged generously.

Lynton sidled up with another glass of champagne. "Just going to watch this celluloid film with the kids, I also got in the same junk shop, called the War Game. A once secret and banned documentary made in the 1960s about how people should prepare for a nuclear Armageddon. Have you still got that old 35mm projector Julian?"

"Yes, of course, down in the large cupboard in the wine cellar, hasn't been used for a very long time though."

"Great, I'll just get it. What fabulous news, Victoria, I can't quite take it in, but the more you think about it the more it makes sense, and answers a lot of things."

"Yes," Victoria replied, still subdued. "What things?"

"Later, later. Aah … Adrian has brought the three of you another glass of champers. This plonk is first rate Julian."

"It should be, cost enough!"

Victoria turned to Abby. "Shall we retire to the drawing room, Lady Warren? I'm done in to be honest, just popping to the loo."

"I think I'll join the rest and watch this film," Julian murmured. "And make sure Lynton doesn't set the celluloid on fire, he looks a bit tiddly."

Abby laughed. "Yes, he's very tiddly; I think we'd better stay over tonight."

"Of course," Julian smiled. "This is your place as well now Abby. See you both later."

Abby wandered through the wide hallway, staring happily at the paintings on the wall of Mauveine and Lydia. She felt like a giant weight was finally off her shoulder, when Maddie came around the corner.

"We did it, Abby," Maddie chuntered, equally feeling a huge relief. "Now I can look forward to my visit to Harvard in the spring. I hope you're still going to come with me like you said before Christmas?"

"Of course … I'm looking forward to that. I've not been to the States for such a long time."

"Good. Actually Mum mentioned that she wants to come too and bring Belle—that would be nice."

"Yes I agree. I'm just concerned that Vikki seems just a little preoccupied and quiet taking the news in, although I suppose that's her way of assimilation. Do you think she'll be okay with it all?"

Maddie's eyes narrowed. "There may just be one issue you and I should perhaps be mindful and sensitive about."

Abby pondered then realised what was obvious if she had been a little more focussed. Victoria was jealous … not of Abby suddenly appearing as a family equal, in most ways that had been the case for so long anyway between them. No, it was Maddie … Victoria was jealous of their close relationship, as if she and Maddie really were sisters. She nodded. "Yes, I get it. We'd better remain alert and see how it all pans out slowly."

"I agree, catch you later. Belle and I will join you and Mum after this War Game film, it isn't very long. I think Ned and Zac, on the pretext of seeing Dottie and Nancy home, are heading to the George later."

Abby laughed and kissed Maddie's cheek. They actually were like sisters and she wanted it to stay that way.

# Chapter Four

March 1841: Marylebone and the London town house of
Charles Babbage

Staring up in the distance towards the magnificently tall
dome of St Paul's cathedral, Morag McKenzie had to stop
for a minute, clasp her gloved hands around her ears, and
try and shut out the incessant racket, particularly of carriage
wheels and clopping hooves on the macadam and cobble road
surfaces. Vacating from noise was an impossible task anywhere
in London and especially walking down Drury Lane in Covent
Garden. Urban life in this mega-cacophony of bedlam and
activity, which seemed to go on twenty-four hours a day, could
not have contrasted more with the genteel and sheltered rural
existence she enjoyed in her Orsbrick village outback of West
Lancashire.

A helpful arm yanked her out of the way as another four-
wheeled cart piled up with masses of old clothes careered past,
the two dirty horses excreting a massive pile of steaming dung
to join the rest piled up on the road.

"Morag, for heaven's sake, you really must take greater care
crossing the road and look both ways," Ada Lovelace screamed
out, dragging her friend towards a pleasing row of shops,
selling pretty, long frocks for the coming spring. It wasn't just
the London noise affecting Morag, it was also the constant,
never-ending smell, which changed and shifted from one
nauseating experience to the next as they walked briskly

through the market. The amount of horse shit cast onto all of London's roads weekly must be an astronomically high volume, she pondered. Fortunately, they had missed the live market. She hated the sight of those poor, sickly looking cows and bulls, battered up and hit continuously with pointed sticks by their disgustingly cruel owners. The animals were clustered into suffocating penned arenas to be sold on, alongside the open slaughtering of squealing pigs and squawking hens amidst blood and gore continuously pouring with its accompanying stench out over the pavements. Cluttering up every available pavement space were the hundreds of ubiquitous street sellers, all poor, working class people, just about making ends meet, peddling everything from pots and pans, matches and fruit to vegetables, old boots, in fact everything imaginable, much of it going for one or two pennies.

Some of them looked very destitute. She knew the match sellers, grubbers and finders of which there were plenty about, scrabbling barefoot in bins and muck for anything sellable, had a truly knife-edge existence only earning a few pence per day. Either they were very old people or very young children, all dressed in shabby rags. She tendered one shilling to a one-legged elderly man, struggling to hold his tray of a few match boxes, balanced precariously on a crutch, his beard long and dirty. It was obvious, once she approached, that the poor wretch had not been near a bath for many weeks. Effusive with the first day's attention, his face beamed into a toothless grin and he thanked her profusely as she carefully took his three last boxes at arm's length. Perhaps that would stave off the workhouse for a little longer. Turning the corner, a tiny, chirping golden canary in a petite silver cage caught her attention. But Ada, knowing Morag's weakness, caught her arm and steered her deftly into the more interesting nearby dress shop.

"No. I've seen that look of yours too many times Lady McKenzie," Ada protested again loudly. "And how on earth would you be able to take that thing onwards to Mr Babbage's house, especially as he is hosting a Royal Society soirée tonight? Apart from an unending mania for astronomy, the other trait you share with my great friend Mary Somerville is you wanting to take care of every sick or caged animal you set eyes upon!"

"Madame, may I interest you in our latest fashion line? I believe you have the perfect figure for that magnificent gown over there."

They both turned their gazes from a row of new, creamy white cotton petticoats to be met by the wide and perfectly toothed smile of a large, well-turned-out woman in her late fifties, her dyed red hair piled up into an elegant bun.

"My name is Mrs Felicity Hope, proprietor of this fine establishment." Mrs Hope was staring directly at Morag, much to Ada's irritation.

"And I am the Countess of Lovelace," Ada responded haughtily, hands on her hips, "and this is Lady McKenzie, from Lancashire."

Felicity Hope looked surprised. It was rare to see women of such a high class inside a shop, especially her shop, in this part of London. Her trade was essentially with the growing professional and middle classes who were now coming regularly to the theatres and opera house, but who, whilst comfortably well off, never could flaunt the wealth of the upper classes. She had never heard of these two aristocrats, surprised they were unaccompanied, but she immediately regained her composure, taking in their expensive clothing in an instant, and of course realising there was genuine wealth to be exploited. She clicked her fingers and a girl of about eighteen appeared from behind the counter. "My daughter, Gertrude. Now Lady McKenzie, if you peruse this dress, my best garment at present, you will see immediately that it embodies all the latest traits of fashion this year."

Morag gazed carefully at the gorgeous, dark-crimson ball gown. She could see the shoulders were low and sloping, quite a departure from the previous decade, with a new-style one-piece pleated triangle from the shoulder to the low-pointed waist. The skirt was beautifully bell-shaped with special sewn tiny pleats which could be seen on the waistline to gather the skirt.

"No need to wear more than two petticoats, milady, to retain the wide shape," Mrs Hope added, seeing that Morag was patently a connoisseur of good fashion. It was an interest she enjoyed sharing with Ada, who also loved beautiful clothes, but somehow Morag always finished up looking just that tiny bit …well … more elegant.

Mrs Hope indicated to her daughter. "Perhaps milady you would like to try on the garment? I can see the size is perfect without alteration." Gertrude immediately led Morag to the changing room at the back.

Morag emerged quickly, preening happily, much to the annoyance of her friend who was clearly jealous. She pranced flirtatiously in front of the long mirror, the curtains now discretely drawn from the outside gaze. She especially loved the way the dress was revealingly off the shoulder, and the narrow sleeves, which had just begun for the first time to fashionably drop from below the shoulder to the lower arms, finished off with flouncing lace to the wrists. The expensive, pearly necklace she wore, a gift from Malcolm the day before he died, looked perfect against the expanse of her pale, smooth skin.

"The fabric, Mrs Holt, it's so soft and such an unusual weft. What is it?"

"A moiré fabric, Lady McKenzie. Becoming quite rare now, I must say, reserved only for the very best couture. In the trade we call it watered silk. The pattern process is called calendaring and is a specialisation I have special access to through artisans at the court in France."

"Mmm … you mean this dress is direct from Paris? Ada, what do you think? Isn't this gown divine?"

"Yes," Ada replied begrudgingly, knowing it wouldn't have fitted her anyway as Morag had a far fuller figure, her eyes flashing with the same shade as her own green dress. "Seriously, of course you look lovely and I'm envious, but I do have some rather nice dresses at my town house so I will complain no longer, honestly!" She ran up and gently hugged her friend, whispering "buy it," in her ear.

"I shall take this, no matter, thank you Mrs Hope," Morag exclaimed loudly. "It will be perfect for our engagement this evening."

Gertrude had by then emerged with a matching, small white linen bag, intricately embroidered in the same crimson colour as well as brightly coloured, brocade silk slippers to set the whole outfit off.

"And accessories too?"

"Of course, wrap them up with the gown," Morag declared happily. "And the final bill?"

"Today is a sale milady for which I will take off ten percent and allow a further discount on the combined accessories, so that will be twenty-five pounds altogether."

Morag looked forlorn, it was a good price for such quality, but she simply didn't have enough cash with her. But Ada, sensing disappointment immediately, delved into her bag and withdrew a twenty pound note. "Here, take this, you must have it. The situation would be mathematically too improbable if you didn't."

"In that case how can I resist the inevitable roll of the mathematical dice," Morag replied giggling and then took the note from Ada's dainty hand.

Whilst Mrs Hope was carefully wrapping up the parcel in string and brown paper, Gertrude was staring at Morag's dark brown hair, parted in the centre and tied in a large bun at the back with a few long bits dangling in front of her ears. Unexpectedly, she piped up in a shy but very posh accented voice. "Lady McKenzie, would you like me to quickly prepare your hair for your special engagement? I have been apprenticed, milady, with Sir Ernest Fanthorpe, hairdresser to Queen Victoria's ladies in waiting. The very latest fashion emerging at court is to keep your centre parting but allow the sides instead to be bunched out into ringlets ... it would look perfect with your gown and your hair is so long and thick. I can do it in no time, half an hour maximum. My tongs are already warming in the oven."

"Ada," Morag cried excitedly. "Do we have time? I really fancy such a style."

Ada looked at the small grandmother clock, ticking methodically in the corner and sighed. "I suppose so, but then we really must make haste, first to my house to get ready and then onwards to Mr Babbage. I shall have to try and call a cab."

"How far are you from Mr Babbage's abode?"

"Only a few hundred yards and James, my driver, will take us then in the brougham anyway."

"In that case, Gertrude, please commence," Morag replied, her eyes flashing with delight, an opportunity to turn up at one of London's most fashionable gatherings, not only with the latest style of gown, but emulating the Queen herself.

Mrs Hope smiled; she had made a substantial profit, unexpectedly for the day. "May I tempt both of you ladies with a pot of hot tea and some of my special home-made buns? I shall wake my husband who will take you both to your destination when you are ready. He is a cabbie, we have a double Hansom with horses at the back, and most comfortable I must say. Where are you heading?"

"Marylebone," Ada replied, relieved she didn't have to step out into the thick mud and effluent outside. Trying to hail a cab in that pandemonium was dangerous at the best of times, especially for a woman. It was foolish to have ventured into the city by train without her driver, but she wanted to be alone with Morag and independent for a change. Being chaperoned constantly by males, whether her husband or her servants, had become decidedly tedious.

"Not a problem at all, Countess. Now, let me see to that tea, I feel quite partial and peckish myself."

*

A continuous stream of carriages clattered to and fro outside the magnificent Number One Dover Street, where processions of mainly male invited guests, a small number accompanied by their wives or mistresses, were formally led inside through the highly lit double-fronted entrance, their top hats and thick coats carefully removed for storage.

Morag, wrapping up her coat tightly from the sharp chill outside as James led her carefully down the steps of Ada's carriage, watched the parade of men, most of them elderly, with interest, intrigued and excited by the assembly of so many distinguished scientists in one evening. This was her first opportunity to mix socially with such a prestigious group in

London, many of whom would likely be active Royal Society members. Her deceased husband, Malcolm, had been invited around the mid 30's into membership of the somewhat controversial Society for the Advancement of Science, but had attended only one meeting in York, always claiming pressure of work. In reality he had been a very poor social mixer of his inventive peers, retaining a close working friendship with a reserved few.

She felt immediately flustered entering such a situation unaccompanied, but noticed a series of overtly admiring glances from one or two of the younger and handsome visitors, looking quite splendid in their dinner jackets and starched white shirts and sporting the stylish hair, long sideburns and moustache for which Prince Albert, the Queen's husband, had been setting a fashionable trend amongst the upper class of socialites. She knew, by the churlish glances from Ada, that she looked stunning in her new gown so immediately felt cheered and confident again. But her stomach remained on high nervous alert, churning over in her mind how she should approach any conversation on science or its merits, and her experiments with any of these people, if they had the temerity to ask of course. She was painfully aware that few men genuinely believed that women were capable of such high thought. Encouragement through education was held in widespread disdain. Without doubt, she would be expected to join the wives for inane gossip and irrelevant social chat.

Well of course, she was actually accompanied … by Ada … but already Ada, in her usual devil-may-care fashion, had dashed wholeheartedly to the door the moment she alighted from the carriage, to be greeted with an enthusiastic, warm embrace by their waiting host, Mr Babbage. This was the first time Morag had met him, tall and distinguished, but undoubtedly already in his fifties. But heaven knows how often Ada over the last years had talked incessantly about Mr Babbage and his great genius for mathematics, calculating machines and all things philosophical. Certainly his output of papers on a huge array of subjects had been impressive, and she vividly remembered arguing all night with Malcolm over the implications of Mr Babbage's controversial publication, 'On the Economy of Machinery and Manufactures' outlining a vision of the future organisation of efficient industrial production. This book had created a storm of protest from all kinds of learned quarters. Malcolm immediately embraced Mr Babbage's revolutionary ideas of the factory ruling over everything made in society to create wealth, with enthusiasm, but she was not convinced. The world of the individual artisan, she believed, would always retain its key place.

She watched the Ada and Babbage greeting with interest, because for a fleeting moment it was evident that the whole world around had been swept away from both, their eyes and attention devoted solely for the other. Without doubt, Ada had needed the challenge of original scientific discourse with a man of high intellect to match her own for so long. Her husband was said to be of little use and her mother's stifling and suffocating attention was burdensome beyond belief. Morag understood that need better than most, especially with the big void evident in her own life. However, she pondered with quiet inner amusement whether Mr Babbage, a widower of some years, or Charles as Ada continuously insisted she used in their private presence, was meeting other needs ... Certainly Ada refused to be drawn even close on that subject, despite some subtle and not so subtle attempts at drawing out the truth. Her friend had a fiery inner emotion, constantly drawn to hyperbole and mischievousness, inherited from Lord Byron, her enigmatic

72

father, a characteristic which Ada's mother had tried so hard to suppress, and undoubtedly, as could be seen this evening, had failed miserably.

A servant carefully removed her coat. Thank goodness the fires were burning hard all around the house, radiating welcoming warmth to her bare shoulders. A loud voice caused her to turn immediately. Ada was approaching and she did look beautiful in a magnificent blue gown, her hair raised in a fetching, high bun and her cheeks radiant for a change. Ada looked ready to be immediately painted in oils and her picture of intellect and frivolity preserved forever. She seemed now to be enjoying a period of sustained good health, hopefully to last, as she strutted over arm in arm with Charles.

"Come over here, don't stand like a wilting violet. May I introduce you to our host, my good and special friend Mr Babbage. Charles, this is Lady Morag McKenzie of Lancashire, about whom I have discussed with you recently."

Babbage stared hard into Morag's eyes, his fast brain whirring. Somewhere there was a connection, vague in the memory, which he should be making, he was sure. Then he had it and smiled. He took her hand and kissed the back gently. "Lady McKenzie, a pleasure to meet you at last and indeed Lady Lovelace has mentioned your kindred affinities for natural philosophy and mathematics often. As for Ada? Well I can only describe her immense capabilities in one way—an enchantress of numbers, now and forever, isn't that so my dear?"

Ada blushed, a deep crimson red. "Why Mr Babbage, I am not worthy of such high and noble praise, in comparison with your vast knowledge and capabilities," she responded formally, but obviously pleased as punch with such a compliment.

Babbage continued staring at Morag, his gaze shifting clumsily from top to bottom, a glance not missed by Ada who looked sternly for a second but immediately forced back a smile. "I believe now I have met your husband one time," he said, "at a manufacturing meeting back in '34 near Manchester to which I was invited to give an attendant short lecture. Lord McKenzie is it? He was introduced by the railway genius Mr Brunel who I know well, a friend and engineering associate. I assume Lord McKenzie was unable to attend this evening?"

Morag gazed for a second at Ada who glanced shiftily to the floor. Unquestionably the facts had been withheld from Mr Babbage, an omission with a deliberate purpose, which, now Morag had correctly assembled her hypothesis, she could guess why. An irrelevance, she pondered forcefully … although she did admire his brain. "I'm afraid, Mr Babbage, that Lord McKenzie passed away two years ago, a rather tragic accident. And it is chemistry and not natural philosophy, if I may be so bold as to be accurate."

Babbage looked embarrassed, a fact he should have known. "I'm so sorry Lady McKenzie, I had no idea. It is totally unacceptable of me to be so lacking in grace. Please accept my humblest apologies."

"Pray Mr Babbage, please do not fret," Morag replied, calmly with a smile. "I take no offence whatsoever. There is no reason for you to know. And I am here to enjoy your evening which has become a notable point in the social calendar these days, so everyone is saying."

Babbage smiled. Undoubtedly Morag McKenzie was a lady of charm, beauty and formidable scientific intellect, an irresistible combination for him. Then he looked at Ada and realised in an instant he had enough on his plate without complicating his life further. "Chemistry you say, Lady McKenzie? Now that is interesting, I have someone here I think you should especially meet. But before we partake of the guest lecture this evening, first we will all indulge in some food and refreshment and I have arranged a little musical surprise to enjoy simultaneously, especially Ada for you."

Ada's eyes widened and a large smile drew across her mouth, she had regained his attention once more ... But who was the potential admirer Charles was lining up Morag for? "Not, I wonder, some early Elizabethan music? With a lute, you mentioned last time we solved those Bernoulli numbers together? I adore such playing Morag."

"No lutes tonight my dear, we will reserve that for another occasion ... Instead I have invited the delightful Rothmere sisters quartet who will entertain us with their mother, Lady Camilla herself, playing a basset with, I am sure, distinction. They will perform pieces from Mozart's Clarinet Quintet in A Major, two violins, a viola and a cello, amazing. They are becoming quite a fixture amongst our social circle in London. Now, may I escort you both to your table ... aahh ... Hershel, my good friend, there you are. Would you care to join our table as I can see you're at a loose end? I'm sure Lady McKenzie here will be curious about your latest photography research, the chemistry of which is quite fascinating."

Morag looked across and smiled politely at the older gentleman, wandering with a rather befuddled look in the wrong direction. The famous Sir John Hershel, astronomer, mathematician and philosopher extraordinaire, but once again not a man she found especially attractive. Quite the opposite, it was clear he was letting himself go. A new suit and a haircut would be in order, with too much time spent in a dark-room or peering through the eye-piece of one of his home made telescopes. However she had heard about his significant recent advances in photographic reagents and had already decided this was a growing science she would spend some time on ... so Mr

Hershel's company at table could at least prove useful and intellectually stimulating, and she was intrigued with his observations of Saturn's moons that he had since named and also that new nebula.

With Ada and Morag linked into each arm, the tall Babbage puffed out his chest and strutted like a peacock down the long corridor, drawing admiring glances from everyone, towards the sumptuous drawing room where around forty guests were being seated for dinner at a number of smaller tables. He smiled in turn at Ada and Morag. "An honour and a pleasure to escort the two most beautiful ladies of the evening by far ... but don't say that to Lord Rothmere will you," he ventured gaily with a large grin.

*

The excellent dinner of roast quail with a huge variety of potatoes and vegetables, followed by imported truffles was enhanced to the delight of all with the interesting discourse of music. Following a superb recital which she enjoyed hugely, Morag was staring at the pencil doodling on a large napkin that Ada, bored as usual, was undertaking next to her, especially as Charles had uprooted himself and was engaging in an intense discussion with Hetty, the youngest and prettiest of the wealthy Rothmere sisters.

"Sponsorship, you know Morag," Ada mumbled, not quite as oblivious as she appeared. "Charles is desperate for fresh funds to develop his next genius creation, the Analytical Engine. Again, the government are not listening whatsoever, particularly that bonehead of a prime minister, Peel. The only thing that fires the man up is his damned stupid police force and their increasingly petty interference in our lives."

"Surely, having a national crime deterrent is an excellent thing. Don't you feel much safer on the streets? What on earth are you scribbling on that good napkin?"

"Charles won't mind. I have just created a new methodology to solve finite difference equations, which will uniquely help his task for the Engine. I do believe that exquisite clarinet playing really did inspire my brain; God, it's truly on fire again. I need another big glass of wine. Pity there's no dancing don't you think?" glancing up at the departing ruffled jacket and untidy wild hair of John Hershel, who was hastily sidling off to find a water closet.

"You do know I had to lever his hand off my thigh under the table, as he muttered sweet nothings in my ear about how fed up he was with having nine young children yelling constantly around him and it was time to marry someone else," Morag whispered vehemently, now hoping that her dinner companion would lose his way back.

"I did hear you arguing about the best compounds of silver for fixing plates," Ada said in a low monotone. "Without doubt Sir John was firing up your ardour with his photography. Has he asked you if he could show you his dark room and take some pictures … you know … those sort of pictures?"

"What pictures?"

"Most men here obviously enjoy staring at you all night long in your ball gown, but I suspect Sir John may have a serious predilection to want to avidly capture you minus the said accoutrements," Ada replied innocently, then burst into a giggle.

Morag gave her friend a dig under the table. "I think you've had quite enough wine … and we still have the lecture to come yet … Best brain behaviour required please. I'm afraid my companion will have more luck peering down his telescope from the wrong end," she retorted quietly, both continuing with a fit of giggles, as Charles glared over at Ada, who he worried was teetering on the edge of another manic phase.

He suddenly clapped his hands and invited everyone into the ballroom next door, which had been fitted out with a demonstration laboratory table in the centre and a blackboard for scribbling notes or perhaps results. Some unusual looking equipment had been laid out for demonstration. It was obvious some sort of experiment was going to take place. The flames in both fireplaces at either end crackled into life as servants piled on a mixture of logs and coal to ensure the large room was sufficiently warm for the guests to sit comfortably. Plush, high-backed velvet chairs had been arranged in three semi-circles around the table. Once the guests rose, Ada grabbed Morag's hand and led her firmly to the front, so they could have a clear bird's-eye view of the proceedings.

"Charles always tries to ensure that his guest speaker presents some original research," Ada said. "These sessions are competing with the regular Friday evening discourses at the Royal Society, except we have much more fun and conviviality here of course."

But Morag was far more interested in the new companion of Mr Babbage as he led in his guest speaker through a side door. He was a shorter man than his host, more, she estimated, her own height and noticeably slim of build. Handsome, with a thick head of curly groomed hair, the speaker had a young face and fresh complexion. However, his expression was of a serious and thoughtful older man, his eyes darting around the room, noticing, observing and drawing conclusions from a myriad of activities, the room humming and bustling with people still coming in and trying to find a decent seat. Morag contemplated him for longer. This was a kind, modest man, comfortable and

78

curious of the natural world, a natural experimenter, her inquisitiveness increasingly drawn to his preoccupations. What was he thinking about? His sharp gaze finally caught onto the attractive and intriguing woman in the beautiful red gown, next to his old friend, the Hon. Augusta Ada Byron. He reminded himself instantly. He must address her as the Countess of Lovelace now.

As Morag looked around, she realised a change of dynamic occurring in the room. "Ada?" she whispered sharply. "Where have all the wives gone? We're surrounded solely by men of decidedly variable quality."

Ada laughed. "Retired of course to the other sitting room to drink tea, flaunt their dresses, denigrate their husbands and gossip stupidly. So totally and utterly boring. Anyway, I know exactly who is fucking whom presently … This is so much more interesting, oh, do say you agree. I so admire the shape of his handsome head, such a stunning intellect, you really should study some phrenology. I have shelves of books on the subject."

"Honestly Ada, please not now," Morag replied, nervously looking around but nobody had heard. "Whose head? Charles?"

"No silly, Michael of course … Oh my goodness, you don't know who he is do you. Honestly, you really do spend far too much time with your nose buried in sulphuric acid and those revoltingly smelly coal tar distillates … You need to get out more, my dearest Morag."

Morag looked blank. "Michael?"

"He's only a very old friend who I haven't seen for absolutely ages. That awful Puritan wife of his, Sarah, wraps his soul up far too tightly in religious chains. The one and only Michael Faraday, the greatest science experimenter this century has yet produced. We're in for a treat. Mmm … Charles is bringing him over, sit up straight."

"My dearest Countess of Lovelace and Lady McKenzie," Babbage announced in a flourish of exaggerated hand movements. "May I introduce my good friend Mr Michael Faraday, who has offered to present our final session of scientific discourse and discovery for the evening."

Morag noticed Mr Faraday's rather charming diffidence, a man plainly unused to seeing two attractive women eagerly awaiting his seminar, or maybe simply unaccustomed to being in the company of attractive women. Faraday took each woman's hand in turn for a gentle kiss.

"I have to confess Babbage," Faraday commenced. "The Countess of Lovelace and I are already well acquainted through lengthy communication of the sciences, although some period of time has elapsed since we last met."

"Indeed my dear Michael, I would say at least ten years and I have now borne three children, but you have not aged one tiny bit … showing how beneficial, hard work and dedication to the sciences are," Ada replied effusively.

"I think more because my good wife ensures I keep to a simple life and regular routine," he replied but his attention and gaze was already fixed onto Morag. "Lady McKenzie, my pleasure. It is unusual to see a woman at these lectures … Are you also a follower of the sciences or perhaps natural history, of which I am especially fond?"

"Well actually Mr F …" she replied in a croaky and annoying voice, why now of all times. "Excuse me …" she muttered with a cough as Ada hastily handed her a glass of water, which promptly slipped out of her hand. She made a hasty and successful grab but sadly the contents poured forth all down the front of Mr Faraday's trousers in a particularly embarrassing location. A servant ran up immediately with cloths to wipe him down, as Morag, mortified and deep red, to the accompaniment of titters and guffaws, tried to apologise profusely.

Babbage, his face showing irritation and immense weariness, shared exactly with Ada, they were well suited with that low threshold of extreme boredom with trivia, exclaimed, "We really must get on Faraday," pulling his arm hard.

But Faraday ignored him, sensitive to Morag's overt discomfort. Instead, he laughed heartily, seemingly quite unembarrassed. "Think nothing of it Lady McKenzie. Getting a little water splashed over us is an occupational hazard of we science experimenters. Davy and I once nearly blew our heads off messing about with chlorides of nitrogen … I know which I most prefer! Perhaps we may have time later before I depart to find out your scientific tastes?"

"Yes please …" she croaked inaudibly as he strutted confidently onto the makeshift platform to begin his experiment and arrange the apparatus into place.

"That wasn't exactly a brilliant start was it," Ada hissed in a whisper. "Too much of that damned absinthe, I knew I shouldn't have handed you the bottle to swig … I can take it."

"Start of what?" Morag replied, her voice having returned.

"Never you mind … gosh, what is inside that box?"

"It's a type of voltaic cell, I think …" Morag replied, staring hard at the table, when the chatter suddenly died down in the room. "Malcolm brought one home to show the children how dead frog's legs twitch when you apply some sparking to them, demonstrated first by Galvani. But that apparatus looks quite different in construction …"

Ada touched her lips with a finger and Faraday commenced in a very clear and pleasing tone of voice, neither harsh nor overpowering, but conveying a strong clarity of purpose which Morag recognised as the intrinsic quality of an excellent teacher and a man confident in his subject matter. If only she could find a governess with the same depth and qualities for son James.

"Gentlemen and ladies pray—my warmest thanks for coming out this bitterly cold evening. But I judge from your contented demeanour that my dear friend Mr Babbage has been treating you splendidly to his usual fine fayre and potent drink. Please … a token of appreciation for our fine host."

A loud clapping and raucous cheering filled the now smoky room, cigars lit everywhere. Faraday hastily unclipped the wiring and then held up the square box containing silver and black elements sitting in clear liquids but within separate partitions.

"Now I know most of you are well acquainted with the practicalities required to generate an electric current, that is to say a voltaic cell. And indeed a small number here I recognise are actively working in this most fascinating of areas, as I too am doing. You may remember, almost twelve months since, a discourse I arranged at the Royal Society for my colleague William Grove to demonstrate his latest, radical variant of a battery cell, which he calls, of course, a Grove cell. This design features a zinc anode in dilute sulphuric acid and a heavy metal cathode in concentrated nitric acid, the two separated by a porous pot. For those who have not experienced this invention, the advantages over a standard voltaic cell are immensely superior, providing the opportunity for a much greater and stable current over a long period of time. Indeed we also demonstrated Mr Grove's other invention … ahh, Wheatstone, I can see you smiling at the back." Faraday gestured to his colleague, sitting with two other distinguished experimenters,

Brande and Harris. "And would you like to tell us what else we saw?"

Morag turned and whispered excitedly, "Mr Faraday likes to involve the audience in his talks, how unusually divine." She finished abruptly as a number of loud shushes filled their ears and Ada shuffled uncomfortably in her seat.

Wheatstone stood up. "An amazing sight indeed, verily I can confirm an incandescent light was demonstrated, powered directly from a Grove cell."

There were loud ahhs and gasps from around the room. For many, this unusual invention had passed them by, the potential of which could be discerned by the buzz of dampened comments.

Faraday continued. "And in recognition of such profound scientific advances, I am pleased to announce that Mr Groves has been accepted as a Fellow of the Royal Society. This evening he was to assist me with this demonstration but is sadly indisposed with family matters, but I believe we should nevertheless show our appreciation and welcome for our new and distinguished member."

Loud clapping ensued as Faraday held the box aloft again. "However, what I want to show you tonight is an example of how, merely in the last twelve months, this arena of electrical research is encouraging a veritable great flurry of innovative outpourings and demonstrates once more how English society, under our great Queen Victoria and in the hallowed name of God the Provider, will advance rapidly with the huge benefit that science and technology is providing us."

He placed the box on the table and proceeded to attach a number of thick copper wires. Morag peered intensely, wishing she had brought her glasses, fascinated by what was to ensue and already attempting to work out the differences. It was immediately clear to her that an unknown variant of the Grove cell was being shown. "What I have here, for the first time on public display, is due to the kindness of its inventor, my German colleague and friend Herr Doctor Rudolf Bunsen who is presently writing up a paper for the said apparatus. Doctor Bunsen has been preoccupied over the last twelve months with shortcomings concerning Mr Grove's battery and has undertaken a number of changes. Now, I will invite comment on said modifications ... Lady McKenzie, I see you have been studying this item intensively in the last few minutes. Would you care to comment?"

Guffaws and stultified laughs drifted around the rows. Nobody was expecting anything to be said by a female, least of all one associated with the dubious Countess of Lovelace in the shape, this time, of a flighty young widow with undoubtedly little else on her mind but entrapment of some unfortunate future husband. Why the pair had not discretely joined the wives elsewhere, a seemly and expected behaviour, was a mystery to all of them, except of course their host. A sharp nudge from Ada shook Morag's mind out of deep, concentrated speculation as the room immediately went into a deathly hush following a request for quiet from Babbage. Why had Mr Faraday addressed her? Was he trying to embarrass and make her appear stupid? She cleared her throat, Ada anxiously reaching for the water again; this scenario was not at all expected. But the croaky tickle had subsided. However, public speaking was not, like most women including Ada, within her experience having been greatly discouraged since being children of being overtly presumptuous, unless groomed of course for the stage. She had to come out of her expected demure shell and appear confident. At least, since being a widow she had made more effort at the task to foster inner strength.

Standing up she drew breath and stared directly into Faraday's twinkling eyes. Mercilessly testing her out as a charlatan or fraud, he undoubtedly was doing what he liked best, whether she appreciated it or not, a trait of character which had become a notorious talking point for years amongst his peers.

"Mr Faraday, thank you for the opportunity to make the first comment," she said, fear having driven out any voice wavering. "I would first like to say that a serious disadvantage of Mr Grove's battery, excellent though it may be, is the negative terminal which although you never said directly is I believe made from platinum, a rare and expensive element. This undoubtedly makes the commercial case for agreeable wider development and distribution seriously flawed. Hence, I am sure a catalyst for Mr Bunsen's research would have been driven by that major obstacle, which implies that he would have searched for a much cheaper and accessible substitute."

A number of quiet murmurs permeated the room again as chairs shifted about on the wooden floor. She sensed she at least had their attention now rather than their belittling scorn. Faraday never blinked, remaining silent for a few moments. "An excellent conclusion, Lady McKenzie. I commend your clear knowledge of Mr Grove's papers on the subject and thank you kindly for your assertion. Of course, answering your point demands a detailed knowledge of chemical reaction, so to spare your embarrassment, I will open the floor to my chemist colleagues … now …" he continued, looking around for Wheatstone again, also in on the performance.

However Morag was not sitting down, nor was she done with Faraday and raised her hand, cutting him off. "If I may be permitted Mr Faraday, I wish to complete my answer as I was only half-way through."

Ada looked up and glared. What was she doing making a complete fool of herself? This unseemly behaviour, especially with a person of Mr Faraday's standing was unheard of, but Morag ignored her altogether, loud gasps of disbelief crackling around the room.

Once more Faraday smiled back. Now he had her once and for all. He remained convinced she was a female charlatan, albeit a clever and pretty one and an admirable fighter, but he also needed to convey a little message to his friend Babbage to take more care with his invitees in future and stick to Royal Society and Institution male members only. "You may be permitted, Lady McKenzie," he replied quietly.

Morag cleared her throat again. She felt hot in the crosshairs and knew her face had become bright red, but she was determined to continue, rightly or wrongly. Male subjugation and unwarranted prejudice against female scientists had to be put right. What were they afraid of?

She recommenced. "The unglazed china diaphragm and the presence of the platinum cathode allow a controlled attraction to take place between the zinc and both sulphuric and nitric acids, creating sulphate of zinc, water and gases, which we can see bubbling forth at present. This releases chemical energy into the electrical particle fluid, now able to flow out through the cathode. Therefore the key requirement will be to maintain the zinc but substitute a cheap and conductive element which also catalyses and maintains the essential reaction of zinc with the said acids. A number of contenders may be possible Mr Faraday but my conclusion, noting the colour of your cathode and from my understanding of related conductivities, is that the said element is black carbon. The form of that carbon would need direct analysis but I am confident I would get to the bottom of it readily in my own chemical laboratory, given the opportunity. Thank you Mr Faraday."

Morag McKenzie sat down to more loud gasps and gazed at Faraday's expression. He had been thrown completely off course with her response, but instantly recognised that a fellow chemist of unusual capability was in their midst. He rather liked the stirred controversy welling up in the room around his unique find, as he was a man unswervingly devoted to encouraging and commending genuine talent in the field, even if she was a woman. He smiled warmly. Wheatstone at the back had meanwhile stood up with a companion at his side, a smaller and quite dapper individual with staring eyes, both clapping profusely. "Well done Lady McKenzie, wonderful analysis and absolutely right," he shouted loudly as the room erupted in cheers, claps and exultations of congratulations, all amazed to hear of a woman with her own chemical laboratory.

Ada, pleased that her friend had pulled off the seemingly impossible, also whispered a congratulatory comment in her ear, but inside remained fuming and jealous that Morag had outdone her at the event intellectually as well as with her new dress. Morag stood up again, turned demurely to the crowd of scientists and bowed her head in thanks.

Faraday held up his hands to quell the applause and looked down at Morag. "To save you unnecessary work, I will confirm that the carbon material is indeed a special form of compressed coke and coal, leaving the field ahead, Lady McKenzie, for you instead to improve even further on the battery design. Do you have any final comment before we move on to the last part of my experiment? I will now demonstrate the running of this small motor which has a new design of my own for receiving and translating electric flow into mechanical motion inside the surrounding magnetic field. And I shall not be asking any further questions of you tonight!"

There were loud laughs and grinning around the room, Faraday was enjoying himself as usual but at his expense which he was always happy to do.

"Only one small point, Mr Faraday. I notice you having to peer closely at your experiment and I assume, like me this evening, you have forgotten your spectacles," she piped up. "However please beware and take care. The gases I mentioned bubbling up will be noxious oxides of nitrogen ... I am sure you would not wish a repeat of your past mishaps with said chlorides of nitrogen would you."

Faraday roared laughing and the room erupted with him. Everyone was very well aware of Faraday's reputation for experimental bravado, amazed that he still retained eyes and limbs. Lady McKenzie, he thought, had a waspish sense of humour as well as scientific acumen ... a very attractive combination, especially as she was so pretty. But she was correct. He needed to keep his head well out of the way, bad for the lungs.

The rest of the experiment proceeded smoothly, the motor whirring into life connected up to the Bunsen cell, with a final discourse by Faraday on some of the latest implications and findings. At close, a large group of men were gathering with Babbage back in the drawing room for a final cigar and a coffee, servants running around madly with jugs of hot brew, smelling strongly. Morag was keen to join them, not normally proper, but she felt, from the glances and quick chats at the end, that she was being treated as one of them for the very first time, and it made her insides feel on fire ... a recognition she would never have believed. The small, elegant and peculiarly intense young man who had congratulated her in the seminar with Mr

Wheatstone had sidled up, at once effusive in the deep mathematics of natural philosophy, and it was obvious from his mode of conversation that his interest in her was not only scientific. But she gave no leeway whatsoever. She noticed Faraday glance over, talking intensely to Babbage who then came across and insisted that Mr Kirchhoff, apparently a close collaborator of the said cell inventor, Dr Bunsen, should join their table for a game of cards and a smoke.

Ada meanwhile was thanking her host for such a splendid evening and then marched over, annoyed that Charles was intent on spending the rest of the evening drinking with his boisterous cronies and not with her.

Morag patted her hand. "Don't worry, you have plenty of time to catch up with him … I think now that we are out of the way they want to enjoy themselves. Do you want to join the wives next door?"

For Ada that was the least appealing notion she ever wished to be doing. "No, I feel a headache coming on … James will be outside with the carriage and I have said our goodbyes for both of us so I think it's time to go, don't you. You certainly made a big impact; Charles thinks it was all quite a success."

Morag instantly inferred from the waspish tone that all was not well, expecting such a reaction at some time or other before they went to bed. "And you, Ada, did you think it was a success?"

"Of course," she replied, quietly linking her arm into Morag's. They walked slowly to the front door, Morag admiring the large portraits on the hall wall of an aged Newton at the Royal Mint as well as Huygens senior aside his telescope, before spotting the welcome sight of James striding in.

"Now I would just like to retire," Ada said. "I feel excruciatingly tired."

The bright mid-day light of a clear, blue spring day filled Lady Byron's morning room, whilst china porcelain plates of cucumber and egg sandwiches, with bowls of fruit, were placed meticulously on the large mahogany dining table. Agnes, head housemaid, performed a final dusting down of the Queen Anne chairs as Morag and Medora entered the room, laughing and giggling. They had enjoyed a wondrous morning together walking Rupert and Sebastian, Lady Byron's pet chows, around the lake in Hyde Park, admiring the large clumps of daffodils springing up everywhere, which had encouraged Medora into a poetical phase, assailing some of her father's poems with gusto to the amusement of Morag. She was pleased that in a short space of time, Medora had come to terms with the revelation that Lord Byron was her father and had not only reconciled her initial distress with her Aunt Annabella, but had decided, at least for the moment, to live with her and accept the benefits of receiving the generous direct support offered by Lady Byron. Certainly her daughter, presently in Ada's old nursery and being tutored by a new music teacher, was very pleased to be in London, already making new friends amongst the wide circle of children within Lady Byron's aristocratic social scene. Sitting under a willow tree just coming into leaf, it was clear to both Morag and Medora, from the happy laughter and boisterous playing of the many children being shepherded by nannies and governesses, that the harsh and unforgiving winter of '41 was giving way to a glorious spring and hopefully good summer, raising all their spirits especially Ada's, who was given to gloom and despondency all too easily, especially with her fragile health.

Ada had of course been preoccupied again with Charles Babbage, both locked away in her study all morning, tearing away at Ada's latest ideas for his so called Analytical Engine which she kept murmuring about every second to the point of tedium. Despite the continuation of heavy drinking with a hardcore of the Royal Society fellows after they had left Dorset Street the previous night, Babbage appeared in fine fettle when Morag and Medora exchanged pleasantries on the way out as he came waltzing in, obviously pleased to be visiting.

Tucking heartily into the egg sandwiches, Medora turned to Agnes. "Pray, do you know the whereabouts of my sister as I believe Mr Babbage has now left?"

Agnes momentarily clammed up shyly. She had something to say but didn't want to say it, when a loud voice rang across the room and Ada breezed in, her eyes flashing and her body manifestly jaunty with exhilaration.

"Heavens, are you two starting without me? You must have had good physical exercise out there, but I prefer the exertions of the mind, and Charles has stimulated me greatly this morning with his final agreement of my latest proposal. He went from begrudging denial to almost erotic acceptance."

Morag and Medora instantly started to chortle. Sometimes Ada got far too carried away into her nether-sphere with mathematics and her language. Agnes shuffled out hastily, her face red.

"Erotic stimulation? Really?" Morag said, unable to resist a tease, as Medora spluttered on her sandwich.

"Sometimes, Morag, your head is so full of test tubes, gases and foul liquids that you fail totally to understand the effect that creating a new mathematical language to enable punch cards to be read can have on two people," Ada cried.

"Especially when they are in love ..." Medora whispered in Morag's ear, setting them both off again.

"I heard that," Ada replied jauntily, "And I will neither confirm nor deny such scurrilous accusations, as if ..."

"As if indeed," Morag said. "Is Lady Annabella joining us?"

"No, I'm afraid Mother is off again to one of her slave abolition meetings. Heavens above, if it isn't that, then she's inside Milbank state prison doing penal reform. They are building another such hideous establishment at Pentonville would you believe? Now Agnes, what is the matter? You look quite flustered again. Where are those flowers from?"

"For you milady. We have a visitor, a gentleman visitor ... but he says he would like to have a word with Lady McKenzie?"

Morag looked up sharply. "Agnes, does the visitor have a name?"

"I'm sorry, I never thought to ask, I'll just go and find out," she replied, dashing out again into the hallway.

"Mother really must do something about Agnes. I think she has a mental deficiency, typical of certain types of the working class. Her physiognomy highlights the issue," Ada cried out.

"Really, Ada. She simply needs a little more domestic training and clear instructions," Medora remonstrated, always ready to support the underdog, especially servants who are wrongly denigrated.

Agnes returned promptly. "His name is Mr Faraday, Lady McKenzie. Shall I ask him to wait in your study, Countess?"

"Good Lord, yes of course," Ada barked. "Please offer Mr Faraday some tea and biscuits. Lady McKenzie will be along shortly, and thank him for these lovely flowers. I'll just find a vase ... So Morag? It looks like you made more than a passing impression on our guest speaker last night. You'd better go and speak to your suitor right away."

"I don't have a suitor."

Medora giggled. "Mmm ... more secrets you haven't been telling us then Morag? Who is this mysterious Mr Faraday and how did he know where to find you?"

Morag sighed, glaring at both of them and went out to find Ada's study, with Agnes tripping and fussing behind. Taking a deep breath, she fluffed her ringlets, smoothed down her deep cream dress and marched inside, whereupon Faraday, perfectly groomed in a very smart suit and necktie, stood up stiffly, holding a small bunch of daffodils, which Agnes immediately took.

"Why Mr Faraday," Morag said, holding out her hand. "What an unexpected surprise and such beautiful flowers which match my dress perfectly. Thank you so much. Now, how may I be of assistance?"

Faraday, normally confident and direct in his speech seemed uncharacteristically hesitant, but finally spoke, clearing his throat into a stern monotone. "Lady McKenzie, I wish to cordially thank you in person for making last night's discourse at Mr Babbage's abode such a great and honourable success. Your knowledge of chemistry is indeed commendable and many are surprised and intrigued how you have gained such a specialised knowledge without formalised university tuition."

Morag smiled. It was plain that he had rehearsed that somewhat wooden introduction to death and displayed overt unease, alone in the company of women. "And you Mr Faraday? Are you also intrigued?"

That wasn't the response he wished for being a man used to asking a straight, simple question and then receiving an equally straight answer. But Lady McKenzie was throwing it obliquely back in his face. "It is unusual for a lady to be so well versed," he mumbled back.

"So you are indeed intrigued. Then I shall consider telling you," she replied teasingly before lowering her voice to a whisper and looking around. Nobody was listening. "I have been solely inspired by two volumes of 'Conversations on Chemistry' by the knowledgeable Mrs Jane Marcet and have digested every nuance of theory and undertaken every practical experiment. Do you have awareness of the said author? Oh please call me Morag, I do insist."

"Certainly I do. Indeed, Mrs Marcet has proven to be a sound educator with her series of 'Conversation' books, I can see the appeal ... err ... Morag. The instructions are set in a dialogue between teacher and pupil, a mode suited most favourably only to the female mind." Instantly he felt a trap being set. He carefully avoided revealing that he too had been significantly influenced by the early edition of that work.

"Oh Mr Faraday, a science genius of such wide experience as you cannot *really* believe that we poor women are capable only of mere light-hearted discursive chit-chat on such serious matters and that original hard research and the digestion of topical papers is beyond are innate capabilities? Surely not."

"Well ... err ... of course not always ... but I may perhaps infer ..."

Morag smiled. He was stuttering again, she had him amazingly wrapped around her little finger. What terrible habits she was picking up from Ada. She interrupted.

"Maria and Mary have encouraged me greatly, and Maria has helped me also with the essentials of running my estate, now I am widowed, which has been hugely beneficial."

"Maria and Mary?" he asked, still aware he was stupidly lagging behind her fast repartee.

"Why, Mrs Edgeworth of course, a most extraordinary novelist and Mrs Somerville who was instructive in advanced mathematics tuition during my childhood, although I must confess, I am not nearly so capable as Lady Lovelace in algebraic analysis. I do believe you are partial to relaxing with a good novel, so I would recommend Maria's latest work, 'Helen', an interesting departure which focuses on her English characters and setting rather than the more moral messages of her earlier writing … although I think you should read both volumes of 'Tales of Fashionable Life'. Such agreeable short stories provide remarkable insights into the true lives and minds of women. I am following such educative practice with my own children, Mr Faraday, and require a new governess who will embrace learning as a positive experience on those so young, where the discipline of education is far more important than the acquisition of knowledge. Children must be entrusted with the responsibility of their own mental culture. Do you not agree Mr Faraday? With your own children too?"

"I prefer Jane Austen," he grunted, drawing breath and thinking fast. He was well acquainted with Mary Somerville, a formidable intellect and a kind and gentle woman, but knowing that his own mathematical capabilities were seriously deficient in both knowledge and application, this was a topic he avoided where possible, especially in the company of Mrs Somerville and Lady Lovelace. It was clear to him now that Lady McKenzie was part of that small but growing clan of assertive and independent intellectual females, with a ferociously penetrating conversation, wide interests and a persuasive personality, not what he was used to either socially with science colleagues, at church, or at home with his wife who he loved dearly. Morag's embrace of science still intrigued him and she seemed keen on progressive educational principles, an interest he did take very much to heart. His innate curiosity, despite her moral danger, was ringing in his head to ascertain more.

"Sadly, my wife and I have no children," he uttered, his expression displaying deep sorrow. "But I do enjoy the company of my many nephews and nieces when I can ... I even showed them how to make a hot-air balloon last weekend."

She smiled back politely. There was a thoughtful silence. Already aware of the fact his marriage was childless, scurrilous gossip abounding, she knew she had gone too far and regretted that pointed interjection. It was time to draw back. She had made enough points in the cause, when he immediately returned to the conversation with a proposal, which did throw her.

"I'm afraid I must leave, I have a pressing appointment at the Royal Institution, another tedious external experiment to assess. Lady McKenzie, may I be so bold as to invite you to dinner this evening, where we may continue our science conversation? Such discourse would be very amenable. Please call me Michael from now on."

Morag felt an instant flush coming on, this request was an unexpected consequence of her rash boldness. She was intending to dine in with Ada, and her husband who had returned from business in Wales, along with Medora and her mother Augusta as well as Lady Byron. But a relaxed evening with Mr Faraday and to hear his latest researches was too good an opportunity to be missed. Besides, she had unease about Ada's family get-togethers, sensing that a variety of difficult tensions remained bubbling under the surface.

"Why ... Michael, I would be delighted. What time do you suggest?"

"I shall arrive here with the Institution's carriage at seven, if that is to your convenience? However, I must confess, Morag, that where we shall go will require some deep analysis. I'm afraid my wife and I lead such simple and routine lives at our lodgings in Albemarle Street that I am quite out of touch with eating places of worth. I have been for far too long, happy to eat in the slap-bangs of the city, decidedly not appetising or appropriate places for a lady." He laughed in a self mocking manner, which she found quite touching.

She had no idea what a 'slap-bang' was but could certainly solve his dilemma. "In that case, I have a solution to your quandary, allowing you to concentrate fully on your scientific jobs in hand later. I suggest a very nice establishment in St James's Street, warmly recommended by a friend and called the Wellington Restaurant. They have large tables and comfortable chairs."

"In place of the boxes and benches I'm sadly used to?" he replied, grinning, his eyes twinkling again like the night before when they were first introduced.

She laughed heartily. "Plus an abundance of clean linen tablecloths and plated forks and spoons, where an edible joint is actually carved at one's table by a person in a white cap and jacket, and there exists even a choice of cheeses and pulled bread."

"Really? In that case we must partake of such a novelty," he replied, still grinning, relieved the conversation had lightened favourably. "Well, I must take my leave now," he added, looking at his pocket watch.

Morag, in her excitement at being invited out, suddenly thought ... care and discretion was essential. There was enough gossip about in London, not least surrounding Ada and her unending male attentions, without adding to it further. She hesitated but said it anyway, quietly. "Err ... and Mrs Faraday?"

Quite nonplussed and purposely self-immune from intrigue, he replied immediately. "My wife Sarah is looking after her ailing sister in Devon presently and will not be back till the month's end, but she is used to my entertaining science colleagues and talking business till late into the night and often morning. We trust in the good Lord and his overseeing blessing that my wife and I share no secrets and discuss all things, praying daily that our enduring happiness will continue and grow deeper."

She felt truly confused, wondering whether she had misinterpreted mixed signals, but was heartened that Mr Faraday saw her as a scientist worthy of further cultivation of ideas. That fact certainly would disarm the gossip mongers, mindful that being out alone with a man of such fame could set numerous tongues wagging in the wrong direction. Not that she cared overly for herself. She lived a life remote and far from the hotbed of London socialising and as an independent widow would please herself, but she felt responsibility towards his reputation. Either his answer, she concluded, was based on a certain naivety or his motives were much more subtly challenging. She needed to quickly do more research on Mr Faraday … who evidently had deep and surprising religious convictions which jarred against her own beliefs. She had long ago, as a child, been influenced immensely by the readings and teachings of the scientific work of Sir William Hershel, the great astronomer and father of that rogue Sir John, who fondled her leg the previous night. Sir William's major discovery of the ninth planet Uranus and his analysis, using giant reflector telescopes, of the distances, age and greatness of star populations, nebulae and comets, had convinced her that somewhere there were other lives inhabiting those far distant places, even likely the moon with its cratered villages and forested slopes. There was no room in her mind for a white bearded Creator floating in clouds, the whole storyline as far as she was concerned, a paternalistic convenience for keeping women in check. Hence, all of it and the bible were a complete nonsense. She knew she was more radical than most but kept her thoughts quietly private, even from close friends. Ada and especially Medora were off-limits for this debate. She respected their religious views they were entitled to them, but as a dedicated agnostic did not share any. Mr Faraday seemed more extreme in his outlook and fervour. Perhaps he could be persuaded by her evidence and then converted. She giggled at the notion, realising she had briefly gone into her own silly trance and both were still sitting around the fireplace. She immediately broke the silence and rang the bell. Agnes came sprinting in, breathless again, her hair all over her face, as Morag stared at such an incongruous sight for a servant.

"I do apologise, milady, and yourself good sir, but I've been trying to catch Lady Byron's chows which have been running mad around the house for some reason … perhaps a rat was loose."

"Okay Agnes. When you've caught your breath, please escort Mr Faraday to the door. He is in a hurry to his next appointment, but we will be dining out tonight at seven on his return. I'll speak to you shortly."

Agnes forced herself to restrain smiling but wondered what would be said to Lady Byron, who would undoubtedly disapprove. "Please follow me Mr Faraday, your carriage is already at the front for you."

*

Back in the morning room, Medora sipped tea, looking demure and relaxed. She had since changed into a becoming, flouncy red dress but Ada was nowhere to be seen as Morag marched in, her face still flushed.

"Ada has had one of her turns again," Medora said calmly. "She's gone to bed with a light fever and taken some potions for her stomach pain. Count William will return in a few hours and Aunt Annabella is stalking around her quarters, mad as hell about something, probably another scurrilous revelation about my poor father. Forsooth, we are heading for a fun evening later at dinner. Mother is the only sane one amongst them, apart from you that is."

Morag was churning over in her mind how to break the news and she needed to tap Medora's religious knowledge which was considerable, especially since the order of Catholic nuns had saved Medora's life when she had entered that dark and desperate period a few years back in France. There was only one way, quick and direct with no fuss.

"Medora, actually I shall be dining out this evening. I must go and give my apologies to Lady Byron and get ready. What do you know about Sandemanians?"

"Aahh ... we thought you might," Medora replied, grinning mischievously. "Don't worry, I'm not upset you'll be missing dinner, my mother and I will give each other the necessary moral support. I'm sure Ada has been scurrilously trying to pair you off and we actually talked about the Sandemanians. I think she believes he may be good for removing your unfounded agnosticism as well as your scientific well-being. Anyway, how did you know he was one of them? To be honest, I'd never heard of them before Ada came forth, quite a secret sect."

"Michael gave me his card which had it printed on ... I didn't like to ask and display my ignorance. A sect? Certainly I discerned very quickly he has strong convictions."

"Michael? You *are* getting on well! Sandemanians were founded around 1730 in Scotland. A sort of breakaway from the Presbyterians who reject the idea of an established state church and believe strictly in the word of the Bible and in

Christ, a sort of primitive Christianity as the apostles practised it."

"You mean it pervades his whole life?"

"Yes, so Ada says. All his experimental work is influenced by his beliefs, that nature actually substantiates the existence of its Creator and that nature must be interconnected as a whole because God created it all … That in Mr Faraday's view is why electricity and magnetism are coupled. He is a fervent preacher, with weekly communion, feet washing and love feasts."

"Love feasts?"

"Draw your own conclusions," Medora said with a smirk. "It appears that Mr Faraday became converted a month after his marriage to Sarah, she was an existing member of the denomination."

"Mmm …"

"Quite."

"But he has no children? Something he said about that … a decided sadness I fear. But I do declare, Michael is a man of kindness, goodwill and generosity to others, which is more than I can say about some of his colleagues."

"Some people have commented whether they have ever done it … you know … perhaps they regard it as truly sinful?"

Morag frowned. "Gossip … is that all they ever think about? I will ignore their obverse ramblings. He seems, I concur, to be very much in love. Anyway, people say enough about me because I enjoy exploring science. I was so pleased Caroline Hershel came to stay last month. An old friend of the family, she has just turned ninety but remains remarkably agile of mind and body, a tremendous role model for women of science learning and practicalities. She brought one of her brother's original brass seven foot reflectors he had built himself in the 1780s and set it up for me in the roof of that old tower, now a working observatory. You must see this most beautiful instrument next time. I'm already sketching the moon and Saturn's rings. Anyway, I had better be off and face the wrath of your aunt … I hope her mood has improved!"

"You have five hours yet before your beau arrives … surely you don't need *all* that time to get ready do you?" Medora replied knowingly.

"Ha, ha, my friend … certainly not. Well okay… perhaps two thirds of it now you ask," Morag replied laughing, getting out of her comfortable chair reluctantly but already contemplating which particular dress to choose. She was glad she had brought her large trunk on the train, despite the weight. "But I must borrow one of Ada's books on electricity and magnetism and read it thoroughly. My knowledge is lacking in natural philosophy and I don't want to be caught out. He is an intensely serious man on this topic of speciality which I am sure will prevail over dinner … but I intend to dazzle him further with my chemistry. Guess what? We're heading for the Wellington, you mentioned yesterday."

"Now I am jealous, a proper restaurant too for your date … be gone wretch. I assume you will wish to sneak out whilst the family gets into combat, so I have alerted Agnes to help you personally this afternoon to look your best."

Medora gave her a large hug, as the two chows bounded in, barking like crazy before shooting off towards Lady Byron's private quarters, knocking over a lamp stand enroute.

*

Once they were seated, Morag looked around the dining room discretely but saw nobody she knew. A surprisingly large number of couples occupied the tables, those in the centre of the room being big and communal with a few families and remarkably quiet children in attendance. They had been led to a lovely, quiet spot near the window. The beautiful and ornate building they were in, number 50 St James Street, was a fine conversion, painted and wallpapered in the most contemporary striped late Georgian style, the head waiter having mentioned that the location was originally Crockford's, an exclusive Gentleman's Club with a raucous reputation 'for gambling and entertainment', so Faraday commented.

Taken aback that he was familiar with such decadent abodes, once again she felt confused with his apparent dichotomies. Perhaps Michael really did separate his oratorical sermons from his electrical laboratories. Did he also do the same with his pleasure time?

It wasn't the best time of year for eating out, the restricted winter menu still prevailed but they settled on the dish of the day, a spring lamb stew cooked with 'unusual exotic herbs and special techniques culled from the orient'. Morag was delighted when a chef, dressed in a white gown and cap, presented them with a sample of the dish to try and some bread and bottled olive starters. The seasonal vegetables of carrots, broccoli and turnip were plentifully added and a quick taste confirmed a delightfully delicate and spicy onion flavour, with some peppers which she had never tasted before, accentuating her hunger. Faraday confirmed the dish was similar to one he had eaten many years before in Naples when he had been on a scientific tour of Europe, as a valet and assistant, and crossed into Italy where he saw Mount Vesuvius. In hushed tones he admitted he had personally met Napoleon Bonaparte, when his master received a medal for science. Morag was intrigued to know more of his travels and soon they were devouring large platefuls of stew from a silver tureen, kept warm with a heating oil lamp. Faraday also requested to be brought the best red claret of the house to savour their food with.

Faraday readily revealed how, before he met his wife, he had been apprenticed to a bookbinder and through much reading and self-education he became more and more interested in science, and decided to dedicate himself to making contacts in London and attending lectures regularly at the Royal Institution.

Morag was fascinated and listened spellbound because unlike her husband who had been formally Cambridge educated, Faraday was completely self taught, exactly like her.

"So how did you end up travelling around Europe on a science tour?" she asked, downing the last half glass of claret and feeling her head going pleasantly woozy, as the chef returned with another bottle and a silver platter, atop of which sat the most beautiful, freshly baked and steaming apple charlotte pudding, sprinkled generously with sugar.

"My goodness Michael, this will make me fat ..."

"Nonsense, you have the slimmest of figures if I may say, plenty of room yet," he replied jocularly, happy with his evening's special company. She blushed and he spooned out a large helping for each, smothering his own with lashings of fresh cream. "So, back to my travels, my dear Morag. All down to finally becoming employed as Assistant, in 1813, to the Director of the Institution himself, one Sir Humphry Davy. He had an insatiable penchant for exotic travel, alongside dedication to the most original science discovery of the highest order, particularly in the field of chemistry, and, I may say," he whispered looking around, "a sharp eye for beautiful ladies."

"And did you follow Mr Davy's example in all those things, Michael?"

"All except the last," he replied with a large grin. "Sir Humphry was my mentor, inspiration and life guide; to him I owe all my success. However, he could also be petulant and temperamental and during the 1820s became critical of my growing work in electricity, claiming plagiarism, untrue of course. But in respect, I ceased such work, continuing with my professorship in chemistry until his untimely death in 1829 at far too early an age. Of course, he was abroad again doing science, in Geneva. Since them electricity and magnetism are my enduring interests."

He looked hard at his companion. He was decidedly boring her having as usual dominated their conversation all evening. When would he learn? It was time for the bill.

Morag had drifted into a dreamy trance, accentuated by her lack of experience with alcohol. But her response was quite the opposite of boredom. Deep in her mind she was weighing up a difficult decision to say something she had painfully kept for so long, and this moment was right, with a person she not only could trust but respected and admired. The moment was sufficiently intimate, something she had not experienced for so long since her husband passed away. But she was apprehensive of new feelings she thought had long since died, unexpectedly flaring up again inside her body, and so many voices in her head were telling her it was wrong and inappropriate. Instantly she returned to the conversation, sensing the lull. Yes, it was indeed time.

"A fascinating account, Michael," she said slowly, fighting every slurred syllable with determined decorum. "I am very keen to hear more, much more. But I have something I wish to tell you … something nobody in this entire world has knowledge of now except me. And it may resolve the pursuit of your original question and why we are here together this lovely evening in your search for an answer."

There was a moment's silence as she brought her thoughts together. "I was brought up alone an only child, in Parbold, a tiny village in Lancashire, by my mother who had returned as a pregnant widow from Italy and bore me there. We lived comfortably in a small cottage alongside the canal on the vast estate of a local landowner. My mother was a gifted pianist and flautist, having been formally trained in a top conservatoire in Rome. As I grew up, she and I managed to live well from both the musical tuition she gave and the special dressmaking she undertook, for she never lost her love for fashion, beauty and skill with a needle."

"A feature, if I may be so bold as to confirm, I think you have inherited from your mother in every way, Lady McKenzie," he replied now silent and listening hard. "Pray, do continue."

"My mother was well educated, not only in the arts and music but the sciences too and had a ferocious dedication to learning. She taught me rigorously all I needed and much more … our cottage overflowed with books, and I was an eager scholar, devouring all. From a child of only three, I displayed a notable aptitude for science discovery and the exploration of nature around me. Her tutoring of the landowner's children enabled her to purchase me a small microscope and telescope too. By the age of twelve, I had sufficient Latin, natural philosophy, natural history, mathematics and chemistry to have entered university, but of course am eternally barred from such pleasures as a woman."

"I sincerely hope one day that the will and love of the Creator will prevail and that this devilish aberration be eliminated so our society will recoup the rewards of equal education and opportunity for all of its citizens. But sadly I doubt if I will live to see such change."

"You may, Michael. I intend to enter a political campaign with others of like mind to effect that change. Such judgement is a moral and social repugnancy, a serious blight on civilised English society."

"With Ada I presume? Who I know shares your beliefs."

"Sadly, I would like her to participate very much but her health remains frail … I could not permit her. This fight will require a robust constitution which I have the good fortune to retain."

"I understand … alas." He sighed. An appearance of grieving drew suddenly across his gaze. "I understand the Countess of Lovelace's burdens only too well. I am afraid I am not too well myself, an over-exertion of body and mind came to a conclusion two years since with a fearful breakdown, which manifests in ongoing depression which I must fight daily with prayer three times and simple living. I am compelled to take it easy and have significantly reduced my workload and responsibilities, although I do enjoy still giving the lectures, and read much with delight, but original work, even in electricity has been scant. Perhaps this condition will improve in due course. I wish you luck and support with your worthy endeavour. Do please continue."

She looked into his sad eyes; his loss of research vitality was a predicament paining him greatly. He was like a bear, wrapped up tightly in chains waiting for his captors to die and an angel to release him. Immediately she felt a strong wave of desire. Mr Michael Faraday needed someone special who not only understood and would match his intellectual needs but had the capability to release those demons and make his scientific mind fertile and productive once more. She would become that angel. She knew instantly she could love him dearly … but how?

"I sincerely believe your great powers will restore soon, Michael, they are merely in slumber, waiting for the appropriate spring tide to release their hibernation."

She patted his hand gently, not thinking, wrong, wrong, wrong. Some dandy, foppish fool with his moll, wearing an old fashioned wig and listening into their conversation, was watching with impertinent delight. She shot a severe glance across, sufficient to draw the man's gaze away. Simultaneously, Faraday drew his hand away, instantly conflicted with intent and necessity.

She drew a deep breath and continued, allaying the embarrassment for both. "Ultimately, through marriage and now widowhood, I became the owner of that vast estate of Orsbrick Hall. However, my mother would never allow me the knowledge to know who my father really was, except that it was not her former husband. For in her eyes she had committed cardinal sin, but her true love and ardour for my father had been all-prevailing and never left her. Only at the end, on her death bed following a premature seizure, she revealed his name. My father, Michael, was Sir Humphry Davy."

Faraday felt a strange chill run throughout his body, like a malevolent ghost of some form had returned. He sat back in his chair, his face drawn and thought in silence, digging deeply into his memories of those enjoyable years abroad with Davy, despite the unpleasant daily nagging of Jane, Davy's wife, who refused to accept him as any more than a lowly servant to the great scientist. "May I be so impertinent as to ask when you were born?" he asked, shyly.

"Of course, it was January 3rd 1816."

"So you were conceived ... in the spring of 1815?" His face went ashen. His mind, still sharp, fell pinpointed onto matters of the far past and immediately recalled a painful and disturbing incident.

Davy's wife had already been sent home when the snows cleared that winter, but Davy had insisted the two of them continue their tiring scientific tour for longer. They had just visited Volta and had incurred very satisfactory electrical exchanges, ending up again in Italy, at Rome. But the nights, on Davy's insistence, were packed with much social frivolity, dances, gambling and of course women, especially as Davy was now outside of direct marital censure. However, one special and sophisticated young woman in her late teens ended up being regularly escorted … tall, with very long, dark hair and extraordinarily beautiful with the most inviting complexion, reputedly half Sardinian and half English. She was married to an English diplomat, a Count and a decorated army officer. Davy found her captivating and witty and became totally entranced … when her husband discovered the dalliance and a duel by sabre was issued forthwith. Faraday, greatly concerned for his mentor who was no match for this swordsman, took matters into hand. He could not conceive of allowing one of England's greatest science discoverers to be despatched like a gutted pig for the sake of an unwise and silly infatuation, and after painful persuasion and much argument persuaded Davy to depart for Switzerland and promised to personally take care of the situation and persuade the Count to drop the matter. However, Faraday's crazy heat-of-the-moment plan drummed up in desperation and shared with no one, least of all Davy, of paying a number of trusted local brigands to kidnap and lightly maim the diplomat sufficient to stop him wielding a sword temporarily and encourage a settlement, all badly backfired when the Count was accidentally shot in the fracas and killed. The body was weighted and dumped in a lake, never to be found, and Faraday had to double the final payment to ensure permanent silence and escape promptly, his own life in mortal danger. This had been the only gross misdeed in his entire existence, for which he had prayed so long and so hard for God's forgiveness.

Only the slow passing of time, his religious devotion, the pure love of his dear wife, and a lifelong dedication to serving the Lord by revealing the ways of His nature to all mankind, had abated the demons within his conscience of such a stupid and regrettable act. All he lived for was to do good work in science and humanity ... and now these revelations of Lady McKenzie had brought that fearful episode and the nightmare back. He had to find out. Taking a full glass of claret, he lit a cigar to calm his nerves, mindful that his temptress opposite was watching and appraising his reaction. No ... no ... he must not think like that, Morag McKenzie was not a temptress of the Devil. Was she instead a messenger from God? An angel of science in disguise? Perhaps he was being gently led to move on from his terrible mistake of causing a faultless man to be killed as well as the blatant lies to Davy to cover the real truth up. His long penance had been served. Was this God's way of final forgiveness, so he could resume his scientific endeavours with the same vigour as before? His mind was in turmoil, but he had to stay rational and ask more.

"My dear Michael, you look a little grey. Are you not feeling well?" Morag whispered, concerned for his sudden melancholy, silence and drawn appearance.

"I'm fine, thank you Morag. A little light-headiness is, I am pleased to say, now going as it usually does," he replied hastily and regained his composure unambiguously. This revelation had been a shock to his system without any doubt. "Sometimes a symptom of my nervous debilitation is to acquire a sudden attack, but a little alcohol and smoke and the menace vanishes," he replied, thinking on his feet. He breathed in deeply and smiled again.

Morag felt relieved having been ready to call over the establishment owner and take Michael straight to a hospital, although that was an experience she wished to avoid in the centre of London, with such dirt, destitution and squalor. Plagues of cholera and typhus were ever present that year, not least in so called places of healing.

"Was your mother's name perchance Francesca? Lady Francesca Appleton?"

She stared. How did Mr Faraday know such a thing, as this was a title her mother would never use in England? "Why ... yes ... but how?"

He interrupted gently. "I was briefly introduced to such a lady in Rome when Sir Humphry and I were at the end of our tour. She was giving a violin recital of works of Haydn, playing in a quartet. Very talented and beautiful with dark hair. We spoke briefly and she was very interested in the latest science discoveries. I think Mr Davy visited her for more conversation."

Morag's face lit up, beaming and ecstatic. Yes, it had to be her mother and that period would have been the time she and her father embarked on an affair. But what a peculiarly strange coincidence that Michael had met her then. Perhaps it was fate, a message from the dark universe that he would become a bright and shining star amongst her collection of dull nebulae. "You met her? But she never spoke of my father when I was a child. Yes, indeed she was a fine musician. Do you know why my mother and Mr Davy, obviously they were lovers, never continued their relationship? All I know is that her husband, an aristocrat, met with some fearful accident and she was left virtually destitute, much debt to be repaid and scraped enough money to flee from Italy to England where she had cousins. That was the reason I was born where I was, in obscurity."

"I'm afraid I do not know, Morag. Mr Davy of course was married and returned to his wife. He never mentioned anything and sadly probably never knew of what transpired or about you. But I am sure if he had he would have been extremely proud of you. You have, if I may say, inherited his gift for science and the beauty and poise of your mother, Francesca. The likeness of her is quite noticeable."

He knew he could say that without lying and offending his Creator because all his lies had been long spent in penance and remorse. But now he had to live with the added burden that if he had been less rash then maybe Sir Humphry and Lady Francesca would have remained together for their daughter. It finally struck him. There was a cause for this revelation, a divine intervention directly by God, bringing his obligation of private atonement for those past wrongdoings to a new phase. He had a duty, an obligation moreover, to encourage Morag McKenzie in her scientific quest and ensure her success. But alas he was inexorably drawn to her. His mind was drowning in a black whirlpool of desire, exactly the way he had violently desired her mother so long ago, but was too shy and inept to compete with his experienced mentor. What did it all mean? He must resist such temptation. He wished his sweet wife Sarah was at home so he could thoroughly discuss and expunge these burning conflicts. She would help him to resolve his moral dilemma without rancour, and steer him to the correct redemption and necessary prayer, as always.

*

Outside Lady Annabella's townhouse, Faraday's carriage had discretely withdrawn around the corner to a side street. He stood with Morag in the shadows under the two ancient elm trees, both huddled in their thick coats from the chill, the tiny gas light outside the door flickering with a smoky, yellow flame.

At midnight, the usual mayhem of the evening with people rushing about endlessly had dissipated sharply. This was a quieter and select area. The poverty and social dislocation where the poor working class lived ten to a room was over half a mile away, although there lingered a faint smell of sewage and smoke in the air from somewhere. A match-seller had been loitering nearby but Morag had once again relieved her of five boxes with one shilling and sixpence, this time to get rid of her. Now she and Mr Faraday were alone. They had been arguing on the way back about the direction of science she should pursue. Morag had amused Faraday with her unexpected disclosure of researches into coal tar dyes, inspired by the properties of benzene discovered in the mid 1820s and was close to some groundbreaking new discoveries with her latest oxidation techniques involving indigo, to extend the coloration range and create a possible artificial dye. She was convinced not only of the potential of coal tar to provide a basis for dyes, but that the commercial opportunity with the textiles industry in Lancashire, the biggest by far in the world, would be huge. But once again Morag displayed her academic isolation and non-interaction with university research, poor access to Royal Society papers and her weak network of collaboration because of her female sex. But Faraday was hugely impressed with her originality and determination, exactly the same characteristic displayed by her father and his mentor, Humphry Davy. They discussed Davy's safety lamp for mines and Davy's regret that he became sidetracked with other interesting work and failed to improve the original design, whose flaws led to unnecessary explosions and lives lost at the coalface. Finally she was totally mortified when Faraday teased her that he was the actual person to discover benzene, a straightforward fact that she was completely unaware of. She listened quietly as he made a renewed plea.

"Your capabilities in the area of electricity and magnetism are already proven to me. So I implore you to leave the dyes and associated chemistry to others and put your effort and time, alongside me, into electricity. I was inspired by your vision, over dinner, of electricity being generated on a massive scale by reversing the motor rotation in magnetic fields using giant dynamos … that being the only way to make progress in the field because of the serious limitations of batteries. Especially, I admire your concept that electricity could run alongside gas and even replace lighting in the home and outside as another municipal service alongside water. It is a vision and insight that is inspiring me to want to work fully again, for the first time in years, but with you alongside me. I could do so much to help you."

Morag blinked. She realised she had the great and famous Michael Faraday eating out of her hand. Move over Ada with her beau Mr Babbage, two can play that game. "Perhaps I can be persuaded, but I must think very hard about it," she replied coquettishly, very aware he was speaking close to her mouth, his steamy breath blowing over her nostrils. It was time to act and seal the deal. Without warning she gently grabbed his head and pulled his lips towards hers. Faraday went into inner shock. He wanted to engage and repel her simultaneously, but she had been whittling away his stoic resistance throughout the evening with her intellect, beauty and composure, until now. His resistance dissolved into a dizzy haze like iron disintegrating in a bath of nitric acid. He had lost Morag's mother to Davy all those years back and he was not going to lose her daughter. Fearful that he would push her away for her gross impudence, instead she felt him respond, the gentle warmth of his lips moving against hers as he grasped her with both arms and held her tightly to his chest, pushing his silk gloved hand through her thick, dark hair under her hood. Below, she instantly felt his excitement pressing against her. He may have a nervous disposition in the head but the rest seemed to be working just fine, making her feel so desirous her body could explode. They continued for a few minutes, but she remained guarded, in no rush to venture headlong into a relationship. There was so much to consider on so many fronts. She drew back and smiled.

"Thank you truly for a lovely evening … goodnight Michael, I must go. Lady Byron's servants will be waiting up for me."

He stood back and looked around nervously. What had taken over him? But quickly she was stepping off over the squelching pavement towards the house as he stood watching, his body shaking and his mind on fire. But God had not struck him down dead. Perhaps he could, in the cold chill of the bumpy ride back to his lodgings at Albemarle Street, rationally reconcile his devil weakness and unthinkable betrayal of Sarah. Or perhaps this was all meant to be.

A few yards further on Morag stopped and turned. "Michael," she said in a hushed voice, once more flashing that dazzling smile which turned his stomach into jelly. "Next week on Monday, I shall be returning to Lancashire. Will you come back with me on the train to Orsbrick Hall and stay for a few days? We can discuss your research proposals and I would like to show you my laboratory? Nine-thirty at Euston station?"

The only rational explanation he could believe was that the Lord God above wanted him to go for the furtherance of science, as he found himself immediately saying yes, he would be there.

Morag was elated and happy ringing the doorbell, unaware that the chink in the downstairs curtain was hastily drawn across and a figure, muttering avowed disapproval of what had just been seen, slunk off into the shadows of the rear. Opening the door, Agnes, relieved to see Morag returned safely, fussed around with a nightcap of hot chocolate, having already laid out her pretty silk and lace frilled, foulard printed nightgown carefully on the bed, admiring the lovely patterns. She had lit a small fire so the temperature in the room was more comfortable to change. This was one of the few houses in London with two water-closets which Agnes had cleaned scrupulously earlier and there was even piped water inside. Lady Byron had been insistent the year before, despite the huge cost. Although where the waste ended up was anyone's guess as Agnes hadn't seen a cess pit disposal cart for months, perhaps everything went straight into the Thames.

When Morag awoke at nine to a hearty breakfast tray of eggs and smoked haddock, Medora couldn't resist any longer and dived into her bedroom to sit and gossip whilst Morag tucked into the hot food.

"I don't know how," Medora began, "but Ada has got it directly into her head all of a sudden, insisting that there is intrigue going on between you and your visitor, Mr Faraday. Sometimes my sister can become so contradictory. I thought she had positively encouraged such a liaison but now she seems distinctly sour and her migraine is back. But I expect you are in neither a confirm nor deny mood, aren't you?"

"Of course," Morag purred, cutting off a thick slice of brown bread. "There's plenty in that pot, pour yourself a coffee. But what I can say is he was a very kind and honourable gentleman over dinner, excellent company."

"And after?"

"Never you mind," Morag replied.

Both giggled loudly. But she did feel concern about Ada's unexpected change of view on her and Mr Faraday. Certainly Ada's health continued to be a worry and Lady Byron's badgering and disapproval of Ada's lifestyle wasn't helping. Perhaps Ada's expectations with Mr Babbage and her constant overzealous mania for mathematical work and study were not in balance. Morag vowed to ensure Ada's well-being where she could … so the less said the better.

# Chapter Five

April 3rd 2026, Good Friday – the cruise ship terminal at the port of Liverpool

Glancing briefly at her watch, Victoria shuffled her bags and downed a cup of hot coffee, annoyed that she couldn't take her time, as she always liked in the morning. They were late. Maddie had decided she needed to recheck her suitcase, having mislaid her phone, Belle was still drying her hair and Abby was helping both of them. The usual morning chaos at Orsbrick Hall, but they really needed to get to Liverpool on time. Today was special. She stared at the heap of dirty cups and dishes left on the table and shouted through the partition to Julian and Lynton, pouring over a large plan on the table in the study. "I hope you two are going to wash this lot up. I knew it was a mistake giving Claire and Danielle a week off at the same time. Where are those boys?"

A voice from behind interrupted her male directed vitriol. "Hello, my name is Sabrina. Do not worry about the domestic discord, I shall take care of it all to your complete satisfaction. May I help your journey time by optimising the route of your driverless car outside?"

Victoria, thrown, turned around sharply. Simultaneously Abby, with Maddie and Belle alongside, waltzed in chatting, suitcases finally ready. A stunned silence pervaded. They all stared, mouths open, at the young and very attractive tanned female, in a crop top and matching short skirt, smiling unperturbed whilst skilfully shuffling all the dirty crockery together at breakneck speed onto a tray. Julian and Lynton were standing at the doorway, chuckling loudly. Her mousy coloured hair was cut in a fashionable bob and her skin, green eyes and facial features were flawless. Except something wasn't right. Victoria, ever the sceptical scientist, looked closely at Sabrina's legs and arms. Her skin was just too suspiciously amazing to be true.

Fast deductions were equally flying through the minds of her daughters. "Gosh, Mum," Maddie whispered. "Sabrina is a robot, but quite unlike anything I've ever seen. Where has she come from?"

Sabrina looked up playfully at Maddie, scrutinising both her and Belle in detail before glancing at Abby. "Hello, you must be Madeleine and Annabelle. I recognise you both from your images in my memory. Please let me take your cases to the car." Deftly she picked up each heavy case with ease and shoving Abby's bag under her arm, marched out through the backdoor.

Lynton, still laughing, took the rest of the bags and followed Sabrina as Julian walked forward and hugged Victoria, who remained incredulous. "Sorry, I couldn't resist. I thought it was a fitting epithet to your grand tour. Sabrina is a state of the art prototype, a closely guarded secret design which has taken the level of artificial intelligence right to its extreme capabilities. You remember Ash Kolinsky, in California at Stamford?"

"Professor Kolinsky, the divorced Hungarian guy in his fifties whose daughters you privately tutored briefly on creative writing?"

"The very one. He's a renowned expert on AI and he asked me, as a favour, to test her out for a month. We're very honoured at Orsbrick, normally they don't get out of the laboratory, but Sabrina is special."

Abby cut in. "I can see that? So how come she's Asian, young and female and wears micro-skirts?"

"Ash rather prefers that type of lady … especially from North Korea."

"Which is why he's divorced I assume," Victoria added waspishly. "I hope she cooks better beans on toast than you do," she continued laconically. "I remember when we first met, you said you loved cooking, but the lack of evidence subsequently confirmed I was in the hands of a con-man!" Maddie and Belle laughed heartily. Abby was deep in thought about something. "Anyway, we must hurry. Let's get into the Beast. I hope Sabrina's programming is better than her dress sense."

Julian gave Victoria a final hug. "But I did compensate in those days by providing the most congenial company ever and did make a bit of money … err … eventually," he muttered playfully. Lynton gave Abby a giant kiss, to cries of "ahh" from everyone, including Ned and Zac who had wandered in, effusively describing Sabrina as a cool dude.

"And you be careful how you handle that robot!" Abby said, in a low voice back to a mystified Lynton. In no time they were off to the cruise terminal in Liverpool.

*

Making full use of the commendable first class facilities, Victoria sat patiently with a gin and tonic, waiting for the arrival and inaugural launch of the Queen Lusitania, a replica cruise ship of the original transatlantic liner from the early 1900s. Not only was she pleased to be going together as a family to visit Maddie's dream Harvard, but they could all have a fun break at the same time, something she had regrettably forgotten for far too long, especially with Abby. So it had been her idea to go across on the liner for a leisurely four days as part of the holiday and then fly back. The Queen Lusitania was built by Kessler Ehrenberg, a rich US industrial dye-maker and descendent of one of the twelve hundred people who died when the original Lusitania was sunk by a German U-boat in 1914. His grandfather Adolf Ehrenberg, an industrial chemist, had been on board. Victoria was a consultant and good friend to Kessler and on the board of his company in New York. She was the first to be told of the concept of the ship three years before and promised to be one of the initial passengers when the project had been completed, all paid for with the handsome socialite Kessler's personal compliments. She enjoyed his overt flirting and constant invitations to dinner, but always resisted temptation, although sometimes she wondered having seen Sabrina. She laughed to herself. Unlike her parents, she and Julian maintained a solid and dependable marriage.

"Abby, you're uncharacteristically deep in thought? A dollar for each of them," Maddie suddenly chimed, swigging down her coke.

Victoria came in immediately. "Yes, out with it, what's the matter? Something's bothering you. You've been far too quiet since we left," tearing open a large bag of nuts on the table.

Abby looked up. "I'm fine … it's just … well … Four male bucks on their own all week with a sexy female robot? Do you think they would …?"

Grimacing, Belle jumped in immediately. "Don't go there Abby, not even my reprobate brothers are that gross. Anyway," she said laughing. "If Sabrina tries it on with Ned, Nancy will pull all her wires out."

They roared with glee and Abby's grin returned, when suddenly she pointed out to sea. A large vessel had just come into view and was heading at speed for the dock entrance. "Hey, four funnels, that must be the Queen Lusitania. Gosh she's massive; I can see at least three decks."

Victoria handed around a picture of the original maiden voyage way back in 1906. "For a short time the Lusitania was the world's biggest passenger liner before the Mauritania her sister ship was launched. We should be on board in an hour and we not only have first class tickets, as you might expect if I do the booking, but I can reveal yet another surprise. Dress code most of the time will be the usual jeans and tops, whatever, but for evening dinner, which will be special each day, formal period wear is requested for ladies. So, knowing your sizes and I think, pretty well, your tastes, I've ordered all of us outfits which will be in our cabins. However, you'll have to allow me some latitude, so no shouting ... and garments will include bustles and petticoats!"

Belle and Maddie gave their mother a hug. "Thank you so much for everything," Maddie cried. "I've always fancied wearing Victorian. It will be so exciting, we'll be able to dress up like Mauveine."

"Will there be formal dances too with eligible handsome suitors?" Belle whispered, lowering her eyes in mock deference.

"Yes, everything is replicated as accurately as possible, but no suitors!" Victoria replied, starting on the large bag of smoky corn crisps. "I do like your new glasses, Belle. The large frames suit your face so much better."

"You'll be dressing up Edwardian actually, but the fashion was very similar. The mega-changes set in after the end of the First World War," Abby added, looking ruefully at her tummy. "I think I might need a corset."

"That can be arranged," Victoria replied grinning. "Let's go to the VIP queue, the walkway has been lowered. Our cases will be taken to separate cabins, home from home comfort and privacy, I insisted on that concession, but this is an authentic heritage experience so no wifi or mobile phones. Get your moaning over now before we board."

Universal groans were uttered, especially from Abby, addicted to Amazon's 3D-Classics. She had been looking forward to 'Star Wars' in bed.

*

Already well out into the Irish Sea, they settled quickly into cabins on the top deck and unpacked before meeting together to take a leisurely stroll around the vast area. Everywhere was fitted out with the same first class luxury provided in1906. Bigger cruise ships built in modern times existed, but the long, sweeping expanse, and plentiful space was impressive. So much to see and this was by far the largest vessel any of them had sailed on. Considering there were no stabilisers, the ride was gentle and the view superb. At least the first day was good weather and the wind remained light. Abby had seriously under-counted initially. There were ten decks, including a fabulous promenade for strolling in reasonable weather. Conveniently their first class cabins were also on this deck, part of the so-called two 'regal' suites, specially reserved for Victoria and family by Kessler personally, with their bedrooms clustered around a parlour, including a small private dining room with waiter service. A shelter deck below was available when conditions were inclement. Walking around, they quickly realised some concessions to modernity had been made. The lifeboats on the boat deck above had been redesigned and equipped to modern safety standards and the engines, whilst made to a similar specification, were running on oil and not coal, now hard to acquire since the 2025 UN worldwide ban on carbon mining. There were other modifications. All the first class rooms were ensuite, but differentiated pricing and basic cabin comfort amongst the three classes had been retained and decks remained separated, Third class basic tickets had been heavily discounted for the maiden voyage and a raucous, noisy crowd from Liverpool inhabited the lower decks. The owners had received an historic exemption certificate to permit a smoking room, reserved for men only, and a reading and writing room reserved for women only. Smoking in cabins and dining rooms was however not permitted this time around.

Victoria suggested they go for tea and cake at the popular Verandah Café on the boat deck, beautifully decorated with ivy trellises and wickerwork, but Maddie and Belle wanted to spend time in the reading room, fascinated by the etched glass windows, carved pilaster wall mouldings and large library of period books.

Sipping tea in a china cup, Victoria was glad to finally sit down and relax. They must have walked at least five miles up and down those decks. She looked across and realised that Abby had not acquired her sea legs yet, especially as they were moving out into open sea and the swell had increased significantly. Abby, in turn had forgotten about her tendency to sea-sickness and fished promptly in her bag for a tablet.

"I know Vikki, but we need some concessions to 2026, at least my stomach does. I'll be fine soon. Actually, I'll just pop out on deck for five minutes and get a breath of air. Your fifty-year-old sea legs need a rest. Stay there, you can have my carrot cake."

"Is it that obvious?" Victoria protested, before grabbing the second slice. "Mmm ... thanks. Sailing makes me hungry, must be the fresh air. Promise I'll go to yoga again with you when we get home, but the pull of the laboratory has been more extreme than usual these past three months, especially as I've been on a roll with the xanthene reincarnation."

The wind had been rising and outside was very blustery. Abby wrapped her coat tightly around and walked up to the rail, staring down hard at the crashing waves as the ship lurched strongly through the water, spray filling the air. Anyone with any sense was indoors, but she was glad for the fresh breeze in her face and sidled up to another lonely figure, dressed heavily in an equally thick black coat, gloves and a large hood pulled over their head.

Staring straight ahead, Abby shouted to her companion alongside, "We must be crazy, standing out here in this weather."

"I was crazy coming here, but it was something we always wanted to do," a sanguine female voice replied, sounding very tortured in the wind.

Abby felt a strange sensation ripple down her back; she had heard that voice before and turned in shock as her companion lowered the hood.

"Mauveine? Oh gosh ... I don't know what to say. What are you doing here? Where's Isi?" She stared at Mauveine's sad and troubled face and immediately realised all was not good, as her head throbbed with that far from welcome psychic indicator.

"Isi never arrived at the departure. We always wanted to go on an Atlantic cruise together in the 1890s but never found the time then," Mauveine replied in that rich Lancashire accent, but this time her diction was clearer and not crackly. "I'm sorry, I have to go Abigail, I need to try and find the reason ... and I must locate Fenella."

Her face was tinged with tears and exhibited a drawn, concerned expression that Abby was instantly alarmed about as she cried out, "But Mauveine, perhaps we can help maybe if ..." but Mauveine walked off and faded away into the misty spray. Who was Fenella?

Abby took a deep breath. Her stomach at least was finally adjusting and she felt much better already thanks to the pills. Her head had also stopped throbbing, when the sharp whiff of engine oil fumes from the two middle funnels filled her nostrils. No way was she going to spoil Victoria's sailing treat by mentioning a miserable Mauveine spotting. This concern would be kept to herself for now … although she realised that Mauveine's appearance may also be made to one or other of them.

"Hey, how are you feeling? I must say that facial tinge of fluorescein green seems to have faded away."

Abby turned to see Victoria with Maddie and Belle alongside and smiled generously, but a glance at Maddie was sufficient to confirm she had not been alone in that unexpected sighting.

Victoria continued. "Funny smell here, I reckon they're using paraffin not oil in those engines." Abby said nothing; the odour was definitely aniline again. Victoria had forgotten, neither was a good sign. "Anyway, I suggest we head back to our rooms and change. You should see the incredible first class dining room, with two levels, absolutely huge and a great glass dome over the top."

"And five musicians, dressed up in dinner jackets, are already playing Mozart, but we've got plenty of time. Dinner isn't till seven, awesome," Belle added excitedly. She was especially pleased to be on the trip and looking forward to doing the Harvard campus tour with her sister whilst Abby and her mother went shopping.

Abby yawned as they walked back to the magnificent staircase which joined the decks up and said, "Sounds good, my turn for a nap too."

Once inside their regal suite, Victoria disappeared for a shower and Belle went off to fetch some bottles of water. They shared an ancient looking fridge in the tiny kitchen, but Belle couldn't remember whether that was a concession or not for 1906, then recalled that efficient fridge like-ice boxes were used domestically in that period.

Maddie, now alone with Abby, spoke immediately. It was clear to Abby she was distressed. "You'll never guess? When we were sat in the reading room, up in a little table near the corner, I spotted someone hunched in deep concentration over a pile of books and when I looked closer it was Mauveine but alone. No Isi anywhere. She looked terribly worried. I stared and she looked back really forlorn. Her eyes had rings around them like she hadn't been sleeping, but ghosts don't sleep so that's silly. I turned to Belle to tell her but then Mauveine disappeared. I'm worried."

"I know ... I saw her on the deck just before you arrived, also no Isi. Something isn't right, I agree, but there's not much we can do and apart from a twinge when I saw her I don't feel like I did when ... well ... when the prism of purpurine drama unfolded. And we're here to have fun, and you have a Harvard course to sort out in three days time."

"I feel fine too. I expect Mauveine will find Isi in the smoking room with all the other guys. I remember he was partial to a big cigar."

Abby nodded, not entirely convinced when a voice called out, "What are you two talking about, muttering around the water-cooler? Well actually a McCray fridge invented in 1887, I think." Victoria and Belle had reappeared with bottles of water.

Maddie glanced at Abby, fast on her feet. "Mum, we all adore our fabulous period dresses, thank you so much."

"As long as that dining room has the heating turned up. You know I'm very nesh, especially as they're so very off-shoulder," Abby added quickly.

Maddie continued. "But Abby and I are not convinced about those drawers. They're sort of weird with the legs not joined properly … like crotchless? Did you have to be that authentic?"

Victoria and Belle laughed loudly.

"Maddie," Belle uttered, holding her sides with mirth. "With all that crinoline and bustle round you as well as a corset, you're a scientist, think. How are you going to get a pair of knickers down? You can now discretely place a bowl underneath when some dashing upper class beau chats you up and you're bursting to go."

They laughed together, Mauveine problem averted, and soon they were sitting demurely listening to Mozart, as the duck à l'orange and seasonal vegetables were brought to their table. The four rapidly caught the unending attention of every passing male and female. Definitely, this was going to be a fun night to remember.

Whilst the mini-orchestra took a well-deserved break and Victoria was ensconced in a slow dance with the persistent Mr Kessler himself, Belle was being chatted up on deck by his nineteen year old son, Abel, who had joined the boat by helicopter. Not exactly 1906. Abby and Maddie stood quietly at the bar waiting for drinks.

"I wonder who Fenella is," Abby said, handing over a twenty pound note.

"Fenella?"

"Mauveine actually spoke, the last thing she said was she had to find Fenella. Any idea?"

"Not a name I've heard or seen anywhere but ... I'm just thinking," Maddie replied quietly, her brow furrowed in deep concentration. "Look, this is a long shot, but Mauveine may have some hidden agenda for being on this ship."

"An agenda? But Mauveine's a ghost. Why would she have an agenda here?"

"Not one now, but one she had back then. Maybe we need to think about where this ship is going, where we're all going? Just something Judy said in the Red Lion the day she got married. She'd discovered in the archives that Robert McKenzie had a second younger sister, born in the priory but hidden away somewhere. She ran away to Liverpool at fifteen and ended up on a ship going to Salem and got caught up in the 1680s witch trials. Judy was speculating that Fiona's mother may even have been Zelda. Whatever happened to her was a mystery. But what if there is another family line somewhere? Perhaps, back at Orsbrick Hall and that Fenella is part of it who Mauveine knew of? A mystery Fenella McKenzie. Someone else to add to the list when we do some family history research in Salem."

"Mmm ... seems a little far-fetched but on the other hand, given everything else that has happened of late, then we should keep an open mind. Something about Vikki tonight ... I think she may also have seen Mauveine and is not letting on."

Maddie grabbed the tray of drinks. "Let's ask her when we sit down. Crikey that guy Kessler is a bit persistent, good job Dad isn't here. He wouldn't be pleased in the slightest and neither am I to be honest."

Abby gazed across and was surprised to perceive the dreamy look of a long ago yesteryear enveloping her friend, dancing slowly in a clinch with the ship's owner. Had Victoria consumed rather too many Lusitania Slings? "I think we should go over. And look. Belle is back too with the billionaire's son, his arm around her waist."

"Agreed, Aidan wouldn't be happy either, and he's a lot bigger!"

Muscling into the chairs back at the table, Maddie plonked down the tray of drinks, whilst Abby shuffled up closer to Vikki and gave her the stare, but the glazed look and silly smile in return indicated that the diagnosis was correct, a more than over-indulgence with the liquors.

"Why, hi there, I'm Kessler Ehrenberg, you must be Abigail and Madeleine. Victoria has been telling me all about you two talented and beautiful ladies," Kessler said in a heavy Southern States drawl. The non-response of a muted yes and two limp handshakes was sufficient for him to decide to retire for the evening gracefully, at least for now, and resume hitting on Victoria the following day. "Well folks, my son Abel and I will leave you all to enjoy the rest of your evening. I'm so glad you love the regal accommodation, best on the whole ship, where the very same King Edward the Seventh himself stayed. Come on now Abel, say goodbye to the lovely Annabelle."

As they sauntered off, Abel turned, blowing a kiss to Belle and uttered, "See you later alligator." They were gone in a flash.

"Bloody hell Belle, what a creep, you can't be serious?" Maddie wailed.

"But a very rich creep," Belle replied softly, with a wink and smile, marking out the future territory of her views on men, distinct from her sister.

Abby had meanwhile tipped Victoria's double gin and tonic into her own and waved the waiter over with a large coffee. "I'm not letting the other big creep, handsome, rich and charming though he undoubtedly is, get you pissed and beddable on your first night. You're venturing into turbulent terrain, Vikki," Abby hissed. "This is just like Saturday nights in Delft all over again."

Victoria nodded, took a deep breath and sipped the hot coffee slowly. Her head swam terribly. "I'm sorry, you're right. Kessler poured me some big multicoloured cocktail, said it had a kick like a Southern mule."

Maddie and Belle were smiling, supping their coke and vodkas. They had never seen their mother, always proper and serious in public, so intoxicated, although they also had to admit she looked very attractive and were not surprised, given Kessler's apparent womanising reputation.

Victoria smiled back and patted both their hands. The caffeine was kicking in, and her brain was returning back to its normal, rational self. Making a spectacle of herself had to stop forthwith. "Thank you all, I'm truly glad the sisterhood looks after its own today. Which reminds me, something happened earlier whilst I was in the ladies adjusting my makeup. Her reflection appeared in the mirror behind me, very unhappy and upset. I was quite startled, but before I could say anything she disappeared."

Abby, staring outside at the deck railings, turned back. "Join the club, I thought as much."

"Hey, me too," Belle cried. "I assume you're talking about Mauveine? She walked past me outside when I was with Abel. I waved but she ignored me totally, walking with her face fixed to the floor, deep in thought, No Isi anywhere which was odd. Abel of course wondered who I was waving at."

They agreed that something was bothering Mauveine but as they had no idea why she was onboard or unhappy there was nothing they could do, so the only plan was to continue to enjoy their trip and keep an eye out for her the next day. A restful sleep in their luxurious environment was beckoning. Soon they were back in their cabins, changed and in bed.

*

Day two, and Easter Saturday continued at a more relaxed pace, with no drinking, quiet reading and indulgence in a Bach concert in the large music room. They enjoyed lunch served in their private dining room and chatted extensively about what they would be doing at Harvard. Maddie had received a ship's telegram from her best friend, Janine, who planned to arrive in the Boston port in her father's SUV to pick up her and Belle and take them to their country house nearby. Both would be staying with Janine's senator parents. Victoria had already decided to leave her capable daughters with Janine to discover and explore Harvard their own way, and find out more about Maddie's course and living there. Over lunch, Victoria then surprised Belle by an announcement which made both girls excited. Julian and Victoria had agreed that if Belle, who was using the opportunity to also find out about medical courses, liked Harvard and passed the rigorous entrance examination in the summer, which Victoria quietly had no concerns about, they would pay for her expensive course and buy a large luxury apartment in Boston that both girls could share. Victoria had reflected hard on her own miserable time escaping home alone to Holland at sixteen and whilst respecting and supporting Maddie's urgent wish to fly the nest and become independent, their circumstances were completely different. They were identical twins and already Victoria and Abby had sensed that Maddie and Belle, deep down, still wanted to be together longer, confirmed by the hugs and thanks and excited chatter afterwards. In the meantime, Victoria and Abby indulged in more tea and cake alone in the Verandah Café, sharing reminiscences about their time together in Holland, laughing at

132

the banal antics of Kessler and son and planning their shopping fest and sightseeing in Boston and Salem. Towards the end of the ten days, they would meet up in Salem again with Maddie and Belle to search some of that McKenzie-Warren history in various archives which Maddie and Judy had been in touch about, with records already identified to delve into in advance.

Evening dinner in the first class dining room came upon them quicker than they realised, sailing in the relative calm of the mid-Atlantic. They felt sad. One more day remained, but they looked forward, especially Maddie and Belle, to seeing America, disembarkation set for early morning of day four. Abby had pre-booked a US version of Beast, a new black BMW X10, so she and Victoria could drive straight to their luxury hotel in the centre of Boston after meeting Janine's parents for an initial chat and a coffee. Everything had returned to how Victoria always liked it; ordered organisation and efficiency. Even Kessler and Abel had unexpectedly taken off again in the company helicopter, much to Victoria's relief, who ordered a bottle of Sauvignon wine to go with the sea bass steaks they had chosen.

Chatting amiably, there had been no further sightings of Mauveine who they put to the backs of their minds for the moment, as the orchestra struck up some Brahms renditions to everyone's delight.

"You know, Vikki, we should do this more often, minus the males," Abby said, separating the bones of her fish, realising this was the first proper holiday she had taken from the gallery in twenty months.

"Yes, good idea. I hope the ground heat pump installation they are supposed to be cracking on with during our absence is progressing. Julian had it in his head that he would do the supervising whilst the others did the digging, but I suspect

Sabrina will have taken over as chargehand and be cracking the whip ruthlessly."

Belle looked up mischievously as Maddie glanced at her. "No Belle," she cried. "Don't even go there." They laughed.

Victoria was relaying more stories about the time she and Eva lived together and had dropped a can of paint over Eva's head, when suddenly Maddie interrupted.

"Sorry Mum, just hang on a second, can you hear that funny noise in the background?"

They stopped eating and listened. A distinct chugging and roaring accompanied by hissing like a steam kettle could be heard above the din of diners talking and the general clatter.

"Sounds odd," Victoria said, "perhaps they're changing the order of the engine running … anyway …"

She resumed her meal when the even stranger sound of a pulsing siren somewhere below could now be heard. At that, the entire dining room went quiet, a faint murmuring and whispering being all that could be discerned, until a siren on the wall suddenly wailed loudly. Diners were becoming agitated when a voice sounded out across the tannoy.

"Passengers and crew please listen carefully. This is the captain speaking, a U-Boat has been spotted. I repeat a U-Boat has been spotted. Do not move or become alarmed, please stay seated. This is a precaution and we are taking immediate action to avert danger."

The ship immediately lurched to the right, accompanied by a thudding sound and a screeching of metal as the level of agitation in the room rose discernibly.

"Do you all realise that the original Lusitania was actually sunk in 1915, by indeed a German U-Boat, off the coast of Ireland?" Maddie said. "By then it was bringing much needed munitions back to the UK from America having been commandeered by the government, but there were still two thousand passengers on board and eleven hundred perished."

"Yes, of course," Victoria replied, seeing Abby's face turning to alarm. The ship had started to lurch from side to side and some people rose up from their seats. "That was why Kessler built the Queen Lusitania, in honour of his grandfather who died. But I must say, this fake enactment of the situation is not in good taste and taking the historic realism way too far … I'm sure the announcement of the end of this poor charade will be on in a minute. I shall reproach Kessler for this at the next board meeting, bad idea, whoever dreamt it up."

But Maddie and Abby suddenly clutched their heads as they each experienced sharp, intense pains. They were being psychically assaulted like neither of them had experienced, not even during the prism of purpurine drama. The wailing of the siren continued and an almighty explosion went off way below, shaking the deck and causing people to tumble and table contents to fly onto the floor.

The tannoy boomed again as the captain's voice rang out. "Emergency, emergency, we have been torpedoed … I repeat we have been torpedoed. Please head in an orderly fashion to the lifeboats on the boat deck. I repeat, head now to the lifeboats."

Maddie grabbed Abby's hand as Victoria instantly put her arm around Belle who had gone white and silent, shaking all over. All she could think of was the film Titanic, her brain was shut down with fear. Victoria held her close, they had to think, coldly, logically and rationally, it was no good panicking blindly. But pandemonium instantly took hold. Screaming and shouting erupted everywhere as the ship lurched over thirty degrees and a mad dash started to the exits. People and children were trampled over, some of the exits had been stupidly locked and tables were being thrown through the glass to create escape routes to the deck. A mad rush to the stairs upwards followed and some people fell screaming through the deck railings in the bedlam, culminating with splashes as they went into the black water. No crew or waiters could be seen, they had been the first to run off.

Maddie shook Abby who had gone inert into some kind of psychic shock with the initial heavy pulsating in her head. "Abby, Abby, please wake up will you. This must be what Mauveine's been about ... but what do we do? We have to all keep together and get to the lifeboats too. Mum, Belle come on, we must escape. Hold hands and head to that other entrance at the end. I remember another way out from the original deck plans I looked at," she cried, her sharp brain revved up into overdrive.

Abby had now come to and pulled Victoria and Belle up, when suddenly there was an even louder explosion, just below their deck. The steel floor burst open in the centre, like a tin can being violently split, throwing them to the floor. The lights had gone completely out, only the dim emergency ones at the door remained visible, as instant darkness and even more screaming pervaded.

Abby still had hold of Maddie, as they both grabbed a table leg bolted down. They had lost Victoria and Belle. All they could see were people sliding towards and disappearing down the huge hole created and a great rush of water could be heard from below. The ship was sinking rapidly.

"Victoria, Belle, where are you?" Abby was screaming at the top of her voice. All they could see were bodies writhing and stumbling around them when a great plume of black water spurted upwards through the hole and covered them in icy cold foam. The large, bolted staff door at the far end suddenly burst open and cold, dark water flew inside. They had minutes left.

Maddie screamed and each, in turn, tore off their bulky dresses, clinging bodily to the table. They would at least swim wherever they could get to whatever it took but still no sign anywhere of Victoria or Belle.

"Shit Abby, look up there on the deck," Maddie screamed, grabbing Abby's arm, lurching in water now up to their chests. Abby flailed around, someone was shouting and grabbing at her legs when she realised Victoria and Belle had found them. They grabbed and held onto each other hard.

"Fuck!" was the last thing Abby said as they all watched Mauveine, standing alone on a plinth silhouetted in the moonlight and staring silently at them, when a huge wave of water rushed in from the other end and carried the four off. Blackness swirled around them as the ship sank like a stone under the waves.

# Chapter Six

**Back in Orsbrick Hall, early morning Easter Saturday**

The sun had barely risen when Julian launched himself out of bed, grabbed a quick shower and then banged on Lynton's door on the way down. If they made haste that morning they could go in time to Leeds and pick up the special cabling required to connect the ground heat pump to the inverter. They had made good progress in the week, digging out the trenching and assembling and laying out all the required components. Having such a large area around the house gave them scope to utilise a lot of potential space for tapping the natural heat underground and then, through suitable electronics, connect to the new electric heaters he had already installed on the ground floor and first floors. The potential savings were large and all the rooms would be given sufficient background heating all year to enable the whole house to be warm whenever, and make full use of all the rooms for the first time. He wasn't concerned about the bill. Money was no longer an issue given the huge amount he had earned through his books and film rights. He was far more interested in piloting the technology to improve energy efficiency and make the environment cleaner for all. His next project would be to trial the new large-scale polymer-ion storage batteries to be linked to a small solar farm using the latest materials which had doubled electrical output from ten years previous, and which he would build near the woods. Unsightly roof panels were an anathema to his conservation beliefs and taste, and anyway were banned on their heritage building.

Julian pulled out the detailed plans to look again at the electrical calculations and the special soldering required for the connectors. He mustn't forget gas for the blowtorch either. As Lynton finally tripped sleepily downstairs, a pleasing waft of bacon and eggs drifted upwards, cheering his returning appetite, dulled by the copious amount of beer consumed by the four in the George the previous night. It was little use trying to raise either Zac or Ned from the dead in their sleeping pits. Despite the bravado, they still didn't have the drinking capacity of their father. But the two brothers had been given the day off, and to be fair, they had worked hard digging and shovelling the whole week.

As Lynton walked into the breakfast room, he caught sight of Sabrina clutching a bag of mushrooms, and deftly waving a frying pan into action with wolfhounds Jeb and Kai beside her golloping their food down. He was glad Julian had brought Sabrina in for the week. She had been brilliant, cooking, cleaning and even helping outside, reading the specs and advising on the digging out. The original plan had been for them to rough it and do their own cooking, but whose reality seemed to entail buying in a crate of beer, and ordering masses of pizzas and Chinese takeaways from Burscough. Much as he occasionally liked Cheung's chicken, egg foo young and fried rice, Abby had spoilt him all those years with her excellent cooking. He wasn't looking forward to time travel back to his student days.

"Good morning Lynton, we also have tomatoes, beans and waffles to go with your bacon and eggs. Please expound your choice," she called out as he eyed her shapely figure and long legs, forgetting for a moment Sabrina was an autonomous

139

robot. She had definitely been programmed to enjoy being leered at which made a change, he thought, a flaw or merit depending on your viewpoint, of the designer's character rather than the final design. "Err, yes please, the full monte, Sabrina."

"That is a film made in Sheffield in 1997, which I believe 89.7% of the population found very funny. Do you wish me to find the DVD or do you want to eat your breakfast naked?"

Julian walked in, laughing hard. "I'm afraid despite the genius capabilities of Kolinsky, she does have a few chips missing. Lynton means add everything," he shouted out into the kitchen.

"Thank you Julian that new information is noted. I assume you would like me to give you everything too?"

"Err … yes please," he replied awkwardly, providing Lynton with the opportunity for his own chuckle.

"I see what you mean. I hope you've worked out those complicated sums, one wrong voltage and the lot goes up like Hiroshima so I'm told."

"I don't know what science fiction you've been reading, my friend, but I can assure you that is definitely not the case and anyway, my new apprentice has confirmed the readings and cable specifications."

"Come on, don't you mean boss? I rather liked the way you were suddenly relegated from supervisor to assistant digger like the rest of us whilst she dictated the pace. As Sabrina insisted, all to ensure maximum efficiency of available labour."

"Okay, but don't tell Victoria, it might give her more ideas. She's all for rebalanced gender roles. Aahh … here comes breakfast, now that looks good."

A smiling Sabrina placed the hot plates of food on the table and returned to walk the dogs. Julian and Lynton watched her depart in the shortest of dresses without a word spoken, each wondering whether Kolinsky had any more like her.

*

For Zac, his father's estimate of bad heads and febrile bodies was wide off the mark. He was out of bed much sprightlier than normal having cycled in his shorts to the twenty-four hour Aldi in the bright sun of a very pleasant day. One of the positive benefits of global warming was the settling down of the early spring and very long summer. Gone were the former turbulent winters, violent gales and endless rain of ten years before, now El Niño had subsided to an annual pleasant circular tour of the tropics, leaving the rest of the temperate zone to bask in old Mediterranean temperatures. In fact it was time to think about growing grapes on the Orsbrick estate and replicate the old priory elder wine brewing habits of five hundred years before, which the monks made and consumed in great quantities.

Unpacking his special picnic basket which he had ordered the day before and laying out a large blanket, he checked where his father and Lynton had got to, linking his i-Glasses to the dinky wireless tracker he had placed under the wheel arch. They left late and were still on the M58 motorway, so plenty of time for him and Ned to have fun. Dottie had already removed her jeans and top, and came prepared, clad in her bikini as they had a quick cuddle, then she dived skilfully into the pond off the makeshift board which he and Ned constructed last autumn. This was how they should do breakfast every day.

Ned meantime was characteristically still in bed with Nancy whilst his father and everyone else were out of the house. Lynton had fortunately persuaded Julian that they take Sabrina with them 'for the experience' to improve her learning capabilities, he had burbled on, not very convincingly. It was obvious to Ned that Lynton desired Sabrina badly. Fancying a robot? As gross, he thought, as one of those 2015 films about sad old men only able to have a relationship with a talking computer. Even Zac wasn't that perverted and he was as nerd-like as they come. Lynton's desire was incomprehensible given how fit Abby was, very fuckable for her age but not quite in the same league as little old Nancy next to him. He rolled over onto her wriggling body under the sheets, probably time for an encore after he had another bacon sandwich first. Later the four of them would cycle along the canal to the Cabbage Inn where he would treat everyone to an Easter pub lunch.

Half an hour went by, all was quiet or at least should have been, until the two wolfhounds rushed into the bedroom barking like crazy, scaring Nancy half to death despite the fact she was a veterinary assistant.

"Jesus Christ you two, what on earth is the matter?" he shouted, leaping out of bed and wrapping the dressing gown around himself. "Go on, off you go … I can see you're both bored, and Sabrina probably didn't exercise you enough this morning. Downstairs now, then shortly we'll all go out on the canal including you."

Nancy hauled herself out of bed and wrapped the sheet around her. "Probably time we got up. Bloody hell, they're back again, Ned. Maybe something's up. Where's Zac gone?"

Jeb and Kai stood there and barked again but more quietly and growled continually, both deliberately pacing the room, they wanted Ned to follow them. "Fuck, what is going on with you two? Zac's down the pond swimming with Nancy. Okay, I'm coming." He started pulling on his boxer shorts and jeans.

Nancy carefully pulled back the curtains and peered out. Perhaps Julian and Lynton had returned for something, shit … then she saw it. The large barn just along from the end of the house, smoke was coming from the roof. "Ned, the barn's on fire … quickly get Zac, I'll call the fire brigade. We need to get the horses out."

"Jesus, right," he shouted pulling over his tee-shirt and jumping into his boots. Next second he was running down the stairs, the dogs chasing after him as Nancy called 999. "Kai, go and fetch Zac, now."

Kai shot off barking towards the pond but Zac, alerted by all the earlier noise, was already running with Dottie, still in her bikini, towards the house and immediately saw the fire from the other side as Ned caught up with him alongside. Dottie ran back to put on her clothes quickly.

"Nancy is ringing the fire brigade, where are the horses? Normally they would be in the paddock now. Christ, they're still inside. Mum always did that job. Fuck, listen to them, we've got to try and get them out before they burn alive."

They ran to the entrance to see huge flames shooting into the air. The situation looked hopeless. They could see the four horses, whinnying and screaming, battering themselves on the thick brick sides trying desperately to get out; two had already wrenched off their harnesses.

"I'm going in, Zac," Ned shouted.

"You can't bro, just look at it, it's too dangerous. The fire engines should be here any minute."

"No, I'm going in … there's no time," but as he was about to run they both stopped dead. Someone was walking calmly out of the barn entrance, stopped and stared silently at them. The culprit who set it on fire? Ned picked up a large lump of wood. This strange looking guy, likely a vagrant by the clothing, won't be walking much further with a caved in skull.

"No Ned, look. Jesus, look who it is," Zac shouted with Nancy and Dottie now alongside, holding the two dogs tightly.

"It's Isi … fucking hell, what's he doing? He's trying to rescue the horses. That was his job a hundred and sixty years ago."

"I don't believe it Zac, what a time for me to see a spook for the first time ever. He's leading the two mares out the back. No time to lose, we can just make it and get the other two, help the spook."

"No, it's madness," Dottie yelled, grabbing at Zac, but it was too late. Both had sprinted through the entrance into the flames, whilst Nancy ran around the rear and pulled away the black and white mares outside. No sign of the other guy in there. Where were the fire engines? In a second Jeb and Kai followed their master, Dottie couldn't hold on to them; they were far too strong pulling her onto the ground. Both leapt off, barking madly into the flames.

A screeching of tyres on the gravel grabbed her attention as she ran around the other side. Julian and Lynton had returned with Sabrina, they had forgotten the specifications in the rush out.

Julian leapt out of the pickup truck, quickly followed by Lynton and stared at the raging fire now taking a firm hold. "What's going on? Where's Ned and Zac?" he shouted to Dottie, crying hysterically. He grabbed her hard and shook her.

Nancy pulled his arm away, desperately trying to remain calm and focussed as her training had taught her. "Two horses are out, some guy called Isi just rescued them. I don't know who he is, but I can't find him or see Ned and Zac. Ned thought this guy had set the place on fire in the first place. They've gone in to rescue the other two and Jeb and Kai ran after them … I've called the fire brigade."

"Well done Nancy," Julian replied. "I'm going in to find them," and without any further ado, he ran like crazy into the conflagration. Lynton stared, shook his head and then followed. He couldn't leave Julian on his own.

Sabrina turned to Nancy, the fire engines were blaring in the distance. They were not far but had a narrow lane still to get up slowly. "I estimate they have 1.27 minutes to get out. It is a dangerous environment for me but I cannot leave my trusted mentors to solve this problem on their own." In a trice she too leapt forward and ran into the blazing doorway and disappeared.

Nancy pulled at Dottie's arm. "Oh my God ... look." They turned to see the strangely dressed man, Isi, not a mark on him, leading the other two horses away from the barn and into the woods as three fire engines screeched to a halt alongside. But as the firemen scrambled from their vehicles, the main front beam dropped down with a great rumble, blocking any escape from inside, followed immediately by a loud roar as the whole roof caved in with a huge ball of flame into the sky.

Dottie screamed and screamed as Nancy tried to comfort her. The lead firemen, in flame protective gear, ran to what was left of the entrance and looked through inside; the water hoses were now being played over the whole building.

The commander walked back quickly and shook his head. "All I can see is a pile of molten plastic. We'll go round the back, see if we can find them there."

Dottie started to wail again uncontrollably. Nancy held her tightly also in shock. She looked towards the house, wishing that Victoria and Abby were here with Maddie and Belle. This was dreadful beyond belief, what was she going to do? She couldn't believe her eyes. That man Isi was standing alone by the front door and simply staring calmly at her. Her blood rose, that bastard maniac had done all this, and picked up Ned's piece of wood. But when she looked back again he had simply and totally disappeared into thin air.

# Chapter Seven

Easter Monday 1841-Parbold Village, near Orsbrick Hall

The moment Morag looked out to the garden from her study desk, it became immediately apparent to her keen eye. The next job that needed doing on this crumbling house would be to make and replace those old sash windows with some new oak ones. Not only did they want painting but she could see a deep, brown rot spreading ominously at the sides, unsurprising the room was chilly and draughty. She put another log on the fire crackling in the small hearth. It may be Easter but that long, hard winter was still trying to hang on in bursts. The day was decidedly low in temperature. However, at least the daffodils were out in full force. She stared fondly down towards the pond at the waving frond of emerged, yellow heads, intermixed with a mass of purple and white crocuses.

Morag perused the large jar of tadpoles on the windowsill which Ellen had brought back yesterday on their stroll from the St John the Baptist parish church in Burscough and smiled. She always attended the Easter service, despite her misgivings and non-belief. Socially it was important given her position in the community, but she was glad they had a private chapel, a good excuse not to be seen in the parish church regularly. She had been married in Ormskirk because St John the Baptist had only just commenced being built, after a generous donation from the McKenzie family matched pound for pound by the Church Commissioners. It took five years until 1832 to complete but looked beautiful, built in the gothic revival style which Malcolm's father, originally trained as an architect, had insisted upon. It was not often one had the opportunity to see a church being built from scratch. Ellen would certainly be confirmed there when she reached sixteen, then she could decide afterwards whether she wanted to believe in God or not. But it was important for Ellen's surety in society to ensure the fullest of future options were taken. Morag contemplated her own beginnings and shook her head. At sixteen she had a three year old son and was already married. She wanted a different life for her daughter, and although a private agnostic she did not feel it correct to impose her views on her children. They had to decide and think for themselves in this life. But reflecting on James, she sighed again. Already at twelve he had firmly rejected a Creator and seemed imbued, of late, with a growing and vehement anti-religious sentiment. Someone was influencing him and she needed to find out who.

She continued to read a paper which Ada had recently sent on further ideas relating to Babbage's Analytical Engine, an obsession which Morag realised would be around for some time. The contents were highly mathematical. Morag was very capable at mathematics, but chemistry was now her real strength and she simply could not understand the intricate algebraic detail. More work and direct discussion was needed, but she realised just how gifted Ada was, not only with abstract reasoning but the ability to visualise how technology could influence the future of society. She very much looked forward to Ada and Medora visiting in ten days time. A knock on the door disturbed her concentration. Agnes walked in sheepishly holding a collection of cleaning brushes in each hand. Morag was still wondering why, on a whim at her last visit to Marylebone, when Lady Byron had stormed in and sacked

Agnes on the spot for gross idiocy because she had confused blancmange with custard, she had immediately offered to employ her on increased wages, and then brought a grateful Agnes back to Orsbrick Hall on the train. That was not only Agnes's first trip outside of London but the first on a train. Morag smiled, remembering Agnes's eyes on stalks with perpetual wonder at the green and smog free countryside they passed through. But on balance, she was happy. Agnes had settled in amazingly quickly, worked very hard and they were all fairly eccentric at Orsbrick so one more, as head maid, would not make any difference.

"Milady, just to remind you, that the new governess, Mrs Hammelaar, should be arriving after lunch. I understand from Mr Williamson that she has daughters so I thought I'd better urgently clean out the adjacent bedroom which seemed to be in a bit of a state. Perhaps some company now for Miss Ellen, Lady McKenzie?"

"Yes, perhaps, we'll see. Excellent, you may take all that junk in there down to the Saturday market for sale. Any proceeds may be distributed equally amongst the servants."

"Why thank you milady, I will do that, your generosity will be much appreciated."

"And will you ask Williamson to bring me another pot of tea. I must get this letter to Mr Faraday written, by lunchtime for you to take to the postal depot."

"Certainly milady," Agnes replied cheerfully before closing the door. Five seconds later a dreadful clatter outside could be heard, undoubtedly Agnes tripping over her own handfuls of brooms, buckets and dusters. Morag shook her head.

She decided to write a long, personal letter to Michael, outlining the new experiments she was working on in her laboratory next door, on rotating a new configuration of coils in a magnetic field, pleased with the three new Bunsen cells which he had kindly sent from the Royal Institution. She was getting the hang of measuring the electricity generated and understood the algebra behind the circuitry perfectly but was unhappy with her instruments, equally determined to improve on their design and accuracy. She needed a technical assistant, someone practical to make equipment. That skill on tap would be very advantageous. As she signed off the letter with 'your very dearest friend and colleague, Lady Morag McKenzie of Burscough', she laughed at Michael's unbelievable ineptitude with mathematics and especially algebra. Even her son James had a deeper knowledge, which made it even more remarkable how great an experimenter her Michael Faraday was. She breathed a deep sigh, fondly remembering his last two visits to Orsbrick Hall, where they argued playfully over their different religious beliefs. Her perspective was very simple; she had none and would not be moved. But she had sensed his resistance to her was wearing down at each visit and that evening, after their wonderful meal at the George, and a second long kiss in her new electrical laboratory, he finally lost his inner battle. But she must not become pregnant, despite Michael's obvious proclivity and desire for children. She was a widow and still needed to retain her standing and position, so had been liberal with the new douching powders which Medora had sent, supposedly being used in Royal circles, which included a small quantity of manganate of potash. Besides, his wife Sarah had returned home and that marital bond was not presently breakable, but she could feel it for sure … she had fallen in love again. She was desperate for next week to come and their meeting in London and would be travelling with the new train from Manchester on the Great Western Railway.

Over at Parbold village, a carriage had just run off the road with its large rear wheel stuck in a ditch, after the driver turned hard down the hill to avoid the canal, perilously close to the track. Desperately trying to unbridle the panicking horses, he looked up at the three terrified faces through the window and asked Mrs Hammelaar if she could find her map in the trunk which he had just taken down because it contained instructions to get to their destination and he was completely lost. Carefully, he helped each one down as they stared disoriented at their surroundings and then tied the horses to a fence.

"Madam, I deign your permission to seek assistance in the village windmill and public house yonder. Please remain here and I will return shortly," the driver proffered in a strange lilting accent, part Irish with a northern overlay.

The man was in his forties or fifties, swarthy and needed a good shave. She stared at his dirty clothes and unfamiliar attire and nodded as he stumped off with a distinct limp. Victoria, Maddie and Belle stared at each other in disbelief and shock, unable to comprehend anything going on around them.

"Where on earth are we?" Maddie whispered whilst Belle hugged her mother hard to check she was real. "My last memory was being swept away in cold seawater in that sinking ship ... next second we're here? We've still got on the same dresses we were wearing."

Victoria immediately commenced her usual process of rationalisation, there had to be some logical answer. "I agree, but we have to stay calm and start thinking quickly. Look at the environment, this carriage we're in and those old cottages with the smoke pouring from the chimneys. Over there a horse and cart loaded with hay and the road, it has some sort of pressed stone surface but isn't tarmac. Whatever truly happened on the Queen Lusitania, we've somehow gone back in time. But

151

where's Abby? One fact remains clear to me. We all said we were worried by exactly the same thing … Mauveine."

Maddie and Belle both took deep breaths. Maddie continued. "Mum you're right. Look we're all scientists, there has to be a reason and a cause for this. I know you hate to talk about Abby and her psychic space-time ruptures but this has all the hallmarks. Both Abby and I felt terrible sensations as the explosions occurred and I'm sure Mauveine is linked in some way. But who are we and where are we? Can we find out before that coach driver comes back?"

Belle had begun opening the wooden trunk, full of period dresses and other clothes, leather books and assorted paraphernalia plus a large leather wallet with documents which she handed to Victoria. "Okay, let's fix the time frame. My history was excellent as you all will have to agree as I got the top grades!"

They laughed uncontrollably, a great release. At least they still all had a sense of family humour which was a good start. Belle continued. "Our long dresses are similar but not quite, look underneath. No crinoline, no bustles, dresses are bulky but not constricting, only petticoats and I've got proper drawers on, we're upper class."

"Thank goodness for that," Maddie said with a giggle, quickly confirming the same. "Oh gosh, look over there."

They stared at a field behind the low hawthorn hedge to see and hear a rudimentary locomotive with four small, covered carriages pulling off into the distance, the chugging and steam emission now discernible. Behind the old farmhouse there was a railway station.

"That confirms it," Belle said happily. "I would guess late 1830s to late 1840s, when those trains were coming into vogue; all matches the dress and the rest around us."

"And the hair buns. Unanimously agreed," Maddie said, hi-fiving her sister.

Victoria glared, rummaging through the documents and reading them quickly. "No, don't do that, rational behaviour is needed for the time. If we're Victorian upper-class, we're going to have to play-act as best as we can, demure, well-mannered and educated in the arts, languages and music. Science is acceptable but whatever we do we must act the time and not give the game away by saying things not invented yet. I hope, both of you, your history is as good as you say. We're going to need to be on our toes until we know what's going on."

"I played Jane Eyre in the school play" Maddie replied. "I reckon I can hack … sorry … I mean handle the predicament we unwittingly find ourselves in Mama."

They giggled again. "Excellent," Victoria said, handing the map to Belle who already recognised the area, despite the changes to most of the surroundings. But the windmill and the pub ahead hadn't changed much. "I know where we are … Parbold village and this map confirms it. The route and the markings lead to Orsbrick Hall. We're heading home!"

"But what sort of home? And who lives there?" Maddie said. "We're in a pre-Mauveine period, before even she was born. Why? One thing Abby and I realised from the library archives, is the time between the late 1780s and 1860 is a big black hole, very little is recorded or was maybe lost."

"Until now," Victoria replied, holding a number of letters. "We know when and where, here comes who. This is a contract of employment. My name is Mrs Victoria Hammelaar, formerly living in Amsterdam and I'm widowed with two twin daughters. So assume your full names and ages, in keeping with a formal expectation. I'm a governess, specialising in science and the teaching of languages and I have a contract to teach the children of Lady Morag McKenzie, at Orsbrick Hall, Burscough, starting tomorrow, April 13th 1841. My two daughters are allowed a room but in turn they will be assigned appropriate work duties. There's a hundred pounds in this wallet, which is a lot really for then so we're not destitute but not … ahh … clarity. Lady McKenzie has added, quote. 'Thank you for the excellent references and I wish to express my condolences for the recent sudden death of your wool merchant husband by typhus. Also, being a widow, I understand fully and hope, now your debts are paid, that you will find the opportunity for a fresh start back in England at Orsbrick Hall.' So I'm English and was married to a wealthy Dutchman who ended up owing most of his money, a serial gambler and womaniser I've decided."

"Spooky resemblance to your real life though Mum, sorry Mother, isn't it? But I think we've got enough to wing it. Belle and I are eligible upper middle class young ladies of leisure, never done a day's work and have been educated at home by you and private tutors. But we've all come down in the world now and you have to work to keep us all," Maddie added, her brain going like crazy.

Belle nodded. "What does 'appropriate work duties' mean, I wonder? I could do with going to the loo and that isn't going to be a wildly exciting experience in 1841. Look, the driver is coming back with a couple of men, one with a large apron around him I assume the pub landlord and someone else is watching further back on a horse."

"Okay, one step at a time. I'll do the talking for now," Victoria responded, finding a pair of flimsy spectacles in the wallet which she put on.

Soon the driver and his two companions, the pub and windmill owners, were gathered around and after apologies for

154

the delay, although Victoria smelt strong drink on the driver's tobacco-ridden breath, they heaved and tugged with the horses until properly harnessed again. With one final lurch the carriage jolted back onto the road whilst Victoria, Maddie and Belle carefully repacked the trunk and dragged it over. Apart from paint scratches, but there were enough of those anyway, no apparent damage was evident. However, the driver insisted on taking the carriage back to the pub to give it a thorough checking over, as his companions heaved the trunk back on. They hadn't heard, with all the clatter and whinnying, the approach of a fourth individual who rode up silently behind to peruse the situation.

"If I may propose madam, I would like to suggest some rest and refreshment at the White Swan for your good self and your daughters whilst your carriage is repaired and the bill will happily go onto my tab."

Victoria turned startled, as did Maddie and Belle. The articulated, posh and educated voice was very familiar. She looked up at the rather dandyish and handsome figure, in tight red trousers, a black jacket and matching top hat, perched on a very fine, white stallion. She gasped, before breathing quickly and thinking fast. "Lynton? Is that really you?"

His puzzled and bemused gaze was sufficient for Victoria to realise immediately. He didn't recognise any of them or was deliberately playacting brilliantly. She reassessed the encounter calmly and logically. Thank goodness she could be a very detached scientist when necessary and analyse the evidence. This man was definitely Lynton and by his expression he wasn't playacting at all, she knew Lynton of old. But for some reason he had returned too, but unlike them had been captured into 1841 time with no memory of his true present. But why? And why were she and the girls different? Maddie and Belle remained silent. Like their mother, they too had realised what was happening.

The man undoubtedly liked the look of the three cultured and refined women before him, staring at each one in turn up and down with intent. "Madam, you appear to know me, but I am at a severe loss, and abjectly apologise as I fail to recognise you whatsoever. My name is indeed Lynton. Dr Lynton Gray, at your service. You have the air of an educated woman. Perhaps you have read my latest book on art history of the eighteenth century? Goodness, I was pleasantly amazed to even find articles about me in the local paper at the inn here, but I never did paint the live battle of Waterloo. It was Borodino. I was so young and adventurous then."

He dismounted smartly and handed her a tatty newspaper before walking over and conferring with the landlord as they moved the carriage. It was the Burscough and Orsbrick Times, which Maddie and Abby had read online when they were researching Mauveine's history. The three immediately shuffled together and quickly perused a full page article on the distinguished Dr Gray, art historian of Southport.

"That's definitely Lynton," Maddie whispered, "but has no idea who we are. He's transferred into this era with a history though."

"Definitely," Belle agreed. "But if Lynton's here, what about Dad and Ned and Zac? There must be a logical reason? Shit Mum, we are in a right pickle."

"We need to play along, hopefully we at least find Abby. We're supposed to be on our way to Orsbrick Hall. Goodness knows what we'll find when we get there, but I'm starving. You must be too, we have to eat and I need a pee as well. Lynton's coming back, I'll chat him up. At least he seems as generous as ever."

"But you don't know how he might view women. This era is not 2026. Any attractive woman was for the taking by the upper class, married or not … mistresses were the norm. Take care Mum, he has a typical aristocratic lecherous eye," Maddie pleaded, feeling anxiety.

"Yes, don't I know and also how to handle it, especially from Lynton, another reason we need to find Abby."

"He's coming back— privies, I remember," Belle whispered. "That's what they'll have. Just don't look down and hold your nose."

"Why madam, I do believe from your smile that I will have the honour of your delightful company. Allow me to escort you to the best table and fayre; you will be pleasantly surprised I can assure you. Now please, tell me all about yourself? Hold onto me, the path is somewhat rough."

Victoria hooked her arm into his and the three, hitching their long dresses as best as they could, walked slowly, chatting continuously, towards the White Swan. Maddie and Belle maintained a quiet demure mode, nodding occasionally, as Lynton was obviously interested in Victoria, especially the moment she said she was a governess. Both girls were flabbergasted with the ease of story-telling and fiction which their mother displayed, making up a complete life history about their life in Amsterdam as they walked along, the tragic death of their father falling into a waterway and their intended new beginning at Orsbrick Hall. Having excellent memories each, they absorbed the essentials and nuances, already feeling more confident. They also learnt that Lynton was a widower with a young daughter not being well educated, only by buffoons as he described her tutors, at home in Southport. Was that Judy? It became instantly clear why his sharp interest in Victoria.

Walking into the White Swan, they were given a warm welcome by the landlord and his wife, which cheered their spirits greatly, and were taken immediately away from the sawdust swept tap-room area where their driver, alongside other guffawing coachmen, was propping up the bar with great flagons of ale. The pub was remarkably full, with many people eating what looked like small pies. A few young women, dishevelled and dirty, one with a snotty child wearing a brown cap too big for his head and holed boots, obviously farm workers by their attire, gazed at Maddie and Belle, glaring. A grandfather clock quietly ticked at the far end, showing it was almost noon, but Maddie had also found a gold pocket watch in her tiny handbag earlier and wound and adjusted it carefully. They ended up in the 'snug' a small room at the back, empty but clean and laid out with tables and cutlery. Lynton escorted Victoria to a large table near the window, where they looked out at a vast expanse of cultivated fields, with men, horses and ploughs working outside and a pleasant, fast flowing stream a few feet away, which ran on in the yard under a couple of small, crumbling brick outbuildings. Victoria looked askance at Belle and Maddie. A steady flow of men, coming and going through the rickety doors, indicated where the privies were. They decided to hold it in as long as possible.

The landlord's wife, a stout woman in her fifties by the name of Gloria, smartly coiffed and dressed in a clean brown dress and wearing a green decorated apron, returned with a smile and announced the menu, in a rich Lancashire accent.

"Today, we have my specially prepared rabbit pie, come for miles they do for that, isn't it so Dr Gray, complete with fresh vegetables out the garden and turnip soup to start."

"I can wholeheartedly recommend Gloria's entire cooking, Mrs Hammelaar," Lynton cut in, winking at Gloria and staring at her ample bosom. "Put in on my chitty please."

"That would be lovely," Victoria replied, as Belle and Maddie nodded enthusiastically. They were so hungry they didn't care, looking out at the large sheltered garden area, full of potatoes, carrots, sprouts, rhubarb and other spring vegetables. "Thank you so much for your hospitality, Dr Gray, we very much appreciate your generosity."

"I stay here often," he replied. "They allow me generous credit. This place is a popular staging point for rest and the ubiquitous change of horses. The landlord and Gloria are doing very well."

Victoria continued. "Do tell us more about your gallery and your art business, it is all quite fascinating. Do you have any work by Mr Turner? His sea paintings are so vibrant."

Maddie and Belle stared incredulously at their mother. She would be a hard act to keep up with.

Lynton went quiet for a moment. "I can see you and your daughters are well educated in the arts, as a governess that of course would be expected. I have indeed purchased two works of Turner and some rare engravings of Constable."

"The sciences too, Dr Gray, and music and languages."

"Pardon?" Lynton replied, shocked and not expecting such a reply. "I am ... well, most shaken with such knowledge. Science is a rare subject for a woman to be well versed in. I know very little of such mysteries, unlike my good friend Michael Faraday. Please feel free to call me Lynton now we have become friends. And, Mrs Hammelaar, your name is?"

"Victoria. You mean you know Michael Faraday? Gosh Dr Gray, you are well acquainted with men of genius. Such an amazing discoverer of the natural world, there is nothing that

Mr Faraday does not know about electricity and magnetism," Victoria replied confidently, as Maddie and Belle continued to stare, mouths wide open. *Thank goodness, Victoria reflected that she had taught A-level physics at Cradleigh Girls for a spell.* "Science is really my special interest, I must confess, and my daughters are also learned in the ways of chemistry. Is that not so, Madeleine and Annabelle? Please speak up for Dr Gray." She looked out forlornly to the privies, but Dr Gray sensed her discomfort and intervened.

"Mrs Hammelaar. If I may be so bold, I suggest you walk another ten yards to the side of the house, follow the stream, where there is a dedicated ladies facility which I am sure you will find much more conducive."

Victoria set off, apprehensively.

Maddie decided she needed to engage in the conversation. She really had had enough of displaying a mutt-like demure, it wasn't her character whatsoever. "Yes, Dr Gray. Annabelle and I have been studying science since small children, guided continually by our mother of course. Recently, in Amsterdam, we experimented with the dissolution of copper in various acids and learned how to produce blue and green crystals."

"And," Belle added, excitedly, to a careful glance from Maddie, "we have also shown how such crystals can grow like exotic plants in solutions of silicate of sodium," then wondered immediately whether that reagent was known in 1841, having a horrible inkling it was first discovered at the end of the nineteenth century. These would be the hazards they had to guard against.

Lynton sat, mesmerised by the unusually erudite conversation from these young, lovely females, who displayed a feistiness of mind, quite becoming to his sensibilities and ardour. The two girls would make excellent companions for his ill-disciplined daughter and Mrs Hammelaar was a very attractive proposition indeed. But he knew from the landlord where they were headed and realised that he would be unlikely to outbid the affluent McKenzie estate for Victoria's services. On reflection, he concluded that Mrs Hammelaar, with her intense and serious disposition, was not really his type for marrying and even less, mistress material. He much preferred flighty, artistic women. But, he was nevertheless enjoying her company hugely and being a gentleman of leisure what else was he to do but pursue life and seek pleasure in all ways agreeable.

Victoria returned much happier than she left, amazed to find that the ladies privy, not only was scrupulously clean and little used and she did look down, but had been filled throughout with vases of newly cut daffodils, masking any odours, but making her sneeze violently.

Maddie and Belle promptly followed. Maddie, to the chagrin of Belle who had no idea what she was talking about, had been dazzling Dr Gray further by quoting from the eminent populist book 'Conversations in Chemistry', written by a female educationalist, a learned tome he had actually heard about from Faraday. It was Maddie's last exam project on the history of science and feminism, for which she had been very grateful to Zac for tracking a Google scanned eBook of the 1812 original.

Victoria sat down carefully, brushing her linen dress gently, when loud shouting began to ensue from the bar area and half a dozen men ran out, carrying something back inside from one of the privies. Peels of bellowing laughter rang out. As Lynton stood up to investigate, the landlord came rushing in and spoke, like his wife, in that odd sounding, deep Lancashire accent, the same as Mauveine and Isi.

"Madam, I'm afraid your driver has had an unfortunate accident. The fool, worse for drink, stumbled inside the privy and fell in headfirst, breaking his leg and is cut badly. Knocked himself out, he did, but we fished the bugger out. We thrown six pails of water over him but he don't really smell good and he need to go to the doctor urgent. Don't know how you're going to continue your journey now. They're ain't no one available."

Victoria coughed, stifling her laugh as Maddie looked away. "That is so very unfortunate, please give the driver some recompense," fishing in her wallet for two shillings. But how could they get to Orsbrick Hall? She pondered hard. Options were short, it was too far to walk and they had that heavy trunk. They needed to get there urgently.

"Victoria, I shall only be too pleased to be of service and will drive the carriage forthwith to your destination."

"But Lynton, I cannot possibly draw further on your good nature and kindness," Victoria replied, feeling both relieved and pleased that she was getting the knack of 1840's speak already, remembering her Charlotte Bronte. Her accent hadn't caused any stir either. So far so good.

"Nonsense, it is a gentleman's duty and my pleasure to continue with you and your two daughters, such delectable company. Also, I have not yet formally met Lady McKenzie of Orsbrick Hall, perhaps a potential patron of my collections?"

"You have a quick and sound eye for business which I admire, being a widow of a merchant," Victoria replied. "I believe we are ready to go at your convenience. Thank you so much, it was such a delicious meal. The Lord will look kindly on your benevolence." Maddie and Belle blinked. Their mother was getting a little carried away.

Lynton stood up and bowed slightly, then took Victoria's hand, as she raised herself from the uncomfortable wooden chair. They walked slowly to the carriage and climbed in. Jumping on top and grabbing the reins, Lynton cracked the whip and they were off in a trice, galloping at pace towards Burscough.

*

Jolting and bouncing along the rough roads, the rocking, noisy ride took some getting used to, although at least, being proficient horse riders, Victoria, Maddie and Belle knew what to expect. Fascinated by the passing landscape and villages, despite the area being so much more rural, they recognised much of what they knew and eventually spotted the unusual, stumpy Burscough church tower in the distance, whispering madly to one another as Lynton continued at breakneck speed. Passing by, they perceived quite a difference. The side wings were missing and the vestry and chancel areas were very different, including the fabulous East stained glass window which was not there, obviously a feature added later. The church stonework looked very pristine, the main building having only been built and consecrated in 1832.

Approaching Orsbrick Hall, they were excited with what they would be seeing, hoping they might find Abby and together discover the purpose of why they were here, and most importantly, how to move forward again in time. But Maddie, correctly, had pointed out that Mauveine and Isi would not be seen or experienced in any way because they had not even been born. As ghosts it wouldn't make sense. But, who was Lady McKenzie with the retained title, which in itself was intriguing?

Rounding a couple more bends with the road in remarkable condition and almost smooth, the familiar sight of their home came into view over the hedges as they headed towards the entrance.

"Wow," Maddie exclaimed. "Doesn't it look so new? The brickwork is pristine. I suppose the place hasn't suffered yet from the effects of localised coal burning and the industrial activity which took place later."

"Of course, Orsbrick Hall was rebuilt in the late 1770s after the great fire so in fact the building isn't that old anyway, but I agree it looks splendid," Victoria replied, her eyes wide, thinking nostalgically about Julian who would be hugely impressed. Was he around too?

Suddenly the carriage drew to a halt as Lynton pulled in the horses. He shouted down. "Sorry, I'm a bit confused with this map, not quite sure where …"

"Another three hundred yards, past two more bends then you'll reach the gates," Victoria replied gaily, then stopped, her heart pounding, realising what she'd said as Maddie grimaced.

"I thought you'd never been here before, Mrs Hammelaar? You sound like you own the place. Are you actually Lady McKenzie in disguise?" Lynton replied, sounding stiff and formal again.

She coughed. "Such fortuity and opportunity will alas never be coming my way, Dr Gray. No, I forgot to say we found more detailed instructions inside, which I am reading to you," feeling her face reddening. Belle and Maddie looked anxious.

He laughed. "I thought as much, let's go," and whipped the horses back into play. Maddie breathed out a long but quiet sigh.

The gates were the first surprise, heavy, cumbersome and wooden, probably oak or elm. They clattered noisily down the drive which was laid out in an intricate series of worn cobblestones, deadly probably when wet. A large, burly man wearing formal attire had already opened the two front doors and was waiting for them as they drove into the coaching area. Another very well constructed and decorated carriage was standing there. Three more servants appeared for their luggage and removed the horses, to be fed and rested in the stables.

Lynton jumped down, opened the carriage door and taking each hand in turn, gently helped Victoria, Maddie and Belle down from inside, making sure they could step forward decorously. By then the burly butler was alongside, thrown by the unexpected appearance of the driver, especially when Lynton spoke with authority to the stable hand. A young female suddenly emerged, running down the steps, dressed in a distinctive maid's outfit and joined them, as they waited for the butler to begin, who looked at his watch churlishly.

"Good afternoon, you must be Mrs Hammelaar, our new governess," he said, stiffly. "Welcome to Orsbrick Hall, I hope your journey has been satisfactory. My name is Williamson and I am in charge of *all* staff here."

Victoria looked at him. She was late, and she took an immediate dislike, neither happy with his rough appearance nor his mannerisms, which seemed uncouth for a man of this position. No way would she be reporting to him but for now she had no choice but to play along. He offered no handshake so neither did she, not being sure of the etiquette.

"Good afternoon. May I introduce my two daughters," Victoria replied in her poshest voice, "Madeline and Annabelle. And this is Dr Lynton Gray, eminent London art historian. I apologise for arriving late but unfortunately our driver met with an accident on the way and Dr Gray, in an act of great kindness, took charge of everything and personally brought us here."

With this, Williamson nodded formally to Lynton and held out his hand. They shook strongly. "At your service, Sir. I am sure Lady McKenzie will wish to thank you for your kindness in attending to Mrs Hammelaar and her daughters. Dr Gray, would you care to follow me to the drawing room for some refreshment." Williamson shot a glare across to the maid who took the cue, whilst he directed Lynton inside immediately.

"Take no notice of Mr Williamson, Mrs Hammelaar, sometime he gets a little brusque but his heart's in the right place. He was decorated at Waterloo, a big sword wound in his side, although I haven't seen it of course. I'm Agnes and head maid to Lady McKenzie. If you follow me, I'll take you straight to meet her, she is expecting you. Now Madeleine and Annabelle, Esther here will lead you straight to your room upstairs and tell you all about the place and where everything is. Then later we will call you for dinner."

Victoria looked at Maddie and Belle; they seemed comfortable with that arrangement. "Thank you Agnes, we appreciate getting everything ready for us. Please feel free to call me Victoria, when of course the time and place is appropriate."

"Yes, certainly, thank you Victoria. Please come this way to the study. Your luggage will all be taken up to your own room."

Walking through the familiar corridor, Victoria stared upwards at the sweeping, white marble staircase, all appeared remarkably similar except the wood was stained darker and the rails a different design The walls were painted with a mixture of crème and green tints and a lot more wallpaper had been hung everywhere, distinctly Regency, with much striping. A large and original tapestry of an ice-skating scene on the River Mersey hung in the stairwell. Wherever had that lovely artefact disappeared to? She glanced through the open door of the ballroom, looking magnificent with the same beautifully decorated ceiling, although the long blue curtains and candle chandeliers were dissimilar to what Julian and she had salvaged when they renovated it for their wedding all that time ago in

2010. But she was forgetting. This was 1841. Everywhere looked fresh and clean and recently decorated, as if a major effort to do up Orsbrick Hall had taken place not long back. Certainly wealth was very evident, with expensive furniture all about. But what was striking were the fewer paintings on the walls, most being of staid rural scenes, fox hunting, hay-making along with a number of unrecognised family portraits from the 1700s, again mysteriously vanished.

They arrived at a very familiar but closed door, her study. Agnes knocked tentatively before opening and Victoria breathed in deeply, not knowing what or who to expect. She walked in confidently, the warmth hitting her immediately, a large fire crackling at the side, to be greeted by a striking, slim woman, her long brown hair parted at the centre and tied back in a ribbon with tufts down her cheeks in an expensive long, pale-pink dress. She was styled in the fashion of the day, that big bell shape and a very noticeable v-shaped corseted waist, which Victoria was becoming accustomed to. But her dress was made from a silk material, vastly superior to the basic linen clothes she was wearing. The top of the dress was also much barer and off the shoulder, quite provocative, with short sleeves darker in shade at the bosom and decorated with green and flowered inlays, all intricately embroidered. She was shorter in flat slippers and unexpectedly had a perfect set of pearly white teeth as she smiled, unlike Agnes.

She held out her hand to Victoria and spoke in a slow and very English rolling upper class accent. "Good afternoon Mrs Hammelaar. I am Lady Morag McKenzie. I understand why you have been delayed, but that is not a problem. I'm simply relieved you arrived safely."

Three things struck Victoria as her fast brain took in every fact and nuance. The fashionable Morag McKenzie was a lot shorter and slimmer. Although very beautiful, she didn't have the typical McKenzie facial features, so must have been married into the McKenzie line of her deceased husband. And she was very young to be a widow with children.

"Good afternoon, a pleasure to meet you at last Lady McKenzie," she replied softly in her best public speaking voice, matching the accent with perfection, that part at least wasn't difficult. "Indeed, my daughters and I had a somewhat tricky moment at the village of Parbold, but good fortune shone its light and benevolence on our predicament and here we are. Thank you so much for the position of governess and I look forward to meeting your children and starting work as soon as convenient."

Morag halted her flow momentarily, surprised with the air of confidence, tall eloquence and cultured poise of Mrs Hammelaar and no trace of that awful guttural Dutch accent. She had remarkably similar features to Malcolm's grandmother an odd coincidence. Whatever her recent tragic circumstances in Amsterdam, this was a woman she could relate to, an English background of education and breeding somewhere … an unexpected mystery to be tackled at a later time. Ada, with her latest phrenology mania, had urged her to 'always make your mind up about a person in the first ten seconds of meeting them.' Morag took an immediate decision about Mrs Hammelaar who would report to her directly from day one. There was no way that Williams would be managing this governess, especially after the experiences and quick departures of the others. The challenge ahead, especially with James, was too daunting.

"We can do all of that in due course. I trust your proposed salary is acceptable? Please do take a seat," Morag replied, pointing to a comfortable armchair by the fire. "May I call you Victoria?"

"Of course, Lady McKenzie," Victoria replied, wondering how far thirty five pounds a year would go. But free board and lodging at Orsbrick for the three of them was included.

"Contrary to convention, Victoria, I have a reputation I'm afraid for breaking societal norms. You will answer to me directly and nobody else. I do not view you as a servant. Agnes will be your personal maid, and I think I would like you to call me Morag from the start please. Furthermore, I would like you to dine with me regularly and keep me up to date with the children's educational and moral progress."

"Certainly Morag, that would be most acceptable," Victoria replied, sitting down and breathing a sigh of relief. No confrontational getting off the wrong foot over Williams was needed for the moment, and breaking conventions she was all for, even in 1841. Whatever she was here for, it seemed like a good start could perhaps be made.

"Now, before we have tea, I mustn't forget to introduce you to my cousin who has been patiently waiting at the window."

Victoria had forgotten when walking in, distracted by Morag's immediate attention, just how spacious the study was. She turned and looked down the far end, at least twenty feet long. In fact the room was even bigger. There must have been some redesign later, with a huge desk, magnificent upright chair and separate sofas down there, in front of a second but unlit fireplace. The mahogany desk, untidily covered in heaps of papers, was even larger than her own. The thickly wallpapered walls were lined from top to bottom with rows of bookshelves, stacked with hundreds of brown and red leather bound books. Striking portraits of scientists adorned her wall including Newton, Boyle, Galileo and a massive painting of

William Hershel, replete with large reflector telescope, over the Adam fireplace. At the far side, a narrow pillared, ceiling-to-floor patio style window, probably, she realised, what was now in her sitting room but much less ornate, was hung with a thick brown curtain, half-drawn. This partly concealed a woman in the gloom, with her back to them, quietly staring out to the garden. She was fairly tall and slim, wearing a long, cream, off the shoulder quality dress, looking like muslin, very bell-shaped and black shiny boots. She had striking thick, red hair parted down the middle, and long, buoyant sausage curls hanging down her face.

Morag stood up to ring a bell for Agnes and the woman swished around, staring defiantly at Victoria, whose expression dropped with surprise. The fashion styles could not be more different but the face was unmistakeable. She had found Abby!

By then Morag had opened the door and frustrated was peering out in the corridor for the missing Agnes. She rang the bell hard again. Abby winked to Victoria and put her fingers to her lips for a second before walking slowly down the room, her dress swishing, with a cultured and natural air, which even for Abby, the natural play-actor, was hard to beat. Victoria composed herself again, inwardly so unbelievably elated. Unlike Lynton, Abby recognised her and likely understood what had happened. Maddie and Belle will be over the moon. But Abby was Morag's cousin?

"Come over, Abigail, we've finished formalities. This is my new governess, Mrs Victoria Hammelaar who I told you about over lunch. Victoria, please meet Miss Abigail Warren. We are rather distant cousins. Abigail's grandparents who brought her up lived in Manchester. In fact, before last week we hadn't seen one another since playing together as children. Sadly, it has been so long, I really didn't recognise her, but you have spent much of your life painting abroad, is that not so dearest Abigail?"

"Err … yes, all over Europe, in between my services to Mr Constable as an assistant," Abby replied in her best, slightly lilting Manchester accent. "I work mainly in Paris where I have an apartment on the Seine. I have built up a steady collection of paintings, some of which I occasionally sell to maintain my independent means. Are you a lover of art, Victoria? I understand from cousin Morag that you specialise in science education, so very rare for a woman. And you have bravely ventured all the way from Amsterdam? I'm so sorry to hear from Morag of your loss which must be hard, especially with two daughters to support. I will be so pleased to meet them later. Sadly I have no children, far too busy travelling of course, for them or men." Abby laughed and waved her hand in a flourish, playing at another convention breaker, but what was new?

Victoria stifled a smirk. Abby was defiantly in her element with embroidered storytelling. "Yes, Abigail, I do indeed teach the sciences, as well, I hope, as any man."

The three of them laughed approvingly, something akin to 1840s feminism apparently shared in common to hopefully bind the cause whatever that was to be. Morag displayed an overt preference for educated independence and free-thinking, patently a characteristic running way back in the McKenzie family.

"And also I am able to provide learning of languages, music and moral direction, but my knowledge of art, compared with your obvious talent and erudition is relatively minor."

"And that is a useful point, Victoria," Morag intervened. "I have already agreed with Abigail to take charge of tutoring art for the children so you can concentrate on the sciences. She will be staying for a while. I trust that is acceptable?"

"Certainly," Victoria replied, glancing at Abby. A smart move for starters.

At that juncture Agnes reappeared, red-faced from further running about, and pushed a trolley holding a giant patterned china teapot, homemade cakes and three matching porcelain cups. Victoria stared hard. She owned that tea set, replete in its viewable splendour within a glass cabinet but never used. Was it really that old?

"Brought from Peking, May 27th 1781, with the first barge of imported goods from Liverpool to reach Wigan," Morag said, pleased to see that Victoria shared with her a love of porcelain. "Dropped off for Orsbrick Hall on special order at our canal landing stage. Which reminds me, I almost forgot. I must go and thank your rescuer, the art historian, Dr Gray resting in the drawing room. I hope he hasn't drunk too much homemade whiskey that Williams will undoubtedly be plying him with. Perhaps Abigail, you may wish to show your work in progress on the easel to Victoria and have a chat? Agnes will wheel the trolley out. Now the sun has emerged, it will be quite warm there."

Abigail nodded. The mention of a Dr Gray had suddenly perked up her attention. Outside, once Agnes had poured the tea and departed, Victoria and Abby pulled up a couple of garden chairs close to each other as Abby instantly devoured a large crème bun, smothered in raspberry jam.

"Just like old times, I see your twenty-first century cake eating habits have seamlessly transferred to the nineteenth," Victoria hissed in a whisper. "Hugs later, but am I glad to see you. Actually you look amazing, who's your period fashion designer? I nearly died when I suddenly found myself inside a carriage in a ditch with Maddie and Belle. So what's happened to us? Your take quickly, a sharp, concise summary as usual please, before Morag returns."

"Me too, you look pretty good yourself. Whatever way this passing through universes has been meticulously engineered, aspects of our inner selves have come along with it, all very clever," Abby said and patted her hand quickly. "Mmm, I see too, Dr Rational Scientist has also transferred over just as seamlessly. Anyway, I found myself lying on a four-poster bed upstairs, one of your guest rooms, in a very pretty chemise and three thick petticoats, fortunately with a personal diary and some letters from Morag inviting me here whose contents I read and absorbed quickly. Then Agnes comes in with a huge breakfast of poached salmon and eggs. Looking at her and as she started to speak, I realised that the catastrophe on the Queen Lusitania had somehow catapulted me through a psychic space-time barrier again, blatantly something to do with Mauveine and her odd behaviour. She knew all along on the ship this would happen, I'm sure of it. I expected to see Mauveine any moment, then realised, when I saw the dates on Morag's letters, that was impossible ..."

"I know because she hasn't been born yet," Victoria cut in, impatient as ever. "Much as I hate to admit it, I'm sure you're correct. We came to the same conclusion. We're here for a purpose aren't we, so we all have to keep playing along as carefully as possible until the reason becomes crystal clear. What else can we do?"

"I'm glad to see the perpetual unbeliever is finally coming round to my psychic world perspective," Abby chided playfully. "Agreed. Now who is this mysterious and chivalrous Dr Gray turning up? Surely to God it's not Lynton is it? He's here too? But how?"

"Yes, it is Lynton … He rescued us from the ditch and drove the carriage here, but be warned right now Abby," Victoria replied sternly, her voice lowered. "This is 1841 Lynton, living solely within this time era, with all the look, manners and characteristics of a gentleman effete of leisure, a well-known and wealthy art historian, not the 2026 version you married and love. And he doesn't recognise me or the girls, repeat loud and clear … not recognised. We've had to play along and improvise with him, really fucking difficult."

Abby felt a deep, inner gloom pervade her from top to bottom, accompanied by an instant flashback to the prism of purpurine and Orsbrick Priory calamity. Then, Julian, Judy and Adrian were taken over by monk-like zombies, but of course only she and Maddie remembered that part of the nightmare. Victoria and everyone else had no memory of the event once the whole McKenzie history cycle became reshaped after evil Rimmer was obliterated and everything returned to normal. Strict silence had been the way she and Maddie had agreed to keep all of that. Explaining what happened had been way too difficult, but this situation was quite different. Victoria, Maddie, Belle and her, trapped inside an early Victorian psychic time bubble but with their real memories and effective future knowledge intact. Lynton has interestingly arrived into the mix, heaven knows how, but displaying no future knowledge and living within the Victorian time frame? Not only did this make no sense but could create real challenges. Most importantly why?

"Fuck," Abby replied softly, glancing through the window. "Morag is returning with someone. Back to 1840s speak … Oh shit, now I see what you mean."

Agnes had opened the study door. Morag glided through gracefully. Victoria realised there was a knack walking sexily in these long dresses, which Abby, plainly, had acquired, but then again she was once a fashion and textiles expert. Lynton was behind Morag and followed inside as Abby drew a deep breath. She stared incredulous at the fashionable narrow red trousers, his tight waistcoat and flouncy silk shirt and the shaved, familiar face; definitely Lynton to a tee. He ignored everyone and immediately headed for the easel to gaze in deep thought at Abby's painting. The moment Morag had presented her with an easel, paint and brushes she needed to portray her own creative style, and remembered that the French painter, Delacroix, was making waves about that time. He had been the great influence on Manet and the Impressionism movement to come, with his violent, seething traditional scenes, bubbling over with colour, dynamism, sex and death. She always loved colour and recalled the artist's unique hatching technique to almost make the visuals daringly three-dimensional. Victoria looked across nervously at the painting, an oriental and vivid murderous scene of concubines with their master, full of nudes and gore. It took your breath away, certainly not reflecting a demure, rural landscape, fitting for the time and place. What was Abby thinking of?

In the meantime, Esther had quietly escorted Maddie and Belle through the study too, and as they stepped outside, Abby glanced up at Maddie with a brief smile. Neither she nor Belle reacted further but were quietly overjoyed. Abby had turned up, thank goodness. Abby was visibly impressed. Both Maddie and Belle looked very pretty. Agnes had done their hair in the same style with thick sausage curls and they wore the most adorable and very bell-shaped green and yellow silk dresses.

"I hope you don't mind, Victoria," Morag said, irritated with Dr Gray's lack of courtesy. "But I took the opportunity to introduce myself to your lovely daughters. I had no idea they were so grown. For some reason I believed they were the same age as Ellen, my daughter. But their elegance, and social confidence is a credit to their upbringing and education by you, I have to say. Now Madeleine and Annabelle, may I introduce you to my cousin Miss Abigail Warren, who is, as you can see, an artist of much merit."

"Thank you Lady McKenzie," Maddie said, her hand outstretched, but before she could step a foot forward they were all interrupted by a loud 'hear, hear' as Lynton strode back to join them, walked between and took Abby's hand to kiss it gently. She could see in one micro-second he had no idea who she was.

"Miss Warren, please stay seated, a pleasure to meet you. Dr Lynton Gray, art historian and curator at your service. What stupendous talent you have with the brush, a most breathtaking composition. I sense a variant of 'The Death of Sardanapalus', oh do please put me out of my misery." He waved his hand in the air with a coquettish flourish.

Abby had to stifle a major giggle, particularly when he followed up with a fervent offer to peruse his etchings in Southport. "Indeed, Dr Gray, Monsieur Delacroix is providing me with new inspiration after my long spell assisting the brilliant Mr Constable with painting landscapes."

"Outrageous I would say, but I see you are a woman who dares to be different, Miss Warren, not least working with the curmudgeonly old goat, Constable. I hope his health remains good. I will buy this for a goodly sum when finished if I may."

Abby swallowed hard inside, the two must not meet.

"I'm afraid you have already been outbid, Dr Gray, by me. I have first refusal and this masterpiece will be going on the wall of my study," Morag replied jauntily, as they all turned to see Lynton's child-like expression turn to mild dismay followed by a playful tut-tut. However, he relished the daring, too, of Lady McKenzie, who had earlier promised him the opportunity to curate a London exhibition of painted engineering inventions of the last hundred years, which she would sponsor, stored in the attic that her deceased husband had previously collected.

Morag continued. She needed to move things on and still had a paper to referee for Michael Faraday. "Now, Dr Gray, I have urgent business to attend to as I am sure you do too. Williams has brought Mrs Hammelaar's carriage to the front for you to return to Parbold forthwith. And here is Agnes with your hat. Good day Dr Gray."

They hastily offered their hands and goodbyes in turn to Lynton who relished kissing each one laboriously, reserving a sly wink last for Abby, which made her blush stupidly, blinking at the incongruous, tall top hat. Agnes led him to the carriage. As he clambered up the side, Morag suddenly ran over and spoke a few giggling words to him. Lynton, 1840s version, was decidedly flirtatious which Abby didn't know whether she liked or not. The situation was so very strange. Would she see Lynton again and for what reason? Victoria was however impressed with Morag's clear thinking and organisational drive, an ancestor and a woman of science after her own heart and style.

"Also, Victoria," Morag added on returning. "Now that you are settled, you have an appointment of course first at the rectory."

"The rectory?" Victoria replied, looking blank.

"Your sister of course, Alice. Goodness me Victoria, have you forgotten? If it wasn't for Alice's suggestion and recommendation you would not be here. I promised her you would visit the moment you arrive. Now, the question remains, how do we get you there? Our carriage is being repainted this afternoon."

Desperate to remain calm and together, Victoria felt a cold panicky feeling run through her from end to end. Her sister? What sister? She was an only child. That didn't compute whatsoever.

"Mama," Maddie intervened gently. "Remember the last letter Aunt Alice sent? Asking to see us when we arrived? I think we may have left it, which is why you forgot."

"Of course, thank you Madeleine. I do apologise Morag, so much has been happening today."

"I understand," Morag replied laughing. "Damned letters going abroad take so long too. Won't it be good when the Wheatstone telegraph can be extended to Europe? I hope you will wish to see the work I am doing on gutta-percha wire insulation for Mr Faraday. He believes good insulation will be the key to transmit for longer distances. Alice and her husband, the Reverend Thomas Langton, have done so much to continue the St John the Baptist building work which I fully support."

Abby suddenly piped up. "Morag, I would be very happy to take Victoria, Madeleine and Annabelle to see Mrs Langton. I can use the opportunity to sketch the outside of that splendid gothic church whilst they have a familial chat. A little exercise and air would be good for us and we have plenty of time before dinner. Do you three ride?"

"Yes, we are very experienced riders, that would be fine," Victoria replied, sensing an excellent opportunity for them to catch up, apart from meeting her unknown mysterious sister. How that would turn out was anyone's guess.

"My dear cousin, such an excellent idea," Morag replied, relishing some peace and quiet for the rest of the afternoon. "It's not too far to the church, the rectory is next door. We always have half a dozen horses saddled up ready." She waved to Agnes and Esther to come over. "Can you go through all the riding gear in the upstairs storeroom immediately and ensure they are dressed in suitable attire. Then take them to the stables for Bertie to pick out a horse each. Victoria is remarkably similar to my dearly departed husband's grandmother, the former Lady Fiona McKenzie, who was also commanding in height. We've kept her entire wardrobe. She also loved riding and although she died ten years ago, her fashion sense is still very modern, forthright and appealing, so you will look the part, if that is acceptable?"

"I am truly honoured, that would be perfect, thank you," Victoria replied, pleased to feel a warm glow becoming part of the family already, and smiled over at Abby. More useful information could be forthcoming.

*

Belle, again, remembered her former school history lessons and warned everyone as they headed upstairs behind Agnes and Esther.

"You'll be found even longer voluminous dresses and top hats, in case you don't know about female riding habits now," she whispered.

Maddie smiled, all sounded fun to her. She was enjoying making the most of wearing these period dresses.

Victoria grimaced. She had no idea, and had assumed they would wear a variant of modern riding garments.

They were all especially grateful, by that stage of the afternoon, to learn from Agnes that Lady McKenzie's love of engineering invention had extended to the unusual installation of three state of the art upstairs water closets, with tanks and a pull chain, filled by hand each morning and also one in the basement for the servants. Somewhere there was a giant cesspit and even running cold water, piped into the ground floor with a tap, from the river. Lady McKenzie, they were told, had insisted no effluent was to drain into the canal, convinced, against the general thinking of most, that scientific evidence pointed to diseases like typhoid and cholera being spread through foul water.

Agnes pointedly remarked that 'Orsbrick Hall was much more modern than any aristocrat houses in London, no sewage in basements or smelly privies except behind the stables for all them outdoor workers.'

The large, white porcelain toilets, with heavy oak bench seats and cast with the newly invented siphon trap U-bend, had been specially hand commissioned from Liverpool by Morag's husband, the late Lord Malcolm McKenzie, but he sadly died before trying them out. 'Cleansing paper,' was supplied following the aftermath of a roof leak which had ruined a section of books in the library. It felt quite peculiar, gently wiping one's bottom with pages off a hook torn from a first edition of Pride and Prejudice. This was the first example Victoria had noted of seeing first-hand how nothing at all was wasted in the 1840s. Everything was habitually re-used, sold on to be made into something else, fed to pigs or recycled. Agnes chuntered on in her cockney accent, 'that the scarcity of day to day food, money and goods during the long Napoleonic era when everything went to the war, had made everyone very frugal to this day, even in big country estates.'

Abby quickly sensed that bubbly Agnes, unlike the morose Esther, liked to chatter and probably gossip more than she should. Once they gained more of her confidence that would be all grist to the mill. She was the epitome of an intelligent working class girl, lost both her parents young, apprenticed into service at twelve but had, exceptionally, been taught to read and write by her first employer, a London Member of Parliament, although she was very reluctant to say why or what she had to do in return. Agnes was undoubtedly an astute survivor within a harsh world.

*

Once out of sight of the house with Abby leading, the four riding sturdy, brown mares drew to a halt near an opening through the hedge down to the Leeds and Liverpool canal. They gazed around at their environment. The fields and hedges were very different and lots more trees dominated, but the lay of the land was familiar as was the canal, although cleaner than they expected and well looked after.

Victoria pointed over to their left. "Isn't that Isherwood's farm over there, where we got Jeb and Kai? Gosh, it looks exactly the same, except the roof is thatched. Amazing."

They were surprised how much longer their dark riding dresses were, which took much gathering up when they walked. Victoria was wearing indigo and the others muted blacks and browns, fetching and comfortable.

Abby pointed to the loops sewn in the front. "Trust a fashion designer who did her masters degree in Regency costume. Slip those around your boot by the outside stirrup, which should stop your dress from flying up. Aren't these black toppers fantastic? Just like Lynton's but smaller. I suggest we try the shortcut down the towpath to the church, it will be much quicker. But let's share thoughts first."

They nodded, dismounted and tied the horses, and sat down on a couple of old birch trunks felled by a storm.

Maddie was first off with the question on everyone's mind. "I just can't figure out who your sister could possibly be Mum, an intriguing dilemma, but we should know soon. So far there seems to be some semblance of logic and relation to our own time. I'm actually much more comfortable than I would have thought. But your sister, the wife of a vicar?"

Victoria nodded. Abby and Belle concurred likewise. Nobody had a clue and nothing had arisen in the library archives, another mystery in the missing gap of seventy years. Belle, who had managed already to gain the trust of the shy and miserable Esther by promising to teach her to read, added more thoughts.

"I've picked up some useful info. Esther told me about Lady McKenzie's children who we meet tonight. She has a nine-year-old daughter, Ellen, who is arty, well behaved and happy-go-lucky and a twelve-year-old son, James. James sounds a proverbial pain in the neck, badly behaved, only interested in being outdoors and misses his father badly. He dislikes his mother intensely and every governess beforehand has soon left in tears because he's so rude and unruly. But, according to Esther, he's very bright."

Victoria smirked. "He hasn't met me, his new governess yet. I won't be leaving in tears!"

But Abby was suddenly deep in thought. "James? He's twelve in 1841? Do the maths. Mauveine was born in 1849 so he would have been a young buck about town then, aged twenty and having every pretty girl around he could, including the boat women, especially if he has an unruly, arrogant streak. James McKenzie was the name of Mauveine's father! A connection somewhere, I reckon. Maybe why we're here?"

Victoria pondered. "Possible but convoluted. He may not be the same person. Actually, Agnes did let slip Morag's age. She's obviously a young widow but of course then, women especially soon looked older than their years, with all that serial childbirth and challenging living conditions, whereas you and me, Abby, look younger than our years. I can see you smirk. I don't mean in 2026, although we do … but especially now."

"I would say Morag is in her early to mid thirties?" Maddie ventured.

"Wrong. She's only just twenty five!"

They all started calculating and gasped. "Fuck," Abby cried. "She was only thirteen when she had James? Bloody hell."

"And probably married Lord Malcolm McKenzie of Orsbrick Hall, becoming Lady McKenzie the same year," Belle added. "You were allowed to marry at twelve then, before the law changed later."

Victoria continued. "According to Agnes, I let her talk whilst we rummaged through the deceased grandmother, Lady Fiona McKenzie's, amazingly huge wardrobe, Malcolm was a lot older, an engineer, who went to Cambridge University. That tradition for McKenzie male heirs has certainly continued and he worked on the first steam trains with Stevenson and the Rocket and even had a factory, which Morag has sold. She is very wealthy. He died two years ago … some grisly accident at Manchester Piccadilly station. There is a line running from Liverpool to Manchester now, that's the train we saw at Parbold."

"But what about Morag's background? Where did she come from?" Abby asked.

"Agnes doesn't know much," Victoria replied slowly. "Morag is a bit of a mystery. All she said was quote, 'a child genius, living on the Orsbrick estate with her reclusive and fierce widowed mother, who was rumoured to be some former aristocrat from Europe who had lost everything.' Apparently Morag was exclusively taught in the sciences by her own mother, hence her unusual interest in the subject and education."

"Fascinating," Maddie responded, trying desperately to pull the disparate pieces together. "It's clear now why she wants you here, Mum. Apart from being the children's governess, she wants her children to follow in her own footsteps, and probably likes the idea of an educated female science soulmate around, but none of it clarifies the purpose of why we're all here. Where is the bigger picture?"

"As yet there isn't one," Abby said, unhitching her horse, and giving his large head a stroke. "We're just going to have to be patient, take each step carefully and keep finding ways to share every relevant morsel of fact and nuance ... at least we seem to have engineered being together reasonably well and we can make use of Agnes and Esther. But I have to say, meeting up with the unreconstructed Victorian Lynton has been a bit of a shock ... which raises another question. Are Julian, Ned and Zac also here and if so where?"

"Oh my goodness, yes, why not?" Belle cried. "It's going to be hard ignoring them assuming they react like Lynton. And he's back for dinner later and he looks like he fancies you Abby. Isn't that sort of weird? Again to what end, beyond the obvious?"

"Back for dinner?" Abby said, confused.

"Yes, I heard Lady McKenzie whisper it to Agnes. Probably meant as a surprise to bring a cheery heart to dearest unmarried cousin Abigail!" Belle replied, Maddie grinning alongside.

"You bet— shit!"

"I've already thought of that and been preparing," Victoria said, scowling and releasing the remaining three horses, as Belle and Maddie grabbed the reins and as lady-like as possible, lifted themselves up into the saddle. "Just play it by ear. In fact I hope I am ignored if Julian and the boys materialise ... makes whatever our task is easier," she continued, rationalising any emotion beforehand out of such an encounter. Lynton was enough of a shock.

They carefully cantered in a line down to the towpath when a couple of farm workers, carrying bundles of wood, walked past and tipped their caps. There was a lot of activity going on down there with a number of barges berthed, men and women, black and grimy boat people with shovels and bags, unloading coal into a big depot on the edge of a cutting with a track going towards the town. Another barge could be seen approaching in the distance, long and low in the water, full to the top with sacks, being slowly pulled along by two hefty shire horses. An unexpected sound of music grew in intensity as they watched a fiddler, one of the boatmen wearing a top hat, play in a frenzy at the front as his colleague steered, stood at the other end with two women and a mixed group of at least six young children sat on the flat deck. They looked old and weary way before their time with long hours of heavy, physical toil, continuous childbirth and meagre pay, life expectancy seemingly short.

"Thank goodness for effective twenty-first century contraception," Abby whispered, pointing in the distance at the quaint gothic steeple. "Let's find this rectory and your mystery sister, Victoria, maybe the next piece in the jigsaw."

"What do they use now? Anything?" Maddie queried, already thinking ahead for any situation which may arise.

"Later, Maddie, you'll be surprised," Abby replied with a grin.

Victoria trotted behind, deep in silent contemplation of what on earth she would say when they arrived. She wished she was back in her laboratory with a science problem to solve, a hundred times easier by half.

# Chapter Eight

Trotting over the wide, gravelled path leading up to the graveyard, they dismounted near the swing gate and tied the horses. Abby and Victoria gazed nostalgically at the beautiful gothic steeple.

"Hard to believe we were married there isn't it," Abby said, admiring the newness of the stone construction and the well kept gardens around the periphery.

"Yes, we passed here earlier when Lynton drove our carriage to Orsbrick," Victoria replied. "The church didn't really register, but look how different it is. A lot more must have been added in the future, although the unusual core design remains."

They peered in through the open door. "My favourite stained glass window in the nave is yet to come," Abby whispered nostalgically, staring at the empty pews and wondering whether they would ever get back again to see the modern inside they knew and loved.

"You ladies looking for anything particular?"

Maddie turned first, to be confronted by a scruffy and overbearing gardener carrying a scythe, his lined and pockmarked face overgrown with a huge red, bushy beard. Seeing their wealthy appearances, he promptly tipped his cap. "Yes, can you tell me where the rectory is please?" she demanded assertively.

He coughed, and she quickly moved out of the way, as he pointed, between unintelligible grunts, to a large, rambling house up the hill. "You looking for the vicar?"

"His wife actually. Mrs Alice Langton?" Victoria interjected.

"Ay, she be there, no doubt." He concluded abruptly and wandered off to begin cutting grass around an unkempt group of gravestones.

Victoria sighed. "Let's go. The quicker we get this over with the better," leading the way gingerly.

The four, walking with difficulty, hoisted their heavy dresses up a steep slope and slippery steps towards a large, dark oak door. The knocker was huge. Victoria rapped it and the sound echoed eerily around the inside … a resounding silence. She rapped again, obviously a waste of time, but then they heard a rustling from behind the door and a series of heavy bolts were withdrawn. The door slowly opened, creaking horribly and four mouths dropped the moment the occupant stepped out of the gloom into the doorway. Even in their wildest imaginations, who they were now seeing could not possibly be.

"Mauveine?" Victoria gasped, feeling Abby's arm gripping her own hard from behind. But this was no ghost standing there, but a real flesh and blood person, beautifully dressed in a pale yellow dress, pearl beads, a black shawl and wearing a trendy bonnet. She carried a basket of vegetables as if she had either just come in or was going out.

"Mrs Alice Langton herewith to you, Victoria. Excellent you all made it. I was so afraid," the woman replied with a grin, in that deep and rich Mauveine Lancashire accent they already knew. Her voice was crystal clear, forthright and strong, with no echo or breaking up. She glanced from left to right outside and then beckoned them inside, and promptly closed the door behind. She led them into the sitting room, resplendent with a beautiful harpsichord, where she pointed for them to sit down. Bach was prominently displayed on the music stand which immediately caught Abby's eye, wondering who played.

Mauveine caught Abby's interest and rubbed her shoulder gently through her dress. Abby stared nervously at Mauveine's warm hand, a physical contact and no ghostly gaps. A realisation immediately dawned. Mauveine had also come back, exactly the same, as part of the 1841 present. But she was as real as them and everyone else but how? Victoria continued to ponder, holding Belle's hand tightly, both silent, their minds churning over at lightning speed trying to piece together where this was all fitting in. Manifestly, Mauveine being her sister was a clever alias in the complex scheme of things unfolding.

It took Maddie to break the ice. She stood up and announced, "Mauveine, may I hug you please? It's so amazing to finally meet you properly, in the flesh as it were."

"I would like nothing better Madeleine. If it wasn't for you and Abigail, none of us would be here at all."

Victoria shot a sharp look across to smiling Abby. What in heaven's name was Mauveine talking about? Unknown to Victoria, Belle already knew the full prism of purpurine story. Maddie had finally confided over Easter, with Belle reacting, as usual, in a matter of fact and unbothered way. Now Maddie wished she and Abby had gathered the courage and told Victoria, but their mother's continued deeply held scepticism of anything psychic, which smacked of new age claptrap and anti-science, had remained a formidable barrier.

Mauveine beckoned her and they hugged warmly for over a minute. That simple act instantly defused the tension, mistrust and shock confusion in the room. Maddie felt her mind float away and detached into a strange and dreamy euphoria. Mauveine was reading her thoughts and soothing her fear.

Abby strongly sensed the same. They had to put genuine trust and confidence in what Mauveine was up to.

Maddie sat down again and held her mother's other hand as Mauveine spoke. "Victoria, before I begin, both Madeleine and Abigail were instrumental, last autumn, in ensuring the highly difficult but final obliteration of the Rimmer evil along with his enduring seventeenth century curse at the Orsbrick Priory. We repaired the McKenzie space-time rift for good. Key to their success was the essential psychic information support which you and Judy provided from afar. We all know and remember intensely everything that happened ... except you. You are and always have been just as powerfully psychic, but your highly rational, scientific intellect puts up a constant communication barrier, ensuring doubt and disbelief to prevail. That's why Maddie and Abby were afraid to tell you."

"Mum, I know too," Belle added. "Maddie told me in secret because I was there in the thick of the action, but I'm not as sensitive as the rest of you and can't remember the detail. But I'm cool about it all. For me these things are a logical and integral part of the McKenzie family legacy, it's who we are, so we just get on with it."

Victoria smiled at her daughter; a very mature and sensible head on young shoulders. But being transported back in time to this 1841 McKenzie family period had already convinced her. All of those years, Abby was consistently right. She just wished she understood the psychic mechanisms but one day she would, convinced the core effect was a transitional jump through multi-dimensional universes involving dark energy. But that wasn't going to help them in 1841. Practicalities must prevail.

The evidence from the past, reluctant though she had been to admit it, was always clear from the moment as a teenager she first saw ethereal purple bodies floating in the canal. She did have the McKenzie female psychic gift and had to believe it now wholeheartedly. The proof was indisputable, stood talking to her. Mauveine was as real as anyone in the room and like all of them living, breathing and existing within a former time period. She believed it. Victoria felt her mind flood out with an array of images, sounds and situations, like watching a film fast-forwarding at a hundred miles and hour speed, as she concentrated hard.

She appeared to go into a strange trance, her face reddening. Abby felt instant alarm watching Victoria and rose from her chair, but Mauveine grinned, putting her fingers to her lips and brusquely waved her back. A faint glow now surrounded Victoria, who was using her formidable analytical brain to make sense of the fast inflow of new information. She could remember the entire shocking scenario. She really did contract bubonic plague, she knew about the wolves from hell, she facilitated the wolfhound attack, listened to Abby sing denunciations like an angel and observed the terrible gory hanging which her son, Ned, almost succumbed to. Finally she watched the degenerate Abbot Rimmer's spirit rise into the sky to be obliterated forever in orange flames. All the scenes of what happened that night in the priory, in 1665, had slotted into place, in a neat and orderly rotation.

Victoria realised and accepted something fundamental for the first time. She always believed that she and Maddie were the closest of mother and daughter soul-mates, but in thinking process and scientific perception she was, in fact, far more like Belle. And now she could understand exactly why. Maddie and Abby were so close and shared exactly the same mindsets, because once, a very long time ago in 1665, they actually were half-sisters. It was a massive relief, after all that time, to finally shed her inner resistance. This turnaround she knew was fundamental if they were ever going to make sense of why they were all here and hopefully to return.

Victoria came to from her trance, calm and as fiery logical as ever, but perfectly relaxed with her new knowledge.

"I believe now you can spare the embarrassment of Abby and Maddie having to relate what happened?" Mauveine said. "You're one of us and finally you know and accept it. My word, I sound like one of those sci-fi films, in your time that Isi and I enjoy on Abby's old iPhone we borrowed. We are often quite perplexed ...especially with 'Alien.'"

They laughed loudly. Abby seriously wondered how Mauveine could cope with spanning three time scales let alone two.

"Absolutely," Victoria replied, smiling. "Mauveine, Maddie and Abby, I think you can say the overdue job is now done and thank you. My brain feels like a five terabyte micro-card of missing data has just been slotted in."

"Excellent," Mauveine replied. "Isi and I could do with one of those cards, no memory left in that iPhone. I think we need to upgrade to ... what pray, do you call that operating system?"

"Err ... Windows," Maddie added, to more laughter.

But no way was this light-hearted conversation going to be repeated later back at Orsbrick Hall.

Victoria glanced at Abby's pocket watch and decided to take charge. Time was of the essence; they would have to return soon and needed answers. "Mauveine, we're bursting with thousands of questions but can I propose that we concentrate on the most essential ones now. Why are we here and what should we be doing? Are you able to tell us?"

"I agree and I will deem it my best to try," Mauveine replied, pouring out a glass of ginger lemonade each from a huge jug.

"But some aspects have not worked out as we thought." She promptly lifted a heavy, brass hand bell and rang it hard, requesting servants or her maid. The door opened and they turned to see a tall, slim figure stride in wearing a dark hassock and a dog collar. The Reverend Thomas Langton, vicar of the parish was joining them, but Victoria, was the first to gasp out loudly, beside herself with amazement. "Julian? Is that really you?"

He stopped and smiled warmly. "I'm so sorry Victoria, but not quite I'm afraid," his voice deep and resonating, a man of presence but the Lancashire accent was decidedly not Julian's.

Belle and Maddie realised immediately. Their mother was wishful thinking. Isi had also returned with a presence as real and flesh-like as Mauveine. But he appeared even more startling as he had always been a very background ethereal presence, in many ways an accompanist to Mauveine's solo performance.

"You finally found Isi?" Abby asked tentatively. She was highly mindful of Victoria's visible disappointment, despite all the emotional rationalising earlier. But Victoria quickly calmed down her feelings. The ancestral likeness was definitely tangible, they were the same height and build but Isi was indeed different. Much younger and fuller in the face, his eyes were a deep blue, in contrast to Julian's dark brown.

"I never lost him, but we did have some worrying moments maintaining our communication," Mauveine replied, beaming and touching his arm, as in love with him as ever.

Isi spoke again. "It is a great pleasure to meet you all. Mauveine and I took a huge risk and a lot of planning to enable your presence here, but I will leave the talking now to her. My dear wife is much better with dialogue than me, although, to my own astonishment, I seem to have developed a good knack with the sermons."

They laughed as he took each hand gently in turn and kissed them, his lips warm and moist, as alive, if that was the right word, as his wife, and evidently relishing his role as a priest. Once sat down, he helped himself to lemonade.

Mauveine spoke quietly. "If you will permit me, I will now explain. Abby, after Abbot Rimmer was destroyed, Isi and I became concerned when you and Maddie were unable to trace any history in the archives of the family between the late seventeen hundreds and my father's letters in the 1860s. It was then that we realised. Obliterating Rimmer has removed the McKenzie curse and everything seemed historically to be adjusted back, but we concluded that a small bubble in the warp of the family space-time remained. Not everything had transferred and a difficult and turbulent period of history has gone missing. But the ramifications have turned out far more serious. This has necessitated your return to the specific year of 1841, with us to guide you. We chose our aliases of the Reverend Thomas and Mrs Alice Langton as a suitable and uncontroversial disguise. There happened to be a handy vacancy, but I do declare that Isi has required to effect some hard studying in the arts of religious thought!"

Abby and Maddie smiled. Mauveine stopped and took a drink, her throat slightly hoarse. "Isi and I had to create a violent rift, something devastating enough to blow a hole in your existing space-time continuum, like applying a high voltage to restart a human heart, as is done in your century. We hated the concept, it was very difficult and dangerous to accept and I truly and sincerely apologise for all the distress, but you will understand shortly why we finally had no choice. Hence my sinking of the Queen Lusitania. May I now summarise?

Unless we can together unlock the reason why that block of history has vanished, and in particular change the direction of Lady Morag McKenzie's scientific endeavours, then Isi and I will not exist because we will never be born and neither will any of you. We don't have much time."

Total silence pervaded the room. Only the spring sound of a blackbird singing energetically outside the window filled the void, as the enormity of what Mauveine had just said began to sink in. Abby and Victoria looked at each other and wondered. At least now they knew why they were here but where do they start?

Victoria instantly assembled a raft of questions and kicked off, because changing the direction of Morag's science felt like it would fall heavily on her shoulders. "Morag has appointed me governess through your clever and I assume deliberate sisterly intervention, so presumably I can gain her confidence, understand what she is doing and influence her and the children, perhaps with Maddie and Belle's help. We've already worked out that Morag must be your grandmother. And twelve year old James is likely to be your father? How can you interact with your own father who is still a child?"

"Correct Victoria," Mauveine replied. "You need to all try and understand the complexity of how the temporary time-rupture we created works. Isi and I have had to work with a set of general happenings, people and events that took place or existed at this time. We inhabit them now and are perceived by the world around as that flesh and blood, as alive in 1841 as we were in our own times. But we have retained the knowledge of our own time and some idea, between us, of the future from here. We breathe, eat, sleep and could die now like everyone else as we embark on this difficult task of reorientation; that may seem strange. My interaction with Morag has been by letter so far. It is preferable that neither I nor Isi, if possible, come into physical contact with my own grandmother nor especially my father as we are not sure if that may trigger another rupture reaction. The incompatibility and bizarreness creates instability. It is easier for Isi and me to adjust and fit into the 1840s than any of you because we are much closer in time. Although I must say, I much prefer the fashions in my own time than now, especially the dresses, crudely made by hand and poorly coloured, with no sewing machines and definitely no decent dyes.

Abby laughed. "We're so far ahead, we actually rather like the fashions, especially this riding gear."

Mauveine smiled and nodded, she understood completely.

Abby continued. "You used the word temporary. How long have we got? And if we don't succeed what happens?"

Mauveine's face suddenly saddened. She remained burdened with taking the decision to embark on this risky venture, and Isi held her hand comfortingly. "I truly don't know but we reasonably concur, success must be within a week or two, before self-repair inevitably begins. Failure and we all remain here as we are. We then live and die in this period of time onwards. There will be no going forward as there will be no future to go to."

They went quiet again … until Belle, always the quick reconciler, piped up. "Okay, guys, yes, we have a real challenge. We know the problem we have to solve and quickly. But, this is something we're all good at, especially you Mum. So let's get to it. We make the news by engaging with the flow."

Victoria, still silent, patted her hand. "Exactly Belle. Well summarised. I've already been thinking. Mauveine, we need to go backwards. Your father was an excellent and enthusiastic dye chemist and turned you, his daughter, into one. But the present James seems to be inclined to nothing, a spoilt and ill-disciplined wastrel, although we were told he has a good brain. I will have to work hard and fast on him, the key lies there. As for Morag, we need to ascertain what science she is focussed on and why or how it needs to change. That begins over dinner tonight."

Isi nodded. "We agree with you, an excellent start. Thank you Victoria. You and Mauveine think so alike it feels uncanny for me. The one thing we do have an inkling of, from the parish gossip, is that Morag's science isn't chemistry."

Maddie raised her hand. She was feeling left out and needed to find a role and a purpose, more than the glamorous, wealthy daughter with a semi-idle life, waiting to be married off to some rich, upper class misogynist. The last thing she would ever want, although she wasn't so sure Belle would object. "Mauveine, you said two things. You've clarified what we need to do and also why it happened. Belle and I will be given jobs in the house, so I propose that she and I try and ensure we do some up to date research in the present archives and fill in the gaps. Information may be there which none of us know."

Mauveine visibly cheered, she hadn't thought of that. "An excellent idea, Madeleine, which both you and Annabelle will be ideally suited for. Make the most of the fact that you are well educated and knowledgeable. Morag will not want you doing menial work."

"Which leaves me," Abby replied now feeling tetchy and marginalised in this game plan that depended solely on the McKenzie scientists. "So, as usual I'm going to ask the awkward questions Mauveine. First off, using your Alien analogy, we are not alone. We've all just encountered one wealthy gentleman bon vivant, a certain Dr Lynton Gray, art historian 1841 style, except he is all contemporary in memory and has no knowledge whatsoever of us and least of all me. So what do I do with him? And moreover, has he arrived enroute with the other males of the family, namely Julian, Ned and Zac and where are they?"

Mauveine's colour drained and she stared hard at Isi who was undoubtedly disturbed. "I knew you shouldn't have done that," she said, softly. "I tried so hard to find you on the ship, now I understand why you disappeared. So what do you have to say for yourself?"

Abby blinked, the reproach was cuttingly targeted. As a couple Mauveine and Isi must have disagreed like any other. Now they were no longer ghosts but alive and fallible, like her and Victoria.

Isi took a deep breath and shuffled position like he was going to actually take the sermon in church. A further silent glare back from Mauveine made him decide to come clean. There were too many astute women around him to fool anyone.

"I take full responsibility. It was my idea solely. I thought if I simultaneously created another time-rupture back at Orsbrick Hall then we could muster the whole family into action and act together."

Victoria raised her eyebrows. "Isi, you mean something awful has happened at Orsbrick Hall?"

He went very glum. "A form of awfulness, I suppose. I created a fire in the barn. They ran inside one after the other, all of them, including Jeb and Kai, to rescue the horses. But I'd taken the horses out already and they couldn't follow and escape by then, a raging inferno had taken hold. It worked, at least Lynton is here?"

"Oh my God," Victoria wailed loudly. "Isi, what a terrible, terrible thing to do. How could …?"

But she was stopped by Maddie immediately.

"Hang on Mum and you Abby before we get over-emotional and start to do a needless blame game we regret. We must stay very clear thinking, just like we did returning to the Orsbrick Priory in 1665. First off, it's happened and Isi took a chance with the best of intentions and we could have all done the same in his place. Drowning in the sea and burning alive in a barn are equally horrible, but it could have been worse because we didn't and neither did Lynton. We've all come painlessly back in time. What's gone wrong is we already know. Lynton is in 1841 minus his real-time memory. Sorry it gets confusing, but we must accept for now what Mauveine has already said. This is our time and also Lynton's time. He has a past too, we don't. So the chances of Dad, Ned and Zac, similarly being here are also high and I believe this is all part of the purpose that we have to work with. We have to turn their inability to know us to our advantage, use it and park our 2026 feelings. Sorry to sound a cold, hard bitch but only that way do we stay sane and crack the problem."

There was silence before Mauveine and Abby each walked across and hugged first her and then each other as Victoria, Belle and Isi followed, tears running down his cheek.

"Thank you Madeleine," Mauveine replied. "Before you spoke I truly believed the confirmation of my and Isi's unwarranted recklessness and that everything was lost before we had even begun. Abby, your job is defined, and it's the hardest and most daunting of all. Because we don't know what it will be except somehow to improvise and manipulate, using all your skills, with all these unexpected factors, like Dr Gray, and keep the whole picture hanging together, with Maddie, as you both did before."

"Improvising and coordinating is my thing, especially if I have to be right-brain creative, as I will," Abby said, feeling positive again.

"Also, look on the bright side," Belle chipped in. "It could be much worse. We're back home, and if 1841 ends up becoming the new permanent scene then I'm sure Morag, with her amazing social network, knows plenty of good-looking, rich suitors to get married to."

"I just knew you would think that," Maddie cried, nudging her sister playfully as the others joined in laughing. "I shall remain blue-stockinged and single thank you very much."

"I suppose there's always Lynton. He did ask me to see his etchings … yet again!" Abby cried, tears of mirth rolling from her eyes.

"And I need to find a proper wealthy scientist, like Charles Babbage," Mauveine said, joining in the fun. "There's no way I want to remain married to a boring, staid vicar!" as Isi's poor face dropped glumly.

"Victoria, I'll try and see if I can find out about Julian and the boys," Isi added, "I have the parish rounds tomorrow. We vicars are not all useless bone-idlers."

Victoria glanced at Mauveine's clock. "Okay, this afternoon has been extraordinary but essential. We need to ride back now, my dear sister Alice. We have dinner at seven and hopefully I'll meet Morag's children. Last question. If we succeed, how do we return in time?"

Mauveine shook her head. "I'm sorry, but I really don't know either. We will just have to hope and pray to our Lord that it happens. But you must all take care not to destabilise the temporary psychic rupture, like telling any of them you're from the future and describing what will happen. I'm certain that could instigate an historic chain reaction explosion, of uncertain outcome."

In a moment Victoria, Abby, Maddie and Belle had saddled up and they were off back down the canal to Orsbrick Hall. Halfway, Victoria stopped to gaze at the view through the fields of her favourite Parbold hill, gently rising clear and unobstructed through the myriad of fields and hedges. The stark background of the grey and clouded Pennines behind was sharply contrasting. Maddie and Belle were intensely studying some unfamiliar wild flowers popping up between the hedgerows in the spring sun.

Abby sidled up. "Almost feels home from home. I must say it is peaceful here this time of the century."

Victoria laughed "You said firstly, what was secondly?"

Abby furrowed her brow. "Pardon?"

"When you asked Mauveine your awkward questions."

"Oh yes … I forgot in the aftermath of discussion. It was part of the reason we are all here. Who was Fenella?"

"Fenella?"

"Remember? On the Queen Lusitania, when I last saw Mauveine looking for Isi? She also muttered that she had to find Fenella."

Victoria pondered in silence for a moment. "Certainly the why of the time rupture is Mauveine and Isi's responsibility, although she never mentioned it. So maybe whoever Fenella is then she's already been found. Unusual name though for this period, I think it's Gaelic."

"Mmm …" Abby replied, reflecting quietly. "We'd better get on."

# Chapter Nine

Fascinated by the bustling activity in the fields as dusk approached, Victoria watched the myriad assortment of workers outside, all shapes, sizes, and ages, with as many women and girls about as males. She recognised a large number who were still there from when she rose at dawn, such a long, arduous day. Some of the men with long straggly beards were very old, painfully bent over, pulling slowly at cabbages with one arm and propping themselves up by a stick with the other. Small, rickety, horse-drawn carts were being piled up with produce and other bits of vegetation, wood and shrubs, anything usable salvaged from the earth. This was the agricultural era of a long and forgotten yesteryear, with little mechanisation and dependent on extensive, hard labour. Other comings and goings were evident at the side door with some young male servants she hadn't seen before, exchanging goods and money, bartering, selling and buying stuff which were piled into or out of small handcarts, pushed by young boys from the town, looking especially lively and rowdy. How Orsbrick Hall had changed.

Her particular surprise had been heightened by the upstairs bedroom Morag had allocated, which was weirdly the same bedroom she and Julian had chosen and renovated all those years back. The Georgian sash windows looked identical, although the frames were heavier, but the room was larger having been extended into the one next door and the small double-canopied bed pushed against a different wall. A separate dressing area with a commode was located in the corner, and the space cluttered up with heavy oak wardrobes, drawers and shelves into which Agnes had hung all her clothes. She eyed the oddly shaped, small cast-iron bath, stood prominently on daintily splayed gold legs, in front of the red and black tiled fireplace. Beautiful pictures hung on the walls, decorated in rich, speckled-green wallpaper of hunting scenes. What was different was the appearance of a wide dado-rail, around a foot down from the ceiling, with a complimentary dark-green intricately patterned paper above. The whole effect gave a very soothing, pleasant touch to the room. Something, she thought, when and if she got back to 2026, for Julian to tackle. Then she sank momentarily into desperate apprehension, whether that would ever happen. She breathed in deeply. She simply had to get on with it, reflecting on the strange reappearance of Mauveine, alive, and the mind-blowing revelations of why this cataclysm in her life had happened.

Where, she wondered, was Morag's personal suite of rooms? Certainly, no expense had been spared. Much money and effort had been expended by a talented Lady McKenzie with an admirable eye for design flair and subtle detail, far better than her own. Orsbrick Hall was going through a period of proud ascent as an imposing local residence despite Morag's early widowhood. Victoria decided she needed to elicit more about that tragic happening. She casually brushed through the many styles of elegant clothes and decided on the expensive gold and red silky dress for dinner, very off-shoulder, then perused with trepidation the matching, hefty white corset, hanging ominously from a rail and adorned by a myriad of complicated straps. The afternoon exertions, physical and mental, had made her both tired and dusty. She could just about sit in that bath and a hot soak was very inviting, but how was it filled?

A knock on the door jolted her thoughts as she called out to come in. Agnes and Esther entered, panting loudly, carrying large pails of hot water from downstairs.

"We've already done Miss Warren, madam and you're next. A good soak after a long ride will set you up nicely for dinner. Normally we would draw hot water from the other tap and tank in the water closet, much easier. It comes up, so Lady McKenzie told me, because of something called convection from a pipe to the boiler in the basement. Lord McKenzie originally designed and installed it himself, but something's gone wrong with the boiler, needs a proper man to fix it, beyond Mr Williams's capabilities. Esther, bring two more pails and then go and see to Madeleine and Annabelle, although they'll have to share the water, running out a bit."

Victoria smiled at the thought. Hopefully her daughters would view the experience like being on an authentic Indian campsite, which they did in America when they were both eleven.

Lying in the enamelled iron bath which was bigger than it looked, and feeling the warmth of the fire alongside, now crackling nicely, felt decadently different. Especially after Agnes poured in a large jar of coloured flakes, making giant suds of soap to luxuriate in. That riding saddle was made from hard leather but she felt the pain across her thighs disappearing. She had struggled momentarily with Agnes automatically helping her out of the myriad of clothes, although without help it was a near impossibility extricating from that bulky dress. The handmade, sewn clasps, tapes and buttons were so difficult to reach and undo. Public nudity was not something she had ever felt comfortable with, avoiding saunas and nudist beaches like

203

the plague but she realised, in this upper class household, this was the day to day normal job for maids like Agnes who thought nothing of it. So Victoria went nonchalantly along as expected, trying to minimise her own shy blushings. Besides, Abby had presumably been doing the same, but then Abby was never self-conscious, always the extrovert. Prancing around naked would have been easy for her.

She glanced at Agnes, carefully laying out her clothes in order, drawers, a chemise, black stockings, that darned corset, three petticoats, the gold dress, a shawl and a black stone necklace. What a palaver when throwing on a simple top and skinny jeans would suffice.

"Agnes, come and have a chat for a minute, will you, and tell me more about Lady McKenzie," Victoria called tentatively, fluffing up the suds.

"Certainly, Victoria," Agnes replied, before giving the dress a final brushing down. She pulled up a three legged stool to sit on, bringing a large white cotton towel at the same time. "Forgot to mention it, but Dr Gray is coming back to dinner tonight, Lady McKenzie asked him on his way off."

"Really?" Victoria replied, feigning surprise. "Does, Abigail know?"

Agnes grinned. "She does. When I told her she looked right excited, she did. I reckon Dr Gray has taken a bit of a shine to Miss Warren, with all her painting and that, don't you Victoria? I saw him wink at her."

"Possibly," Victoria said, mischievously. "Now, as you know, Lady McKenzie has asked me specifically to tutor some science to her children and wants to show me some work she is doing for a Mr Faraday … Is that a Mr Michael Faraday?" Victoria asked, hugely intrigued with the possibility of an involvement with such a great scientist of the past but then she jolted her own mind. This isn't the past. "Does Lady McKenzie even have a laboratory?"

"Yes, she does, downstairs next to the morning room and adjoining her study. Esther and I have to clean it carefully every morning and sometimes she asks me and Mr Williams to help with her experiments. Much better now all them smelly dye liquids and glassware are out of the way, place is full of wires, jars, instruments and the like."

"Out of the way?"

"Well yes, Victoria. Not that long back, me and Mr Williams we were suddenly told to pack the chemicals and the apparatus away safely in the basement. Lady McKenzie said she was going in new directions. I'm sure it's all down to her friend Ada, who is well acquainted with Mr Faraday."

"Ada?"

"Oh yes, they've been friends for many years now. The Countess of Lovelace, she's the daughter of Lady Byron, my former employer, who I was with for many years in London before coming here. I liked working for Lady Byron, but she could be so very up and down and of course, it's common knowledge, Victoria, she hated her husband, always obsessing about him, even now still and with such vehemence, like I've never seen in a lady. The poor man's been dead for nearly twenty years. After he cleared off abroad, they was only married twelve months, she never saw him again and in between, well that was when Ada, actually she was fully named Augusta Ada Byron but never got called Augusta, was born."

Victoria, wide-eyed, was astounded. Morag was very well connected. Was Agnes talking about *the* Ada Lovelace? The amazing mathematician who invented computing with Charles Babbage? Agnes seemed so matter of fact about them. "Did you actually meet Lord Byron?"

"Well yes. I worked for them, him and Lady Byron, as a scullery maid, I was very young then, much younger than your daughters, down in their house in Piccadilly Terrace in London. You see, I started in service with Lady Byron's parents, in their London summer house, when I was orphaned as a child. My mother was a cook there and my dad looked after the horses, but they both died of cholera, it was a bad year. I liked Lord Byron, he had a witty turn of conversation and was very good with us servants, especially me because I could read, and could he talk, Victoria, and write such amazing poems, I still got some of his writings in my desk. Such a charmer with all the women and gambled a lot, the talk of London and the whole country by then. Between you and me, what he saw in Lady Byron, I never could see. She was so serious and proper, so quiet and very religious. He was exactly the opposite, life and soul of a party, but she must have loved him or she wouldn't still be feeling so aggrieved by his former behaviour. He ran up loads of debt you see. Lady Byron is from a very wealthy family and they kept paying if off apparently, but in the end he runs off to Europe with some fancy woman and was never seen again on these shores."

"Heavens!"

"Anyway, that water must be getting cold. Time to have you dressed and ready," Agnes continued, standing up and holding the large towel. "Up you get now, careful ... that bath can get right slippery with all them soaps."

Victoria did feel a distinct chill but hadn't noticed listening to Agnes and her fascinating stories. What an amazing and envious experience Agnes had. She stood up shyly, her mind focussed on any relevant information passing, whilst Agnes, quite unperturbed, threw the giant bath towel around her and wiped her dry. So Morag had a laboratory, that was very useful but she had obviously turned away from chemistry, evidently doing something once with dyes. But in 1841 all dyes were plant based and natural, so what was she doing? Morag was now working in physics, electricity and magnetism by the sound of it, which made sense, associated with Michael Faraday. Shit … she had to take care with the terminology and not use physics but natural philosophy. Why the switch? That had to be quickly identified and the reasons which had turned Morag off chemistry. Moreover, why wasn't son James interested in anything academic? Even his beloved father had been a nationally successful steam engineer. Perhaps James's petulant behaviour was a reaction to the rebalancing of parental order and his mother not behaving 'normally' and he was becoming a moody teenager, to add to the present mix of disturbed emotions.

"Why Victoria, you've gone into quite a trance. Deep in thought are we?"

"Sorry, Agnes, just thinking about science."

Agnes laughed and went to bring over the drawers and chemise, holding silk stockings in the other hand. She pointed to the thickly upholstered Queen Anne chair to sit on. "Science, I don't know, just like Lady McKenzie. I think for the first time you'll be a governess she'll get on with well, if you don't mind me saying so."

Victoria smiled. That was exactly what she desperately needed and fast, carefully taking in the order those clothes had to be put on.

"And, I can say," Agnes continued, handing over the first bits of underwear, "Lady Lovelace is even worse, a real fanatic especially for them there mathematics whose symbols and squiggles I don't understand at all." Agnes laughed. "Countess Ada, she thinks about science twenty four hours a day if let, a real fanatic I daresay, not at all like her sister Medora, who I'm sure you'll also meet in time. Medora is completely different, and I would add, Lady McKenzie's best friend. I think you'll like Medora very much, so easy going. But then her and Ada, they share the same father, Lord Byron, but … that is a strict secret Victoria, you must promise not to tell a soul or the Lord above will strike me dead into hell."

Struggling but finally succeeding in getting the chemise on, Victoria nodded, highly intrigued. She always loved secrets just as Abby did.

"Well, Medora's mother, she be Lord Byron's sister, Lady Augusta Leigh and was married to Colonel Leigh then too. He brought her up as his own daughter. Most people in society had suspected for years, and I was certain because I … well I just knew being his maid, but I had to stay discreet of course, but it only came out, not public like, but in the immediate family, just before I came here."

"My lips are totally sealed Agnes, you have my word," Victoria whispered. She had no idea of the specific histories of the Byron families but could understand how incest then was probably not uncommon. The immorality and laxity of the eighteenth and early nineteenth century was only beginning to be overtaken by the Victorian religious prudery to come. Lady Byron's time was finally arriving.

"Now, I know it can be a bit uncomfortable but breathe in deeply, Victoria. I've put so many of these things on over all these years, I have acquired a definite knack … petticoats next," Agnes muttered, wrapping the corset around her and pulling the straps hard at the back.

Victoria winced, her insides felt like they were being stretched by a giant black hole. This 1840s dressing experience was going to take some getting used to, no more laughing at Abby.

*

A pre-dinner sherry in the sitting room had been organised so that Victoria, as well as Abby, could meet Morag's children. Victoria suddenly had a coughing fit. The sherry was not the same as she was used to one hundred and sixty years later. Abby whispered it was homemade by Mrs Williams, a rotund, hard looking woman, who was the head cook. She and Mr Williams had met both serving in Wellington's army during Napoleon's Peninsular campaign, and she had learnt the black arts of Spanish distilling then.

Nine year old Ellen arrived first, a pretty little girl, her hair in bunches and dressed in an elaborate dome-shaped white dress, all frills, lace and ruchings. Her feet, in white socks and flat cloth shoes, poked out of long pantalettes with frills at the bottom. Victoria stared, quite fascinated. Even girls endured the same over-elaborate profusion of clothing as their adult female counterparts.

"Long drawers, popular with children until the 1860s," Abby whispered in Victoria's ear. "And at least two petticoats, but she's been spared the corset. Shit can you breathe? I can't."

"Barely," Victoria whispered back, "but where's James?"

Ellen was brought forward formally by her mother and did a small curtsey. "Good afternoon, Miss Warren and good afternoon Mrs Hammelaar. My name is Ellen," she said nervously, clutching a large sheet of paper.

Abby, as always very easy and natural with children, knelt down and smiled. "Hello Ellen, and what have you got in your hand?"

"It's my latest drawing, Miss Warren, of my favourite apple tree with Bruno asleep under it. Would you like to see it?"

Abby took the picture and looked at it, a beautiful charcoal sketch revealing a significant depth of talent and maturity of technique for such a young child. Victoria watched the two of them. Ellen was so alike in features, a Warren to the core, and it was clear she had made up her mind already that Abby would be her favourite tutor.

"Art is my most likeable subject, but I also enjoy music, especially the harpsichord and I can play a little Bach," Ellen added, in such a clear, unsullied diction, Victoria thought, that even the BBC would have been envious of.

Morag interrupted. "Alright Ellen, that's quite enough for today, now would you go with Esther and eat your dinner please in the nursery."

"Yes, Mama," she replied, and walked away slowly. But suddenly she turned and looked back at Victoria. "I like natural history too, Mrs Hammelaar. Can I show you my new microscope tomorrow?"

"Yes of course, Ellen," Victoria replied, smiling warmly. "I would like that very much. We should try and find some frog spawn in your pond."

"Yes please," Ellen replied excitedly and then continued on quietly out of the door, holding Esther's hand. Victoria looked across to see Morag in a heated conversation with Williams the butler. Still no sign of James. Williams went off hurriedly and Morag walked over.

"I must sincerely apologise to you both but James, despite my warning him so many times today to be here on time, has disappeared again. I'm at my wit's end what to do with the wretch. Williams believes he is over, yet again, at the blacksmith's cottage on the edge of the estate. The boy seems to spend night and day there, anything to be absent from his studies and parted from me as much as he can endeavour. I hope, Victoria, you can take him in hand. I am failing badly in my duties, I must confess."

"I shall certainly do my best, don't worry Morag," Victoria replied, but was feeling apprehensive about the challenge. Without doubt, this tearaway was going to need a very firm hand indeed. But she had her ways, thinking back wistfully to Ned when he was twelve and equally then a total pain in the proverbial rear.

Morag spoke again. "I have never had occasion to meet this blacksmith man. James calls him Rocket, a name of affection, because apparently the individual has formidable engineering capabilities with the metals, like his godfather Robert."

"Is that Mr Robert Stephenson, the famous railway engineer who developed the Rocket locomotive train for the initial Liverpool to Manchester railway line? The first with the revolutionary 0-2-2 wheel arrangement?" Victoria asked, as Abby blinked, surprised at Victoria's detailed knowledge.

"Why, yes. My goodness, Victoria, do you have detailed understanding of the physical and mathematical sciences as well as chemistry?"

"Err … yes, reasonably."

"Impressive, I must say, most impressive. I am sure my good friend the Countess of Lovelace will wish to speak with you in depth. Alas, Mr Stephenson, who was a close associate and friend of my dearly departed husband, is too preoccupied with looking after Frances his wife who is not at all well, to take my son in hand. I am very worried for her frailty. Although Mr Stephenson has offered the boy an engineering apprenticeship in his factory, an excellent opportunity, when he completes obligatory studies at Cambridge like his father. An academic tradition of the McKenzie family, Victoria, but only of course for the men to enjoy."

That engineering possibility had to be stopped in the bud, Victoria immediately thought, glancing at Abby who had read her mind instantly.

Williams had walked back in and interrupted brusquely. "Milady, I have ridden to the blacksmith, found the boy as you suspected and he will bring James back here immediately. I think the blacksmith wishes to make his apologies directly."

"Good," Morag replied, her expression like thunder. "I wish to give this man a stern piece of my mind, face to face.

"As you wish, milady."

Morag turned back. "Now Victoria and Abigail, pray, I beseech you to try this new sherry which Mrs Williams has made for me. It has a kick like a proverbial Spanish mule." She poured out another large glass as Agnes walked past with three bottles of red wine. Victoria looked askance. She was already light-headed; she needed some substantial food in her stomach soon.

Another fifteen minutes passed and they were joined by Maddie and Belle, both looking delectably sophisticated in new dresses, barely worn cast-offs from Lady McKenzie, which Esther had picked out. Their slim waistlines had not required the tortuous reining in which Abby and Victoria had endured. Belle was distracted by a shelf of recent novels, sidled up and pulled out her spectacles to read the titles, when Victoria realised they had time transferred as exactly the same modern design, with the large black polymer frames that Belle left home with. As Mauveine glibly said, there had been some glitches along the way. Victoria had noticed the few spectacles seen, including Morag's, were all thin wire frames with large circular lenses, quite unflattering to females. She spotted Morag talking to Agnes. Morag immediately noticed the design and pondered rather thoughtfully, plainly amazed.

Victoria wandered over to Belle, whispered quickly in her ear and continued, a pre-emptive strike was necessary. "Radical new design, Morag, trialled by a lens maker in Amsterdam for women," she said, casually. "An acquaintance of my former husband. They are probably not robust enough to last like yours. I bought them for Belle before we left."

Morag looked far from convinced, displaying the same stubborn attachment to evidential rationale as Victoria herself. "How very strange. Verily, I have never seen anything like them whatsoever, even in the best shops in Piccadilly, London. But I agree they are so flattering. What is that odd material of the frame? Neither metal nor wood?"

Victoria could feel anxiety rising again. It was so easy for this situation to happen, think, think, think. "Err ... a form of carbonised rubber, like gutta-percha, Morag. A unique process of manufacture being tested and patented, I daresay, before future release," she replied watching Morag's thought process. But fortunately a distraction ensued.

"Aah ... the arrival of the prodigal son. Well, when they're out in the shops I want a pair, Victoria. Now, who is that interesting looking man accompanying him? Surely not the blacksmith?"

They both turned. Meanwhile Abby and Maddie, led by Williams, had already gone into the dining room with Belle. A tall, handsome man, well-built and muscular and in his mid forties, with a thick head of wavy black hair, stood prominently in the doorway. For a blacksmith, his clean shaven facial skin was soft and clean, sporting a pair of fashionable sideburns and a clipped moustache like the royal consort, Prince Albert. His clothes, smart and well pressed, were fashionably similar in style to that worn by Isi, a type of brown corduroy. He held a matching cap in his hand. Alongside him a tall, lanky boy

213

brushed past towards Morag, his blonde hair flopping over his eyes and an air of arrogance and disdain immediate in his face. This was the last place he wanted to be, instantly eyeing Victoria with a glare, working out that the bitch governess had arrived.

But Victoria was not interested in James right at that moment because her face had dropped like a stone staring incredulous at the dapper blacksmith. He was unmistakably Julian, but not the staid and familiar Julian of 2026 married to her for the last seventeen years, but a dashing 1841 variant who seemed to have undergone cosmetic surgery to look like when they first met in Liverpool in 2009, in a youthful spree of unexpected lust and discovery. Where the fuck had Abby, Maddie and Belle disappeared to?

"Victoria, do you know this man?" a voice rattled in her ear, realising now that Morag was speaking to her. "A somewhat more interesting creature than I imagined for an artisan, don't you think?"

"Err ... yes. I do apologise Morag. He reminded me of my younger brother for a second, sadly drowned in the Zuider Zee," she replied, making it up as best as Abby might, but also seeing displayed by Morag, that decidedly flirty and desirous look again as with Lynton. Morag, patently and teasingly, enjoyed the affections of men, awed by her great beauty and widowed wealth. Williams had marched up to Julian, said something and Julian tentatively walked across, confident but wary.

"Stay with me please Victoria," Morag whispered, ignoring her son James who was standing beside her sullen but silent. "I think the delectable Mr Blacksmith will be coming to proffer his apologies in a suitably grovelling fashion, I hope. What fun isn't it?"

Victoria's mind was in turmoil, her face flushed crimson. So much for her rational decision that she would keep cool if Julian ever appeared. Now he had appeared she was totally flummoxed and wanted a nice big sink-hole to suddenly open up in front of her. She wished she hadn't drunk so much either. In a trice Julian was there and, hands behind back, he bowed deeply like Morag was a Japanese Empress, much to Morag's amusement. He ignored Victoria totally. Not only, like Lynton, did he not recognise her, he was not in the slightest bit interested. Julian had eyes solely for the esteemed lady of the house, and Morag was lapping up every second of it. Victoria gazed first at him and then at Morag who was decidedly taken with her new catch, looking more dreamy than desirable, as Victoria's mind ran through endless scenarios of every imaginable variant of Lady Chatterley's Lover. She was not the slightest bit comfortable with handling this.

"Good afternoon Lady McKenzie," he said, speaking with precision, his accent as upper class as Lynton's, which threw and intrigued Morag in a micro-second, expecting the usual thick Preston variant. "My name is Fazackerley, Julian Fazackerley, general blacksmith to the Orsbrick parish and as of yesterday also your estate milady, following work which Mr Williams has kindly offered me. It is an honour to meet you."

Morag put out her hand for him to kiss, not the usual act towards a servant. He didn't linger but she enjoyed it. "How interesting Mr Fazackerley, as I had no idea that Mr Williams, without my permission, was gifting work to anyone he saw fit in the parish?"

Williams coughed and went to gather up the bottles of wine and other delicacies, and marched off back into the dining room, indicating to Victoria to follow but she ignored him. Victoria was determined to remain by Morag's side and be introduced, but quickly saw that wasn't going to happen. They were solely and queasily preoccupied with each other. But she was still not moving. The whole bizarre situation appeared like watching a returning cine-reel of her first encounter with Julian. Son James remained standing next to her, also intrigued by this encounter and pleased to see his friend, Rocket, impressing his mother. Victoria looked down at James and he looked up at her as if she was a piece of smelly horse dung he had just walked into. Surreptitiously she felt behind for his arm and gripped it hard making him wince, too proud and arrogant to cry out or say anything in front of Rocket as tears rolled down his cheek. She relaxed her grip and looked down again, smiling as he shot a resigned and surprised grimace back and wiped his eyes. First point was to her *and* she was a lot bigger.

Morag continued. "However, Mr Fazackerley. Are you at all adept with a hot water boiler?" she asked mischievously. Time for the final put-down, certain that such a rare plumbing commodity in this part of Lancashire would be outside of his sphere of understanding. Only dearest Malcolm understood such technical intricacies. She was already resigned to having to bring in a specialist from Manchester.

"I am indeed familiar, Lady McKenzie. I worked on the first installations of hot water heating for Mr Charles Hood of London himself in '37 and rewrote a number of chapters of his manual for the same as a result of the experience. I've already perused your problem, thanks to Mr Williams. I see you rely of course on the thermo-siphon principle for heat transfer, using gravity, milady. The boiler requires a new cast-iron heat exchanger which I can make, and if I may be so bold to recommend, if I change those old thick pipes to new thinner ones, the circulation will be much more efficient. I believe I could thus extend the water flow into some radiators and heat your bedroom and a few others."

Victoria stared. How did he know all this? 1841 Julian was good, very good and already, by guiltless guile and charm, astutely gaining the confidence and respect of the desirable Lady McKenzie, and maybe he wanted more. Shit, he was trying that old boiler line with Morag, exactly like when he seduced her for the first time over the modern gas boiler he installed in 2010. This was not how it should be.

"Oh my goodness, if it isn't Lady McKenzie. How wonderful to be back again so soon and how extraordinary that you have already acquired those exciting paintings of Mr Turner on your wall, when I had only recently curated such items at the Royal Academy."

Victoria and James turned around, the voice as recognisable as the day itself. Lynton had entered the room in a whirlwind of effusive rhetoric, arms whirling and voice outpouring, and immediately thrust himself between the serious Julian Fazackerley and the bemused Lady McKenzie. He too had acquired a thing about the desirable Morag, thought about in detail on his ride over, and was not going to let this oaf spoil his ambitions. Victoria could see in an instant he and Julian didn't know each other.

"Why, Dr Gray, I'm so pleased you arrived at last," Morag said, flustered by the sudden interjection.

But she spoke no further. Julian, his muscles bulging and overbearing height fully evident, had stepped in front of Lynton barring his disruptive intervention. A deathly silence cut the air like a knife, as Dr Gray tried to push him away, but failed when the rock-solid Mr Fazackerley simply held his arm in a vice-like grip rendering Dr Gray immobile, who shook himself free.

He looked up. "You sir, how dare you, the impudence is beyond reproach. Who do you think you're addressing? I know you, that damned smithy living in Cinderblack cottages with those ruffian boys. Presently, I would add, both inebriated to the gills in the White Swan. Damned ignorant boat people all of you."

"I'm very sorry sir, I don't believe we have actually met," Julian replied calmly. "But I haven't finished my conversation with Lady McKenzie yet, if you don't mind?" His muscles were tensed and his eyes fixed malevolently on Lynton with that steely, unmovable and dangerous gaze that Victoria had encountered intimately many years before when they first met and dated. 1841 Julian Fazackerley was a man as immovable when riled as her Julian Endersby-Finnis in back to the future. Who were his sons? Were they Ned and Zac? Shit, this scenario was getting incredibly out of hand. Julian and Lynton, literally at each other's throats, ready for blows and a duel over Morag? And she was totally helpless to do anything about it.

Morag was thinking the same and hastily surveyed around for Williams who had inconveniently disappeared. James meanwhile, grabbed hold of Victoria's hand, unaware of what he was doing, eyes popping from their sockets, engaged with glee at the big fight about to emerge and secretly willing on his hero Rocket to tear this fop's head off.

Lynton stood back. "Your impudence and insult Fazackerley is intolerable. You don't speak to me, a gentleman, nor a lady in this manner. You've forgotten your status, blacksmith. Outside, with sabres, and I'll teach you a lesson you're not going to forget!"

Victoria paled. Suddenly a voice called out from the other end. Abby, hearing the commotion and recognising Lynton's voice had run in with Agnes, Maddie and Belle right behind.

She glanced at Victoria who shook her head for a second, and assessed the crisis correctly, as did Maddie and Belle who said nothing. Agnes had run downstairs to find Williams who had disappeared to the kitchens and scullery below to check the food with his wife.

"Dr Gray, how wonderful to see a real gentleman," Abby called out in her confident tone. "I do insist you join me now in the dining room. There is a most agreeable and unusual drawing on the wall by a Mr Ruskin that I would value your excellent opinion on."

Lynton turned around. Miss Warren looked stunning in that crimson dress and he realised, seeing her face, that he was going too far. She was right. "Certainly Miss Warren, I would be highly honoured to sit with you," he replied with genuine conviction. She was a lady of significant allure too. Besides, his sabre fighting was not his strong point by far, more like sabre rattling. Realpolitik must prevail and a tactical retreat. "Lady McKenzie, I would like to offer my most sincere apologies for my lack of manners as your guest. My stomach has been most disagreeable today after raw eels for breakfast but I am confident your renowned drink and fayre will set me to rights once more and dispel my rare mood of unwarranted tetchiness. Fazackerley, I withdraw that request forthwith. It behoves me as a gentleman, to show how one should behave in the house of such genteel and erudite company as Lady McKenzie and her lovely companions this fine evening."

"Accepted, Dr Gray," Fazackerley replied smiling and held out his hand. They shook hands, reluctantly but firmly.

"Now, Miss Madeleine and Miss Annabelle? If you would, please?" They hooked into each of Lynton's arms as he walked off gaily with them and Abby to the dining room all jabbering and laughing nonsense on the way out.

Victoria breathed a sigh of relief and poor James, stunned with it all, remained next to her, not a word spoken.

"Well, James, I see that you've now made your acquaintance with Mrs Hammelaar," Morag said gleefully, gazing at him and Victoria still holding hands. James suddenly realised and let go with a flourish and an accompanying scowl. "We've had enough excitement for one day. Tomorrow you will start your first lessons with your new governess at nine a.m. sharp, clear?"

He looked at Rocket, who nodded sternly. "Yes, Mother, understood and goodnight," he replied and shuffled off, disappointed, to the nursery for his dinner.

Williams, accompanied by a few other male servants, had begun taking the hot food into the dining room.

"Mr Fazackerley, I am sure you have a wife and family to return home to. You're hired. Please make the boiler repair and proposed heating extension a priority but I wish to oversee your designs first. Williams will see you out."

"Certainly, Lady McKenzie," he replied, bowing once more. "I shall start immediately tomorrow. I can see Mr Williams is very busy, I know my own way out, thank you again. Good evening."

Without a glance at Victoria, he strode out. Morag turned and smiled. "Well, a bit more of a fiery start to the evening than I anticipated, but at least you got to meet James, a little chastened I believe. Start with science tomorrow please. That man Fazackerley, he is imbued with much deeper mystery and is no ordinary blacksmith. I can see he is unusually well educated and cultured. What blacksmith have you met who can read and write and radiates such intelligence? I intend to find out more. He is somewhat attractive Victoria, don't you think? Certainly strong of will and muscle to be sure, just like my poor Malcolm, God rest his soul."

"Well, err … yes, I suppose he is," she replied. So much for Morag tearing a strip off the blacksmith earlier.

Morag linked her arm into hers. "You don't sound over-enthusiastic. Now, we widows need to stick together where men are concerned don't we," she replied with a giggle. "Time for a nice meal and I'm sure Dr Gray's stomach will settle quickly in the delectable company of my cousin, Abigail. Don't you? They are like brushed peas in a painted pod, in raptures already so Agnes reports, over some ancient erotic artist called Botticelli. Although, I must say, I can't make up my mind whether Dr Gray is a ladies' man or a sodomist. Let's go."

"I guess you're right Morag," Victoria muttered thinking only one thing under her breath. Fuck.

# Chapter Ten

Bright sunshine and clear blue skies greeted Victoria the following day as she stumbled sleepily out of bed, pulled the curtains back and peered out of the window. Not a bad night's sleep for a horsehair mattress. Six in the morning and already heavy carts were rumbling past, with numerous farm labourers going about their daily business. A small brougham carriage had drawn up and a boy ran into the front door with a pile of packages and letters. That must be the daily postal service, she thought. Certainly they were up and about early.

"Comes five times daily, Victoria," a voice rang out. "Special like to Orsbrick Hall. Lady McKenzie receives many letters. She is prolific with the pen, always writing about something or other to her correspondents."

Agnes walked in with two large pails of hot water, pointing to the copper basin near the commode, which itself had rather a minimal appeal that time of the day or in fact any time of the day. Victoria needed to find the water closet down the corridor.

"I'll leave you to wash," Agnes continued, pouring the hot water in. "Fresh towels are over there and I've reordered your clothes for the day in the end wardrobe. First lesson with James I understand. What a kerfuffle last night. I was terrified for a few minutes but Mr Williams, he was quite unperturbed, said it would blow over without consequence, happens all the time in the army and Dr Gray is no fighting man to be sure. Breakfast will be served, as always, in the morning room, porridge and scrambled egg. Lady McKenzie insists on that every morning. Now, I must wake Miss Warren." Agnes headed to the door before quickly turning and giggled. "Dr Gray left very late last night!"

Victoria sighed. Abby would undoubtedly dish the dirt later, deciding her priority was to work into a routine for the unfamiliar morning ablutions. Some scientific systematisation was the only way to keep sane in 1841. Although she did admit that the food, at least in this upper class household, had been surprisingly good. Mrs Williams was extremely fastidious with only the best ingredients.

*

After coffee, before the children's lessons commenced, Morag insisted on showing Victoria her laboratory, the place where she wanted their science classes to be held. As Victoria walked down the corridor past the morning room and the ballroom, the lack of familiarity with the layout confused her as they turned a corner which in her mind didn't exist and a large, unfamiliar door at the end confronted them. She gazed around again, then realisation hit. This was the area which she now used as the kitchen and also adjoined Uncle William's original ground floor bedroom and small study. He must have extensively reconstructed this part of the house after he had become reclusive in the 1930s. Morag opened the door and they walked into a very large and airy room, with windows to the back where there now existed a solid wall. The adjacent scullery, which had a door to the outside that Victoria used as a back entrance for the dogs, was a form of storeroom where all kinds of apparatus, some chemicals and other materials and a host of instruments and tools of varying kinds were neatly shelved. Against the long wall of the main laboratory was yet another floor to ceiling bookcase, packed full of more old leather books, alongside folders and notes bound together with twine. A small writing desk stood in front of the window, from where one had a pleasant and clear view of the pond ahead between the trees. The brick outbuilding that Julian used as his workshop was completely absent.

Three hefty and well-made benches of a quality hardwood, possibly teak, stood in the middle of the room, on a wooden floor. Lots of space had been made to walk around and a huge porcelain sink stood conveniently nearby with an actual cold tap. A thick lead pipe drained to the outside, through the wall. A rusty steel pipe ran from one bench along the floor, also to the outside with an intricate brass tap, flanged onto the end. Gas? Surely not possible? She stared incredulous.

"I see you are admiring my new gas supply, Victoria," Morag said, very pleased with herself. "The trustees of the Burscough town municipality, as part of my community support fund last year for the poor, are beginning to install gas lighting in the main streets to improve safety. A small coal gas works is now operating. We can of course obtain a plentiful supply from Yorkshire using the canal. I know we are a long way behind London in these rural parts but we will arrive there eventually. Then, I want gas lighting in all homes. I'm so sick of these kerosene lamps and candles, but the smoky flame and smell of the gas light is not good for health. We must find a way of reducing the soot and improving the light ... I need to talk to Mr Faraday about that line of research. What do you think of his latest burner?"

Victoria stared at the device, like a crude Bunsen burner with a pipe and collar, but far too complex and big, which Morag was screwing into the threaded gas tap. She picked up a box of matches, the sticks huge with large phosphorus tips.

"My vendor came this morning," Morag cried out, striking one hard on the sandpapered side. It burst into life with a huge fizzing flame before she proceeded to turn on the gas tap, which hissed and sputtered into life. Victoria winced. Recognised gas safety standards were still a very long way off and the revolting smell of coal gas, almost forgotten, instantly permeated her nostrils as Morag thrust the flame over the burner. It lit with an ominous whoosh, a smoky yellow flame a foot high shooting into the air.

"We female scientists have to be bold, Victoria, and demonstrate we are as fearless as any male operative, remember that," Morag exclaimed, tweaking at a stiff side valve in the base with a pair of pliers. The flame reduced, becoming less smoky but no real blue-flamed heat ensued like any common or garden Bunsen burner in a school laboratory. "I am testing this device out for Mr Faraday who has a keen interest in such matters, but he needs to work on the valve design. Better, but I'm sure we could improve the heat output further." She turned it off again, much to Victoria's relief.

But she faced the extraordinary dilemma she had dreaded most. There were so many scientific facts she wanted to say and couldn't. She didn't dare for fear of what Mauveine had warned, a premature cataclysm occurring before it should, and also raising suspicion. She had to play a very difficult and careful pathway with her own science expertise, not made easy by her shaky knowledge of much history of science. The problem of obtaining decent burner heat in the lab was so easy to solve with a pin-hole gas exit into the tube and a throat collar around a slit made in it, let alone the addition of a thorium dioxide gas mantle to create real light. But that would have to wait another fifty years. She struggled momentarily with mid-

Victorian history and remembered that Robert Bunsen's invention came later.

Also looking around, there was scant evidence of any serious chemistry; this was decidedly a physics laboratory. A number of different sized glass jars with wires attached lay around, which Victoria surmised from the grey, zinc-like metal inside, were some sort of crude voltaic liquid batteries. A number of experiments in progress were set up, with old fashioned dialled gauges connected, presumably measuring electrical current, resistance and pressure. Crude coils, the wiring badly insulated with paper, were set up in frames inside large iron magnets. Victoria quickly worked out that Morag was indeed totally preoccupied with electricity and magnetism. She had kept mentioning Michael Faraday which now made sense. Obviously she was undertaking experiments, either under his supervision or with him in collaboration, maybe both. But why? And why had Agnes been instructed to suddenly remove all the chemical paraphernalia into storage?

Before she had time to formulate some questions, Morag had gripped her arm and with a "come Victoria, I must show you this but in great secrecy you understand," led her to the far bench. Two experiments were set up. In the first a complicated shaped loop of wound wire was held in a rotatable frame, through which a magnet above could be lowered. Additional wiring connected the apparatus to a rudimentary measuring dial. In the second, a similar loop of wire, but with many more turnings, had been wound onto a hollow metal cylinder, welded around an iron shaft and fastened by a crude bearing into a wooden frame. The shaft could be rotated by a handle. Victoria perused the first experiment closely, recognising in an instant a demonstration of electromagnetic induction through which Faraday was best known and praised for its discovery.

"Do you know the principle of that experiment I have made?" Morag asked in an inquisitor tone, obviously, Victoria sensed, testing out the depth of her science knowledge but not exactly subtly. Care was needed.

"I do believe," she replied slowly, "I am seeing for the first time a practical demonstration of the link between electricity and magnetism which I believe Mr Faraday was the first to discover." Victoria moved the magnet up and down between the coil and the needle flickered, with some kind of ammeter measuring the current flow.

"Excellent. I am impressed that your knowledge of natural philosophy is as good as your chemistry, which your sister had vouched for in detail. Now, instead, keep the magnet still and move the coil around it."

Victoria complied. She knew the effect. This was elementary physics she had once taught thirteen year-olds at the Cradwell School for Girls, but feigned surprise as the needle flickered again. "Goodness me Morag, they are interchangeable, I mean the magnetism and the electricity."

"Yes indeed, an excellent analysis. This interchangeability is at the heart of what I am working on for Mr Faraday. I am so honoured to have the opportunity to take his discoveries further, don't you think?"

Victoria gazed at Morag's face, all lit up and beaming, her eyes flashing at the thought of her great mentor. "Is Mr Faraday guiding you with your studies or a collaborator with whom you are jointly producing papers?" she asked, then wished she had phrased that differently. The question sounded far too personal and professional. But she was concluding that whatever was behind Morag's dislike of chemistry and the giving up of her mystery dye work had a close link to Faraday directly.

Morag remained unaffected. She was only too pleased to talk about him and his work. She was so glad Victoria had turned up, who could subject James to death-like torture with tough learning for all she cared. Most importantly, for the first time, she could talk to another woman dispassionately who understood the science. Ada and Medora were far too intimate with her, especially knowing her feelings.

Morag talked for ten long minutes, without a break, about Michael Faraday and the inspirational kick he had given her following the resounding praise from male science researchers and great names she had received at the Royal Society. She described the lecture with glee, when she clarified the chemical mechanism behind the new batteries being produced. She then revealed that she, Ada Lovelace, Mary Somerville and Caroline Hershel plus other women Victoria had never heard of, were on a secret political crusade to get women recognised properly for their scientific achievements and be allowed university tuition.

"But, the task has become hard going and there remains so much patriarchal resistance to all reasonable argument and the clear evidence of great economic and social benefit for England. We want the newly crowned Queen Victoria to back us up in Parliament, but so far a royal reluctance has been made very clear."

The drive and energy within Morag for women-led science was patently catching. Victoria felt a flush of pride for her ancestry, for this was what Morag really was as a person. How odd that such a vibrant chunk of time and action had gone missing from the McKenzie archives.

"And, as for the answer to your original question, Michael is both my mentor and my collaborator. A kindly and thoughtful genius, he feeds my entire soul. Also, he needs me badly to help him get better and overcome his inertia after a long period of nervous exhaustion and overwork."

Victoria, watching Morag's face lit up and radiant, could not fail to discern the obvious. Michael Faraday was more, much, much more to Morag. Was she actually in love with him? The evidence was substantial as Victoria grappled in her mind with her knowledge of Faraday's history, never having been a lover of biographies. She was always a doer and maker of original science not an historic observer or a writer interpreter. She spied the untidy pile of letters on Morag's desk, all with the seal of the Royal Institution which Faraday led or the Royal Society at the top. They were in constant communication, Lady Morag McKenzie with one of England's greatest experimental scientists at the pinnacle of his career. Long letters from him, page after page covered in drawings and diagrams were scattered about.

All Victoria could really recall was that Michael Faraday was a simple and private man, sought no high office all his life, was very religious of the hell and brimstone type and remained married until his death, all of which seemed quite incongruous set against Morag's strident personality and personal ambitions. Whatever was going on between him and Morag was decidedly secret and private, unlike the highly public, even in 1841 and forever written about, tête à tête between Morag's friend, Ada Lovelace, and the mathematician Charles Babbage. In fact Julian, in one of his successful earlier steam punk novels, had even used Babbage as a key fictional character. The challenge which Mauveine had outlined was becoming intractable by the minute.

"Of course, Mr Faraday has been equally prolific and original in the fields of chemistry experimentation too," Victoria said in a flash of inspiration, taking the opportunity to divert Morag back into chemistry. "I recall he invented benzene from coal tar, such an interesting and radical structure. I'm sure benzene will become very important for the making of dyes in the future. We will then move beyond the natural indigo and madder plant dyes to other exciting ... err possibilities." Victoria stopped; she was getting beyond herself already. She didn't know the dye history well enough and was muddling the time frames again. If only Abby was here who did know, but that wouldn't be any use as Abby was now an 1841 fine artist not a textiles specialist.

Morag hesitated and went into a deep reflection. Her face displayed immediate and total astonishment. Her own sharp scientific analysis had begun working overdrive on what she had heard. Victoria felt sick. She knew she had overcooked that statement somewhere, and Morag was far too clever to be fooled ... shit ... shit ... shit ... she felt her face redden.

"My goodness Victoria. I have to confess, you do have the most ... well, fanciful of imaginations. You mean that you truly know about my former secretive dye work on indigo using benzene? But I never published any papers? And what do you mean by a radical structure? Even Mr Faraday has no idea of the constitution of his baby which he distilled from oil. And of course he named the chemical bicarburet of hydrogen. It was that plagiarist Mitscherlich, no Frenchman can ever be trusted, just look at Napoleon, who renamed Michael's prized discovery benzene after distilling benzoic acid, not exactly original. I am astounded that you know all that."

Victoria had to think very fast, deep extrication was needed and desperate measures. "Err ... well, I'm sorry I must confess. I don't want to get her into trouble but Agnes did casually mention that she had packed away all your chemicals into storage including lots of a distinctive blue liquid which I inferred was likely an indigo dye. Are not coal tar and oil the same thing for benzene, such unique binding being solely the two elements of carbon and hydrogen?"

Morag laughed. "No, of course not, an elementary mistake Victoria, but don't worry. In fact Agnes assists me often in the laboratory. I'm slowly providing her with new knowledge and skills. She is by far a rare housemaid, cleverer than she may appear, which is why, when Lady Byron summarily dismissed poor Agnes, I took her on immediately. And, like you I do think there may be a future many years off yet, with dyes produced artificially and I have, unsuccessfully, been experimenting with indigo to do so, with a little progress. However, I do like your skills of synthesis and deduction, Victoria, so akin to mine. So, once again no. Oil and tar are not the same by far. Oil is rich in potential chemical discovery, as Michael elicited, whilst coal tar has no future value whatsoever. An undesirable dreg and waste product of coal carbonisation, which for sure we will need more and more pits to bury the obnoxious stuff into. There are other compounds of carbon and hydrogen equally radical. I must however teach you more advanced chemistry if I may, and do feel free to borrow any of my books from in here."

Victoria breathed a huge inner sigh ... too close for comfort. Next time she may not be so fortunate or so slick of tongue. "Thank you, I would love that Morag. Self-learning and education throughout life is so necessary. I must go I'm afraid. Nine a.m. is approaching, to begin James's science tuition."

"Yes of course, I suggest you initially test and ascertain his knowledge for a few days in the nursery. That wretched boy does have a brain in his head somewhere, but hides it deeply under an impenetrable bushel. But before you go, please look quickly at the second, my latest experiment."

Victoria watched as Morag turned the handle rapidly on the shafted coil. No meter reading of course. Then she rummaged in a bench drawer and pulled out a semicircular piece of iron, set in an adjustable clamp, and carefully secured it around the wired cylinder, a magnet.

"The reversibility, the mirror image idea," Morag said, "which Michael has been grappling with for years. But since being sick for the last few years, his mind has weakened temporarily, just when he almost saw it before. Instead of moving the magnet in the coil, I am moving a bigger coil, much harder near a powerful magnet. Look at the reading. A strong current, as rich as that produced by a Volta cell, but the needle flicks from one side to the other. Plainly the current alternates as the coil reverses direction when meeting the magnetic environment. Now watch again."

Out of the drawer, Morag pulled another type of carefully engineered and sprung copper collar with wires attached and tightened it gently onto the other end of the shaft. Victoria then noticed the collar was carefully serrated and some rubber material inlaid in segments. In an instant she realised that Morag, for the time period, had entered another level of her science research altogether. She really was as innovative as Faraday had declared, maybe as original a genius as him, but in her own fashion. Morag had created something which wasn't announced for at least twenty years on, maybe more, Victoria wasn't sure. But did it work?

Morag turned the handle round and round with a flourish and the needle jumped sharply to the right, and stayed there with a slight flicker. Morag was demonstrating an original early direct current dynamo, Victoria was astounded.

"Heavens above, Morag, a commutator! You've made an actual commutator, this is a dynamo!" she shouted above the screeching of the metal as Morag turned the handle as fast as she could. She stopped.

"What was that word you used, Victoria? A commutator? What is that?"

Victoria drew breath. "Sorry, I said communicator. You are communicating the electric current directly; this has the potential to replace these batteries."

"Yes, exactly, which is what I promised Michael I would show was possible. He didn't believe that the current could ever be strong enough and would always have a useless fluctuation. He has been for so long obsessed with motors but I am obsessed with their inverse, dynamos. He is wrong. Gas lighting is not the future, Victoria. It is incandescent electric lighting, run like this but on a scale unimaginable at present. I need to do more work before I provide him with a paper. Please keep this strictly to yourself but I needed to show it to someone who understood and was sympathetic. Now you'd better find the nursery. The children will be waiting."

Victoria smiled, pulled her folder together of class notes and set off. At the doorway she turned back to watch Morag, totally engrossed with her new apparatus, making further change measurements and noting the new results. "Congratulations Morag, you really are an amazing experimenter. More material I would suggest, towards the cause of we women doing bold science?"

Walking briskly towards the nursery, Victoria felt badly conflicted. Was it morally justifiable to try and pull Morag back into chemistry? Her dedication and love of what she was doing in electromagnetism, work of immense originality in this year of 1841 was paramount. And Morag was in love with Faraday. That much appeared obvious. Reversing all of it would be a Herculean task, needing real guile and subterfuge. She hoped

Abby would be down in the nursery too, they needed to talk and fast.

*

Abby arrived breathless in the nursery and an hour and a half late to be confronted by Ellen waiting patiently reading a book. Alongside sat a sullen and disengaged brother James being grilled and tested mercilessly on his level of mathematics and the chemistry of iron, seeing as he was so entranced with the notion of becoming a blacksmith like his idol, Rocket, down in the cottages. None of his learning was anywhere near up to scratch as preparation for Cambridge, or even the Bluecoat School he was expected to be boarded at soon, which for Morag the quicker he went the better. Victoria had assessed, from some searching questions, the essential drivers making James so difficult. He had replaced his real and adored deceased father with that of Julian Fazackerley, the substitute father figure and he despised his mother for cleverly taking over so effectively as the figurehead for all the wealth and influence of Orsbrick Hall when that should rightfully have been his role to play and have fun with. And he hated her for being a woman so young because she was not likely to be dying off any time soon for him to inherit his father's title.

"Ellen," Abby said. "It's such a pleasant day outdoors. I would like us to go to the pond, do some drawing and talk about perspective and then find insects and things to look at under your microscope which you can also sketch. Then Mrs Hammelaar will teach you the biology."

"Oh, yes please, Miss Warren, that sounds much more fun than I've ever had before with my tutors."

"Okay, now Agnes says you both normally have a break time now, and a glass of milk," Abby replied, fixing her gaze onto Victoria. "I suggest you both do that and be back in fifteen minutes."

"Off you go, James," Victoria added, as he hauled himself reluctantly out of the chair, slammed the book shut on the history of metals and sauntered off, that chip on his shoulder magnified ten-fold meeting up with the Governess from Hell. It was going to be much more challenging to intimidate her than any of the others before, who soon cleared off crying. He would have to think of more devious ways. He would have preferred a mid-morning jug of ale with Edward and Zacharias, which they always indulged in when Rocket had left the forge on a job, rather than a glass of milk.

"How come you're so late?" Victoria queried, shuffling through her lists of curricula she wanted to follow next.

"He wouldn't leave until after two, then tried to undo all the buttons on my dress but failed miserably … he wanted to, you know, there and then over Morag's desk in the study."

"Lynton?"

"Who else … and blabbering on about all the aristocratic women he's seduced. I had to push him off sharpish."

Victoria laughed. "Why? It's not like you haven't done it before with him? It seems Lynton is a real ladies man at heart although Morag thinks he also runs with the hares."

"Very funny. I'm not amused with the lascivious Dr Lynton Gray in the slightest; a somewhat more appealing part of his character might have transferred. Mind you, the intense and ever so manly Mr Julian Fazackerley seems to have the all lowered eyes for her gorgeous ladyship, as does every other male in the vicinity. Not much of a look in chuck was there?"

"Fuck Julian Fazackerley, arrogant shit."

"That's more like it, so we can both agree we need new men in our lives. Oh and here's your mail."

"Mail? For me?"

"Well open it. Some more intrigue might cheer us up."

Victoria picked up the letter opener and carefully slit through the top of a very pretty yellow envelope, pulling out a short note. "It's from Mauveine. She says she and Isi won't be available for a day or two because he's had to retire to bed with a fever and she's looking after him, but he has to be right for the sermon on Sunday. Oh my God, she says we might have only five days to ensure James becomes a scientist and not a decadent country squire with too much money and no purpose. Every step forward there seems to be two exponentially growing, monumental steps back. One thing though I have ascertained is that Morag's flight from chemistry is intimately associated with Mr Michael Faraday."

"Really? The man who invented electricity? By intimately you mean shagging?"

"Hush," Victoria replied in a whisper, looking around furtively. "They don't know that word in 1841."

"They do plenty of it though, don't be surprised," Abby replied with a grin. "So what do you mean?"

"I think Morag is in love with Faraday. You only have to look at her doe-eyed demeanour when she talks about him and his work. It feels totally wrong to me … disrupting that emotional bond and diverting her obvious talent in what are the beginnings of true electrical engineering."

Abby went silent, once again confronted by Victoria and her moral dilemmas, a constant feature of their friendship going back decades. "Do you want to stay in 1841 forever?" she said slowly and deliberately. "By your face the answer is very clear. But I agree. We might need to work on that angle somehow. Hey, Ellen and the reprobate Orsbrick squire are returning.

Back to work I'm afraid. Gosh, here's Agnes too in a bit of a tizz."

Agnes came tearing around the other corner as the children waited quietly by their desks. "Have an urgent message from Lady McKenzie," she stuttered, panting hard. "She forgot to mention earlier, came in the mail first thing. She has an appointment at the Royal Society Lecture tomorrow afternoon in London with Mr Babbage and Mr Faraday and she wants you both to go, and the children, and she wants Mr Fazackerley as well to keep an eye on James and it appears that Dr Gray popped in earlier and has invited himself. Might be for a few days, so you'll be able to stay at the Countess of Lovelace's town residence, a very splendid place I may say."

Victoria looked at Abby, who nodded. They needed to go with the flow of events and there could be opportunities. In any case they had no choice. "But what about …"

"Don't you worry about Madeleine and Annabelle," Agnes interrupted. "They'll be fine with me and Mrs Williams. Esther will be journeying too, keep an eye on things. Besides, they're both talking with Lady McKenzie now who'll be giving them their promised jobs in the house. Must get down to Parbold station with Mr Williams and book the tickets for everyone. Looks like you'll be going by train, a real treat, should be a lot of fun." She shot off through the other door, leaving Victoria and Abby pondering and a grinning James, slyly assuming that he'd get plenty of opportunities to duck out of the way of dragoness Hammelaar.

"Miss Warren, can we go and paint now please?" Ellen pleaded, sidling up to Abby.

"Of course, see you later at lunch, Victoria," Abby said, and departed promptly, holding Ellen's hand.

Perusing the volumes of books and papers in the library upstairs, Maddie was racking her brains to try and remember anything new which she, Abby or Judy had previously not seen or catalogued. An extremely difficult task as the whole collection of materials was haphazardly scattered about, in no sensible order or structure. Piles of very dusty books and tattered diaries were piled up randomly on desks and chairs, alongside and interspersed with artefacts looking like they were kept in former dilapidated ship's trunks. A small brass telescope on a tripod stood in the corner, partly clothed. But she did spot a large heap of books on steam engineering and railway construction. That was new, potentially promising to reveal any vital information and history of the present time which Victoria and Abby might need.

She and Belle were quietly waiting for Morag to return with a collection of local maps she wanted them to look at. In a moment, Morag walked briskly back with rolls of parchment under her arm.

"Now, young ladies, I have been thinking carefully about the most suitable occupations you should undertake in this household. As you may know, I have agreed with your mother that you shall both partake in necessary work in exchange for my generous allowance of free board and lodging."

Belle glanced at Maddie, both thinking the same thing. The idea of assisting Agnes and Esther or Mrs Williams with cleaning water closets and peeling vast amounts of vegetables was not exactly appealing.

"You have a very interesting collection of books and family heirlooms up here in this large library, Lady McKenzie," Maddie said quietly, in her most erudite sounding and poshest accent. They needed to put distance between themselves and the servants.

"And, may I ask, are those actual medical implements in the ship's trunks?" Belle added, not to be outdone but gauging the theme running through her sister's head. "Perhaps they are spoils from exotic visits abroad, or wars which earlier McKenzie ancestry have participated in?"

"Mmm …" Morag said, analysing further their capabilities and backgrounds to align with something useful which needed to be done. "I believe you both have benefitted from a sound education, received at the hands of your mother whilst in Holland. How are your reading skills, can you write too? And what about your sewing skills? I am wondering whether you have made your own clothes."

"Yes, Lady McKenzie," Maddie replied, wincing at the thought of hard hand-sewing; this was an era before Singer machines had been invented. "But our energies have been conspicuously directed mainly to the academic, our mother insisted. We had servants for dressmaking, common in the Netherlands. Our reading and writing has been tested to a high standard, we believe, and our education is liberally broad, as a woman of well bred and ambitious parents should aspire to, milady. We are proficient in knowledge of the arts, literature and music."

"And the physical sciences and mathematics too, as well as chemistry," Belle said, averting a wary glance from Maddie. Belle had now decided against what they earlier had agreed. She and Maddie needed to be bold but careful, to appeal to Lady McKenzie's own interests and inclinations and gain her confidence independently of Victoria and Abby. Certainly they should not play down their strengths.

Morag smiled. The manner by which they spoke with eloquence and clarity and their overall deportment was a credit to Victoria's abilities as a mother and teacher, another verification of a good choice as governess. She had enough servants to do all the menial work. Such an initial idea suggested by Williams would be discarded. Perhaps this very room instead held the remedy for her dilemma, but first she needed to know more about them, and whether their knowledge was as sophisticated as both Madeleine and Annabelle had made out.

"So, what can you tell me of the solutions to x squared minus x minus six equals zero?" Morag uttered triumphantly, never prepared to give any leeway and one hundred percent confident they would stare into space dumbfounded. But they at least might know the formula for the area of a circle.

"Why, an equation of the quadratics, Lady McKenzie, with a solution of x equals three and x equals minus two," Maddie replied, instantly factorising in her head. That was easy.

Morag was thrown, unexpectedly but pleasantly so. Their algebraic levels had been inculcated more vigorously than she expected and Victoria had taken them much further in mathematics than was normal for young women. "Correct, but what about x squared plus one equals zero?"

Maddie looked at Belle. This would have to be her baby as she had taken them down this pathway, against their earlier agreement.

"A more difficult problem, Lady McKenzie, but only if we restrict ourselves to the real numbers because no such number when squared can equal minus one. But such an equation is soluble using the discoveries of Mr Bombelli, an Italian mathematician of the sixteenth century, where we extend the number plane and apply the concept of an imaginary number, i, which is defined as the square root of minus one. So the solution is plus or minus i, which can be represented pictorially on a two dimensional Argand diagram. Of course these imaginary number studies have been taken much further with contemporary work using the calculus by Mr Euler, Mr Gauss, and Monsieur Legendre amongst others."

Cool it Belle, Maddie thought frantically, staring at her sister, feeling a distinct, cold discomfort run through her body. You're running away with your maths enthusiasm as usual. One more step and they will be squelching into the desperate unknown.

Morag's eyes narrowed, she was dumbfounded. She understood the broad gist of what Belle had described but would need the expertise of Ada or Mary Summerville to question them any further. Their knowledge of mathematics was very advanced. Moreover, exactly like their mother, they used idiosyncratic terms she had never heard of. Where had they all really been educated? Mrs Victoria Hammelaar and her daughters, like the delectable Mr Fazackerley, also purveyed elements of interesting mystery ... she would need to get to the bottom of that too in due course. However, practicalities must come first. These two young women were a significant intellectual asset; they definitely would not be put to mending clothes.

"Excellent," Morag replied, displaying no emotion. "I can see you have achieved high standards in your science and mathematical studies, but your modes of expression and correct terminologies must be improved ... by me. I have two tasks for you which I believe is appropriate to your aptitudes and knowledge. First, the environment around you. This library is frankly a disgrace; neither my deceased husband nor I had the time to sort out a hundred years worth of accumulation. I would like you both to clean, sort and catalogue the mess into something the family can be proud of visiting and using. Second, I wish you both to train further in the physical sciences and assist me in my electrical experiments, setting up apparatus, measurements and general laboratory maintenance which will allow me more time for in-depth analysis and synthesis of my findings. Is that acceptable?"

Madeleine and Belle beamed. That result was way better than they could ever have expected and an excellent routeway to information for their mother and Abby. "Thank you so much, Lady McKenzie. May I humbly say on behalf of my sister and me that it will be a great honour and a privilege to be allowed such beneficent servitude."

It was Belle's turn to blink. Where did Maddie acquire the flowery language? It must have been all the Jane Austen she used to devour. Belle much preferred proceedings from the Institute of Physics.

"You both look excited, that pleases my heart," Morag replied, smiling warmly. "Now, as it happens tomorrow I will be away for a few days with the children, your mother and Miss Warren to London. We have appointments with the Royal Society and to meet Mr Faraday, Mr Babbage and the Countess of Lovelace. In due course I would wish you both to enjoy the same, but for now I would like you to make an immediate start with the library. Tomorrow, I shall leave a folder on my desk of some of the latest electricity and magnetism experiments Mr Faraday and I have been conducting here, for you to read and try and acquire an understanding of the laboratory work."

Morag sighed wistfully. "One of our most difficult challenges is that Mr Faraday and I can measure from the Volta cells that there are electrical pressures causing current flows which are meeting resistance in the wires, but how on earth we can quantify that into a coherent and systematic framework so everyone can repeat the same and we find laws and behavioural relationships is beyond me."

"You mean like electrical standards?" Belle said, thinking instantly of the definitions of volts, amps, ohms, watts, and more but realising from Maddie's knowing look that these were not terms in use in 1841 and shut up. They needed to do some very careful thinking together.

"Yes, absolutely ... a standardisation. Excellent thought Annabelle, I like that concept. I shall mention it to Mr Faraday directly tomorrow. Now I must leave you, I have many letters to write before the next post."

In a flourish, Morag dived out through the door and clattered down the stairs, nearly knocking over Agnes who was walking through the door with a tray of tea.

"Her ladyship is in a hurry, off to her study no doubt. I'd better get after her. So has Lady McKenzie agreed your new jobs?"

"Yes, first she wants us to sort out the library properly for the children and family to be able to use," Maddie replied.

"Well, this place is a pigsty no denying the fact, and a tidy up is long overdue. That will keep you both going for months, see I told you to make sure milady knows you can read and write, like me. I knows she has a soft spot for ladies educated. I'm sure Mr Williams had other ideas but as usual she overrules him. Must get off, here's your tea, sounds like you need it. And the second?"

"Oh, and we ..." Maddie began, but was interrupted brusquely.

"Lady McKenzie was thinking about other possibilities, maybe dressmaking in the future," Belle said.

"Ah ... that would surely help Mrs Williams. She's excellent with a copper pan but useless with a needle and thread. Right, I'll leave you ladies to it ... lunch time soon, I'll ring the bell."

As Agnes disappeared around the corner, Maddie turned round annoyed to her sister, who already had the answer. "Mum mentioned that Agnes has been helping in the lab up to now. We need to work out an angle for our involvement and make sure she doesn't get upset, we really need Agnes on our side."

"Good thinking sis," Maddie replied, now with a grin. "Gosh, a great outcome this morning; can't wait to start, but we really have to be on our toes with all this. I thought you'd blown it going on about complex numbers and Argand diagrams."

Belle sighed then smiled. "So did I. Although Monsieur Jean-James Argand has been and gone twenty years before so I was confidently on safe ground. But she was flummoxed, you could see it in her face. I think Morag is more of an original experimentalist than a theoretical mathematician. Tell you what though, if we get to meet Ada Lovelace, her friend, we really will be tested out. She's a super-brain genius for the time, humility and deep curtsies will be the order of the day ... well humility anyway!"

They laughed loudly as Maddie rummaged through a dusty pile of early nineteenth century encyclopaedias. "I think Morag is an early feminist. I really admire that for 1841, although she's rich enough to manage it. We'd better start with finding Esther for clean dusters and pails of water!"

*

"Miss Warren, would you like to come and see the forge down at Cinderblack cottages, where James's friend Rocket lives? There are a lot of interesting things to draw," Ellen shouted across the pond, finishing off her detailed anatomical drawing of a dead carp in the reeds, which Abby had carefully laid out on a rock.

"Give me your basket, we'll take this dead fish back for natural history lessons before it goes off. Mrs Hammelaar's daughter Annabelle is very good at dissecting with a scalpel and will be able to teach you all the different organs of a fish and how it breathes water."

Ellen grimaced but then cheered when Abby said she could sketch the pieces and they would start a natural history scrap book. "I really like Annabelle. She wears very pretty clothes and read me a chapter of a story called Oliver Twist in bed last night from one of Mama's old magazines. The man who wrote it visited us a few weeks ago. I would much prefer to be like Annabelle when I grow up rather than Oliver or his friend the Artful Dodger. Are all Jewish people as horrible as Mr Fagin?"

Abby laughed. "I'm sure you'll grow up just like Annabelle, Ellen, but you have to study hard like Annabelle has."

"I will, I promise."

"Alright, we'll pick up the fish on the way back. Show me the forge, fold your paper carefully."

Walking along the peaceful canal towpath towards the edge of the estate which bordered onto the town, Abby gazed around at the environment, still remarkably familiar, although far fewer cottages were evident along with the occasional small farm holding. A long, narrow boat, piled up with sacks of cotton and pulled by an old shire horse, eased past them, the old coxswain raising his cap with a toothless smile. She thought how remarkable it would be if Charles Dickens turned up again. She loved his books, an amazing repository of the social history of this time. In fact a re-read was a good idea, although at the time his novels were published as serialisations, not books. In 1841, Dickens would have been a relatively young man, of the same generation as Morag. What in fact was the connection with Morag? Was he a close friend? She would ask later, it could reveal more answers.

Soon they turned off the canal and walked down a narrow lane with a few dilapidated cottages standing. A bunch of scruffy farm worker children were playing ball outside. The Orsbrick estate in 1841, Abby realised was far larger than what Victoria had inherited. All those cottages and smallholdings must generate significant rental income for Morag. Someone in the family at some stage later must have sold off a lot of land, perhaps to pay off debts. Then Abby saw where she was, now arriving at Cinderblack cottages. Victoria had lived in Cinderblack Lane as a child, this must be it. Only once had they both been here, on a reminiscence wander with Maddie and Belle when the twins were Ellen's age; Victoria always maintained a serious reluctance to return to her disturbed childhood days. Shortly afterwards, the whole area was redeveloped with a new solar powered eco-housing estate, including the demolition of her parent's old cottage.

Ellen, running ahead, waved as they turned a bend, and there it was, standing apart from the others but looking almost new, with whitewashed walls and a fresh thatched roof. Victoria's old childhood cottage, except there were originally three small ones, linked together. Heavens above, Julian actually lived here? In Victoria's former childhood home?

Approaching, she saw smoke coming from the rear and an acrid, pungent smell permeated the air. Also two of the cottages were obviously being used as workshops, the end one displaying curtains and a lived in appearance. At the side were piles of rusting, twisted metal, pieces of wood and the remains of dismembered carriages, an 1841 scrapyard.

Grabbing her hand, Ellen shouted for Abby to follow her as she knew the way because James was always down here.

246

Carefully hitching up her dress, Abby strode through some long grass along a narrow path at the side to be greeted by much hammering and banging, with three burly figures hunched over coke furnaces and anvils, battering at the metal with huge clubs. She could see a large pair of metal gates was being made and something else, circular, sitting red hot in an open oven, flames roaring around it.

Abby stopped; Ellen was already sat on a log, sketching away with a piece of charcoal, ignored by the workers. The nearest man looked up, his face and large leather apron covered in soot and wiped his sweaty face. It was Julian, no, she had to remember, this was Mr Fazackerley. Crikey! She stared at the other two, fascinated, definitely Ned and Zac but beefier especially Ned and having hardened appearances much older than their years with dirty, wispy beards and old caps. Suddenly they pulled the large piece of metal out with giant tongs and deftly dropped it over a wooden spoked object on the ground, before quenching the red hot metal with pails of water. Clearly Ned and Zac were repairing a carriage wheel with a new iron rim.

"Can I help you miss?" Julian called out, approaching. Abby stood her ground, her hand on her bonnet to stop it blowing off as her mind ran through the best way to handle this meeting. He didn't recognise her that was for sure, neither from last night or normal time.

"Rocket, this is Miss Warren, my new tutor at Orsbrick. She's an artist and is teaching me to draw correctly," Ellen cried out, running up to the pair of them as Julian wiped his face and hands clean with a cloth and stared. "Is it alright if I sketch that wheel Edward and Zackary are making?"

"Yes of course, but be careful, don't stand too close, it's still very hot," Julian replied.

"Thank you, Mr Rocket."

She ran off and started drawing, laughing and joking with Ned and Zac, now drinking a large flagon of ale each, and who were quite uninterested in Abby as a visitor, apart from Ned's initial up and down scrutiny of her.

Julian held out his hand which she shook tentatively and pulled a pair of delicate looking wire-rimmed spectacles out of his apron, which he rubbed carefully, much to Abby's inner amusement, before putting them on. "Of course, Miss Warren. I do apologise, now I can see straight. The heat makes my vision a little blurred. You were the lady who kindly removed that irascible oaf, Dr Gray, in the nick of time before I shoved his head into a coal bucket. A very timely intervention which brought rational sense to his brain. Thank you."

"Dr Gray appeared to me to be a much finer art collector and historian than a swordsman, Mr Fazackerley, so I felt it my duty to encourage his strengths and ability rather than to see his potential wasted at a stroke," Abby responded with a grin.

The irony was not wasted on Mr Fazackerley, who roared with laughter. "Quite so, Miss Warren. I must say, your wit is far sharper than Dr Gray's apparent rapier. May I offer you a tea or coffee? I certainly need one, especially after finishing the shaping of Lady McKenzie's new boiler earlier today."

"Err … yes that would be most pleasant," she replied, watching Ellen happily sketching the large luxury carriage behind the furnace, minus its rear wheel. The intricate design on the doors and woodwork would take her a while. Without warning, the corner of her eye caught two large shapes bounding out of the backdoor and she instinctively grabbed hold of Julian's arm in alarm.

"Jebediah, Kaiser, no, you both know better with visitors," he shouted in a commanding tone. The two aggressive dogs stopped dead, growling quietly and Abby released her grip. Jeb and Kai? How could they have been transported back in time? But it certainly appeared that way, the two wolfhounds every bit as identical to those she knew and loved. But seeing Abby they suddenly switched mood in a moment, barked affectionately and with huge tails wagging, lolloped over. They nudged her affectionately, each wanting their ears caressed as she always did. The dogs had recognised her, truly strange.

"Well now Miss Warren, how very odd. These animals act like they've known you for years, not seen such a thing before. Normally, they'd happily tear a limb off most people. You must be a real dog lover, wolfhounds are very sensitive," he said, puzzled.

"I guess that is true, Mr Fazackerley, and I have owned a few wolfhounds myself in the past, a superlative breed, but these animals are very fine specimens."

"Excellent, well, follow me please and I'll see to some warm drinks. I can recommend a particular blend of Earl Grey, which I receive regularly from Fortnum and Mason. Thank heaven for trains nowadays, don't you think?"

"Yes please that would be very nice, thank you," Abby replied, walking behind with the dogs trailing alongside, now understanding precisely why Morag was both intrigued and attracted by the mysterious, cultured and handsome Mr Fazackerley. Somewhere, Julian had a secret. Perhaps his own heritage was not as prosaic as the wayward boat person reputation in 1841 circulation, which Dr Gray had insisted was so. "Err … Mrs Fazackerley? Has she gone to the town for vegetables?"

Julian's face darkened as he quietly ushered her into the doorway and placed a kettle on the hot wood burning stove inside.

She shouted to Ellen. "Are you alright for fifteen minutes? Have Edward and Zackary left you then?"

Ellen sighed. "Yes Miss Warren, this carriage of Dr Gray's has very complicated carvings to sketch, he must be very wealthy. They've gone to the George for a pie and more ale. James often goes too but don't tell Mama or she will become very angry with him, and he punches me if I tell tales."

Abby shook her head. Not much changed with Ned that was for sure. "I promise I won't tell Lady McKenzie, but Mrs Hammelaar must know so she can find him if he doesn't turn up for class."

"Alright, that should be fine, I like Mrs Hammelaar. She's the first governess James is scared of."

Abby laughed. Victoria was making some progress, and returned to Mr Fazackerley who was pouring out a large teapot of Fortnum's special Earl Grey into china cups, not what she expected in a blacksmith's cottage. The room, a combined living and kitchen area, was quite large and sparsely furnished with basic wooden items, although they were well made. One good and well upholstered armchair, with a large candle floor reading light alongside, was sat on the clean wooden floor, conspicuously, in front of the fireplace. A large bookshelf behind was filled with a mixture of European and English history, including politics as well as some contemporary fiction. A few books he was reading at the moment lay opened with markers on a small coffee table. But the white painted walls were beautifully adorned with pictures of all sizes, mainly Flemish and Dutch seventeenth and sixteenth century obscure artists, of colourful religious and landscape scenes, presented in the most intricate of frames. She stared hard. These were no ordinary choices; he had an eye for good and expensive art. Julian indicated for her to sit, and pulled out a heavy wooden chair, as she sat down, still not yet having mastered the art of Morag's eloquence in those long and heavy period dresses.

"No, is the answer Miss Warren as there is no Mrs Fazackerley, I'm a widower. Ophelia died in childbirth, complications, having those two sons of mine, twins you see, when we were living in London. They were big boys even then and the doctor had to cut her open in the end, the labour went on for so long and they wouldn't move themselves. They're still lazy tykes if let. She lost too much blood. Please call me Julian."

Abby felt thrown, the plot had gone in an unexpected direction. Who was Ophelia? Definitely not a boat person. And he said London? "I'm so sorry Julian. Please forgive my ungracious ineptitude. Have you brought them up on your own? Oh, and I am Abigail."

"Completely. Don't worry, many ladies are surprised that I remain solitary. I am very independent and organised, although I must admit the George has a more appetising menu for the lads than my cooking and rather prettier barmaids."

Abby grinned, chewing at a stale bun. They could definitely do with some of her kebabs.

"All the furniture and picture frames that you peruse, I have made by my own hands over the years. I enjoy skilled practical work in all trades but especially metal and wood so have never been short of work. But I haven't shunned female company all those years, Abigail," he replied quietly with the famous Julian come-on smile which Morag had received the benefit of in spades last evening. "I'm still waiting for the right woman to come along though for marriage."

"And I see you also enjoy literary reading and the fine arts?" Abby replied, now distracted by his reading of an eighteenth century copy of Boswell's 'Life of Samuel Johnson.'

"Indeed, I have had the benefit of a good education, just as I'm sure you have enjoyed too, without which no man will ever raise himself above the common lot."

"Or woman, Julian."

He laughed loudly, that exact raucous laugh she was so used to over the years. There was a purpose to Julian being here … but what? To seduce Morag? That was not a notion that had any appeal whatsoever to suggest to Victoria.

"Yes indeed, I very much support that proposition. Anyway I must get on. Lady McKenzie's requirements demand my attention. I can see the boys reappearing on their velocipedes to finish off the broken wheel repair on Dr Gray's personal carriage. He came to see me this morning. You appear to have had a cheery influence on his demeanour. I can unhesitatingly understand why," he replied, with another seductive look.

Shit, Abby thought alarmed, Julian is chatting *me* up too. Definitely this is not something whatsoever to share with Victoria. What is it about men in this period of time? Or, actually have they ever been any different? Probably not she concluded, rising with difficulty from the chair and patted the dogs that were lying at her feet, stretched out. "Thank you for the tea, Mr Fazackerley, I must see to the prompt return of Miss McKenzie."

"Of course, good day Abigail. I do hope you will pop by again, although I am sure we will meet at Orsbrick Hall, I have much work to do there."

Calling Ellen, she departed quickly. She needed to find a moment alone again with Victoria and provide feedback, well, most of it.

# Chapter Eleven

General chaos with servants running back and forth occupied the early morning as numerous trunks filled with essentials and clothes for the London trip were brought out by Williams and his helpers, whilst Agnes and Esther did a final dusting down of the inside of the two carriages. Excursions to London were not for the faint-hearted even amongst the wealthy, although it was patently clear to Victoria, from what Agnes insisted be packed, that there was an expectation of their attending dinner parties and maybe a ball, as well as meeting an array of aristocrats and wealthy, upper class gentry. So, sufficient dresses and gowns had to be taken. Abby and Victoria stood near the front door, patiently waiting for Morag who seemed to be taking a long time coming down. A smaller wooden box full of Morag's latest scientific papers, tied around with thick leather straps, was thrown inside the first carriage.

Dressed in their best outfits, James and Ellen emerged and without a word spoken they were led by Williams into the first carriage as Esther climbed in with her small case of clothes for herself. James had been especially sullen that morning and glared at Victoria as the door was shut. She was making no headway to gain his confidence, but after working him hard the entire previous day, she was now clear that his knowledge and education were at a better level than she first thought and he knew more science than he had initially let on. However, his overall attitude, especially to her, remained appalling.

"He displays a paradoxical mixture of childish ambition and truculent perspective coupled with a suave and swaggering man of the world charmer," Victoria muttered to Abby, who had managed to quickly give some feedback about Julian, Ned, Zac and the dogs in the evening. "He's bright, street-wise for his years and cunning. I can give him no leeway whatsoever and don't intend to. When it comes to a battle of wills …"

"Then I'm sure he's met his match, like everyone else who got in your way years ago. Not renowned for taking prisoners are we," Abby whispered, with a wide smile.

"Ha-ha, but no, that's true and certainly not ever with James McKenzie. I've been thinking long and hard about the Julian Fazackerley family set up. It's heartening to hear about the kids but frankly, I find Julian so unpalatable and this insatiable fawning over Morag, you should have seen him this morning. I can't work out what part he has to play, if any. All of them and Lynton may be an accidental by-product of the four of us and Mauveine and Isi coming back together in time. At the moment I'm happy to keep a wide berth. I need to keep focussed on Morag and James."

"Yes, I understand where you're coming from," Abby replied, sensing a deep emotional unease from Victoria, much worse than her own. "Look, leave them to me, and maybe Maddie and Belle, I think it's probably easier. Whatever they're about, we'll try and get to the bottom of it."

"Thanks, still my best friend even in 1841," Victoria replied, happier. "We'd better climb into the carriage. It appears that Messrs Julian and Lynton are already travelling independently to Manchester, together would you believe, and will meet us at Piccadilly station. Where is Morag? We're going to miss the train if she doesn't hurry up, it's hardly the regular half-hour Maglev to King's Cross. To be honest she seemed very down over breakfast, like she's been crying. I wonder if something has happened."

"I'll go and find out. I have the family status to instruct and demand from Williams, just hang on."

Abby walked over to him. "Mr Williams, my cousin seems to be a little delayed. Is everything alright? Is she feeling unwell?"

"Lady McKenzie should be down any minute, Miss Warren. She was out of the house very early this morning on business, I expect her ladyship is feeling rather tired. Is everyone on board the carriages?"

"Yes, thank you. Mrs Hammelaar and I will wait in our carriage."

"As you wish, Miss Warren. Aah ... I can hear Lady McKenzie now; I shall just check the horse harnesses."

Abby walked into the hallway to greet Morag coming down the stairs, her hands full of mathematical calculus books.

"I need these in London when we meet Ada. Can you take half of them please Abigail," Morag said brusquely, missing the bottom step and dropping the lot, distraction running angrily across her face. "Hellfire and damnation, may the Lord condemn all sinners."

Abby bent down to pick them up with her. "Dearest cousin, you don't seem yourself this morning. Victoria and I are concerned for your well-being, are you feeling unwell?"

"My health couldn't be better," Morag replied, both walking briskly to the door. "No, something truly awful happened this morning or should I say I found out about the bombshell in the middle of the night. A servant knocked on my door with an urgent note which had been delayed. I've dealt with it and don't wish to converse further on the topic. We should be enjoying the day and I intend to. When I am more favourably disposed, I will speak further about the incident with both you and Victoria."

"Of course cousin dearest. The best seat awaits … oops I think Victoria climbed into the carriage before you," Abby replied, curious about what had happened and deciding it was time for some light-hearted behaviour. There were too many serious goings-on with everybody.

Morag laughed at long last. "Yes, I have to be on my toes with you two around but I hope this trip will prove fruitful and enjoyable for everyone." She reached the carriage where Williams helped them in.

"Move over Victoria, you're not allowed all the best space," Morag cried with a giggle, mindful that she needed to act normal, despite the devastating news received. The door was finally slammed shut, the horses whipped and they were on their way.

*

Once alighted at Parbold Station, they waited patiently for the train. The paucity of the station was very self-evident, with a small hut standing on a length of garden decking planks, containing the ticket master and his assistant. Another larger wooden building with holes in the roof, for shelter when required, stood alongside, although the day was dull but dry and reasonably warm for spring. Ellen was running around excitedly, pointing out various wild flowers growing around the planking to Abby, but James sat apart on a bench, sullen and disengaged, likely wishing he was with Rocket and sons down at the George public house. Esther was busy checking that the trunks and luggage were secured properly for when they embarked. Victoria noticed a severe frostiness by Morag towards her son but the relationship between the two was so strained anyway this was expected, as the likelihood of James not wishing to come would have been very high. However, Morag walked across to him, said something and his face lit up.

"I've just told him that Mr Fazackerley will be joining us at Manchester. It's about the only thing which conjures up any joy whatsoever to his countenance," she said to Victoria and Abby. "Well almost, but taking his position and responsibilities as the future McKenzie male heir seriously, remains bottom of his priorities, that much has become very evident. Thank you, Victoria, for taking him in hand so quickly. Your teaching approach has been a decided shock to the system, a badly needed jolt of reality, long awaited. Look, yonder up the track, I can see the train approaching. Is this your first train journey Victoria? You look a little apprehensive."

"Err ... no, they are building railways around Amsterdam, but my first in England," Victoria replied, cautiously eyeing the great plume of belching smoke and steam approaching with an ear-splitting racket.

As the engine slowly drew towards the station on rickety looking tracks, the fact that they were at the beginning of the railway era was evident by the engineering on display. The last time Victoria had seen anything resembling this small, shiny green locomotive was in the York Railway Museum. It was pulling four carriages, only one of which had a roof and windows, the three others had no roof and the rear one, packed with piled up goods and people was open sided, with women and children sat frozen on the middle of the floor, wrapped in blankets and huddled closely together in groups.

"Of course we have purchased first class tickets so we'll be at the front," Morag shouted, as the train slowly came to a halt with a squealing of brakes and huge plumes of steam, the engine being put into neutral. A fierce red glow of coal and coke could be seen burning under the boiler. Even James looked more animated, walking up to the engine to examine it closely, with Ellen sketching furiously. "The poor must make do at the rear, in third class where tickets are a few pence only. I am lobbying my Member of Parliament, as a priority, to force the railway companies to put sides and a roof on all carriages and proper seating like second class. The situation they face for travel is inhuman and unjustified, when these companies are making vast profits. Railways and education are the future and will change society immeasurably for the better. Don't you agree? I am also lobbying with others for a removal of third class altogether."

Victoria nodded. A liking for liberal and forward thinking values and tolerance seemed to have been an integral characteristic of the McKenzie family for many generations. As their luggage was loaded on board they all alighted into the first class carriage, empty apart from an elderly gentleman with a tobacco stained beard who doffed his cap politely. Ellen ran straight to the front, followed by James ambling along, hands in pockets, and they settled into quite comfortable wooden seats. Fifteen minutes elapsed whilst a fresh load of coal and boiler water was initiated and then with a lurch and a chug they were off, slowly gathering speed to about twenty miles per hour.

Abby immediately tried opening the hinged window to alleviate the stuffiness and musty smell, but Morag instantly intervened.

"We must keep that shut, I'm afraid. The smoke and ash can be most injurious blowing in and very unpleasant … the vicar's curate lost an eye last year as a result of a red hot ember," Morag remonstrated, before rising from her seat to check Ellen and James were comfortable and safe.

"This reminds me of being on a giant version of the children's steam railway in Southport," Abby whispered. "But at least inside here is quite reasonable, apart from the rattling and shaking. Bit of a boneshaker isn't it?"

Victoria smiled. "This pantechnicon on tracks is probably state of the art, don't knock it. They haven't quite invented computer controlled, damped wishbone suspension yet," she replied, opening a flask of lemonade. "We're being treated by the great McKenzie wealth today too. Normally, you'd be sitting on the floor at the far end with the donkey. I think we've reached maximum speed, I'd say we were doing around forty miles per hour. There must have been a big leap forward in railway design in the next thirty years for these Puffing Billys to finally resemble our childhood memories of old steam locomotives like the Flying Scotsman."

"I heard you say Puffing Billys, Victoria," Morag's voice resounded, as she carefully made her way back, hanging on tight to the ceiling poles as the carriage rocked from side to side. "There is plenty of science, engineering and geography to discuss on this train journey so I've made some space at the front for you, and later Abigail, to be able to tutor James and Ellen. I'll join you. What nobody knows, including James, is that the locomotive at the front, the Star of Manchester, is one of my husband's creations. I recognised the design when it pulled in. I think that should keep his attention. I assume Victoria that you have a basic knowledge of how a steam engine works?"

"Yes, thank you, Morag. An excellent idea, ideal for the children to refrain from boredom and for James to learn some chemistry of combustion."

"I'll stick to geography if I may, please, cousin dearest," Abby replied. "I'm afraid my engineering knowledge is somewhat lacking in depth and substance."

Morag laughed. "Good. Now, whilst we enjoy the scenery and some refreshments and snacks which Esther has packed, as I have just mentioned the technology work of Malcolm, this is a good opportunity, Victoria, to tell you in detail about him and what he achieved. Malcolm was an outstanding railway engineer and a great innovator," she continued, her eyes animated and sparkling with the chance to talk about her husband.

"Yes … I'd like to hear about Lord McKenzie very much," Victoria replied, weighing up the potential useful information and glancing at Abby for a reaction, but she was distracted completely by the remarkable rural scenery flashing by as the Pennines approached. Next station, in around twenty minutes, was Wigan, which for Abby would be fascinating, being her early childhood home.

*

Changing at Manchester Piccadilly was more of an ordeal, not made easier by Morag's discomfort on arrival, at the station where her husband had died. Abby gazed around in wonderment as the station was merely a large shed with a number of lines running in. Agnes's whispered aside over breakfast had been running in a loop through Victoria's mind. '*Rumour abounded that Lord McKenzie had jumped rather than fallen but her ladyship would never accept it. For what reason, she kept saying. But them in the know said he had a mistress.*' Was James aware of the surroundings of his father's death, another cause of his dislike for his mother? Victoria had the strange impression James was not aware at all of the facts, unmoved by his surroundings unlike his mother, nor was his

260

father spoken of any further. She would bide her time on the reason for that conundrum.

Fortunately, a distraction came to hand with the sudden arrival onto the platform of Mr Julian Fazackerley and Dr Lynton Gray, now seemingly bosom buddies who provided sufficient wit and mirth to distract Morag totally, especially alongside the attention lavished on her presence by Julian. This behaviour was beginning to grate nauseatingly with Victoria, as apart from a grudging good afternoon, she was ignored once more.

Victoria understood but found it hard to accept. She was not Julian's type for some reason relevant to 1841, although Abby strangely seemed to be vying alongside Morag as a recipient for his attention, an issue which would need an urgent discussion on London arrival. Lynton had completely lost interest in Abby already and had worked his way, not very subtly, to the end of the platform to chat to a lone and young aristocratic looking lady in a white, voluminous dress and matching cloak and bonnet, wafting a sun parasol around stupidly whilst fluffing her long, black curls. James became animated for the first time at the arrival of his great friend Rocket. Soon they were boarded onto a larger and apparently faster train, with ten carriages including two of first class, joined together by a cloth framed tunnel and pulled by a black locomotive. They set off at a pace. The carriages were noticeably larger. This train, Victoria pondered, really was state of the art, soon reaching speeds of between fifty and sixty miles per hour, the estimated journey time being four hours to Euston Station. The service had only recently opened and was packed out, especially second and third class, with standing room only, resembling, Abby remarked, old Indian trains travelling though Bombay, when she was there as a student. Their comfortable first class carriage contained numerous business people and other wealthy landed gentry types with a few families and children, but sufficient room at the front prevailed for Victoria and Abby to continue some more lessons with the children, under the stern watchful eye of their mother. Julian had taken a seat a few rows behind next to a young businessman and they chatted avidly, whilst Lynton, wearing a bright yellow jacket and blue trousers, was ensconced at the back, holding his top hat, with his aristocratic new paramour, waving both arms and gabbling loudly, trying to impress her with his knowledge of the latest art by a Mr Turner and inviting her to invest. She, seemingly, did not appear overimpressed.

Two hours in and Victoria was flagging with the science of carbon combustion and coal gas manufacture when James, staring inattentively out of the window, suddenly shouted back in a loud voice to his friend.

"Rocket, look outside, what's going on? Bandits?"

Everyone who heard stared alarmed out of the dirty windows to watch four masked horsemen, holding long pistols, shoot out from a clump of trees to ride madly alongside the train. They had only just departed from an extended stop at Leicester for a major refuel and water top up. The boilers were slowly working up to full steam pressure again and the train had barely reached ten miles per hour. One tried to board the locomotive but the burly coalman in the cab swung a huge shovel and knocked him off his horse, the driver shovelling coal into the boiler at a fast rate. The other riders continued and one took a shot at the cab and fired but missed. The train was slowly gathering speed and the lead rider, sensing they had to act fast, drew alongside the first class cabin.

"What are we going to do?" James cried, getting up to join Rocket and rudely pushing Victoria out of the way, who fell over and banged her head on a wooden pole, as people in the carriage began to shout and scream and Abby held the petrified Ellen tight.

"Lady McKenzie, my pistols, down in the bag at your feet please," Julian yelled, pointing to a large black holdall on the floor. Immediately she yanked open the top and pulled out two gleaming pistols whilst Victoria, rubbing the side of her head, watched wide-eyed as Morag fished quickly inside, pulled out a pouch and a tin of gunpowder and primed the first pistol, like a veteran soldier, with a round ball of ammunition. She lurched over to Julian, who had pulled the window open.

"Pass me it," he demanded, their faces close and intense expressions locked together. In a moment he had the pistol, pointed it towards the rider about to clamber onto the side ladder and fired. Instantly the horse buckled and fell onto the ground in a great cloud of dust, throwing the rider headfirst into the air. By then Morag had primed the second pistol and Julian repeated the shot at a second horse further away and the same happened.

"Shame about the horses which likely will have to be put down," he barked to Morag. "But it should provide a salutary lesson to the rogues chancing it. The glory days of the highwaymen are well over."

Victoria watched in amazement. Julian Fazackerley was a fine shot and a brave man. By then the train had gathered a fast pace of steam, outrunning a horse, and the remaining rider, who, seeing the misfortunes of his comrades, turned and rode away smartly into the distance.

To a loud tumultuous cheering and clapping, Julian stood up and took a small bow, his arm held tightly by Morag, encouraging the applause and with James at his other side, grinning proudly. He blushed surprisingly shyly with embarrassment and a large top hat was already being passed around from an elderly man in a dark tweed suit, which was gathering coins and notes in rapid succession.

"Thank you so much, Mr Fazackerley, you have saved our lives and the rest of the train. The passengers are rightly praising you but I will ensure you are especially rewarded," she said, deliberately loudly for both Victoria and Abby to hear unambiguously. The way they gazed at each other was sickening enough for Victoria, still nursing her throbbing head, which had subsided a little with a wet compress which Esther applied. She would have a small bump there to be sure. But what alarmed her most was that an entanglement between Morag and Julian was going to complicate matters hugely … It was certainly obvious that Morag liked desirable men, and the more they fawned over her the more she liked to manipulate them. But Victoria was plotting and analysing as dispassionately as possible. Julian had some long term plan in mind, and going by the feedback Abby had earlier made, he was looking to secure a new wife, someone with class, intellect and wealth and also fun to be with. Morag was a high contender for Julian's masterplan. He had therefore to be distracted somehow whilst in London by somebody else as beguiling. But who? She glanced at Abby, also deep in thought. A naughty idea had suddenly flashed across her mind.

Abby however was concerned with something else more pressing. "Mr Fazackerley," she screamed out over the noise. "Where is Dr Gray, he's disappeared? Has he been shot or taken?"

Julian looked back and clapped his hands. "Order, please everyone, quiet, if you will … my friend the eminent Dr Lynton Gray has vanished into thin air," he cried out frantically as everyone went still and looked about mystified, the clackety-clack of the wheels over the tracks being the only sound permeating the air.

A slow creaking sound broke the silence as the passengers turned en-masse to see the lid of a huge trunk at the back being raised and a red-faced Dr Gray struggle out, holding the hand of his lady-friend, equally flushed. She climbed after him somewhat inelegantly and wearing little underneath, doing up the buttons on her dress.

Lynton stared nonplussed at the audience, never one to miss an opportunity for a grand entrance. "Dearest passengers, my good friends, I say a gentleman must always do his duty," he announced in his eloquent voice accompanied by a florid bow. "And shield a lady from distress in time of war."

A huge roar of laughter and whooping with more claps rang around the carriage as Lynton continued his flourishes whilst he helped the embarrassed female aristocrat back to her seat. Victoria and Morag, along with Julian were laughing loudly too, enjoying the spectacle, but one person further on grimaced sharply.

"Stupid little prick," Abby hissed in a whisper to Victoria, forgetting her voice carried, unaware that Morag caught her exclamation and pondered very puzzled. What in heaven's name was that strange expression her dear cousin had used? And Morag wasn't the only one.

"Miss Warren, what's a prick? Is it another name for a big Silly-Billy?"

Abby grinned, realising. "Yes, Ellen you could say that. I picked it up from Europe when I was painting."

*

Back at Orsbrick Hall, Maddie and Belle were working hard in the library having cleaned up an enormous pile of books and papers, which they were now assembling into sections ready for some logical categorisation. The fact that Belle had been school librarian for one year and learned the basics of bibliography, with Judy's expert assistance, was immensely helpful, so they decided to organise this content, exactly as they had done in, as they now called it, 'real time'.

Piled up in a heap in the corner, were a large number of old textbooks from the eighteenth century on astronomy, with notes, sketches and drawings of observations from a telescope, which Agnes had hinted was still locked up in the observatory, all covered in cloths and ready to be used with the children at any time. Another three trunks contained further engineering and design books, including the most fascinating original editions of clothing machinery and textile mill layouts, from hand to steam driven production. Diagrams and explanations of costing up, licensing and installation of Arkwright's Frame, Hargreaves's Spinning Jenny and Crompton's Mule, written in antiquated English with peculiar spellings, were scattered about. These books were augmented with economics and political tomes, espousing the benefits of industrialisation and the sharing of profits amongst workers. Maddie picked up and perused a few of the most recent 1830's economic treaties and realised that these critical ideas of the political economy being espoused, had sowed the seeds of the work of Karl Marx, Das Kapital and the basis of the idea of communism to arrive in the 1850s. A number of the books had annotations and comments written in by a George McKenzie, and going by the dates, he was either Malcolm McKenzie's father or maybe grandfather. The comments showed that the seeds of the McKenzie adoption of the ideals of a socialist and cooperative working community, underpinned by steam and coal technology, were sown at the beginning of the nineteenth century, influencing the drivers and ethics of Morag's husband and undoubtedly

Morag herself. Old diaries and accounts books for the missing periods between 1770 and the present 1841, piled up at the rear, would fill many of the time gaps they had never seen previously.

How or where had this archive lot disappeared? There was plenty of work to do and parallel reading to keep them busy for a long time, but according to Mauveine they didn't have much time so they had to focus on any specific family material, science or newly revealed connections and hidden answers which could be used by Victoria and Abby. The quest was like looking for a needle in a haystack.

Belle drew Maddie's attention to the large number of books, drawings and plans relating to textiles and clothing factories. Notes abounded on automating Jacquard looms further and the required power of steam engines to run rows and rows of spinning machines, which again George McKenzie had focussed on.

"This would explain why Morag's work in chemistry was focussed on dyes. Somewhere and sometime in here, ideas were discussed on setting up a textiles factory on the Orsbrick estate, probably spinning and weaving cotton, which was endemic in Lancashire at the time," Maddie cried, gripping her sister's arm excitedly. "And Morag saw the direct connection between science and manufacture by taking on the inadequacy of natural dyes if automated production ramped up output hugely, which of course it would."

"This future venture for Orsbrick Hall must have been in the mind of her husband too, but something turned his attention away from factories onto railways. Perhaps he saw more money could be made," Belle continued, both musing hard. They worked well bouncing ideas off each other, their capabilities nicely complimentary.

Maddie interjected, flicking through some papers. "Morag meanwhile still remained academically interested in and wedded to researching the chemistry of dyes, rudimentary though it is presently … until widowed. I'm sure she must feel lonely inside. She's only twenty-five and has a lifetime ahead of her, being wealthy and upper class, and then she meets the great Mr Michael Faraday and suddenly goes all physics and electrical engineering. I tell you what Belle, if I meet anyone and ever get married, which is highly doubtful, I would never sacrifice my career and academic passion for a partner's foibles."

"Hear, hear, Madeleine," a soft voice rang out. Maddie turned swiftly in dismay then smiled, realising it was Agnes, with some tea and fruit buns plus homemade jam.

"I would have done the same, but nobody ever bothered to ask me to marry them except some illiterate clod-head coachman in Lady Byron's employ and I told him where to get off, in no uncertain terms. Like to be independent, I do. My goodness there are a lot of books up here," Agnes exclaimed, picking up a history of the Napoleonic Wars and browsing through.

"Borrow that one, Agnes," Belle said, taking the heavy tray. "Keep you busy for a week or two at night in bed."

"Why thank you, Miss Annabelle, I do declare you have a heart of gold. My grandfather served in the Peninsular, then at Austerlitz and finally the Battle of Waterloo, like Mr Williams did, but sadly he never made it … buried there somewhere."

"A bit like War and Peace," Maddie blurted out, then realised with one sharp glare from Belle. Tolstoy was a long way to come yet, damn, it was so very easy to let slip.

"War and Peace, Miss Madeleine? What book is that then?"

"Err ... no, I was meaning first you have war and then peace and then war again and so it goes on in a perpetual cycle, which was how Napoleon ran his campaigns, keeping everyone on their toes, wasn't it," she muttered, trying hard not to blush.

"I guess so, never thought about it that way. You do have a sharp brain, young lady. And, combined with those looks, both of you will be married off in no time, mark my word, especially once her ladyship takes you down to those magnificent balls in London."

They laughed and sat around the table munching a bun each as Belle poured out the tea. Agnes then moved onto another topic with more serious concern.

"Now, I need to warn you both, Mr and Mrs Williams are both mad as hatters that you girls have been let off the hook so to speak, by working in this here library. Mrs Williams is forever complaining about repairing her ladyship's clothes and needs more help in the kitchen. They don't want me talking to you either. Mr Williams tried to order me to stop but he knows he can't enforce it with me being her ladyship's and now your mother's personal maid. He was looking forward to seeing you both scrubbing floors. Be careful is what I say, you can't trust Mr Williams especially if he has a bee in his bonnet. They will both be out to try and disgrace you to Lady McKenzie, so keep sharp and don't fall out of line."

Maddie looked askance over to Belle. "Thanks Agnes, we do appreciate you warning us, we'll be careful, I promise."

"Good," Agnes exclaimed. "Now if you don't want the other half of that extra bun, I'd better make good use of it, waste not want not, and I need the energy ... got them outside latrines to clear out as Esther's not here."

Maddie gently pushed her plate forward, screwing up her nose. "By all means, Agnes."

Belle stifled a giggle. But Maddie was also pondering the warning. They had in fact, in one day, narrowed the gap in the missing McKenzie history. Now it was only between 1841 and 1860, twenty eventful years, with Mauveine at the centre. Was someone behind that original erasure? Maybe even Williams?

# Chapter Twelve

Gathering together around the collection of carriages outside Euston station, Victoria gazed wide-eyed at the normally familiar surroundings. She struggled a little in the breeze to hang onto her bonnet, she hated hats. Morag, as annoyingly eloquent as ever, was fussing about the best arrangements and talked earnestly to Julian and Lynton, whilst Ellen sat quietly on a trunk with Abby and Esther, chatting. Victoria felt wistfully reminiscent. Both she and Abby had spent far too many days over the years when the children were small, travelling up and down to London by first class train from Liverpool Lime Street. In those days, they were each intensely occupied developing their respective businesses in art and dyeing, always on the go, whilst Julian wrote his books in the attic and Lynton pursued the expansion of his legal practice more often in the Ship and Mitre or down the Rotary Club. For Victoria those were golden years, before the extent of Julian's writing career became apparent and took off. Her McKenzie legacy of millions of pounds kept them both totally worry free and the growing family, two sets of twins, she had ached for after her miscarriage, materialised in a house they loved and nurtured with endless care and affection.

Certainly this Euston station, the original design and only four years old according to Morag, was mightily impressive, despite only having two tracks inside for incoming and outgoing trains. Morag had become very animated earlier about a new station at Fenchurch also being built and due to be opened that year, for which Malcolm had contributed to the drawings. Abby had whispered that London Bridge was the very first London station, opened in 1836, and was serving the burgeoning south east region and Kent. Victoria hadn't a clue. So in 1841, only three railway stations existed in London? This period really was early days for train travel, but the hordes of people, especially the poor who crowded endlessly on the long platforms, demonstrated a steam led technological future across all England was set and irreversible. That vision was likely what attracted Morag's husband to become a railway engineer.

She stared up at the massive stone arch commanding the Euston entrance, at least eighty feet high and held up by four fluted marble pillars in a Doric style, modelled on the entrance to the Greek Acropolis. Whatever had happened to this beautiful piece of original Victorian architecture? The existing Euston station, modernised so called in 2020, was a garish glass and metal fronted monstrosity in comparison. She wished she had a camera, but then noticed a small group of people stood around a large object on top of a tripod. A man was standing beneath a black cloth ... goodness, an extremely early photographer, maybe a pioneer, with his cumbersome device pointed to the arch. The exposure time seemed to be endless.

"Mrs Hammelaar. Do you know how making pictures with a camera obscura works? I would like to know the chemistry involved."

Victoria was momentarily startled by the deep voice, breaking fast, of James stood quietly beside her and pointing to the photographers. Certainly, he had become quite chastened since the bandit episode on the train. Following a sharp dressing down by Rocket, he had unexpectedly apologised to her for being rude and pushing her over by accident. The journey had continued very quietly and the bump on her forehead was barely visible thanks to Esther's timely dabs of rose scented water and a little blusher.

Victoria thought fast. Perhaps a window of turning point opportunity was arising where she could slowly gain some respect from this intransigent boy, and build on from there. She cast her sharp mind back to Maddie's GCSE science project which was based on the development of photography, and Maddie, being a keen history student, had written a lot on the early evolution. A pity Maddie wasn't there.

"Well James, in a nutshell, a few years ago, it was discovered that a chemical called iodide of silver, when exposed to light, darkens and the silver metal comes out. By coating this on a glass plate and placing that at the focal point of a lens in a camera obscura, then when the shutter is pressed for a certain length of time, the image pointed at is captured by the lens on the plate. But for the picture to be kept permanently, the image has to be fixed. So the plate is washed carefully in a solution called thiosulphite of soda, a process only very recently invented. This creates a negative where white is black and black is white, but by printing onto special paper, a positive image is reproduced."

James was for once spellbound. He not only instantly appreciated the opportunities such a technology could bring, but was thinking through how this could become a future McKenzie activity. Despite his love for his father, he had no inkling whatsoever to become a railway engineer, but photography was something novel and exciting, with much to be invented.

"That is a very clear description, I understand the process. Thank you Mrs Hammelaar," he said, his gaze remaining fixed on the photographers. "How long do they have to sit under that hood?"

"Err … well it depends," Victoria replied, not sure.

"About ten minutes is, I believe, the necessary exposure time." A voice behind interrupted them as Morag thrust herself in-between. "Too long and everything becomes black. Too short and the picture is not defined. Photography requires much patience and trial and error, James. Perhaps while we are down here, we will follow this up further?"

"Yes please Mother. Do you have the chemicals Mrs Hammelaar mentioned?"

"No, but I'm sure I can acquire them and perhaps we could do some experiments? Now, will you join your sister and Esther please in the first carriage? As the man in charge, you are to ask the driver to take you to number twelve St James's Square in Mayfair where the Countess of Lovelace will be expecting you. This should be sufficient." Morag handed him some coins.

"Is Rocket not coming with us?"

"Mr Fazackerley will accompany me to the Royal Society where he has some urgent business nearby, so he tells me, and will return to St James's Square to join us all later. Off you go."

Morag rejoined Victoria, both watching Abby repositioning her bonnet and fluffing out her red ringlets for a five minute pose before the hooded tripod, after a brief conversation with the photographers who had erected a sign for 'fashionable ladies and gentlemen.'

"My dear cousin has always wished to be seen in the limelight. Originally she was, I believe, an actress at Drury Lane before realising her true vocation was with the brush and easel."

274

Victoria nodded and thought hard. However they had transferred into this time period they must have come with a history, seamlessly coherent as seen by the external world, including Julian and Lynton of course. "Dr Gray and Mr Fazackerley appear to have vanished, Morag? Do you know where they are?"

"Julian has gone back into the station to find Dr Gray, who was last seen pursuing that dreadful trollop on the train down the platform. Do you know who she is? Lady Helena Windelbar, the wife of Lord Windelbar of Chelsea no less, a landowner of immense wealth. He is housebound now, decrepit with the gout and pushed around in a bath chair whilst she floozies herself about every eligible male stud society can offer her. It appears she fled like the wind down the departure track, too fast for Dr Gray to catch, and has escaped on the new train to Bath. Even for her whoring standards, rollicking in a trunk was a step too far … She will need to be away from London for a month or two until the scandal dies down. Anyway, they will make their own way in a hansom cab."

Morag waved towards a line of luxury carriages and one of the drivers gently urged his four horses and large brougham over, as Abby rejoined them excitedly. "I'm going to be in the next edition of the London Post … I have to look for my next commissions," she blurted out. Victoria's eyes narrowed. Was Abby already factoring in exit from 2026 on a permanent basis? Perhaps she was beginning to actually like it in 1841.

"Where to milady?" the driver shouted, in a distinctive cockney accent, before jumping down and opening the large door.

"The Royal Society in Carlton Street, please," she replied before climbing in first. Quickly they were off, the ride in this carriage being much smoother, despite the rutted roads and potholes everywhere. Fascinated by the sudden change into the urban scenery of the most populous and busy city in the world, Victoria stared at the never ending parade of carriages and carts, all shapes and sizes that careered in and out of the main highway, many pulled by hand. The number of horses was huge, evident by their waste piled up in great stinking heaps amongst the mud. Everywhere, there were hundreds of people walking and wandering about, many distinctly poverty stricken in rags. Street-sellers abounded between shops of every kind, ten to the dozen. Up and down the main highways, animals roamed loose, chickens ran around, cows, pigs and even sheep were being herded to markets or slaughter-houses, often whipped mercilessly by tiny children or very old men. London was a vibrant place, reminding her, with its huge rich and poor divide, of being in a city like Mumbai but having classy architecture everywhere. Districts changed back and forth dramatically, from one minute clean and expensively upmarket to suddenly become run-down and decayed with tumbledown infrastructure. A number of buildings and landmarks were very familiar, having barely changed over the last 180 years. She easily spotted the unmistakable magnificent dome of St Paul's cathedral rising in the distance. As they ventured deeper into the city, the faint murkiness around Euston station, still relatively rural, was descending into a much thicker, yellowish fog, with a distinctive smoky smell, mixed with sewage, both exacerbated by the muggy weather not being especially sunny. This was the London of the 1950s on a bad day, the proverbial pea-souper of old, except every day was the same. Morag pulled the window up to keep out the incessant racket everywhere and the smell.

"You get used to it but it takes a day or so," she shouted to Victoria. "There are advantages and disadvantages living here as I'm sure you are weighing up, judging by your expression. On balance, I suspect, Victoria, you are a country lady at heart preferring Orsbrick to Piccadilly," she added with a grin.

Victoria nodded. That hypothesis held in 2026, and was decidedly strengthened in 1841. But to visit London then was a unique experience not to have been missed. Thinking of Mauveine's warning that they were now living in the time and could die in the time, she was mindful of the obvious insanitary conditions and health hazards abounding in an environment where even antibiotics were a hundred years off. She and Abby would have to be very careful and keep watchful, with all of eating, drinking and social mixing.

"Dear cousin, you seem much recovered from this morning. Do you wish to tell us of your trouble?" Abby said, as the carriage lurched around a corner taking a narrow short cut, the Thames very visible in the foreground. A myriad of tiny ferry boats scurried up and down the dark, murky water, loaded with passengers, obviously water-taxis and popular. Another waft of unpleasant odours entered the carriage; sewage control must have been almost non-existent.

Morag moved the handkerchief away from her nose and mouth, her face troubled. She remained silent, gathering her thoughts. The carriage returned to another main road, levelled with some kind of fine stone surfacing and the surroundings had become very upmarket. The general noise had also died down with the worst smells of the sewage, although the pungent smog lingered, reminding Abby of Beijing on a windless day. Victoria recognised a number of buildings. They were passing through Mayfair.

"Yes … now both of you. I want to share this but in the strictest of confidences. Do I have your word?"

"Completely, dearest Morag," Abby urged, "Pray do tell, I can see that your well-being will benefit from sharing your distress."

"It's about James. Late at midnight, I learned he had become a father, the baby born is a day old."

Victoria and Abby's mouths dropped. James's academic brain may have been on idle but the rest of him was physically in fine fettle for a twelve year old.

"But who is ..." Abby started, however Morag interrupted.

"A boat girl, sixteen years of age, quiet and pretty, from one of the relatively respectable Wrigley families, who control the tobacco imports from Liverpool and own a dozen barges and warehousing in the area. All of course are maintained within the family."

"You've seen her ... and the baby?" Victoria asked, astonished.

"Yes, last night. Her elder brother came to the house and knocked up Williams who woke me discretely. We rode out to their barge with the man. At first I was incredulous, I mean, the boy is still only twelve years old. He of course has no idea whatsoever. Apparently the poor girl was lured by her wayward friends to visit the George public house ... which again, unknown to me, James was visiting regularly to drink ale with Julian's sons, Edward and Zackary. The girl repeated that those two had cajoled and teased James to take her out the back and become a real man like them. She had no idea what was going on and then much later realised she was with child which was kept quiet. They wanted compensating with no fuss and had credible witnesses who would testify if need be, and I could see immediately that with the large number of existing children on board of mixed legitimacy, some dark-skinned would you believe, one extra mouth to feed was unwelcome. But there was no way on God's good earth that baby would be landing inside Orsbrick Hall. So I took an instant decision, and upped their expected compensation considerably on one condition. That the baby girl was to be removed onto the next tobacco ship sailing to America and that no mention would be made again or there would be serious consequences for their business. If asked she would be declared stillborn. Two family members, a young married couple, were to depart next week to join the Puritans. I also paid extra for their sailing and a dowry for the baby. All this was not her fault poor mite, but she should be with them now. End of situation and goodbye Fenella, to hopefully a better life."

"Fenella?" Abby asked instantly as her eyebrows rose, glancing slyly at Victoria.

"Yes, odd name, I must confess."

"Err … it's Gaelic with Scottish roots. Perhaps, Morag, the Wrigley family thought such a name would be appropriate."

"Mmm, indeed, although I've never heard of it before. Look, there's Julian having a cigar outside with Dr Gray, Abigail. Rescued from the clutches of that snake Helena you'll be pleased to see, they've arrived already."

Abby looked distinctly unimpressed.

"Are you not angry with Mr Fazackerley, Morag, for not keeping an eye on his sons?" Victoria asked, equally queasy with the new Julian intimacy emerging and secretly wanting to kick him in the testicles hard.

"Oh no of course not. The man's a widower, he evidently needs a strong woman around him for that sort of thing and boys are boys, they have to grow up some time. No, not a word to Julian will be said either. We've all moved on."

After a hasty goodbye, Julian stamped his cigar into the mud, gathered the time from his pocket watch and leapt off down an alley. Where to, as his destination remained undisclosed, was anybody's guess. But for Morag it was, as she whispered jubilantly to Victoria, likely to be part of his mysterious background to follow up later. Victoria realised something for the first time. Julian's London period in the twenty-first century had never been openly discussed either, always cleverly diverted. She parked that knowledge carefully.

Entering the impressive building, Morag instantly shepherded Victoria towards the Royal Society afternoon lecture, being given once again by Michael Faraday. They left Abby to peruse the interesting paintings on the wall. In another room at the rear there was an exhibition on the topic of how art and science intersect in the natural world, which drew her enthusiasm far more than electric motors. Unfortunately, a problem of how to get rid of the loquacious Dr Gray, whose arm she was being forced to hold, was an urgent requirement, especially as his amorous rejection at Euston had reignited a suffocating bombardment of renewed affection for her as the consolation prize. Much as she loved contemporary Lynton, this transmogrified idiot was decidedly more pain than asset. And he had been drinking heavily, his breath smelt and he was slightly slurring. She looked around for a convenient lonely lady to direct his attention towards … but was met only with dismay. There were none. A loud, 'hail fellow well met' grunt from behind, however, distracted both.

"Good heavens, Gray, what are you doing here? Had a mysterious conversion to scientific erudition? I though the Royal Academy was more your bag, you old reprobate."

A tall and impressive man, dressed smartly in a black suit and white shirt, with a high forehead and a stare of forbidding concentration, which immediately fed Abby with 'beware - highbrow intellectual,' signs, glanced her way, eyeing her red curls and flamboyant dress and bonnet with lustful interest. "I do beg your pardon madam. Dr Gray is a very old friend."

"Babbage, I might have known you'd be around. Moved into the building yet have we or maybe bought the Royal Society outright to house that crazy calculating machine of yours?"

They both roared with laughter, slapping one another's backs as Abby and this man's companion, a much younger and shorter man, stood back, neither knowing quite what to do. Presumably, Abby thought, this must be the very same Charles Babbage, extraordinary mathematician and close associate of the Countess of Lovelace, Morag's friend they would be staying with?

"Miss Warren. May I introduce you to Mr Charles Babbage, a well known scientist and philosopher inside this building. However outside of it I'm not so sure," Dr Gray interjected with a roar, everyone passing looking quite shocked. "Miss Warren is an artist of prodigious talent who I am proud to be sponsoring as her personal and sole agent."

Abby grimaced at Lynton but decided to say nothing right then and shook hands with Babbage, a firm and confident handshake.

"Well, I declare Miss Warren," Babbage commenced. "That announcement may be of some interest to my companion here, a Mr Ruskin, recently returned from a painting tour of Italy, with your parents I believe Mr Ruskin?"

Abby gazed into his handsome, fresh face. He was slightly shorter than her, when she realised immediately. This was the very same, the famous John Ruskin who she had studied prodigiously for her BA degree dissertation. Only one early sepia photograph of him was in circulation when he was a little older but she recognised the features. They shook hands politely as she switched her brain into a warp three overdrive, trying desperately to recall as much of the early Ruskin as she could. In 1841 he was still at Oxford, so Effie Gray, his future wife, was only thirteen years old, his disastrous marriage some way off yet, and he was very much exploring poetry and literature too at this time.

"Miss Warren, it is truly a pleasure to meet you. Tell me. With what style do you project your innermost thoughts and desires onto paper?" he said with a penetrating, deep voice, his gaze transfixed solely onto her face, disarming Abby for a moment. Here was a man whose brilliant future as the greatest art critic of Victorian time, who understood art for its creative and inventive ideals, lay ahead, but the foundations of that focussed, intellectual passion were being dug at a very early stage. Already, she remembered, he had started to make his mark. An unexpected frisson of excitement passed through her from top to bottom, a bizarre confluence of circumstance with Lynton, distracted and ill at ease, stood next to her. But before she could answer …

"Good Lord above, I am most confused with what I see," Lynton suddenly shouted, spitting over Babbage who backed off promptly. "There, down the passageway. Isn't that Mr Turner? What in heaven's name is he doing here? I must seek his counsel immediately." At that, Lynton, without a glance at Abby, tore off into the distance and disappeared down a corridor.

At last, this was her chance to ditch Lynton. "Mr Ruskin? I believe you are the very same John Ruskin who recently won the prestigious Newdigate Prize at Oxford for excellent poetic endeavours? I understand you shared the presentation platform with Mr William Wordsworth, another fine poet. I spent many an enjoyable evening, comparing and contrasting styles."

Ruskin smiled, his teeth were white and near perfect, but she really had to stop obsessing over teeth. His thick hair flopped in a cute quiff over his large forehead and the rest of his face sported the mutton chop sideburns presently in fashion. "I am impressed, Miss Warren, that you are knowledgeable of my literature work. I assumed you are a mere painter."

Babbage looked from one to the other, sensing immediately that he had become the third one out in a crowd and grinned quietly. A highly attractive, older woman of style and intellect would be a fitting distraction for his friend Ruskin, who had become far too tied to his mother's apron strings and was worryingly obsessive of late with the moral rights and wrongs of the world. "John, this seems a good point for me to leave you. I need to attend the lecture, which commences in five minutes."

Ruskin still hadn't taken his gaze away from Abby. "Charles, that is perfectly fine, perhaps I will find you later?"

"Yes, but don't worry, no necessity. Bridge at the club, Saturday?"

"Of course."

Abby interjected. "Mr Babbage. If I may be so presumptuous but do you know Lady McKenzie who is here today?"

Babbage reacted surprised. "I certainly do, I'm just going to find her. Why pray do you ask?"

"Would you please tell her that I will make my own way to the Countess of Lovelace's residence for dinner and meet her then."

"Good heavens, do you know both Morag and my learned friend Ada?" Babbage replied, quite startled.

"Lady McKenzie is my dear cousin. I came with her today but I have yet to make the acquaintance of Lady Lovelace. I am looking forward to being introduced this evening."

"My word, what a small world encircles us, I do declare. I must challenge Ada to work out the probabilities. I'm sure, Miss Warren, you will find her company and deportment very much to your liking. Anyway, I must find Morag, but that should be easy as she will be with Michael Faraday, my other good friend who is lecturing this afternoon. Good day, Miss Warren. Please give my regards to Lady Lovelace and that I will be replying to her latest missive this evening."

Abby nodded, watching Babbage stride off eloquently towards the lecture hall, a man very comfortable in his own skin with his wealth and position in society. She returned to John Ruskin, waiting patiently beside her. "I apologise for my long, delayed answer. Please do call me Abigail. My innermost creative desire is that an artist should observe and reflect nature in its stark purity, and render both moral and material truth onto the canvass, devoid of composition and historic stricture."

Ruskin stared, saying nothing. He had never heard a woman espouse his personal beliefs so lucidly and complimentary. "Like Mr Turner, Abigail?"

"Exactly like Mr Turner, John," Abby replied with a grin, having worked out that Turner had come here for fresh ideas in the exhibition because Ruskin, who was already an ardent devotee and supporter of Turner's controversial approach, had likely asked him. She had no idea except selfish inner desire, why she was engaging with this man and what value it would be, when she reflected in a moment again. There was a distinct purpose. To remove herself from Victoria's space and allow her to interact, distraction free, with Morag and Michael Faraday. In the meantime she had cleverly swapped nauseating Lynton for someone far more interesting if she played her cards right. Lynton obviously was unaware of the connection between Turner and Ruskin and in any case, as usual, he had wandered off to pastures new.

"Abigail, may I offer you the opportunity for a personal guided tour of the Royal Academy, where perhaps we can jointly examine the directions future artistic merit will take us? We have sufficient time and also to take tea later before your dinner appointment. I have my personal carriage outside?"

"I would like that very much," Abby replied with her warmest smile, linking her arm into his. She looked around hastily, no sign of Lynton as they strode out of the door together.

*

Panting to keep up, Victoria struggled with her heavy, long dress and restrictive corset, and rushed through one dingy corridor after the next. Morag was assailing each door with animated urgency as they flew past a variety of startled people, some in familiar white coats, carting around science equipment and other materials.

"Should we be down here Morag? That's the third door labelled private, keep out," Victoria cried, finding her breath and finally catching up with her.

"Ignore all that nonsense. That is where we are heading," Morag replied, pointing ahead.

In front of them, a door was half ajar with a person visible in narrow beige trousers and half-bent over, but his face hidden. As they approached, Victoria caught the sign Michael Faraday FRS etched onto a small brass plate.

"Michael, dearest, are you available quickly?" Morag called out excitedly, fiddling with the new bunches in her hair.

Victoria stared and decided in a second. Yes indeed, they were having some sort of affair. There was a silence, then a deep but quite stentorian voice called out, "Certainly, do enter please." The upper half of the tight- trousered person stood erect and Michael Faraday poked his head around the door, but his warm smile reserved for Morag decidedly faltered seeing Victoria unexpectedly alongside.

"Aah ... you are not alone Lady McKenzie."

Morag, irritated by all this odd formality, strode straight into Faraday's office as Victoria smiled, wondering what was going on here. Michael Faraday stood shorter than her but undoubtedly he was a handsome man, with laughing eyes and a friendly disposition. That much was plain in an instant as he held his arm out for her to enter too.

"No, and evidently neither are you Mr Faraday," Morag uttered, in a disappointed tone. A slim, smart woman in a large, floppy bonnet and blue dress was staring out of the window into the rear garden, and slowly turned.

"Alice, dearest sister, what a pleasant surprise. What are you doing here?" Victoria responded, thinking at lightning speed on her feet. Mauveine was for sure up to something radical.

"Mrs Langton?" Morag spluttered, thrown virtually dumbstruck.

Faraday, stood to the side, hands on his hips, perplexed but bemused with this entourage of women, each one surprised by the other. "Perhaps I should unlock some of the mystery, and then we can all be introduced. Mrs Langton is here on behalf of her husband, the Reverend Thomas Langton of Burscough who corresponded to me about ..." But Mauveine gently intervened.

"Our latest research into how science and religion and the faith of our Lord God, Jesus Christ, can support one another.

My husband and I became aware of Mr Faraday's intense interest in such matters and wished to share our thoughts. I had no idea you were in London, dearest sister. And a pleasure to meet you Lady McKenzie."

"And very interesting it is too," Faraday replied, holding up a thick bundle of written papers, which had been the subject of his close scrutiny the moment they walked in. "Now, may I ask, your name, please madam," Faraday continued, gazing up at Victoria.

Morag had regained her usual composure and eviscerated any sign of disappointment. "This is Mrs Victoria Hammelaar, my new science governess, Michael, who I wrote to you about in my last letters a few days ago? Mrs Langton and Mrs Hammelaar are, as you now know, sisters. Victoria has a formidable practical knowledge of electrical matters, as do her daughters Madeleine and Annabelle who will be directly assisting me in the laboratory with our experimental researches."

Faraday blushed and pointed to a pile of unopened post on his desk. "I most humbly apologise but I have been very remiss opening the mail. However Victoria, may I call you Victoria? It is a great pleasure to meet a fellow science discoverer like Lady McKenzie, sadly too rare in a woman."

Victoria shook his hand warmly. "The pleasure is all mine Mr Faraday. You are the nation's greatest scientist, the integrator of electricity and magnetism which will benefit English society more than any other recent discovery. I am honoured and humbled indeed," she replied, gauging that flattery and praise rather than honours and money, looking at his rather worn but quality suit, would appeal most.

She was not disappointed. His smiling eyes twinkled and he grinned like a little boy receiving a giant lollipop. He had an almost indefinable and handsome charisma, a Nelson Mandela of science who could turn his hand to so many experimental and practical challenges and discover innovative laws of physics and chemistry everywhere. Shame about his conflicted religiosity but the rest of him was a towering mega-intellect, unmatched in the contemporary time she was in. Victoria immediately knew what was turning Morag on and sensed from the corner of her eye all the body language and expression of instant jealousy because she and Morag shared exactly the same analytical mind-set, including about men. Faraday was not exclusive in his attraction towards intellectual female scientists and Morag could see it. Victoria could almost hear his heart beating alongside her own. It was so very, very rare for a man to have this charismatic effect on her too, but then in 2026, scientists were one great, boring, homogeneous mass of anonymous team working and ultra-specialisation. The days of the prodigious Universalist, excelling in all types of science or mathematical disciplines and discovering jaw-dropping generalisation after generalisation had ended long ago, probably finally with the mathematician Poincaré's death in 1911. Meeting Faraday face to face was an individualistic religion all by itself, albeit, for her, a very sensual one. And Victoria was astute enough to notice that she was also having an explosive effect on him, which would need playing very, very carefully indeed.

"However, Mr Faraday," Victoria continued, turning and smiling to Morag, "I think it is important to emphasise the genuine reality. Lady McKenzie is the true science discoverer, especially in chemistry. I am a mere educationalist who follows pioneers like her and you."

Morag's eyes widened, and her posture changed, the stiffness dissipating and a wide grin appeared across her face.

Victoria breathed a silent sigh of relief. "Why, Mrs Hammelaar, how generous is your flattery, thank you. I certainly like to hope I may become a leader in my work, particular in electricity under the watchful eye of the grandmaster here, Mr Faraday."

Mauveine quietly watched the interaction, saying nothing but formulating a tactic. Victoria was creating opportunity.

Faraday glanced at his grandmother clock ticking slowly over the collection of batteries by the wall. He had had enough of this back-slapping, unctuous sanctimony and needed to get to the public lecture and get on with demonstrating some sorely needed practicals. His assistants had taken the motors already. "Aahh ... but Victoria, I have not failed to notice your unusual use of the word scientist, which means you are one of the very few to read Whewell's review of Mary Somerville's excellent treatise in '34 on 'The Connexion of the Physical Sciences' so perhaps you are a pioneering educationalist then."

They all laughed, even Morag, who was still uneasy about Michael's sudden informality addressing Victoria but decided to move on. Jealousy was not her strong suit and was so illogical given her status and that of her governess.

"Michael, I realise we have to make our way into the hall, especially you, but may I have a very quick word in private please. This will have a bearing on your lecture, I do believe heartily," Morag interjected, waving her folder of papers she had brought.

"Of course, let's adjourn next door," he replied as they both disappeared and shut the door.

Victoria turned to Mauveine. "How did you know I was here? In fact why are you here? How is Isi?"

"Much better, he will be pounding the pulpit on Sunday. I called in to Orsbrick Hall first thing. You had all left but

Madeleine explained you were here and why and updated me on her library findings. We have the gaps filled until this year which is excellent news. I knew before you arrived that Morag and Faraday were 'close' and Isi, bless him, had the brainwave of writing the paper on religion and science, as a gateway for me to meet him. I took the next train and came on the hooves, as we say."

"So did we. Pity there are no phones though or even the telegraph universally yet."

Mauveine smiled, and pulled out her iPhone. "Definitely, Victoria. I have to confess, Isi and I have much more empathy with your time than this one!"

Victoria's eyes widened. "How did that get here?"

"I don't know. It was in my bag when I arrived. We haven't figured out how to use it here though."

Victoria laughed. "Yes, a very unique phone indeed. Apple would be very pleased."

"Anyway, I shall have to get back home. From my earlier chat and observations, I can see Mr Faraday has a serious weakness in his relationship with Morag. His Sandemanian faith and the strict Old Testament interpretation is all embracing for him, alongside his loyalty and genuine love for his wife, Sarah and is conflicting his desire for her. Morag, I believe, has some hold on him. I don't know what, but it may hold the key to why they are attracted to one another."

"Do you think their relationship is … err …?"

"You can say it to me." Mauveine grinned. "I grew up liberally remember. Physical with intercourse? I'm not sure. She is a very compelling magnet for his iron will."

Victoria laughed. "I like your symbolism, Mauveine."

Mauveine continued. "Without doubt, they have a deep affair of the mind and emotion, but that is equally difficult for him so his logic may be that he may as well fuck her anyway. Each is as bad as the other. A third party breaking into that intimacy of his conflicted soul could change the parameters of the equation and break the bond. You need to do whatever it takes, Victoria."

"Whatever it takes?" Victoria whispered, an apprehension running through her body, although maybe? Could she?

"I don't need to repeat myself, start with the lecture. Take great care but if you get the chance, use your privileged knowledge to make some impression on him as the speaker. He has a reputation for championing females, probably how Morag came into his sphere of influence. She's been a regular at these lectures for some time through her friend Ada, the Countess of Lovelace."

"Whose house we're staying in and who I'm meeting tonight with Abby, although where she's gone I have no idea. Probably exploring the art and science exhibition with Lynton."

Mauveine smiled again. "Actually, I saw her leaving the building as I came in through the other door, arm in arm with a very delectable looking gentleman, somewhat younger than her, and certainly not Dr Gray."

"Really? Oh my God ... typical. She worries me in that frame of mind."

"I'm sure it has a way and a purpose," Mauveine replied, her lips pursed in amusement.

"That is exactly what concerns me. Listen, Morag and Michael are returning. We'll see you when we get back."

Victoria and Mauveine stood patiently as Morag and Faraday returned in silence, both red in the face and hiding agitation. Something had been said between them or he had overcome his mental anguish and celebrated quickly over a lab bench.

Faraday spoke as Morag sullenly put down her folder onto his desk. "I'm so sorry. I must away to the lecture hall now, please close the door behind you. I hope, Mrs Hammelaar, you will be accompanying Lady McKenzie?"

Victoria smiled. "Of course Mr Faraday, I have been looking forward to it."

Waving to Mrs Langton, who hurried off at the same time, he disappeared, running fast down the long corridor. Morag breathed in deeply, plainly trying to shake off something distressing.

"What is the matter, Morag?" Victoria asked, softly.

"I said something foolish, it is of no consequence. We must hurry and ensure a good seat at the front, Ada and I always take the same preferential places."

"Do you love him?" Victoria suddenly offered, wishing in an instant she could bite her tongue off.

Morag stopped and stared. Then at last she smiled. Victoria was already proving to be a potential and astute friend, someone she should confide in eventually but not yet. She needed to talk to Medora though tonight.

"As I said, it's of no consequence."

*

Back to her composed self, Morag with Victoria behind, strode into the auditorium which was filling up fast and headed to her two favourite seats, spotting Charles Babbage already sat alongside. Immediately she approached he stood up, charming as ever and kissed Morag's hand, then introduced himself to Victoria, who could only mutter a vague pleasantry, feeling overawed with the icons she was meeting. Babbage, yet another giant of the science and philosophy world. He and Morag were exchanging the latest on his Analytical Engine development and on Ada too, Babbage remarking that Ada's recent physical health was giving him cause for concern and that she should reduce her intellectual labours for a while. Faraday appeared on the podium to a tumultuous applause. The large room was now packed out, with every seat filled and little standing room left at the back.

Babbage suddenly turned to Morag, catching Victoria's attention simultaneously, sat in-between. "I almost forgot," he whispered hastily. "Message from your cousin, a Miss Abigail Warren? She said to tell you that she will arrive separately at Ada's tonight for dinner and not to worry. She is in the company of my friend Ruskin this afternoon."

"John Ruskin?" Victoria whispered back, eyes narrowing.

"You know him?" Babbage said, handing her a glass of red wine from the trolley circulating.

"Err … only the name, an art critic?" Victoria replied, incredulous that Abby had wandered off with a complete stranger, even if it was *the* John Ruskin.

Babbage laughed. "He has to get to that stage yet, although he would like to think he was. A little way to go, I'm afraid to say!"

*

Striding quickly along Pall Mall, his bag of pistols over his shoulder, Julian smirked at his good fortune. His sister, whose London townhouse he had just left, confirmed that the Countess of Lovelace would desire him to visit immediately. Caitriona had done a remarkably good job, persuading her friend Ada that she had a brother who was 'highly adept and skilled' at the diagnosis and repair of the latest central heating systems and would 'be conveniently in town today.' Well he was adept at such matters, a useful entrée into the rich Lovelace household. He had a long and acrimonious score to settle once and for all, with Colonel Leigh who was visiting with his wife

Augusta, Ada's aunt, during the afternoon. There would be no way the Colonel could wriggle out of his ten-year-old poker gambling debt this time, and the stakes were high; twenty thousand pounds, with legitimate interest.

He rummaged casually through his pockets for the piece of paper with the address Caitriona had written down. His dismay increased, finding tobacco, coins and a boiled sweet, but no paper. "Damnation and hellfire," he cursed out loudly. He must have dropped it earlier. And Caitriona would now be on the train to Brighton for her weekend holiday. He knew it was St James's something or other but was it Terrace, Walk, Street or Square? And he wasn't sure of the number either. He kicked at a mangy cat scurrying past, missed and cursed again. There was only one thing to do. He would have to return to the Royal Society fast, find Morag and obtain Ada's address. Well, he could use the excuse he had forgotten to ask precisely, earlier, and would be making his way separately to Ada's residence after business. The fact that the business was there would be coincidental.

Reaching Carlton Terrace again, he hurried into the building, panting hard, and rubbed his glasses carefully before gazing around at the huge melee of visitors, gathered in groups and parties. Where should he start? Then, stood quite alone from the rest, perusing with intensity a splendid picture of the three pioneering initiators who had set up the first Royal Society meeting in 1660, he spotted a very beautiful lady, perhaps, he mused, only in her early twenties. She was dressed in the most expensive silk and taffeta dress he had ever seen, exquisitely embroidered and drawn tightly into her astonishingly slim figure. Her short, brown hair, tucked into a pretty, matching bonnet, dropped casually in sensual bunches around her cheek. She radiated the most blooming of health and to his attuned eye, one another interesting attribute, great wealth, noting the large diamond rings on her hand but no wedding ring, as well as copious strings of pearl beads around her neck. A couple of servants stood discretely nearby holding her three tiny spaniel dogs.

Always alert, perfected to a fine art as any intelligent man would run a business, to expanding his network of potential female suitors, especially rich, aristocratic widows, he decided to introduce himself, having reasoned that as a proposition in her own right she was irresistible, but also could well likely be acquainted with Lady McKenzie. He strode up ignoring the aides who stiffened and lowered his top hat.

"Madame, please excuse my intrusion, such a fine picture you are perusing. I couldn't help but notice your most beautiful outfit and wondered if you may be able to help me locate an acquaintance? I have lost her in this panoply of people. I am confident you may know the lady."

She turned, slowly and graciously, eyeing up the rather dashing and enigmatic man stood before her. He was sufficiently astute and experienced with females to sense that he had indeed caught her eye, a great encouragement, and the closer he had become the most attractive she appeared, with a cute, small nose and her reddened lips to die for and kiss. She also had an intelligent demeanour of authority and poise, a characteristic he had sought so hard to find. Without a doubt this woman was a serious contender to the lady at the top of his list to marry—Morag McKenzie.

The servants moved forward ominously, but she summarily waved them away and they stood discreetly back, still holding the dogs. A number of people had stopped and were watching them curiously from a distance, as he felt many eyes upon him.

He took a deep breath and continued unabashed. Why should he care about a bunch of nosy scientists and artists?

"And, Mr …?"

"Fazackerley, madam. Mr Julian Fazackerley at your service, art purveyor and master metal maker."

She smiled, taking in his features with a very knowing determination. "Interesting occupation and you have an unusual name. So, tell me, what do you know about Messrs Wren, Boyle and Wilkins, Mr Fazackerley?"

Fortunately for Julian, his breadth of reading, history and literature always seemed to stand him in good stead with beautiful upper class ladies, as his discussions with Morag on the train confirmed. He enjoyed cultivating a dichotomous air of mystery and confusion, knowing they could never resolve his cultured knowledge with his physicality and occupation, always an aphrodisiac for subsequent conquest. This lady would be no different.

He took off in a deep voice, weaving a detailed diatribe of the early architecture of London, the Great Fire and the need then for a moral, economic and scientific renaissance for the city and the new political atmosphere which the three seventeenth century pioneers had decided such a society could provide. She listened intensely at the erudition, saying nothing but happily admiring his dark eyes, manly physique and intelligent exposition. Without warning she suddenly raised her hand.

"It was rude of me, I almost forgot. You wished to know if I am acquainted with your friend. Who may that be?"

"Not wishing to mislead, madam, I wouldn't quite say a friend, well she is in some ways but I do work for her. She is Lady Morag McKenzie."

The woman giggled. "You exhibit a little enigma and coyness, Mr Fazackerley. Either Lady McKenzie is your friend or isn't. So what is it to be?"

Julian felt himself reddening, she was smart and astute. "Well ... err ... I suppose she has now become a friend."

"Exactly as I surmised," she replied smiling. "You are in luck, sir. I do know Lady McKenzie, as it happens very well indeed. I shall have her brought out."

He realised she must be in the lecture which had commenced. He needed to sneak in and catch Morag's eye, get his address then clear off quickly. And, he especially needed to give this desirable female his calling card for later. "Thank you so much Madam, but now I know where she is I can find her directly, she will not wish to be withdrawn," he said gently but she ignored him.

"She will come for you Mr Fazackerley, I can guarantee it."

Before he could utter another word she walked smartly over to one of her servants, wrote a swift note and handed it to him, before returning. The servant ran off into the lecture hall, whilst Julian watched. It was too late.

"You were saying, about King Charles the Second sponsoring the initial Royal Society. Do you think the present monarchy should do the same? I am not a great fan of this monarchy, Mr Fazackerley. I'm a bit of a revolutionary at heart, are you? Rather an ostentatious and mawking display of affection between the Royal couple I fear?"

Julian laughed. She was a lady of high birth, undeniably, but an interesting rebel and becoming more fascinating by the minute. Hopefully, Lady McKenzie would resist the request and stay put; he needed to extend this chat a little longer. By the number of people still staring, she was well known, so he must not forget his card; probably, he suspected a famous actress. He would answer her question first then request her name.

"I'm sure the Queen would not wish to bother her silly head about such serious matters. Continuous child bearing seems to be her preoccupation, and she should leave this important decision for science solely to her wise husband, Prince Albert, a person of true standing and economic vision. I must confess he is a man who I could do business with in turning this country into the greatest leader of empires ever. Now, may I request the pleasure of knowing who I am addressing, dear lady?"

The woman giggled and then pointed to her servant who was accompanying Lady McKenzie. "Your friend is coming exactly as I said, Mr Fazackerley. Goodness me, she does look a little unhappy, I would suggest you treat her with caution."

He smiled. "Of course," and turned to greet Morag who brushed him aside rudely, thrust the note back in the servant's hand and walked slowly to the woman.

At that point, the colour drained out of Julian's face as he watched Morag give a gracious curtsy.

"Your Majesty. I sincerely apologise, ma'am, with all my heart for this erroneous intrusion."

Julian, his mind in a whirl of disbelief and his stomach pounding, stepped forward with a deep bow. "Your Majesty, I too apologise for my contemptible and stupid lack of recognition … I had no idea …"

But Queen Victoria cut him off and waved him to one side. Morag stared with disbelief at his idiotic red face, but she was the one to be severely embarrassed. The aide quietly sidled up to him and surreptitiously back-handed him the note.

Queen Victoria, her face beaming with delight at a rare intervention to break up another boring exhibition visit, summoned Lady McKenzie closer. "Don't be so fretful Morag, I do understand, given your position," she whispered with a smirk. "He is rather erudite and truly delectable and I'm quite envious, but I strongly advise … watch that man like a hawk. He is a serial womaniser beyond any doubt."

"Thank you, ma'am," Morag replied quietly, fuming like gunpowder about to ignite.

"Now, my carriage awaits, I must be away, I have some child bearing to deal with, Mr Fazackerley." The servants and aides immediately gathered alongside some ladies in waiting and others who suddenly sprang out of nowhere from the shadows. "McTavish," she called out to the most senior. "Take Mr Fazackerley's card out of his trembling hand and fix up an appointment with His Royal Highness Prince Albert. I think they have some empire building to discuss."

Her aides and hangers-on tittered.

"Don't look so glum Mr Fazackerley," she continued. "I must say, I was amused, very amused. Good day to you both."

In an instant Queen Victoria was whisked away through the main entrance, hidden amongst her entourage, as Morag and Julian watched her depart, both mortified.

She turned violently towards him. "What on earth in God's own name, Julian, do think you've been doing?" she hissed. "I'm ruined, the laughing stock of London society. Are you really so inept? And I've missed one of Mr Faraday's most important lectures."

He looked quickly at the note and blanched. Fuck.
*Dear Lady McKenzie. Your iron man lover is waiting in the foyer for you. With kind regards. Victoria Saxe-Coburg-Gotha.*

"Oh Morag, I really had no idea whatsoever it was the Queen herself, she looks so young. I'm so genuinely sorry, an unforgiveable mistake. What can I do to make amends?" he replied, wishing he could blow his head off immediately with one of his pistols. "Actually I'm sure the Queen was merely engaging in a little trivial distraction and fun. The novelty, like the news in yesterday's eel and chip papers, will have disappeared and be forgotten in a day or two. Everyone will know it's a joke."

"You can start by addressing me as Lady McKenzie from now on," she whispered curtly, looking around desperately, but fortunately, as the fun and spectacle was now over, the gorping bystanders had all drifted off. "A bit of fun? Am I hearing you correctly? For your sake, you'd better be right, and a joke, in the worst possible taste, it undoubtedly is. What on earth you said to the Queen is beyond my imagination. I'm going to find a carriage and ride out somewhere, take some air and reflect. Fuck you, Mr Fazackerley, for ruining my day totally."

She stormed off as he watched, his mouth gaping as she ran outside and jumped into the first carriage. He hadn't seen such venomous anger directed his way from a woman for such a very long time and from Morag, of all the people he wished least of all. He too needed some air and think. Then he realised, the real reason he had returned and he still didn't know the Countess of Lovelace's address. He would start with St James's Square, only a short walk away. Somebody there would know her number, angrily picking up his bag of pistols. He was going to blow Colonel's Leigh's head clean off his body.

*

**Earlier, and inside the lecture hall:**
The applause had died down and the room went silent as Faraday opened his address. Morag appeared happy, especially when he glanced her way with a special smile.

"Ladies and gentleman, I thank you warmly for attending today, I see many familiar faces. Although I must be careful that I don't say too much or I'll have no material left for my next Christmas Lecture."

A buzz of laugher spread around the room with a few appreciative claps.

"I would like to start by relating something I wrote in my diary, many years ago as a young man. An important requisite for a lecturer, though perhaps not really the most important, is a good delivery, although to all true philosophers, science and nature will have charms innumerable in every sense of address," He glanced fleetingly at Victoria, who blinked hard. "Yet, I am sorry to say that the generality of mankind cannot accompany us one short hour unless the path is strewn with flowers. Or, as Newton once said, we must be grateful for our endeavours, only borne by standing on the shoulders of giants before us."

The room erupted, they loved his every word. Faraday, Victoria thought, was one of the first science celebrities to enter the popular psyche. No wonder Einstein once had a painting of Faraday in pride of place over his desk.

"Now, onwards to more intensive matters. I wish to unveil my most advanced electric motor to date … and hypothesise that we may one day substitute these wonders of electricity for the hot and dirty steam engines of the locomotives we are all now beginning to experience and love."

Victoria delved deep into her past physics knowledge, running though her understanding, many years back, of how Faraday's basic observations on electromagnetic induction had underpinned the development of motors, generators and transformers. She had eventually specialised in physical and organic chemistry, but her mathematics was always first class and she was one of the few in her group at university who properly understood and could work with Maxwell's equations.

When was Maxwell? As Faraday demonstrated his motor, looking like it was based on Morag's new wound coil design, and hooked onto around fifteen battery cells in series, she quickly harnessed her knowledge of these early discoveries into some logical order. Maxwell was definitely a step too far. His famous field equations were published in the 1860s, but the principle may not be. Faraday was running the motor over twenty-five volts, perhaps with the power of a modern portable drill Julian perpetually carried around, and by using a worm gearing, it was slowly pulling a heavy weight across the table, showing the significant inherent torque available.

The audience, as ever with Faraday's demonstrations, were mesmerised and Morag beside her was transfixed into a daze, pleased as punch that he had read some of her letters after all and had merely been teasing. Victoria glanced at Charles Babbage, busy writing line after line of mathematics. She knew some of his biography and that he had been, in his final year, the top mathematician at Peterhouse College in Cambridge but some religious dispute disallowed him from being formally examined to claim senior wrangler. Perhaps he was a non-believer. She saw he was trying to formulate Faraday's words and ideas as Faraday spoke, directly into a form of advanced calculus, integrating and differentiating various functions and attempting solutions, but lacking the correct vector tools to pre-date Maxwell's success. But she could work out that Babbage already was putting into mathematics the basics of what would become those field equations, a formidable intellect, live in progress beside her.

Babbage caught Victoria methodically concentrating on his scrawling and realised she had a talent and a grasp of what he was trying to do. "Sadly, Faraday is no mathematician, even basic algebra is beyond him," he whispered, as a number of people at the back were asking questions and a noisy debate ensued. "I see from within your mind's eye, you are erudite in advanced mathematics. Faraday continues to spout all this fantasy of lines of force as proof of an electric field but until someone puts his experimental genius into more concise mathematical terminologies, then few will believe him. Do you agree?"

She nodded and amended one of his formulae with her pencil, forcing him to grin. Morag glanced over annoyed that she didn't catch either the gist or the conversation.

"So Mrs Hammelaar. What is your opinion, please, of my electric train hypothesis? A future fact or mindless fiction? But, rules of the game here, you must justify your response."

The room went silent and Victoria looked up and around. Faraday was standing before her, hands folded and waiting for an answer. Morag crossed her legs angrily. Michael was at it again, teasing unsuspecting women in the audience but he always had directed the questions to her of late. How unfair and disrespectful to pick on and make fun of a lowly governess. Muttering and tittering were now permeating the room.

Morag whispered in her ear. "Victoria, if you have anything to say, you stand up and face the crowd. Otherwise, as I believe you must, say nothing and he'll move on. I'm sorry he's deliberately embarrassed you, I will have words later."

Victoria however felt her hackles rising. That was the trouble being a McKenzie female, they take no shit especially 1841 patriarchal male arrogance. She drew a deep breath. This could be an opportunity as well as a challenge 'you must do what is necessary' still ringing in her head. And she stood up.

Morag felt instant alarm as Victoria turned to the silent crowd, mustering up her confident public speaking persona. "Well Mr Faraday, thank you for the opportunity to comment.

If you do what I suggest you will not only foretell the future but make lots of money and perhaps become famous. But if not then you will indeed be remembered as a serial fantasy science fictionaliser."

There were gasps and then laughter from the audience. Such a forthright and witty reply was completely unheard of from a woman. Even Morag sat back and re-crossed her legs slowly, stunned. Her instinct was right all along. Her governess used a language unlike any woman she ever knew. She really did have to find out Victoria's true past. Babbage smiled. Fireworks were in the air again, such fun. Faraday smirked awkwardly but remained unfazed. His instinct was also correct, and he too had expected it.

Victoria continued. "I believe Mr Faraday that we first need to manufacture a staging point, let us call it a half-way house, a hybrid even to test your hypothesis as good scientists must. We already know battery power is limited and costly. You will therefore need to embrace the reversibility of the electro-magnetic field and build a scaled-up dynamo in the same manner as your motor, to the design specifications which Lady McKenzie here has already experimentally proven work. Then, using simple gearing, a slow moving steam engine will drive the dynamo to a high speed which in turn will power your electric motor, which in turn will drive all the wheels on the track independently and increase frictional forces and reduce slipping. Lady McKenzie has also demonstrated that an electric motor pursues a high torque right from start-up and thus costly gearboxes, mechanical linkages and other weighty additions can be eliminated, making locomotives more efficient and faster. I hope Mr Faraday that you like my vision for future rail travel."

There was a stunned silence in the room. Victoria gauged she had gone as far as she could without raising incredulity, and used the opportunity deliberately to promote Morag once more as a credible scientific investigator. However, she had not appreciated the cultural disbelief with her provocative and unheard of female challenge of a male science icon of the time. What she had said and how she presented it was far more revolutionary than even Morag had attempted.

"Hear, hear," Babbage shouted and stood up. "I think, Faraday my good friend, with Mrs Hammelaar's Rocket Two, you have been well and truly strung up by the proverbials on this occasion as we say in the navy. I'm afraid the ladies are coming en masse gentlemen, you'd better be on your guard."

A roar of laughter, approval and clapping commenced. In the raucous commotion, someone had sneaked in and caught the attention of Morag, whispering something in her ear, whereupon she stood up, face like thunder, and departed quickly out of a side door, watched with some concern by Victoria.

Faraday, in his usual way, was far more intrigued by Morag's new and beautiful companion. In fact he was more than intrigued. This woman was supposedly a governess, but with an intellect and fiery passion unlike any female tutor he had ever met in his entire life. His emotions were being stupidly ripped apart. He needed to explore more about Mrs Hammelaar immediately and decided the time was ripe to shut off the lecture.

"Well gentlemen, I had better quell this female revolution in our midst before it's too late by asking no more questions. We have come to a timely end. Mrs Hammelaar has provided much serious food for thought, so I would like to thank you all for your forbearance. The Royal Society will see you next month and the bar and art exhibition remain open. Good day, all."

As everyone rushed off, Victoria finished chatting and shook hands with Charles Babbage before looking around for Morag. Still no sign of her anywhere. What message had got her out of the lecture hall so suddenly? A couple of Faraday's technicians had just finished talking to him when he suddenly jumped down off the podium and strode straight towards her, his laughing eyes twinkling with delight.

"Mrs Hammelaar, I would be honoured to hear more about your ideas. Your unexpected contribution today brought the roof down, metaphorically speaking, and I have to tell you, I am old and wise enough to believe that underneath your beautiful bonnet lurks a formidable brain of technological vision and mathematical substance."

"Mr Faraday, you are so very kind, but Lady McKenzie who I am accompanying has strangely vanished. I need to find her."

Faraday waved his arm. "Finding Morag is of no consequence. May I call you Victoria? You are a widow I believe?"

"Err … yes to both, but I'm afraid I must …" Victoria spluttered, wondering how he knew, and she felt suddenly desperately conflicted with a huge and unexpected desire to continue the day with Michael Faraday.

"No need, Victoria. Morag has unfortunately left the building in a hurry and departed on elsewhere. It appears that one of her employees, a certain Mr Fazackerley, made a rather embarrassing nuisance of himself in the lobby, which has had … mmm … unfortunate ramifications. She has gone to settle the matter urgently. But let us not trouble ourselves about Lady McKenzie. Would you like to come to my room for a celebratory sherry and I would love to personally show you the splendid library and other facilities in this wonderful building. Finally, I will take you personally in my carriage this evening to your next destination that Babbage tells me is the Countess of Lovelace's residence, which I know very well. It's not far, walkable even, but I really wouldn't want you to spoil that lovely dress in the mess outside."

She smiled coyly. What, she thought fast on her feet, had stupid Julian done to cause Morag to abandon her like this? Going after her in an alien London made no sense. Where would she start? The only rational decision was to calm down and indulge herself for the rest of the afternoon, with a sensual gentleman giant who was turning her on in quite ridiculous ways, but so what? And, with a guarantee to be graciously returned to Ada's house later where Morag would end up anyway? The decision was a no-brainer.

*

Journeying to the Royal Academy building on Piccadilly took far longer than Abby anticipated, partly because a long trail of large pigs, crossing the road on St James Street, broke loose and pandemonium took hold with stallholders and traders scattering as the pigs ran amok with their owners chasing them blindly from one side to the other. This greatly amused her and John Ruskin whilst they sat tightly in their carriage, the driver keeping a firm rein on the horses. Ruskin instantly recited one of his ironic poems on the intelligence of animals versus the common man, causing her to laugh hugely when the side rocked precariously side to side, as a giant sow with at least ten small piglets brushed past squealing. She was instantly thrown into his chest, and he held her protectively, gazing into her eyes and smiling with that impish grin and their lips met. Fuck idiot Lynton, he had his chance, was the last thing running through her brain as she responded with passion. The carriage rumbled on slowly towards its destination but the rest of the surroundings disappeared into a blur, until they stopped outside the Academy. She hadn't had a kiss like that for over twenty years. She knew their age gap was considerable but Abby neither cared nor counted, and it seemed to have no detrimental impact on Ruskin's ardour, demonstrating a strong desire for an older woman. But, as she would be quick to point out to anyone who asked, especially Victoria, an older woman very far from being mutton dressed as lamb. Where fashion and looks were concerned Abby had kept up the same slim and sultry appearance in 1841 as in 2026.

Fumbling amongst the swathes of long, thick clothing and undergarments, was a significant challenge, for even the most ardent and athletic Ruskin, and she firmly decided this was not the place for detaching anything either, but pondered that they were planning to head for his home later. However, in the interim he certainly knew where to find her bare thigh, beyond stocking top, and direct his exploring fingers with fast precision. As she gasped, he simultaneously murmured Aphrodite, whence reels of flashback ran headlong through her mind of John Ruskin's disastrous marriage to come. The eventual unpleasant and public divorce denunciation of his marital problem and this reality in the carriage, live and lively, did not compute in her brain whatsoever. As arms and hands flayed and fumbled, he pressed tightly against her in those yellow, drainpipe trousers, looking like they would split any second. The court battle myth of his contested impotency and marital non-consummation that led to immediate divorce, had just been exposed to perfection, confirmed by a judicious fondle. Poor Effie Gray must have been doing something seriously wrong on that infamous wedding night, especially because her paintings were of a very attractive young woman.

But then his ardour for Effie had begun when she was only twelve. In fact he had earlier declared that he was already writing poetry for his good friend Effie, but that he would compose sonnets twice as long for the lovely Abby.

The answer to the enduring Ruskin mystery now seemed totally clear to her. Darling John had casually muttered, in one passionate exclamation, what all the literary analysts for the next hundred years had debated and strenuously argued over.

Feeling the carriage shudder to a halt, she gently pushed him away, accompanied by a vintage Abby smile and adjusted her clothing. They had serious art to peruse and debate. He grinned, jumped out of the carriage, plonked his top hat on and opened the carriage door with a flourish, holding out his hand for his new lady. This was a habit she could distinctly get used to. A line of carriages cluttered up the drive, numerous females of all ages, some looking quite prissy and cantankerous, were also being led out. But whether it was his singularly dashing appearance, with a style that made most of the men around look very dowdy, or whether she looked more naturally lascivious than normal, she wasn't quite sure. Probably both because the incoming visitors all stopped and stared quietly, and a couple of attendants ran out of the entrance to greet him. If looks could kill, but that had never bothered her in all of her forty-five years. Being the centre of attention, unlike Victoria, was her natural default.

"Mr Ruskin, sir," one of the footmen cried out, controlling the crowd. "I have the last two tickets left for the special exhibition by Angelica Kaufmann. The Director says they are on the house if you would like to supply the Gazette with a hopefully favourable critique of our curation?"

Ruskin gazed at Abby. He was smitten in that intense artistic way she hadn't experienced since doing her doctorate.

"Well my darling. When love and skill work together, they can expect a masterpiece can they not? When you and I build, let us believe we can build forever."

Abby nodded, mesmerised. He was genuinely a man of lovely words as well as images. Little wonder she was turned on.

Ruskin took the tickets promptly. "Tell Worthington that we accept his kind offer and a piece will be jointly written by me and my talented new artist discovery, Miss Abigail Warren."

"Certainly, Mr Ruskin and Miss Warren. Do come this way please. The crowds are huge today, but I will direct you both straight inside, as Mr Worthington requests."

She linked his arm and they strode majestically, like Royalty, past the long queues and into the special exhibition room, where various paintings were on display along the walls.

"It was unforgivably remiss of me, Abigail," he murmured into her ear, "but I should have queried and confirmed your opinion of Angelica Kaufmann's art before we entered."

"On the contrary, John, I am happy to defer, as your guest for this wonderful afternoon, to your choice and personal desires. Your eyes instantly sparkled when her name was raised, so it would have been most impudent and improper of me to even dream of contradicting, when enthusiasm for this artist glowed radiantly from your temples." Shit, she thought, she was beginning to match Victoria already for eloquent bullshit.

He gently took her hand and kissed it. "All that is good in life, my darling, is the expression of one soul talking to another, and is precious according to the greatness of the person that utters it. And I wish your opinion above all other. What do you see about you? Give me your impressions from the heart with your sweet voice that is all I want to hear. When a man is wrapped up solely in himself he makes a pretty small package."

He handed her a welcome glass of wine, as she carefully studied the paintings. She had a familiarity with this artist but no deep knowledge and even that was a long time back. Eighteenth century female artists being exhibited were rare, but the pièce de résistance effused from the canvases in an instant. She knew formalised practical training for women, in shape, perspective and colour at that time, was virtually zero, like all other modes of education. But these pictures by Kauffman displayed an originality and perfection that jumped out from the walls. She gathered her opinion carefully, concentrating with intensity and quickly reconstructed her approach to fine art analysis for which she had gained a top degree. "I will say this John. Angelica Kauffman's work is one of the finest examples of history painting I have seen."

His eyes narrowed. What unheard of expression was this?

She sensed the need to clarify and spoke slowly but measured. "In my opinion this art form is the most elevated to create in the Western world and for a woman who would have had no access as you have had to practical training, the work is remarkable. She is an artist of genius, a prodigy no less. By history painting, I mean work defined by its subject matter not its artistic style, a representation of human action based on themes from history, religion, mythology and literature. Look around you at these wonderful depictions. She has self-learned extensively in biblical knowledge, art theories and human anatomy, but the most remarkable are the subjects … lots of nudes. I love nudes, all perfectly produced, but they are male nudes, access to which she would have been denied, because of the over moralistic attitude of today. This work, I believe, should be highly sought by patrons for its originality. So we have an opportunity to draw attention to her brilliance and, if you so believe and I am drawn to the possibility that you do, we can extol the virtues and benefits for encouragement of formal training for women, giving them equal opportunity to cultivate their artistic talents by showing, through this exhibition, what is possible for a female artist to achieve."

He stopped and smiled. "I can truly see, hear and smell your passion for both learning and art. I assume, dear Abigail that you too have had to strive to perfect your skill inside a deep well of lonely imagination and lack of the bonhomie we male artists discover together, whether being creative or critical. What is your source of inspiration?"

"Colour, dearest John. Bold, inventive, frightening colour, as used by the brilliant Monsieur Delacroix."

"I understand completely. A worthy challenge, I do declare. I am desperate to see your creations, curated by that odd man Babbage and I met earlier, Dr Gray."

"I would prefer for you to take that rein solely and whip me into desirous production. Dr Gray has no formal or legal exclusivity; it is in his mind and talk, not my reality. Would you consider such a proposition?"

She bit her tongue. Her enthusiasm and desire for Ruskin was taking over her sense and rationality, she had to cool and calm it. The time had come to depart, but he sensed too that moments together were slipping away and intervened.

He held her hand, oblivious to the gossiping nearby of such a flagrant public demonstration of his passion for her. "Of course, I would love nothing better, dear Abigail. I suggest we talk of this again in the very near future. Your analysis of the artist around us will be my completed journalism and I have no need to amend. I shall write all this up exactly as you have perfectly spoken and submit it to the Gazette forthwith, after giving a little more concentrated thought to the subtleties of distinction between history and historical painting. I believe,

Miss Warren, you have invented a new genre for we critics to percolate amongst the hungry public. Let us depart. I am mindful you have an evening appointment and my residence, well I must confess, my parent's residence presently but only for now whilst I complete my studies, is around the corner. Tea? To finish off such a wonderful day?"

Abby thrust her arm back into his. "Yes please, Mr Ruskin," she whispered with a smile, but wondering whether his parents were around and whether they had time to get to know one another more intimately.

They arrived and alighted at a magnificent row of identical but large four-storied terraced townhouses plus a cellar-basement, each residence resplendent with a frontage of matching marble pillared entrances and beautiful small gardens. Ruskin's house was in the middle. Indubitably, this part of Piccadilly was one of the most upmarket in London. As they approached, the door opened smartly and a large, rotund butler welcomed him in with a great roaring voice.

"Jackson," Ruskin bellowed back, each pleased to see the other. "This is my companion, Miss Abigail Warren, an artist of great repute and standing. Are my parents available? I would like very much to introduce her."

"Welcome milady, it is a pleasure to meet you," Jackson boomed with genuine delight, eyeing Abby up and down with some precision. "Please come this way, the chill is beginning to set in Miss Warren. Allow me to take your coat. Now Mr Ruskin, I must tell you that your mother and father unexpectedly departed this lunchtime for a Billingsgate market meeting and they are not expected back until later in the evening. Shall I ensure dinner for Miss Warren is also prepared?"

"Sadly, not today Jackson as Miss Warren has an ongoing engagement, but I am sure she will be returning soon. Will you not Miss Warren?"

"Yes, I very much look forward to meeting your father, a successful sherry and wine importer so I am told," Abby replied softly. "And I love sherry."

John Ruskin smiled, pleased that incredibly she knew so much about him, a remarkable woman.

"I must confess," he continued. "My mother is the true enthusiastic tutor and educator in the family, and to her I owe the essence and foundation of my entire knowledge and enthusiasms for art and literature. Although sometimes I must remind Mama that she has to release my shackles and let me fly off like a bird."

Abby winced. Meeting his mother would need to be treated with delicate caution, potential cries of baby snatcher immediately sprang to the fore. Then she pondered. Was she too old yet to still have a baby?

The butler remained standing, patiently, as Ruskin turned back to him. "In which case, Jackson, I will take tea in my rooms. I wish to show Miss Warren some of my latest drawings and discuss her collection I wish to curate."

Abby caught a whisker of a smirk cross Jackson's mouth. "Of course, Mr Ruskin, you go on right up, sir. I won't disturb you and will leave a tray of refreshment and cakes on the table outside." He nodded and disappeared around the corner, his booming voice bellowing instructions to the maid, Peggy.

"I'm afraid I'm up in the eyrie," Ruskin murmured. "But I have a nice suite, with gorgeous views over the park. I hope you don't mind the steep climb; the final stairs are a little narrow. Please, follow me."

Wishing she had taken up Victoria's advice and renewed her gym membership, Abby stifled her panting and entered a magnificent suite of rooms, including a small study, mostly taken up with a massive mahogany desk off a very comfortable sitting room, replete with a large sofa and two armchairs. Warm rugs were scattered over the polished oak flooring. As expected, floor to ceiling shelves, lining the stripe papered walls, were stuffed full with books of all types and sizes. The covings on the walls were intricately decorated as was the painted ceiling with gold inlays, the steep rise of the roof constructed above. The attic design was unusual, probably, she realised, an extended and elevated roof with sloping windows one side and large Georgian windows on the other. She peered through the end door to see a huge, luxuriously covered four poster bed sat atop a highly patterned Persian carpet. Another small door was visible inside.

"I see you admiring the unusual layout, Abigail. I actually designed the suite myself and father paid for the roof to be raised and altered as per my drawings. Architecture is as much of a passion as water colour painting and sketching. We even have recently installed the first water closets on the terrace, in fact we have four in the house, one of which I insisted be built up here as an ensuite, a concept which I believe will become popular in the fullness of time. But we really must, in London, start to build proper sewers. The river stench is becoming untenable for healthy living."

Abby nodded impressed, staring out through the tiny window panes at a wonderful view of a small park with mature lime and elm trees just coming into leaf, although she was unsure where she was looking. Perhaps this green space no longer existed in London. Ruskin had a mature foresight for his years. She smelt a faint whiff of cheroots in the air, noticing his desk, covered in handwritten papers and sketches, with an ashtray full of stubs, undoubtedly a man for the cigar when composing his thoughts.

She needed to get her thoughts together immediately and decided there and then. Time and tide wait for no woman. A rustling and clattering outside suggested that tea was being left.

She turned slowly and smiled, happy that he too was gazing all over her. "May I suggest that you bring in the tea, whilst I use your water closet … and then lock the door?"

He breathed in deeply and his face reddened, a positive sign for what she no longer had any qualms about doing. On emergence from the most positive freshen-up she had experienced, she walked across, watching him fiddling with the china cups and saucers and a slab of fruit cake. He looked up and she thrust her arms around his slim body.

"Would you like your Aphrodite to dispense with all these encumbrances and spread out over your irresistible four poster bed? And my Adonis, disposal of unnecessary clutter applies to you too I'm afraid," she purred, undoing the stiff buttons on his silk shirt and pulling mischievously at the black hairs.

"Perhaps we should dispense with the tea," he blurted, breathing heavily.

"And you can put that pencil down, sketching comes later."

"Aphrodite and Adonis, you mean like Titian painted?" he murmured softly, moving his lips to hers.

"Even better than Titian," Abby replied, hastily tugging off his belt.

*

Julian Fazackerley turned the next corner and stared, bemused at the opulence of St James's Square, a very grand complex of houses indeed. Caitriona was right; the residence of a wealthy Countess had to be fitting to match her status. This had a good chance of being the correct street. Ada Lovelace sounded like a woman he should have got to know aeons back. He grimaced momentarily, as he recalled with disgust the fiasco he had launched earlier, stumbling into a right Royal mess of his own making indeed. He may have to accept that he had permanently burned his boats with the beautifully poised Lady McKenzie, who he had been falling for in a significant way. He remained incredulous that he must have been the only person in that damned room who didn't recognise the Queen. Little wonder everyone stared, although being the perpetual optimist he did conjecture whether she actually would tell her husband, Prince Albert. Something no doubt to amuse both of them in bed, an activity they indeed cloyingly spent a lot of time indulging in, so Caitriona's gossiping lady friends bitched about.

The question was who to discretely ask for the correct number. But immediately he spotted a suitable street-seller and with the lure of half a crown, five boxes of matches and three candles, which he shoved peremptorily into his bag, he continued towards the impressive frontage and bright blue door of number twelve, one of the biggest of all the town houses around.

He pulled the long handled bell and after an extended silence the door creaked open and a very elderly man, with snow white hair and a stooped figure, stood before him. His hands trembled in a very distracting manner, which Julian was immediately drawn to stare at.

"Yes sir, what can I do for you?" he whispered in a croaky voice.

Julian tipped his hat. "Good afternoon, my name is Fazackerley. I have an appointment with the Countess of Lovelace, a certain problem with the central heating?"

"Sorry sir, you'll have to speak up if you may, hearing is not what it was."

Julian repeated himself as the man picked up a large ear trumpet and shoved it to his head.

"Can you repeat that again sir, only no need to shout, you be waking up the dead over the road, if you please?"

Julian, feeling a wave of severe exasperation suffuse through his entire body, was beginning to believe this nightmare day was never meant to end, and perhaps he should depart forthwith. He repeated the whole thing concisely for the definite last time.

"Thank you sir. I expect plumbers are always aggressive by nature, walloping pipes all day."

"I'm not actually a plumber," he replied, but the old butler either couldn't or didn't want to hear him.

"Jeeves, who on earth is at the door?" a stentorian female voice bellowed out, which he did catch immediately, also making Julian jump. He stared up the long corridor.

"Her ladyship is expecting you Mr Fazackerley. Give me your hat and coat and follow the sound … fourth door on the left. Countess would like a word first. Shall I take your bag of tools to the scullery?"

Julian picked it up hastily. He had indeed brought some tools from Caitriona's place, but hidden underneath a large cloth were the pistols, primed and ready. "Err, no thank you Jeeves, I can look after them."

"Please yourself sir," Jeeves replied. "Whisky? I shall be bringing her ladyship's regular malt anyway as the time has reached three o'clock already."

"Yes please," Julian shouted, now seriously wondering what sort of a place this was.

"Good, something cheered you up anyway," he mumbled and shuffled off down the corridor with Julian's belongings.

Tentatively looking into each empty but seriously opulent room as he passed, and hearing giggles further down, he came to the fourth door, partly ajar and knocked.

"Please come in Mr Fazackerley," a soft but firm voice replied, not at all like the bellow he had heard. It couldn't have been the same person. He entered slowly to be greeted by a tall and very pretty woman, dressed in a blue and white complicated, patterned silk dress, wrapped in a shawl and scarf with an unusual motif, hanging down her back. He was drawn instantly to her ample figure, smooth pale skin and unusually large coiffure of two brown curls hanging down each cheek. A decorated headband with a prominent brooch above her broad forehead, held the rest of her hair, piled up and adorned with tiny yellow flowers from the garden. Caitriona, as ever, was absolutely correct, having insisted the Countess of Lovelace was a woman he would be immediately attracted to. She had not only immense style and fashionable appeal but radiated an intensity of intellectual thought, unusual for a woman, matching that even of Lady McKenzie. Caitriona had said the Countess was, amongst other things, a very talented mathematician and that her husband was rarely at home.

Lady Lovelace stared right through him and instantly analysed this very handsome man from tip to toe, working out exactly what Morag saw in him. Normally she would not have countenanced ever seeing an artisan. He would have been sent to the job straightaway, but this was no ordinary tradesperson, just as she suspected. A brother of her adorable friend Caitriona was worth meeting face to face, especially as Caitriona had never mentioned she had a brother in the last twenty years of their acquaintance. And Morag had alluded, in

319

a titter that gave away in a second far more than Morag intended, that 'her blacksmith' had an unusual liking for and knowledge of English literature and fine art as well as being an inventive metal engineer. In Ada's mind that mixture of male talent did not compute without further scientific investigation.

And, she was bored and tired, especially with the debilitating bleeding and stomach ache that continued to thwart her after her third child, although lately she felt much better. Such a difficult birth, she would not be having any more if she had her way and besides, she hardly saw husband William these days, always off to their grandiose Ockham Park estate in Sussex or gadding around the country with some obsessive building project and the buying of even more property. And Charles Babbage was becoming equally elusive, either enmeshed in gearwheels and drive shafts or permanently camping out at number ten Downing Street for yet more eye-watering handouts from the government. She would set some intrigue in place to amuse herself. Morag would be coming later.

She held out her hand which he kissed delicately, always a good start and Ada invited him to sit with her near the small fire burning in the grand Adam fireplace, which took up half the wall. Jeeves walked in with a fine cut glass decanter of whisky and poured out a generous helping in the two matching glasses, before departing slowly and shutting the door behind.

"Now, Mr Fazackerley. Like Lady McKenzie I am not a great lover of formality, only in my mathematical studies. So what name, pray, may I be calling you?"

"Err … I am Julian Fazackerley, Countess."

"Please Julian … do call me Ada. Everyone else does apart from my husband who insists on calling me always by my first name Augusta and I hate the name with a vengeance. Do you think it is an awful name Julian?" she replied with a tiny smile.

Instantly he realised. A trap, this is a woman of intelligent cunning and guile who likes her own way where men are concerned, mustn't do a repeat of the fiasco earlier. Have to try and be just as smart.

But whilst he was contemplating, she suddenly took the opportunity to dive across to his bag and in an instant opened the top and delved inside as he watched in horror. "Now what have we here Julian, of course, tools of the trade. I adore tools, they have an aesthetic appeal all their own, do you not agree?"

She grinned mischievously. "You may play with my boiler later. My diagnosis will prove correct; pressure loss is creating the reduction in latent steam fluidity necessary to provide convection to the required room temperatures. I have done the heat calculations three different ways and reached the same result … I'm sure the tightening of a few pipe collars in the primary output circuits with this foot-print will do the trick," she continued, waving a wrench triumphantly in the air. "The rest of the idiot plumbers who have already visited have no understanding of calorific theories and wouldn't believe me, especially coming from a woman. But your sister, Caitriona, vouches you are a little different from the common artisan. Is that correct Julian?"

He suddenly realised that he had gulped down one glass of whisky and she had topped it up full again but had hardly sipped her own, and that best Scottish malt was very potent, like explosive nectar.

"Well, I do believe …" he replied, desperately trying to stitch a coherent sentence together when she rummaged headlong into the bag again as he stared, helpless to prevent her given the circumstances.

Facile with her fingers, it took her a micro-second to realise there was more to Mr Julian than even Caitriona had hinted at.

"Now what tools have we here ... mmm ... a secret compartment? My word Julian, what a fine pair you have." She giggled again, waving a pistol in each hand madly in the air.

Alarmed, he pulled himself up sharply and tripped over the pet spaniel sat at his feet, catching himself with a wobbly grasp of the standing lamp. The three candles fell with a thud onto the floor, just missing the dog who yelped off onto the couch. "Really Ada, please be most careful, the pistols are primed," he cried holding out his hand delicately to take them.

"I can see that Julian. Don't worry. I do know intimately how to use a gun, the longer and thicker the barrel the better the shot, don't you believe? Here, perhaps you had better put them away now. We don't want to frighten the servants."

She handed them and the wrench back to him as he carefully packed them inside again. Now what was he going to do?

"Most unusual for a man of iron to be carrying such very fine pistols around in the middle of London. You remind me of my uncle, equally rash."

"Is Colonel Leigh visiting this afternoon Countess?"

"You know Colonel Leigh? Two army men of mystery I suspect."

"Err ... same regiment. I was ... well ... I was a major in his East Anglia platoon. Our last engagement was putting down some of the Swing riots, when Lord Melbourne insisted that the army bring in the Norfolk ringleaders for hanging. I didn't agree with such harsh penalties, those men and their families were starving. The cause wasn't the rise of new technologies in agriculture; it was, please excuse my unintended insolence, rich landowners not paying living wages to their tenant farmers. I resigned my commission thereafter and concentrated on metallurgical engineering. I make a good living as a specialist fabricator and have invented some new machinery for cutting and shaping. I really need to seek patents, but have been too busy. Excuse me Ada, I'm going on far more than I should."

Ada sat and listened intently. Her hypothesis was confirmed. Mr Julian Fazackerley consisted of far more than the mathematical sum of his parts, a delectable and able thinker and rather a nice body. Swinging heavy implements kept him very fit and presentable. She had found out far more in two minutes about this so called mystery man than Morag had done in a week.

"So you believe in liberalism and social justice, Mr Fazackerley?"

"I do, very much, Countess."

She smiled. "Good. Now, I was indeed expecting my uncle but unfortunately he was called back to barracks. Some unfortunates, including his two top officers, have been run over by a recoiling cannon. I had warned him that he needed stronger springs and provided two full pages of calculations to prove my point, but alas, I was ignored, as ever. My aunt did call but has departed for the residence of Lady Byron, my mother. So demonstrating your old prowess to Colonel Leigh with a pistol will have to wait another day, I'm afraid Julian. Which reminds me. Julian is an unusual name. Why did your parents call you that?" She looked at him sharply again.

He smiled, cursing inside. An opportunity well gone again. No Colonel to shoot his legs off, so only one thing left to do, as the conversation was becoming interesting. Ada was far feistier than Morag, but then Caitriona had heard she had a tendency to be rather flirty and informal with men. Rumours of affairs but no tangible evidence had been circulating for some time, especially around the intense affection she seemed to have for that arrogant bounder Charles Babbage, who it was said strung her along like a lapdog on a lead. The Countess of Lovelace deserved better, much better, given her prodigious intellect, as equal, so his sources insisted, as Babbage's. But that was not to also diminish her great wealth, always an attraction for him at the best and worst of times. He glanced around the room, full of books, including science, mathematics, some art and lots of literature. Ada Lovelace was the most fascinating and intellectual woman he had met for a very long time, if not ever, with a mindset like him.

"I'm sure the Colonel and I will catch up soon … err … Ada."

She finally drank her whisky at last and topped up his third large glass. "Shall I ask Jeeves to prepare a place for dinner? You will stay won't you, Julian? Lady McKenzie, her cousin and her governess will all be arriving later."

Despite an enveloping alcoholic fuzziness attacking his brain, he was sufficiently together to decide that it would be politic to depart before then and return to Caitriona's. Some time and distance needed to be placed between him and Morag, and allow the ill-feeling to gradually die down. James would be disappointed but then again he would soon be off to boarding school and needed to get his academic act together. Edward and Zachery had been far too much of a distraction for the boy and he should have curtailed the excessive time they had spent together and not turned a blind eye to their furtive trips to the George. But more importantly, his emotional feelings were being unexpectedly assailed by the woman sat demurely in front of him, and the last thing he needed was to be sat between her and Morag in an embarrassing evening. He needed time away and to gather more information about Ada directly.

"Regrettably, I have another business engagement this evening but perhaps another time?" he replied, smiling warmly.

"Perhaps, Julian, perhaps. It will be dependent on how well you tweak my pipes?"

He laughed loudly, all kinds of bizarre and unsayable in polite company scenarios were running through his brain. "My parents were great lovers of poetry, Ada. As a child, I was told I was named after the special poem 'Julian and Maddalo' by Percy Bysshe Shelley, who was, I understand, a personal friend of my father. I've inherited a similar love of verse and the prose of the novel. You have a fine collection of books, Ada, so very admirable. I could spend many hours in this room in deep solitude, reading, in your case I see by gaslight, from dusk until dawn. I would love to hear more about your father, Lord Byron. Did you never meet him?"

Ada's face lit up. Julian Fazackerley was connected with Shelley? And knew of her father? "You actually read literature in-between beating metal to death then Julian?" she replied, as both laughed heartily. "If you like I will tell you briefly about my father. He was great friends with Shelley and they shared many special moments together. Sadly I never got to meet him, as after my birth he never returned to England but I have always missed his presence and I am sure his love. I'm afraid my mother and I disagree heartily on this issue, but I remain steadfast with my own views on Lord Byron. And at twenty five years of age and three children following my marriage, I think that is very reasonable and logical to love your father, despite his shortcomings. He was also very thoughtful, kind and sincere but, like a number of men, needed to live a racy and intensely literary life, unable to settle down quietly to one woman. My mother's serious moral piety and his gregarious love of life and adventure were always going to be incompatible, but she would never accept it and never forgave it either. I will tell you a strict secret Julian. When I die I will be buried with him in Nottinghamshire. He and I are so very alike, if you swap mathematics for poetry."

Julian smiled softly. Somehow, unintended, he had touched a raw nerve. She wanted to talk about herself, something perhaps quite rare, certainly it would seem to a man. He had to see her again and nobody would stand in his way this time, eyeing his pistols again. Listening mode was needed immediately, something he was good at when necessary and as he listened she talked more about her father, his rise from obscurity to become England's greatest poet and how he had been, in her view, misunderstood and maligned for far too long by her own mother. She described his poetry, recited word for word a number of favourites and his life as she knew it when he lived abroad and why he couldn't return.

She pulled out three volumes of his work and Julian then offered to read some selected works to her, interpreting, as he understood the subtleties and clever quirks of such brilliant language usage. Tea was brought in and they shared a large bun which he cut into two and spread jam all over and she squealed with delight when it ran over his face, not having had so much levity for ages past. Noting she was presently reading Jane Austen's 'Sense and Sensibility' he ran through his own critique of the novel, comparing and contrasting her views with the many literary articles he had once written as a journalist for the Times before he enlisted in the army.

Then she finally and cleverly turned the tables and asked him about his own life, his ambitions, the death of his wife and the long struggle to bring up two boys on his own, why he lived in a tiny cottage on Morag's estate and most important and the most difficult question for him to answer. She wanted to know why he had not met a new woman in his life to marry.

This was the first time he had opened up his own inner secrets, fears and disillusions to anyone, least of all a woman and virtually a complete stranger. Only his sister Caitriona, as equally secretive as him, knew and understood. Perhaps having a dry run the other day with Morag's attractive cousin, Miss Warren, had provided a new flow of rational thought he could put finally into words.

As they continued to talk for two solid hours he realised he really had to leave and he still hadn't fixed her boiler. Ada finally gave him permission to wield his wrench and reluctantly they finished the afternoon with another kiss of the hand and a firm handshake. Jeeves led him away to the scullery and exactly as Ada had foretold, he did find three loose collars inside the sealed outflow box, where steam was escaping. He tightened them up and the pressure returned promptly, although Ada's so called revolutionary heating made him reflect hard about the efficiency of these steam systems. Wouldn't a continuous flow of heated water to the radiators be more effective and cheaper, but how could the water be pumped around? Before the clattering of horses returned again in the evening he was gone, a yellow pea-souper fog having descended in force, allowing him to creep stealthily away into the dusk, coughing badly, back to his sister's home in Mayfair.

Ada, arranging her latest papers for Babbage, swigged down another whisky, took a deep breath and sighed. She had also firmly made up her mind. Mr Julian Fazackerley was a unique man who would not be leaving her life, ever. She had the wealth to indulge and would buy 'Morag's blacksmith' and bring him and his family down to London as soon as possible. Julian had asked her to apologise to Lady McKenzie for not being able to stay, but Ada had other plans. She would not be mentioning Julian whatsoever, and especially that he had visited her during the afternoon. Fortunately, Medora and her lively artist friend, Lady Katherine DeBeers, and the amassed collective of joint children had been occupied at the other end of the house and rear garden, being amused by some tedious and odious friend of Morag's and her cousin with the name of Dr Lynton Gray, who had invited himself unannounced to dinner. Only Jeeves, a bastion of discretion, knew of Julian's arrival. Not only did he never hear anything he saw nothing either, but then he had been senior butler to her own mother when she and her father lived together briefly and understood the family idiosyncrasies better than anyone else living.

*

One large and one small carriage swung one behind the other into St James Square. Both headed for the same destination; number twelve, drawing up in front. The combination of the dense fog, the silent, windless air and deep dusk descending, made Ada Lovelace's town house barely visible. The terraces with lamps inside now being lit rose like hulks into the sky and the street gaslights displayed eerie coloured halos around their flickering flames.

Two fashionable women, their bonnets pulled down hard and cloaks wrapped tight, alighted carefully onto the pavement from each brougham and waved respectively to their top hatted male companions before the horses were whipped and the carriages shot off, both drivers fearful that very soon they would be unable to see to return to their master's houses. Fortunately, the pavements in this area were spotlessly clean as they hitched their dresses up, eyeing each other's ghostly forms in the murky air, and then realised they were both walking to the same address.

"Vikki, is that actually you? Jesus Christ, who was that man in that carriage you were kissing?"

Victoria laughed and embraced her best friend. "Abby! Interesting timing as ever. I heard you had departed the Royal Society, arm in arm with a certain Mr John Ruskin ... and by that rosy glow on your cheeks, I suspect, recalling our past experiences in Rotterdam, that you've rediscovered the elusive ardour back. What's it like being a Victorian cougar then?"

Abby giggled. That was an understatement. "Okay ... hands up, I fucked him rotten, you would never believe the ..."

"Mmm ... gory detail later please when we're out of earshot of everyone. I assume with shit Lynton's antics, you concluded that what's good for the goose is good for the gander in 1841 speak?"

"Absolutely. So ... what have you been up to? Sounds to me like that metaphor may be extendable, present company included? So who was that delicious looking older man with the laughing eyes then?"

"Faraday."

"*The* Faraday, of Michael Faraday fame? Revered scientist and love of Morag's life, alongside shit Julian of course?"

"Afraid so. Mauveine turned up in his office-lab in some academic religious guise. I have to give maximum credit to her and Isi, they are very resourceful. Anyway, she told me I had to do what it takes."

"So did you?"

"Err ... something rare took hold of me, I still don't know what. Michael is a most amazing intellect, then I inadvertently overcooked my electrical predictions contribution to his lecture questions, so easy to do, and brought the house down and he became instant putty in my hands and asked me backstage for a sherry. In the meantime, Morag left the lecture hall. Shit Julian had turned up again, upset her badly with something, and they both disappeared and never returned. I'm assuming she's already arrived here … I hope so."

"Well? Did you?"

"Did I what?"

"Jesus Christ, Vikki, spill quickly, I'm getting cold out here, so I don't have to feel so guilty on my own becoming an upper class whore."

Victoria took a deep breath and grinned. "I have to say," she whispered, "I've never done it before on a lab-bench. All his newly designed gas burners were flickering in a row either side, it was like being ravished on an altar. In his wild pent-up passion, like his body would explode, he shouted I was the devil incarnate and he couldn't resist the mental torture any longer … so perhaps the imagery was logically apt."

"Bloody hell. A bit different from the top of your boiler then? So in a few short hours, you've managed to steal Faraday away from Morag, she's alienated herself from Julian and we've both had some well-deserved fun for a change. Life in 1841 has its upsides. Oh fuck … play dumb. Morag's coming out of the door," Abby whispered as they both turned sharply.

"Victoria, Abigail, I'm so pleased to see you both at last." Morag called out of the gloom, running up to them. "I was severely worried that we all inadvertently got split up and you wouldn't know your way back to Ada's residence, especially now this fog has descended so thickly."

She hugged each one warmly, a butler's cloak wrapped around her from head to toe.

"Not a problem, cousin dearest," Abby replied. "I had the address written down so at the end of the day, after of course tea, cake and various discussions, we both took a carriage together before we were stranded. An excellent art and science exhibition prevailed."

"Morag … are you alright? I too was worried after you suddenly rose from the lecture theatre and never returned. Mr Faraday and Mr Babbage both reassured me you were fine and that an urgency of business must have come up. So he kindly showed me the wonderful science library and gave me a tour of the building, most educational, until Abigail and I got together again. I will discuss this unique experience with the children of course as a lesson topic."

Morag sighed. "Alas, it was no business exigency. Do you actually know who that dastardly bastard is?"

Victoria and Abby stared, incredulous with the venom and anger. "What bastard?" Abby replied, wide-eyed.

"The mysterious Mr Julian Fazackerley. One reason I never came back is I had to call on some close friends and dig out the facts, once and for all?"

"Facts?" Victoria whispered.

"He's an imposter. I knew all along there was more to him than met the eye, none of his behaviour made any full sense. Julian Fazackerley is the illegitimate only son of Lord Endersby of Liverpool, a wealthy landowner and shipping merchant and has a whore of a half sister, living here not far away, a Lady Caitriona Endersby, well known in more polite society for her dalliances and subterfuge, with more money than sense. Julian was once a well respected journalist for the Times would you believe and was a commissioned major in the army too, hence why he is so good with a pistol … How on earth he has become who he now is and lives the way he does and adopted the name Fazackerley is beyond me."

"Maybe," Abby ventured, looking at Victoria, whose brain was going ten to the dozen, "As his father was in shipping, linkage to the Leeds and Liverpool canal? Perhaps his mother was one of the Fazackerley clan of boat people, hence his name."

"Oh God in heaven strike me down dead," Morag retorted. "What a mess. And on top of that, the poisonous Fazackerley behaviour has even spread its pox to my own son. That girl might even be directly related to Julian, heaven's above, well at least she has been dealt with and out of the way. To be honest, Julian Fazackerley's illegitimate upper class background wouldn't normally be of any great concern to me. There are many landed gentry around like him, part of English life let us be fair and I'm sure he's a good man at heart and very capable and erudite. It was what he did this afternoon. An unforgiveable deed."

"What did Julian do that is so terrible?" Abby replied, her face wrought with curiosity but Victoria remaining silent and ponderous.

"Made a complete fool out of himself and me … with of all people in the country, only the Queen herself in the lobby who he hadn't recognised. How could the man be so sharp one minute and so desperately stupid and deceitful the next."

"You mean he … actually …?" Abby speculated.

"Yes, it appears he tried to proposition her and then implied of all things that I was his lover obviously not knowing that I have been a regular fixture at all the Court balls since the Queen and Prince Albert married. His glasses must have been well and truly steamed up."

Victoria laughed but instantly turned it into a cough. "The fog is getting to my chest, maybe we should all be going inside. I'm so sorry Morag, a truly awful thing to do, but I suspect Julian is feeling very apologetic for himself and the inadvertent distress caused."

"I'll be a laughing stock in London, I don't want or need his apologies and … I think I may be pregnant."

Abby shot a glance across to Victoria. "Pregnant?"

"If I am with child I'll deal with it. Thank goodness I have one thing nobody can take away … my wealth. And I have my science to keep me occupied. Yes, let's head inside and find warmth but I don't want Ada to know anything whatsoever of all this. Julian is not here apparently, he seems to have vanished into thin air, probably back to Lancashire with his tail between his legs. Anyway, I suggest we put all this behind us and enjoy the dinner. The Countess of Lovelace has quite a wonderful cook."

Jeeves opened the door and took their coats, panting with exertion. "Jeeves at your service, Lady McKenzie. Lady Lovelace has suggested that you may all wish to retire to the drawing room and take a pre-dinner brandy. She will join you shortly with her sister Medora. Freshening up facilities are down the corridor, third door on the right, downstairs bathroom and water closet. Your trunks are all in your rooms if you wish to change. Dinner will be at seven-thirty sharp and Harriet, head maid, will see to your needs."

"Thank you, a brandy would be most welcome," Morag replied, Abby nodding enthusiastically, whilst Victoria was trying to work out what was in his hand.

He shoved a small ear trumpet to the side of his head. "Sorry, milady, a little deafness afflicts me. Had to come out of retirement at the request of the Countess, normally I do a day a week helping out at Lady Byron's residence. Poor Mr Doubleday, her head butler, was taken to the Chelsea hospice, stricken down with pox. Doesn't sound like he will be coming out of there, poor devil."

"Mmm … thank you Jeeves, and the children? I haven't seen mine yet?" Morag said.

"All are being looked after and fed in the nursery at the back by Miss Newton, the Countess's new housekeeper, milady. Quite a crowd today, but she is very thorough and a real disciplinarian. If you wish I can take you there now?"

"No, that won't be necessary, I can wait till the morning," Morag replied, having no great wish to see James yet. "Actually, I have changed my mind. I think we would all like to change for dinner first, and then a brandy. Perhaps we could find our rooms?"

"Certainly milady," Jeeves replied and pulled a long string hanging from the ceiling. A loud bell resonated downstairs and in a few seconds Harriet and an under-maid ran from the scullery and escorted them up a wide and sweeping ornate staircase, similar to Orsbrick Hall, to the first floor.

*

"This is a very beautiful drawing room, Morag," Abby whispered, admiring the small tapestry and various paintings along the thickly papered wall, with a harpsichord stood in the corner. They slowly sipped their generous portion of old Napoleon brandy Jeeves had poured out into large blue balloon glasses.

"I do so heartily agree, Abigail," Morag responded, eyeing the three volumes of Lord Byron's published work lying on the table. "Ada has such exquisite taste and chooses everything personally with precision. I don't know how she finds the time."

"By being highly organised, Morag dearest, and succinctly methodical. Eat well, study well and buy well, that's my motto, oh … and drink well too, cheers everyone."

They turned to see that a smiling Ada, in a dazzling yellow dress and blue shawl, had breezed in unannounced, carrying her own glass of brandy.

She smiled warmly at Victoria, who instinctively sensed a kindred spirit; there was something distinctive about female mathematicians. Ada was quite striking in appearance and exuberant in personality, an aristocrat who obviously liked to socialise, keep up with the latest fashions and enjoy the challenges of a scientific intellect, decidedly a woman after her own heart. It was clear why Morag and Ada were such good friends but she could see a difference immediately. Ada was undoubtedly a woman who could enter a room and become the instant magnetic centre of attraction, and without effort dominate the attentions of males and females alike. Morag was far more reserved and restrained.

"You must be Victoria, Morag's new governess," Ada said, ignoring Abby, who quietly watched, fascinated by the body language. "I have heard much about you, not I will add, from Morag, who is far too discrete, but I understand you made rather a stir at the Royal Society, and as a fellow able mathematician and equal enthusiast for the physical and electrical sciences then I have been told I should keep a careful eye on you. Mr Faraday was not the only one hugely impressed. Is that true Victoria?"

Ada shot a mischievous glance over to Morag who reddened, either by surprise or annoyance.

Victoria sat up, her instincts were right. Ada had a very sharp and eloquent naughty turn of dialogue, but then having Lord Byron as a father and a mother who was apparently an excellent self-taught mathematician too, her formidable presence and intellect should not be surprising. It was evident that mobile phones were totally unnecessary in 1841 London society. Gossip and information flashed by in an instant with the plethora of notes and letters circulating all day long. That was quick, very quick. Charles Babbage must have been the villain spilling the beans, hopefully not Michael Faraday, at least not all of it and not yet. She would have to be smartly on her toes around Ada Lovelace.

"A pleasure to meet you Lady Lovelace and what a lovely home you keep here, really quite splendid. It was quite fortuitous that I had been reading some chapters of Jane Marcet's 'Conversations on Natural Philosophy' to aid my teaching of Lady McKenzie's children, which perfectly coincided with Mr Faraday's lecture question he directed to me. We women scientists cannot afford to be caught out in such a place of prestige as the Royal Society."

"Well done Victoria," Ada replied with a knowing but satisfied smirk. "Please, don't feel you require any need for formality in my house. Call me Ada; we are all on first name terms."

Victoria knew in a nano-second that Ada had seen right through her and probably knew more than she was letting on. She clearly enjoyed a little jousting and teasing in company, as did her father before her.

"But before I forget, I have something for you," and ran briskly to a shelf, to grab an old leather bound book and what looked like an academic paper. She handed both to Victoria who gasped in disbelief. A first edition of Legendre's popular Eléments de Géométrie published in 1794 and a copy of his 1828 famous paper on polynomials and how to use them to solve differential equations.

"This tome will provide a focus for your mathematics teaching of James. Immersion in Euclid is the ideal way to fire up his imagination. Such learning provided the necessary stimulus for both me and my mother, and also for our friend, Mary Somerville. I tested his algebra this afternoon, far too weak in understanding and application. He must improve his factorising and practise basic equations. Then he should be ready for that boarding school Morag wishes to send him too. As for the paper? Perhaps you need a few new tools to address Mr Faraday's predilections … of electrostatics of course." She grinned again over to Morag who remained polite, silent and fuming.

What game exactly was Ada playing? Victoria thanked Ada profusely and pondered carefully. Why, when Ada likely knew of and maybe encouraged Morag's affair with Michael Faraday was she sowing some subtle alternative implications? Perhaps Ada already knew much more than she should and was using that knowledge for some other purpose, entirely with Morag in mind.

Ada suddenly sprang towards Morag's chair and hugged her warmly. "You look a little peaky, darling, but some mail has come to cheer you up … with a Royal stamp. Must be important," she cried, handing a large letter over. Morag looked at it with apprehension. "Well go on, open it and tell us all," Ada continued with a flourish before turning to Abby, by now quite absorbed with this devilish and cunning woman.

"Miss Warren, a pleasure to meet you. I heard so much about you this afternoon, you have an extraordinary talent for art and music, the plaudits of your work simply flowed in profusion from your exclusive agent, a Dr Lynton Gray? A credible purveyor and seller of art he may be, but I would suggest there are so many more attractive and literate young art critics in this part of London who would find your wares and special talent quite irresistible. I would be only too happy to introduce you to one or two." Again, Ada followed up with a mischievous grin.

Abby reddened uncharacteristically as Victoria swallowed a large gulp of brandy, stifling her own smirk. Both of them were in the firing line. Abby had concluded that Charles Babbage was again the culprit. Ada and he obviously shared a love of society gossip as well as mathematics.

"You have met Dr Gray? Is he here?" Abby asked, now curious how and why he turned up at the residence of Lady Lovelace.

"Yes, he arrived earlier, invited himself rather rudely to dinner but I must confess he has a way with children and has amused them with tales and stories all afternoon. Do you have children, Abigail? Certainly Dr Gray has all the charms of a potential doting father, although his only daughter, Fenella, is apparently of age to be coming out for marriage. He implied she was a little, how shall we say … wayward?"

Abby looked across at Victoria who put down her glass gently. Another Fenella? Lynton's daughter? What was this all this about? Neither would say anything but they both looked at Morag who was also reflecting; decidedly too many Fenellas in the last forty-eight hours. Morag suddenly tore open the letter to read the spidery handwriting as impassively as she could, dreading the contents:

*My Dearest Morag*

*I just wanted to let you know that I was only teasing today. I happened to meet Caitriona later who explained about her brother and that he had only just returned from service in India, and was a little disoriented with his English surroundings. The foolish incident is of course completely forgotten already. Prince Albert and I look forward to seeing you at the next ball. Please call in at Buckingham Palace next time you are in London, as he*

*wishes to discuss a posthumous award to be made to your husband for his outstanding service to the railways. We miss him as much as I'm sure you do.*
*Victoria Saxe-Coburn-Gotha*

"So what does the Queen want then Morag?" Ada started off again, looking down at her pile of Byron books and wishing Julian was still there. A lilting, friendly voice suddenly spoke up from behind Morag.

"Nothing, just an invitation to the next ball … When did you last get a handwritten invite from the Queen then, Countess Lovelace?"

Everyone turned. A tall and very beautiful woman had appeared quietly from nowhere, standing behind Morag and had been surreptitiously reading the note. She proceeded to hug a smiling and relieved Morag affectionately from behind. Medora, her best friend had come in. Victoria and Abby immediately realised who she was and it was so very plain how close Medora and Morag were, and Medora was not under any circumstances going to fuel Ada's obsession with gossip any further either.

Ada grimaced for a moment and decided to change tack. She wasn't quite finished with the unappealing foppish Dr Gray. "As I was saying, sadly Dr Gray left earlier with Lady Katherine DeBeers. Morag, you remember Katherine of course." Ada flashed a knowing look to Morag, whose eyes narrowed, remembering the one-time rumours about Lady DeBeers and Malcolm. "She insisted on wanting to show him her husband's latest collection of Goya canvasses … however as she buried her husband a month back, I doubt whether Dr Gray will be returning this evening. I hope you are not too disappointed Abigail that your friend will be absent?"

Victoria tittered, and then coughed. "Lovely brandy, Ada, thank you, a rare display of wonderment to the taste."

Ada laughed loudly as Morag and Abby both stared silently, neither sure what the subtleties of the joke were. Medora was used to these antics whenever guests appeared, especially concerning men. "Indeed Victoria, indeed. Now Abigail, will you play the harpsichord for us? Dr Gray insisted you have the touch of an angel. And then we will convene for dinner. I do love a little Bach before eating, don't you?"

Victoria's face dropped. Since when had Abby played a harpsichord, or even a piano?

However Abby stood up and smiled. "It will be a pleasure, Ada," and glided confidently to the stool, fishing out some suitable music. Unknown to everyone in the room, especially Victoria, she had been tutored at sixteen, for two terms, on a harpsichord during her wanton days at her school for girls, one of the more unusual skills acquired when boarding. It was only when she decided that art would be her career direction and Miss Brimley, the music teacher, had made a Saturday afternoon sloppy pass at her that she stopped. It may be the 1840s rather than the 1990s but Bach was Bach and the music notation seemed identical. She picked a composition with an accompanying choral song, and started to play with gusto, singing with her loud soprano voice for all she was worth.

The room fell silent. Morag's face dropped as did Victoria's, both surprised for their own reasons. Half a dozen servants slunk into the doorway to hear the creator of such dulcet tones followed by Miss Newton and all the children of Ada, Morag and Medora, all except James of course. They crowded, headlong, into the room.

Unexpectedly, Morag picked up an old lute from the corner and joined her with another sheet of music. "Abigail, may I accompany you? This particular aria from Bach? Can you sing the words in Latin?"

They played and sang together, their voices and playing ringing around the room in an unrehearsed but virtuoso duet. Rapturous applause ended the dazzling performances. Abby had always been proud of her singing. She wished Mauveine had been there to hear.

Ellen broke away from the other children and ran forward to hug her favourite teacher. "Will you teach me to sing like an angel too, Miss Warren?"

"I'm sure she will, Ellen," Ada cried. "Like the Angel Gabriela. Now I believe the time has arrived for dinner. Children back to the nursery please and continue your meal."

Morag stood up and caught her daughter as she skipped off. "Ellen where is James? Why is he not with you?"

"He was not feeling well Mother. Miss Newton made him some eggs and put him to bed. He said he felt feverish probably from jumping into Aunt Ada's pond this afternoon after a dare from Dr Gray. We were playing a silly game."

"That man! Alright Ellen, thank you, you go and eat now … I'll tuck you into bed later and see how he is."

Morag caught up with Abby in the dining room. "Cousin, you have the most wonderful musical as well as artistic talent, I had absolutely no idea. It makes me realise how little I know about you. Between you and Victoria, who uses the strangest of words sometimes and has an almost unreal and extraordinary knowledge of science … it is like you both come from another planet in the universe," she said laughing.

Abby felt a cold wave run down her stomach. She and Victoria needed to moderate. Also, she wondered how Maddie and Belle were getting on back at Orsbrick Hall, with the wonderful Agnes looking after them.

341

"My goodness, Ada is always a woman of constant contradiction," Morag continued, staring at the dining table. "Will you take in these formal place names, written in gilded pen? It appears that Lady McKenzie is designated to be formally sitting next to Lady Lovelace. I'd better move up the table, I see Medora is on the other side."

Abby waited for Victoria who finally came in chatting happily to Medora. In facial features she was very similar to her half-sister, Ada, but in temperament and character, they seemed poles apart. Medora, slightly younger, was a very natural and normal conversationalist, easy to talk to and very engaged with her children, although no father on the scene was mentioned. A gifted linguist, she also spoke fluent French and Italian, Abby was impressed that Medora had lived on and off in Europe for years.

She sat down and Victoria joined her. Jeeves hastily removed place names for both Dr Gray and Mr Fazackerley and rearranged the seating, to include Miss Henrietta Newton; B.A. the pleasant and serious young governess of Ada's who was joining them to balance the numbers. Abby pondered thoughtfully. Ada had known Julian was expected but said nothing to anyone, including Morag. She did have an agenda, but what exactly?

"But that's not possible," Victoria remarked to Abby, distracted by Henrietta's qualification. "The first female honours examination graduate, even at Oxford, was not until 1877, and it was only in 1920 that women actually were awarded a formal degree and matriculated."

"University of Padua, in theology so she told me. Europe is somewhat further ahead it seems, and she has rich parents."

Victoria shook her head, returning to a more light-hearted theme. "Medora reckons the Angel Gabriela is one of the fallen angels."

Abby grinned. "I know exactly how Gabriela feels! Anyway, the food looks delicious, matches the meals I do for you at Orsbrick Hall, well almost, she's missing the kebabs. To be honest I have to say, I rather like Ada ... she has a mischievous temperament."

"Mmm ... a fellow soulmate isn't she," Victoria whispered gaily. "Morag and I are too serious and straight down the middle; we don't easily do second nature devious. Gosh, I think Ada is going to ask us to pray. I never thought she maintained religious beliefs, must be one of her mother's influences that she never fully rejected ... on the positive side I suppose we're going to need all the help we can get!"

*

After such a lavish four course dinner, Victoria was desperate to be relieved of that awful corset and excused herself towards an upstairs bathroom, only to find Abby already ahead of her. They emerged beaming with relief and threw them into Victoria's bedroom.

"I don't know how the others manage, I simply cannot adjust to this aspect of Victorian fashion," Abby whispered.

"It was enlightening watching them eat, they pick at their food, an acquired social art. You were too busy shovelling Peking duck inside you to notice. Ada was watching you quite bemused, although she makes up for it with the red wine. And they may not look it but they are somewhat younger than us."

"Mmm ... true. We need to talk about Julian."

"I know. Tomorrow when we're back home. Ada and Morag have arranged a card game in the sitting room, so you need to

343

keep sober. No virtual reality 'Game of Thrones' splayed on the sofa to finish off the night I'm afraid. How's your charades?"

"A little rusty. Last time I ended up with no clothes on. I don't get the impression the others are into that, with or without males. Mind you, all that scurrilous gossip from Ada and Morag was fun. I had no idea how the 1840's upper classes were such a closed and incestuous society and so socially interlinked day to day with the Royal Court. Everyone seems to be bonking everyone else except those they're married to, in the quietest and most discrete privacy, until the women become pregnant … shit Morag too?"

"Not a word, Abby."

*

Lying quietly in bed, Victoria couldn't sleep. Abby didn't relinquish her clothes but she did lose five pounds she could ill afford to Ada who was remarkably slick in the betting stakes at poker. The room and the mattress were very comfortable but her brain was on fire, trying to bring together all the events of the day. She tossed and turned some more. Eventually she gave up and lit a candle. The Legendre book gift had rekindled her dormant mathematical spark and she decided to read a little downstairs in Ada's library, a habit from Orsbrick Hall which always cured insomnia.

Slowly stepping down the marble stairway, trying to avoid the creaking section of banister and with the candle balanced precariously on a saucer, she carefully opened the heavy study door and crept inside, only to be met with immediate horror to see the end of the room lit and a gowned figure, wearing a heavy woollen bed-hat, hunched reading in a chair, a small fire burning in the grate.

"Do please come in Victoria … I was quite expecting you to appear, hurry before your hot chocolate gets cold," the figure announced in a cheery voice without looking up as Victoria stepped closer and Ada's friendly face, now minus the hat, loomed out the gloom. "I must confess, watching you while we were playing, I decided you are a woman much closer to my heart than I first thought. We mathematicians have a bad habit of burning the midnight oil, our heads always full of speculations to write down and ponder over. Please sit … here is your cup."

Victoria sat down in the opposite armchair, still wary of the many candles everywhere, contrasting her thick and ungainly grey flannel nightdress with the very sleek and silky blue garment, with a hand-sewn flower motif that Ada was wearing underneath her brown dressing gown. She crossed her legs demurely, her matching linen slippers enclosing small and delicate feet.

In silence, they both slowly sipped the welcome hot chocolate which Victoria had missed as a night time beverage. Ada lived a lot more of an opulent lifestyle than Morag, despite the equally beautiful furnishings in Orsbrick Hall. She enjoyed excess.

Squinting at the title of the heavy old leather tome Ada was holding in her lap, Victoria had to ask. "What are you reading? That book looks distinctly taxing for this time of the night."

Ada smiled. "The later the night, the thicker I like it."

They giggled, Victoria now enjoying that ironic and pointed humour, exactly and familiarly mirroring Abby, who was indeed absolutely correct. Ada was fun, beautiful and brilliant, but more importantly what exactly does she know?

"I am rereading a well respected treatise on differential equations by a Cambridge friend of Mary Somerville, a Dr James Harvington, you may not have heard of him. You probably know from Morag that I spend much time assisting

Mr Babbage with his calculating devices. At present he is working on the design of his latest and very complex creation, an Analytical Engine, which you will not understand, but I have a crazy idea."

Victoria pondered, finishing off the delicious chocolate. Another science moment was arising. She needed to speak very, very carefully, especially given how astute with the slightest nuance, Ada appeared to be.

"If I may comment," she said cheerfully. "I do know that Mr Babbage's Difference Engine is a geared calculating machine which turns numerical multiplication and division operations into staged addition and subtraction steps. Turn a handle and out pops the answer. But from what little I have gathered about the Analytical Engine, this mechanical device would take computation to a much higher level, ultimately to enable the operator to solve an algebraic problem by numerical means, using instructions. I believe, Ada, that you have suggested using the same system of punched cards to Mr Babbage as used in a Jacquard loom? Certainly if Mr Babbage can build and make work this engine, then it will be a process of quick computation to calculate, for example, logarithmic tables from infinite series, one hundred percent accurate and to as many places as you and the government desire, whether for navigation or warfare."

Ada sat bolt upright. Her instinct was one hundred percent good. Victoria's physiognomy, the moment she had walked into the house, had told everything needed combined with Charles's feedback from the Royal Society. Mrs Victoria Hammelaar was an outstanding scientist, this was no ordinary governess. Victoria was masquerading way beneath her capabilities, probably because she had fallen onto hard times, as a widow. She had been a clandestine beneficiary of a much deeper, academic education somewhere. Foolish and naive Morag with her vague suspicions had grossly underestimated Victoria right from the beginning, and she was a very likeable person. Moreover, this woman could keep secrets to have survived as a widow the way she had, play a long game and take risks, equally aware of the tough fight for science education equality she, Morag, Mary and an increasing collective of others were having in this grossly paternalistic and nannying society.

But more importantly for Ada was how desperate she felt to have a woman of her capability to confide in. Mary Somerville, her very old friend, was excellent but far too homely and steeped in past traditional roles to be a revolutionary and even Morag, committed to a point but she was not a true mathematician, was already making a silly fool of herself with Faraday. Ada smirked inside. Her spies had been out already and perhaps that emotional dynamic was not so iron-clad after all.

"You are remarkably informed," Ada replied pointedly, wondering exactly how Victoria could have picked up the Jacquard loom instructional concept. She was certain that it had never been shared beyond Charles Babbage. "My crazy idea is in fact linked to the instructions. Want to hear it?"

Victoria nodded.

"You see, Charles, that is Mr Babbage, well he and I have had a long, collaborative friendship and we have been toying with the necessity of using recursive formulae, where one term in a sequence is calculated from previous terms."

"An iteration."

"Do beg my pardon Victoria, but that is not a word I have ever come across, Morag says you do speak some odd science syntax occasionally?"

"I'm sorry Ada," Victoria replied, thinking fast. "A Dutch translation, I still haven't completely readjusted my language since returning to England, I must stop mixing the two."

Ada grinned, another mystery solved, which Morag hadn't even guessed, because Morag lacked good old Byron family guile. "So, my reason reading this tome. I am looking to research an explicit function which could be thus worked on by the Engine, independent of human head and hand. I have been thinking of a generator for Bernoulli numbers. Such an example would have the gravitas to make the idiots in Whitehall sit up and give Charles his desperately needed funds to build it."

Victoria had to rack her brain hard what Bernoulli numbers were, then remembered they are rational numbers generated using an exponential function but defined through an infinite series so capable of being iterated. She wished Maddie was here because at least Maddie knew Ada's history in better detail.

"An excellent example I believe. Perhaps you could also try an infinite series which generates the irrational number pi as a demonstration programme?"

Oh shit. Victoria winced inside as Ada immediately looked hard again, but then grinned profusely, putting down the book and grabbing her quill pen and a sheet of paper.

"Yes indeed. Mmm … I rather like the word 'programme' rather than instruction … a computational programme. I must try that out on Mr Babbage," Ada mumbled, dipping her quill furiously into a pot of black ink and scribbling madly, line after line of words, equations and diagrams as Victoria watched mesmerised at the fanatical speed and skill of Ada's brain in action. Finally Ada looked up.

"Examples captured. That piece of feedback provides my letter for tomorrow completed, in outline form anyway. I will work on it further when you have retired. Thank you, an excellent contribution." She put the quill down and stared intensely into Victoria's face, before asking in a whisper. "So Victoria. What other ideas for the Engine do you have? Will Mr Babbage ever indeed build it, even if he is successful in raising sufficient funds?"

Victoria took a deep breath. This was the same behaviour Faraday had pursued. Ada had been tipped off. "My humble opinion, from the top of my head but please don't take me seriously, is that the biggest impediment Mr Babbage faces presently is the enormous engineering challenge of forming, shaping and cutting the gears, shafts and bearings to sufficiently fine tolerances. And I fear so many moving parts are needed that the time and cost of manufacture and assembly will be huge."

"Agreed, I keep telling Charles this … So?"

"Err, sorry Ada … so what?"

"You don't want to end there do you? You have another idea up your sleeve … I can read it in your eyes."

Victoria could feel Ada cleverly cornering her. She had to delve right in and hope the world wouldn't explode.

"As I said to Mr Faraday in his lecture … the real key to future success on the railways is to replace mechanical steam with electrical energy to drive motors. Equally, for the Engine, you need electrical computation and not mechanical, so the problems I have highlighted are eliminated." Victoria stopped at that point. No talk of switches, on-off and binary. She had thrown a bone to Ada, hopefully enough for her to ponder on, for a very long time.

Something triggered immediately because superfast Ada had once again grabbed the quill and scribbled furiously for another half a page.

"Mmm … a very interesting concept, I must admit. I need to distinctly mull over that but it confirms that you and I both share an innovative, analytical approach to such matters. Science and engineering require mathematics to progress. We can't depend totally on the experimentalists, some of whom are very amateur; too much money and not enough theoretical brain. This is why I am far more attracted to Mr Babbage than Mr Faraday, although the latter was a dear associate once."

Victoria's eyes narrowed. My goodness, was Ada about to confirm that her relationship with Babbage was physical? But Ada was quicker off the mark, a deliberate comment to evoke a subtle body reaction, and Victoria had twitched. Ada smiled mischievously and intervened.

"As we have now become friends, I would like to share some confidences. May I believe in your total discretion?"

"Of course, we women of science must support and believe in each other … and I love secrets," Victoria replied, deciding to take a chance and talk to Ada like she was Abby, time relevant though.

Ada's eyes sparkled. She laughed and lit three more candles. "Excellent. What I am about to say you may not agree with, but I have come about my conclusions with the deepest analysis and respect for all concerned. You may be aware that Morag, one of my oldest, dearest and ablest friends, has a growing, mmm … shall we say rapport with Mr Faraday. Two things are wrong. One, she is heading to make a big and deluded fool of herself. But I'm sure, like me, you have already divined that Mr Faraday's exclusive religious conviction does not render the same ideal with regard to women."

She stopped for a brief pause and a coquettish stare, as Victoria coughed slightly, maintaining her gaze on Ada. The dice was thrown. Ada knew for sure what she had done with

Faraday. No getting away from it. The cough would be acknowledgement. Victoria could happily play a similar mind game. Intellectual guile was something, unlike with Morag, she and Ada decidedly shared and was implicitly understood already of the other.

"He will never leave his beloved wife, Sarah. They are locked together for eternity in heaven or hell, depending on your perspective. Second, but equally important, Mr Faraday, for his own selfish ends, is subjugating her true talents as a scientist. Lady McKenzie is not a second rate experimental engineer but a first rate innovative theoretical chemist ... and needs to be re-guided to find her metier back. I now wish young Kirchhoff, who had the desire but not the timing, had found and fucked her first. Electrical theory is the battlefield for you, me and Mr Babbage, Victoria, so *we* can use the experimental genius of our mutual friend Mr Faraday towards the world your vision is dictating, and which I fully agree with. What do you think?"

"An interesting hypothesis, Ada."

Ada grinned. "You may already have heard rumours that Charles and I are lovers. It may keep the gossipmonger tongues wagging in my society network and the Queen amused but the truth is quite different. Despite his sensual attraction in all ways, and I can sense you understand that perspective having met him, I actually took a reality check and gave up many years ago on that false premise. My mother believes I suffer from moral incontinence. Not so, I'm far too logical. The Engine and the intellect are his all-consuming life ... physical needs he has none. We are genuine collaborators of equal capabilities although Charles, being a staid and traditional male won't quite accept that ... yet!"

Victoria laughed, amazed at the openness of discussion Ada was prepared to share. "I really do understand and admire your position."

"Good, because you're the first woman I know who does. Sadly, neither my sister Medora nor our friend Mary has any idea what I talk about and my sister is too close to Morag as a friend to accept it anyway. So I will endeavour to nudge Morag back to her metier, by whatever means I can, as I care for her and believe it is the right thing. Victoria, I'll be frank and open. You are wasting your extraordinary talents as a mere governess. I have the means to change all that and would be happy to support your relocation, in a manner compatible with your taste and expectation, down here to London with your two daughters, who I understand are also extremely talented and knowledgeable for girls so young … I have my spies in Orsbrick Hall too. You would engage with me on accelerating the Engine and your electrical theories. Mr Babbage and I will establish you as a renowned scientist. I would like you to think about it, not for now, but at an appropriate time soon that we both gauge is the right one."

Victoria's mind was racing in circles. Ada, with one of the most highly-tuned, cunning and far-seeing minds she had ever come across had just made her a proposition so mindblowingly attractive, she should go in an instant and change the course of history. But that assumed all was lost, and a return to 2026 was denied because time was running out as Mauveine increasingly suggested and that she, the girls and Abby were locked into this time era forever. Shit, she wished Abby was there as a fly on the wall. Ada was not putting her under immediate pressure, but already a schism inevitably would be drawn with Morag, who she still liked very much and who was family. But, on the other hand, would that have any meaning or relevance in due course?

Just like Lynton and Julian didn't feature as expected in their lives? She needed to buy time, think hard and discuss with Abby and Mauveine? Hellfire.

"I will seriously and in complete confidence, consider your proposition, Ada, but I do request time," she replied.

Ada smiled warmly. "That is all I ask. Excellent. One more thing. I can see you're becoming tired and I have a few hours of work left yet. I posit that you will now sleep soundly for the rest of the night. I mentioned lovers … you are a woman of the world and subtlety. My husband and I have a good friendship and I have borne him three lovely children. He now has an heir and I hope to bear no more, physically the experience has drained my vitality. Our interests over the years have diverged and we live, as you may have gathered, quite independently. He much prefers life in the country on our Sussex estate and is buying others around the country as well. That is his life but he supports and encourages my intellectual endeavours, always against my own mother who irritates me often, and he makes no value of interfering for which I am grateful. But I enjoy the company and stimulation of men as well as women and need, how shall I say it … variety. Please don't laugh, I don't mean to combine such an expression with lascivious crudity."

Victoria intervened. "I empathise completely and bear witness to treat your frankness with the honesty and confidentiality it requires."

"Yes, I know," Ada replied with a wide grin. "Or I wouldn't be telling you. I have met a man, who you already may be acquainted with and he fires me with an intellectual and physical passion. His name is Mr Julian Fazackerley. His sister, Caitriona, is a close friend, rather wild but excitingly unpredictable, whereas Julian is a gentle, learned and cultured man. Already he feels as a soulmate and I want him."

Victoria felt a distinctively sharp chill. Somehow she knew that something like this was coming but not quite so overtly soon and not from Ada Lovelace but from Morag. "Yes, I am acquainted," she replied, biting her lip. "Mr Fazackerley accompanied us down to London. He lives on Morag's estate and does work for her. I think he and Morag have become …"

"No longer, Victoria. Recent events have conspired to become a permanent barrier to Morag's carnal desires, not that I blame her. I intend to buy her blacksmith and family and bring them here to start a new life. He has already started on my boiler."

"Buy?"

"I know what he needs and I know and understand his true background and what he desires … with a little financial incentive that can and will be arranged. In due course he will inherit vast wealth anyway."

"Really? I had no idea, I assumed he was a simple Lancashire artisan."

"I assure you Victoria, nothing is further from the truth. Do you have designs on him yourself? You are an attractive widow, although sadly his priority is access to cash and lots of it."

"Err … well no … Mr Fazackerley is an attractive physical man, I agree, but his inclinations do not veer in my direction and nor have mine in his."

She couldn't believe what she was saying, but in truth that was the bizarre reality of the world she had now been thrown into. If only Ada knew. Certainly she had ascertained a lot about Julian in a short space of time.

"I thought not. Morag will know very soon … I will tell her myself appropriately. Now, it has been most satisfying having this chat but I must finish my calculations. I suggest you take your book and rest your head swiftly on those soft pillows, I only purchase goose-filled. We both have sweet dreams coming. And please feel free to have a good look around my library before you depart tomorrow, after lunch. You may borrow anything which is to your liking."

Victoria nodded and rose from her chair, picking up her Legendre book. She was very much embroiled between a graphene rock and a diamond hard place much sooner than she could ever have dreamed possible. What had Mauveine unleashed?

"Thank you Ada, I look forward to your company much more in the future. Good night and sleep well. Don't over exert yourself."

"I must work hard whilst I have the energy because I feel it may not last as long as I would desire. Good night Victoria."

Victoria crept upstairs, hoping she would wake early and find Abby.

# Chapter Thirteen

The dawning of the spring morning could not have been more different. Instead of the cascading songs of the pleasing myriad male blackbirds, out-performing one another across the trees from her Orsbrick bedroom window and competing with the cooing grunts of paired turtle doves, a cacophony of shouting, neighing, wheel rumblings and animals shrieking assailed the ears, causing Victoria to leap out of bed petrified the house was collapsing. London in 1841 was doing its usual awakening.

Servant staffing shortages due to illness was somewhat evident, so washing bowls remained empty of hot water. After closing the window, she poured a large jug of cold water into a basin and washed herself all over as best as possible. At least Ada's Egyptian cotton towels were thick and fluffy. Now becoming much more adept with mastering correct attire with the cumbersome clothing, she picked the prettiest madder-red long dress with the fewest buttons from the trunk and threw it on over a new chemise, three petticoats and proper drawers. She could feel a chill in the air plus a long and draughty train journey ahead and shoved her feet into a nice pair of ankle length black boots, lacing them up smartly.

Opening her door to the wide bedroom corridor, needing a good lick of paint, she was assailed with complete nothingness. An eerie silence permeated upwards and downwards, only a distinctive smell of familiar bacon cooking filled her nostrils.

She spotted Jeeves hobbling into the breakfast room with a bowl of boiled eggs in one hand and a frying pan of bacon and sausages in the other. He was improvising badly; multitasking was not something he did well. She quickly caught up with him, putting out a sole set of plates and cutlery and pouring a hot coffee just for her. It was six-thirty in the morning. Where was everyone?

"Heard you coming, madam, would you like some toast with your eggs?"

"Yes please Jeeves, but where is everyone? Am I the first person up?"

"No madam the last, bar poor James who remains in bed rather poorly. Just you and me left standing so to speak," Jeeves replied with a croaky guffaw.

Victoria blinked and rubbed her eyes in disbelief.

"The Countess has taken a carriage already … gone to see Lady Caitriona Endersby on urgent business. She said she will be back to see you all off immediately after lunch. Unfortunately, cook slipped on horse muck outside and twisted her ankle so she's gone to the apothecary and the maid is poorly. Hope she ain't got the same as the butler, but she had spots and gone to her mother's place. Looked to me like measles. Lady McKenzie has gone to Harley Street to call up the Countess's doctor, she's not happy with her son's fever, don't blame her, but I saw much worse at Waterloo, madam. Lad will be fine in a day or two, he's a strong'un."

"Medora?"

"Her other ladyship took all the children with Miss Newton out for an early morning ride to the estuary mud flats on a Thames steamer, see the sea birds nesting. The older ones will have to sketch and write an essay."

"Well I know Miss Warren will definitely still be in bed."

"No madam. A carriage came for Miss Warren at six am sharp. A very fine young gent called by the name of a Mr John Ruskin. She wanted you and Lady McKenzie to know that she won't be returning, but not to worry and she will journey separately back to Orsbrick Hall later today on the train. Left a note here, thanking Countess Lovelace for her hospitality. I'll leave you to your breakfast madam. The Times is here if you want it?"

"Thank you Jeeves, yes please," Victoria replied, tucking hungrily into the bacon and toast. Hell and damnation, she instantly thought. Of all the times Abby has to go missing just when she needed to talk about Ada and last night's revelations. She may as well read the Times from cover to cover. But that pleasure came to an abrupt end as Morag marched into the room through the back door accompanied by a large and rotund elderly man, dressed from head to toe in black, with matching top hat. His long beard was yellowed around the mouth to match his teeth, with excessive smoking. He adjusted his small wire-framed glasses to the light and coughed, a deep racking sound, placing a small suitcase onto the table, which he promptly opened with a bang.

"Victoria," Morag shouted as Jeeves shuffled in quietly from the kitchen. "This is Dr Aaron Samuels, Ada's renowned personal physician from Harley Street, who has kindly come over immediately. I am very concerned about James; the fever doesn't seem to be subsiding."

"Good day to you Mrs Hammelaar. Now Lady McKenzie, where is the patient? I haven't much time especially if we want to give him a good bleed."

Victoria peered into his cold eyes, bulging through thick lenses, quite alarmed and uninspired by his mannerisms. It was little wonder that poor Ada suffered chronic illnesses. She knew enough about the state of pre-antibiotic and pre-vaccination medicine in 1841 to remember that basic biochemistry and endocrinology were unknown and that anatomy knowledge was pretty shaky. In particular, the reasons or remedies for many serious ailments, which were either endemic like tuberculosis or epidemic like cholera, were seriously facile or plain wrong, making the patient even sicker.

She turned swiftly to Morag. "May I come up with you please?"

Dr Samuels winced, the fewer around him the better, especially women. Morag pondered. "Well, I don't know why but if you must, come along then."

The three entered James's bedroom where he lay, quite inert, a thin sheet over him, still sweating and decidedly feverish, a high temperature evident. Any remainder of his usual maternal indifference had vanished. He propped himself up and groaned. "Who is this man, Mother?"

"Dr Samuels dear, he's come from Harley Street to make you better."

The windows were propped wide open and the temperature very chilly, the stench of coal burning and sewers prevailing strongly. Victoria went immediately to close the windows.

"No, no madam, leave them be," he shouted. "We need to purify the toxic vapours, plenty of fresh air needed."

"What is coming in from outside smells a lot more noxious than inside surely," Victoria countered, "and the room is far too cold."

"I'm sorry madam but are you a physician?" he rebuked in an offensive and condescending tone. "If not then I demand you leave immediately. I will not abide wilful obstruction to my diagnosis."

"I'm a scientist, Dr Samuels, and I am not leaving," Victoria replied, staying steadfast, looking him straight into his watery eyes. Morag stiffened. She was unused to seeing a medical practitioner challenged, and especially by a woman; such behaviour was simply not done. Victoria had to show some respect. This man was a senior doctor and even attended the Queen.

"Lady McKenzie," he bellowed. "Have her removed please."

Morag, now uneasy, looked hard at Victoria who shook her head firmly. She respected Victoria's capabilities and doubts ran through her mind. "I wish Mrs Hammelaar to remain but she will comment no more. Please proceed Dr Samuels, I will pay your fee immediately you finish."

His eyes brightened. "As you wish, Lady McKenzie." He listened to James's chest with an old wooden stethoscope and felt his forehead. "How are your bowels, boy, eaten any cucumber or melon or been raging at your mother lately?"

"Loose, sir, I've not eaten anything since last night, only dry bread, and I am a boy of very calm temperament sir."

Victoria stared in total disbelief. "He jumped into the pond yesterday. Did you swallow any water, James?"

"Yes, a few mouthfuls, Mrs Hammelaar."

"That is of no consequence, boys will be boys Mrs Hammelaar," Dr Samuels muttered, glaring again at Victoria. "The boy is entering puberty which often causes rabid fever when noxious elements of childhood lurk, especially in the liver. No liquids for forty-eight hours. I'll purge his bowels fully with some chloride of mercury to be sure we have evacuated all fetid elements. Can you turn him over, Lady McKenzie? I need to cut his back and bleed the liver clean. We need a bowl. A few pints out should be enough. Should be right in a day."

Morag looked at Jeeves who stood apprehensively in the doorway.

"No, no, no," Victoria shrieked. "You will not do this. Your diagnosis is absolute and complete nonsense and those remedies are downright dangerous and will kill him rather than make him better."

Dr Samuels spun round, his face bright red and bloated with anger. He moved to slap her hard across the face but stopped himself as she backed off. Morag stared horrified with both of them.

"This is outrageous. You damned impudent woman," he bellowed. "How dare you speak to me like that? Have you any idea who I am? Outside immediately, I demand it. Remove yourself now before I throw you out with my own hands. If you were a man I would horsewhip you instantly for such intolerable behaviour. Now Lady McKenzie, stand aside, I need to do my job and not listen to this ridiculous hysteria."

Victoria strode to the door and turned. "I don't care who you are, Samuels, you are not doing that to a McKenzie, especially James McKenzie."

"Victoria, what on earth are you talking about? Have you gone totally and absolutely mad?" Morag shrieked back as Samuels pushed James, howling with pain, roughly onto his distended stomach, and pulled out a large, dirty scalpel from his case.

Victoria ran out down the corridor blindly, not knowing what to do, when Jeeves suddenly confronted her from out of Ada's bedroom. "You're right madam. Get rid of the bastard quickly, he's done nothing for the Countess either; he just wants his fat fee. I've seen enough maladies in the army to know that boy has now become very sick overnight. Take this and just point it … he'll soon move his backside. Then I suggest you get James home on the train quickly. I have an old bath chair in the basement, you can push him in. We'll wrap him up properly." He thrust a shiny brass pistol into her hand. "It's loaded and primed madam."

She held the heavy pistol carefully and thought immediately of Julian. If he can do it so could she. "Thank you Jeeves, you are a star in the making, believe me, you've just saved his life."

She ran back into the room. James was screaming for his mother to stop everything, his back covered in leeches from a jar on the bedside table, as Dr Samuels mixed a glassful of orange powder, the scalpel now fixed between his teeth. Morag was standing by the window, immobile, silent and petrified.

"Dr Samuels, move away from James, now. Take your case and leave, and don't ever think of returning to this household again," she shouted, pointing the pistol, two handed straight to his chest. His face whitened and he put down the glass and the scalpel, slowly shutting the case, whilst keeping his eyes peeled solidly on his assailant.

"Victoria, what in heaven's name are you doing? Oh God in heaven, please have mercy on her poor demented soul."

"Morag, please believe me, I have not been more sane in my entire life. And if this man doesn't move himself, I shall blow his bollocks right off without hesitation."

James had by now struggled to turn himself around, the leeches tumbling off his back onto the floor, and sat bolt upright, in total disbelief with what he was seeing and hearing. For the first time in twenty-four hours a genuine grin appeared across his face. His governess had as much bottle as Rocket.

"Lady McKenzie," Dr Samuels whispered in a much softer croaky voice. "I am leaving forthwith, but I cannot begin to describe the untold consequences of this unheard of action by this maniac, once I report back to the Countess of Lovelace and her husband."

Morag looked straight at Victoria. "I'm sorry for the inconvenience Dr Samuels, but your services are herewith terminated. Jeeves will give you half of your agreed fee on your way out. Good day."

Hastily, Samuels stepped quickly from the room and clattered down the stairs for his hat and coat, followed by a smirking Jeeves.

Victoria put down the pistol and immediately closed all the windows, leaving only the side vents open. Fluffing the pillows properly, she tucked him under the sheet and put two light blankets on top before stamping on the leeches hard. She felt his forehead, his temperature remained high but he was alternating between bouts of feeling very cold inside and feverish and his stomach was slightly distended, looking painful. A pale rash could be seen on his lower abdomen.

Morag sat quietly on a chair by the window and watched.

"James, when did you last eat and drink?"

"Not since last night Mrs Hammelaar. I've had nothing because Miss Newton said I mustn't and the doctor was coming, but I had the runs badly first thing this morning, just made it. I've still got stomach pains. I'm very thirsty but I don't know if I can drink anything because my throat feels so sore."

Victoria wiped the end of a spoon clean with a napkin. "Open your mouth." She gently pushed down his tongue and noted the inflamed swelling, as well as his neck glands. "You need to start drinking, right away. Boiled water and I want you to have some soup and some mashed potato, just a little but often during the day."

Jeeves sidled out of the room to boil some and promptly removed the pistol carefully at the same time.

"Do you understand James? You have to have plenty of fluids down you, even if it hurts to swallow. That was exactly what Rocket did when he was ill in the army, so you must do the same. Agreed?"

"Did he really, Mrs Hammelaar? Yes, I will try, and thank you for removing Dr Frankenstein, that man was a hideous abomination. And I hate leeches when they're on me!"

Victoria laughed, she had to think when that novel was published, plainly earlier in the century than she realised. "Have you read the book then?"

"Yes, last year. I wasn't supposed to but Aunt Medora lent me it. Rocket also thought it was very funny too."

"Do you talk a lot about books to Rocket?"

"Yes, he has a fantastic library and is very well read, not like a normal blacksmith. We even read Shakespeare together."

"Good … now when this cup of water has cooled, drink it all down. It won't taste nice but that doesn't matter."

"Why do you boil the water?"

"To kill any germs, so you won't get sicker."

"Germs? What are they?"

"Little tiny creatures which make you ill and carry diseases, boiling the water kills them off."

"Can you see them under a microscope?"

"Sometimes, like tadpoles, but they are very small so you can't see them with your eyes."

"I hope when I get better that we can do some photography, Mrs Hammelaar, I'm looking forward to that."

"Alright. Now Jeeves will feed you some of his vegetable soup he's brought up and then you have a snooze. I need to have a talk with your mother."

Morag, intrigued and puzzled, walked from the room with Victoria behind, down to Ada's study, where a smiling new maid in a brand new uniform, Rhona, Mr Jeeves's young niece drafted in, was waiting with a pot of tea, china cups and a slab of fruit cake. They sat down carefully, each eyeing the other and slowly supping the tea. Victoria could sense that Morag's analytical brain was alight desperately trying to make logical sense of what had happened, exactly as Victoria herself would be doing. Their minds worked so very similar. But at this stage, Victoria was far less concerned with that and more bothered about the symptoms which James was displaying.

Morag coughed, cleared her throat and spoke softly. "Victoria, I want you to know, that I do believe you. I was stupidly taken in by that man's purported status and gravitas but in fact, by applying a little scientific process, his examination and conclusions were inept and his attitude to women and us deplorable. I know, for far too often, I've accepted this state of affairs with overbearing men. It is hard to shake the burden off, and I must adjust my outlook … you would think I'd know better being a widow. But Ada convinced me of his credentials, yet look at her treatment? She never gets well. But I must know now. You do and say strange things which I have never ever encountered before. How do you know all this science and these facts? Where and how have you learned so much?"

Victoria blanched inside. She needed to keep Morag focussed on James's condition; this was not the moment to meander into awkward territory. One thing above all else was paramount. James cannot be allowed to die, here in London, in this house. They have to take him home promptly to Orsbrick Hall, then she can attend to him with Maddie and Belle alongside and do everything possible to get him well, no matter what it takes, even if she has to encroach into futuristic science or medicine. He cannot die, or everyone, starting off with Mauveine, will never exist and there will never be a future.

"I'm nothing special, Morag. My knowledge is simply the benefits of an unusually thorough initial education and a lifetime of science learning, like you and Ada. And as for James, I've experienced those exact symptoms first hand, when Madeleine caught the identical lurgy in Holland as a child. That is why I was so adamant in my protestations."

Morag smiled. She wasn't entirely convinced but it didn't matter for now. What was important was doing the correct actions for her son, and in comparison to Victoria she knew she was equally inept at such things. "I'm pleased you did what you did, despite it being a little ... well, unorthodox."

They giggled. Morag was coming around to practicalities.

"So what is your diagnosis? What do you think James has got?"

"If I'm right he's been likely incubating sickness for a week or two. Falling in the pond has just exacerbated the condition. Has anything happened to him over the past two weeks or has be done anything stupid?"

"You mean apart from the usual behaviour, like despising his mother and being an ignorant little bastard, but he is my son and I don't want him to die. And I can sense you're making a positive impression on him, which is excellent. Let me think ... oh yes, one thing. Apparently a few weeks back, those idiot sons of Mr Fazackerley were larking about and pushed him into the cesspit. They fished him out and poured three buckets of water over the fool and Mr Fazackerley washed and dried all his clothes ... I only heard from a barmaid at the George who had spoken to Agnes in passing."

Victoria drew a deep breath. "The cesspit was the culprit. I believe James is in the early stages of typhoid. We must take him home immediately Morag before he worsens and he will, and care for him properly at Orsbrick Hall. Ada's house is lovely but the environment here in London is not at all conducive to good health. We must leave now. Jeeves has offered us a bath chair that we can wrap him up warm in and I'll push. We need to retrieve Esther from her sister's house. Between us I'm sure we can manage. We can be back home at Orsbrick Hall, with clean fresh air and water by nightfall. Oh gosh, I forgot, there's also Ellen missing, she's gone out."

Morag nodded and stood up. "Fine. We will of course not see Ada who is gossiping around town as usual but I do know her well, she'll understand. Look, there outside, the children are down the road and coming back with Medora and Henrietta. That's our Ellen problem solved. Pile your dresses and things into the trunks. I understand Abigail is making her own way back and is surreptitiously indisposed presently."

They laughed again. Normality was restoring.

She continued. "We'll be in a carriage in fifteen minutes. I'll ensure James is dressed ... Now where's Jeeves gone?"

"I'm here Lady McKenzie ... and look who we've got too," as he pushed James in the three-wheeled bath chair into the study, already dressed and wrapped up in a blanket, a weak smile across his mouth. "I'll just get a couple of lads from Lady Courtley next door to lug those heavy trunks downstairs and we can borrow their large carriage, so we'll have you at Euston station in no time, I'll be driving. Train is in three quarters of an hour, direct, I believe, straight through to Liverpool and passing Manchester so no need even to change, milady."

Pandemonium quickly caught hold with the children rushing in and running around everywhere, shouting and laughing. Morag beamed. "Jeeves you are an absolute treasure. If you decide you would like to see out your retirement in the countryside, there will be a most pleasant home for you and your wife at Orsbrick."

He grinned, a large toothless smile. "Lady McKenzie, I may seriously take you up on that kind offer. I'm getting a little old for all this excitement. Rhona has gone to fetch Miss Esther, so let's get the wagons and horses hitched as we used to say at Waterloo."

# Chapter Fourteen

Returning on the train, Victoria and Morag took turns to keep James warm and comfortable, bathing his forehead with cooling lint, whilst Esther looked after Ellen, still sad and concerned about her only brother. Jeeves had packed a substantial picnic lunch, with bread, sausages and fruit plus a large bottle of boiled water to assuage James's thirst. The first class passengers were told that the train was the most modern yet built by the newly-merged railway company, certainly the long journey felt much smoother and quieter. A guard and his female assistant provided boiling hot tea and coffee off a trolley from a special hot plate on the locomotive, the carriages all furbished with roofs, interlinked with a flexible cover. Happily the guards also heated more cold soup up for James, who Morag spoon fed slowly and sporadically throughout the journey. To Victoria's great relief, a new water closet had been constructed at the end of their carriage, down which a regularly filled pail of water could be thrown, the contents disgorging onto the tracks. Two gentlemen nearby helpfully assisted James inside when more bouts of intense diarrhoea and pain assailed him.

Back in Orsbrick Hall, James's condition continued to worsen, but he was finally back in a warm, comfortable and odour free bedroom. On return, Morag had jumped straight onto her horse and rode into Burscough to find her doctor, a young and very affable man, well dressed and courteous who had not long completed his training at the flourishing medical school of the Liverpool Royal Infirmary hospital. Dr Emmanuel Kirkby, youngest son of the Duke of Kirkby, had opened his local practice only six months before.

Returning with Morag, Dr Kirkby concluded that Victoria's diagnosis 'had a serious semblance of true possibility' that James's illness could indeed be typhoid, but as Victoria knew, despite his up to date knowledge and modern attitude, he could offer little in terms of a cure except the use of camphor poultices around James's distended belly to relieve the pain. Knowledge of germs had still to wait until 1861, but Dr Kirkby condemned the common application of leeches 'as a medieval abomination' and strongly discouraged the routine use of bleeding and purges. Despite the vociferous opposition within the medical fraternity, he was scientifically convinced that something within dirty water, or lack of cleanliness and bad sanitation, carried both typhoid and cholera, following an intern spell in a hospital abroad in Paris. But he discounted cholera because vomiting and excessive continual diarrhoea were absent and the patient lacked the telltale clammy skin and sunken eyes, which he had seen in droves amongst the dying of the poor in the districts of Montmartre where a bad outbreak had taken place.

Victoria kept running backwards in her own mind to her recent reading of the early years of Virginia Woolf, when her beloved brother Toby caught typhoid in Turkey in 1906. They got him home safely but doctors stupidly misdiagnosed appendicitis and he died, suddenly, prematurely and unnecessarily, of intestinal bursting, after falsely appearing to improve for several weeks. Dr Kirkby was especially intrigued with Victoria's insistence of the liberal wiping down of everything using a dilute solution of 'coal-oil acid', known of course to Victoria as phenol, which Morag had made in her laboratory. Only discovered seven years previously, coal-oil acid was one of the compounds prepared from her plentiful supplies of coal-tar that Morag had been researching for dyes before her obsession with Faraday's electricity took over. Once again Victoria used the justification that this was a proven help to reduce infections spreading, which had recently been tried in Amsterdam. She was now very mindful the Dutch excuse was wearing thinner and thinner, as each time Morag stared at her sceptically. Time was running out maintaining pretences, but she had to do all she could to save James.

Still too there was no sign of Abby. Morag came in with some letters including one from Abby, confirming that she was staying for at least three more days with Mr Ruskin's parents with whom 'much empathy and sociability had been sustained'. Victoria was becoming irritated with this situation. It was as if Abby had definitely decided to give up and go hell for leather at making a life out of this 1841 here and now rather than support Mauveine. Or, was it possible that Abby had genuinely fallen in love? Damn it, that was never originally conceived of but Victoria understood why, only too well.

Also, another situation had arisen, where Abby's support would have been a huge help. It became quickly apparent that during their absence, relationships, between Maddie and Belle with Mr and Mrs Williams, had well and truly broken down, especially after a mysterious fire had broken out the day before in the library. Maddie and Belle had been accused of 'exhibiting negligence and incompetent behaviour' by stupidly leaving candles burning amongst the books. Agnes, however, had spotted Mrs Williams creeping out of the library that evening, before then raising the alarm, after Maddie and Belle had completed their day's work and relaxed downstairs. One

371

almighty row had ensued with Mr Williams losing his temper. In the end, Agnes had gone to the rectory for help and asked the vicar and his wife, the Reverend and Mrs Langton, to come and reconcile the situation in the absence of Lady McKenzie. Mauveine immediately realised what was happening. She had been far too familiar with inter-family rivalries between servants, and Williams regarded Maddie and Belle as exactly that, servants and no more. With her experience, Mauveine managed to quell the tension but without agreement as to who or what caused the fire. Fortunately, the flames had been quickly extinguished, the damage restricted to the unfortunate destruction of copies of early writings by Anthony Trollope, some volumes of poetry by Wordsworth and Shelley and a few eighteenth century books on elementary algebra which Maddie was about to record. However the bad feeling and atmosphere remained which was making Victoria quite uneasy. Morag insisted to Mr Williams that the priority library cataloguing must continue for the time being. Agnes however, promised Victoria that she would inform Morag, as soon as the time was right, about what she actually saw.

James's fever continued to rage, with Dr Kirkby's endorsement of Victoria's treatment plan. Rest, liquids, keeping warm and regular soup and boiled rice would be maintained. Also, Dr Kirkby agreed to provide two nurses, one for the day and one for nights, who with Agnes and Esther would form a continuous twenty-four hour shift to watch over him. Morag was more than happy to pay the heavy costs for as long as necessary.

But Victoria had to do more, increasingly concerned about his intestinal pain, which was one of the most invidious outcomes of the disease, exactly as happened to Toby Stephens, Virginia Woolf's beloved brother. As well as Abby missing, there was no sign of either Dr Gray or Mr Fazackerley. Lynton had disappeared amongst the social elite in London, cavorting with his new aristocratic belle. Julian had reappeared in his cottage and resumed work quietly, but despite James's pleas he was keeping well away from both Morag and Orsbrick Hall. And from Morag's perspective that was exactly how she wanted it, especially following the letter she received from Ada, which she refused to discuss with Victoria.

Day two came and went. James's fever had stabilised but he remained very ill indeed, the nurses, night and day, busy with everything necessary. Victoria, in-between, gave more lessons to Ellen as well as consoling Morag. She had also spent time quietly in the library with Maddie and Belle, as they discussed and relayed each other's experiences over the previous two days, the three of them increasingly concerned that despite the acknowledged progress, some sort of breakthrough like Mauveine had demanded was needed but not forthcoming. However, the biggest cause of concern remained James, his life still on a delicate knife-edge. At one point, after Agnes ran in, red in the face with anxiety, Morag had even bolted out of Orsbrick Hall and ridden straight to the rectory, to bring back Isi and prepare for last rites.

Early in the morning of day three, Victoria, Maddie and Belle rode to the rectory to confer with Mauveine, who was now very concerned about James. Events were moving fast in real-time and James could catastrophically die in a moment. They met over tea and cakes, all extremely despondent. They decided to brainstorm new ideas. Mauveine brought in a large blank hymn sheet and a pencil, time to aggregate the McKenzie brainpower and scientific knowledge. Mauveine commenced, bringing forward all her knowledge of the late nineteenth century medicine to combat diseases, when germs and antiseptics were known and the use of plant based remedies and poultices extensive. Sadly, apart from honey and carbolic acid, much of what happened later in the Victorian period, including finding the specialist plants, was presently frustratingly inaccessible. But it was Belle, always thinking quietly away from the mainstream, who came up with an interesting suggestion.

"Mauveine, when you were talking about innovative plant remedies in 1890 that were used for the first time and effective initially with bacterial infections, has sort of made me jump further with that concept."

Mauveine patted her hand. "I hope Belle, no matter what happens to us all, that you pursue a career in medicine. You have a bright future ahead of you as a doctor, I know it. By 1860 female doctors even commenced formal training. You might have to do the Crimea though and make an impact."

Belle blushed as Victoria and Maddie beamed. Mauveine still displayed exactly the same sense of a determined McKenzie female destiny as she once had, and may also have to acquire again too, if James dies.

"Well, do go on then Belle, don't keep us in suspense," Victoria cried impatiently, as Mauveine laughed and cut four pieces of her freshly baked raspberry jam sponge cake, a firm favourite in her own time, with Isi running in and grabbing a slice before dashing off again to prepare the next church service and keep up appearances.

"Belle? Are you thinking what I'm thinking?" Maddie intervened slowly. "What we really need are antibiotics."

"Yes, but I've been racking my brains about that conundrum. Mum, you remember when we had that panic last year, when you became ill and we thought you had bubonic plague and were shipped off to the isolation ward?"

"Sadly, I was out of it of course most of the time and missed the fun," Victoria replied, "Especially when Dr Lee confronted a naked Ned with a foot long needle to inject into his stomach!"

They laughed; even Mauveine admitted she and Isi had watched it all through the window, highly amused.

"Dr Lee and I talked a lot about ancient diseases and the fact that pre-antibiotics, many people, even then, did survive serious illness and epidemics. The ones who succumbed mostly had poor immune systems, or were very young and elderly."

Mauveine nodded, "Absolutely correct. And public health measures improved dramatically between 1850 and 1900, another key factor. Here, in 1841, they are still relatively in the dark ages, although amazingly Morag has had the foresight to install effective sanitation even if she doesn't know yet the reasons why it works. And Victoria, you've instituted a kind of localised sanitary environment by encouraging all the hand-washing and carbolic acid."

"Not without some initial resistance, but even Mr and Mrs Williams are now advocates and helping. Thank you for the intervention incidentally, we seem to be back to normal around Orsbrick Hall."

"All part of the service, so to speak, but it was Isi really who facilitated the breakthrough. He does have a remarkable talent as a mediating vicar. I fear he may want to take this up permanently … if we remain." She sighed. "I know we don't want to give up but McKenzie women have always been very pragmatic and realistic. There is no harm in considering our options if we fail."

"Abby is certainly exercising that possibility well in advance presently," Victoria added, still exasperated with her lovesick friend's critical absence.

They all giggled. Victoria had spilled the gossip earlier.

"Actually," Mauveine responded, "this may be serendipity, because I am beginning to conclude that we need to focus on hard science now, which is we four alone. Let Abby have fun, I think she deserves it after all she's done."

Victoria smiled and nodded, she couldn't really argue against that hypothesis. She turned and looked hard at Belle. "So? Your conclusions please?"

"Right, well since Dr Lee's chat, I've done a lot of reading on the history of antibiotics. Given that we are in 1841, where nobody in the population has any experience of antibiotics in their bodily systems, that means if one was used, even if it wasn't clinically by our standards very good, the chances of success would be high. So why don't we make one in Morag's laboratory?"

"What, Penicillin? Like Fleming in 1924?" Victoria replied, impressed by Belle's lateral thinking but immediately dismissive of the practicalities.

"No, too difficult, but what do we know about Prontosil?"

Mauveine went quiet. Belle was now outside of her personal knowledge and time barriers.

"Prontosil? … Gosh I've heard of that, let me think," Victoria cried, her fast brain revving into overdrive, alongside Maddie who as ever arrived first.

"The first sulphonamide drug, Belle, wasn't it?" Maddie replied. "Discovered in 1932 by a German team working for Bayer and very effective for a time, viewed as a magic bullet although it only worked against certain strains of bacteria. Lots of replicas emerged but they were all quickly superseded by penicillin which could operate more widely."

"Pretty good sis, gosh Mum's getting slow in her old age."

Victoria glared. "Not that slow, because I know what is really at the back of your mind here, Belle, and I'll give you top marks for lateral thinking. Many of the early compounds from which these nascent antibiotics were made had close links to dyes ... same chemical core bonding. Drugs and dyes, certainly from the First World War, went very much hand in hand. As I recall from my organic chemistry, Prontosil can be produced as a by-product of the first azo dyes, all the progenitors of the brightly coloured, yellows, greens, reds and orange as far as fluorescein."

"Hold everything exactly there please," Mauveine suddenly cried out, back into the debate, her eyes animated and her brow furrowed in deep concentration. "I made some of those dyes, including fluorescein, very early in my career, before they were formally announced in science papers. Goodness me, I was only around fourteen or so down in the basement laboratory, but had a bout of major inspiration from reading some papers from Germany I was not supposed to look at, and then I oxidised various coal tar distillates with chromic acid and other reagents. It has all come back to me, like yesterday. Xanthene ... we have to make xanthene as the azo dye basis of this so called Prontosil. This was even before I met Isi ... mmm."

"Xanthene, of course, which I recently reproduced from your original papers, Mauveine," Victoria added, equally excited.

"I know," Mauveine replied. "And I was so pleased to see your work Victoria and planned to come into the laboratory alongside you to see and advise you further, until our predicament here suddenly came into sharp perspective and Isi and I became sadly distracted."

"But, we can surely do it again?" Belle interjected. "Mauveine and Mum, just to be clear, Prontosil is a brand drug name. It is, in fact, the dye itself. Prontosil and xanthene are essentially the same thing. The antibiotic properties were accidentally discovered when someone in Bayer injected the yellow-red dye into mice."

There was a silence, as everyone pondered what they had just come up with.

"So our flight from the Queen Lusitania ship is … well, a flight for xanthene," Mauveine interjected. "What are we waiting for? We all need to return to Orsbrick Hall and start work. Morag showed me her chemistry store, and I did a rapid automatic stock check, old habits die hard. She has pretty well all the required chemicals and with some improvisation, enough equipment, although I don't like her Bunsen burner one little bit. We will need to acquire some coal tar but that can be obtained from the gas works in Burscough. I'll just saddle my horse and tell Isi. Victoria, you need to lead with all of this, I mean with persuading Morag, who will become highly suspicious. You have her confidence presently, but we must have a story ready which also includes why I am with you."

"Okay … I'll think of something on the way there, you'll all have to play along with it though," Victoria replied. "But this may be our only chance before James's intestines burst."

*

A difficult sell was probably an understatement. In the end Victoria had to strongly appeal to Morag's fears to overcome a raft of suspicions, doubts and disbelief.

"Alice and I are now convinced that poor James is in the most serious of dangers and we have discussed an unusual remedy, which we saw formulated during the days when Alice and I volunteered together in the fever hospital in Amsterdam err … in '35, is that not so, sister?"

"Yes indeed Lady McKenzie," Mauveine added, as bold as daylight. "I was visiting Victoria and her family for three months on an extended holiday, when our neighbourhood was overcome with an epidemic of fevers. A horrible disease took hold, similar in symptoms to that of James. Nurses were short in supply and Victoria and I volunteered to help. They were desperate … and that is how I met my dear husband Thomas, he was administering to the dying and praying for their souls."

Maddie blinked and glanced sideways at Belle. Mauveine was as good as Abby at making it up as she went along.

Mauveine continued. "I too am well versed in chemistry like my sister, although these days of course my wifely duties, as should be, are confined solely to assist the work of my husband. But my sister and I were invited to help a doctor from the Far East, to make an unusual compound in his hospital laboratory that he had learned of in the Americas. On completion, the reagent was used on the sick, and a high cure rate was facilitated. I noted the process carefully … and have it here," She began to wave her original xanthene paper in front of Morag for whom it too would be incomprehensible, starting with the chemical notations written all over, but not used yet in 1841.

Victoria cut in. "Do you trust me Morag? I have only ever had your interest and James's welfare at heart since he became ill."

Morag went silent and reflected quietly. Once more, Victoria was acting and speaking bizarrely. "Do you really mean to tell me again that the world of science in Holland is so much more advanced than in England? You know I have no means of verifying that, but the word of your sister, a respected wife of a preacher, I do respect. Always Victoria, you talk in ways and riddles I find most difficult to assimilate, but I can't deny what you have done and my gratitude is immense. Yes, I do trust you and I know we have reached such a critical and dangerous point in James's cycle of illness that any mother would wish for an immediate solution and cure to be found, as I truly fear his imminent death within the next twenty-four hours. Which is why, Mrs Langton, I have asked your husband to be ready … to guide his soul towards whatever the Lord God becomes in the next world."

"He is praying hard for James's recovery right now, Lady McKenzie. The power of prayer will help and my husband has bid me to come too and assist you in the methods Victoria suggests."

"And, Lady McKenzie, Annabelle and I will also support my mother and aunt in their scientific proceedings," Maddie added in a whisper.

Morag laughed. "So we have a house suddenly replete with five female scientists. If only Mr Faraday were here he would not believe his eyes. So what do you need Victoria?"

"Four scientists, if I may suggest please Morag. We agree it would be best if you continue to provide comfort directly to your son, and we will do the necessary work. Your emotions are too overwrought to think well. We need a few buckets of coal tar from the gas works and the key to your store room to find suitable apparatus and chemicals. Have you ever heard of the saying 'too many cooks spoil the broth?'"

"Yes of course I have Victoria, a phrase extant since 1597, my English happens to be excellent also," Morag snapped back. "But I accept your collective proposition. If you need me you know where I am. Agnes has the key and I will send Mr Williams forthwith to the gasworks. Now I must return to James, the pains in his abdomen grow worse, only the poultices have provided some relief."

*

Once the window shutters were opened, a stream of afternoon sunshine flooded through the store window, enabling

Mauveine and Victoria to carefully work through the labels on the bottles and find the range of chemicals needed.

"Mrs Hammelaar, I'll just carry this flagon of sulphuric acid up to the laboratory. Do you need any more of this glassware on the other table for Madeleine and Annabelle? They are very fast assembling things, quite takes my breath away, you must be very proud of them … real scientists I do declare."

Victoria smiled. "Yes, I am proud Agnes. Does Lady McKenzie require you, or can you help us? Please, when with my sister and daughters, do still call me Victoria and Mrs Langton, my sister, is Alice."

"I'm alright presently, Victoria. Esther is taking the day shift until seven then Mr Williams has volunteered until midnight when the night nurse will arrive again."

"Alice, have we got all the compounds here? Is there anything missing?"

Mauveine squinted hard at the labels. "Benzene, we need benzene. At least I've found dichromate of ammonia."

"Lady McKenzie did have some of that benzene stuff but she made me throw it all in the cesspit … smelled terrible. She said something about it reminding her of the wrong half of Mr Faraday, whatever that means."

Victoria grinned. Morag's mind worked in some odd ways. "I can distil it from the coal tar, Alice. We need to make a fractionating tower from those glass tubes over there. I didn't work in a refinery for nothing."

"A refinery, what is that place, Victoria?" Agnes queried.

"Oh … err another Dutch name, for making oil of coal," Victoria replied, catching a smirk from Mauveine. "Agnes, can you ask Mr Williams to double the amount of coal tar, we will need more now."

"Straight away, Victoria. I'll then check how your girls are progressing."

*

In one sense this was the most bizarre situation Victoria could possibly have imagined. Maddie, Belle, her and Mauveine, all working busily together as a team, with makeshift white coats on in an early Victorian laboratory, creating a dye. Once again, what was Abby missing? Mauveine was fantastically adept at shaping glass tubing, a skill she had learned as a child, once she decided to modify, in frustration, Morag's smoky gas burner. With a hammer and punch she carefully knocked a thin, wide hole into the vertical tube and with tin-shears cut out a piece of zinc sheet, which she moulded into a collar.

"It's so easy, Victoria," Mauveine cried, as they all watched the yellow flame turn into a sharp, hot and familiar blue one. "All this complicated valve nonsense … that fool Faraday should stick to electric motors and leave the chemistry to Bunsen and Kirchhoff."

Victoria grinned and Maddie and Belle laughed loudly.

Soon, working to Victoria's sketching, Mauveine created a working distillation tower with condensers, run-off taps to collect various distillates and cooling tubes leading to a water tank on a ledge. The large metal retort, connected to various flasks, was carefully filled with thick coal-tar as they opened every window wide; fume cupboards were unknown back then.

On the other bench, Maddie and Belle, working from Mauveine's paper, had constructed a crude mini glass chemical processing plant, with retorts connected to various flasks and beakers, clamped together with wooden stands, the stages corresponding to the oxidation and distillation processes from coal tar to pure xanthene, which should drip into the final receiving container. They needed another burner, but Victoria found an early model in a box, which Mauveine once again modified and connected to the gas supply.

Maddie, struggling with the final connections, turned to Belle. "Can you hold that Woolf bottle? I wish we had rubber tubing; this flexible metal stuff is really hard to bend properly, ahh … that's got it. Mum, Mauveine, I think we're done our end."

Victoria moved the burner towards the retort. "Okay, let's go. First we need the benzene and one or two other distillates that Mauveine doesn't know about yet. Now, I don't need to say it twice. Every process and action with this makeshift equipment is very hazardous, the fitting tolerances are not what we're used to so fire, leaking gas, and potential explosions lurk. All this is highly dangerous. Belle can you bring those sand buckets over and if anything happens just throw it over the lot. And watch your eyes, no safety glasses."

Mauveine interrupted. "Don't forget, I am used to this type of laboratory and my equipment in the 1860s wasn't much improved. I will have a better sixth sense of how far to go than any of you, so let me do the heating part, Victoria, you check the distillates as they condense. First we need benzene."

Mauveine shoved the burner roughly under the retort, Maddie and Belle watching very warily. "Remember all of you, Orsbrick Hall was still standing when you arrived, so I didn't do too badly. Only had one explosion which singed my hair off, but it re-grew," she cried, very patently back in her element doing chemistry again.

One hour of nervous time passed by. They had opened the store windows as well and a welcome draught blew through, minimising the fumes accumulating, as their coughing stopped, but the air was still far smellier than would be allowed normally. Mauveine, impervious to the stench, was completely absorbed by the fractionation of the coal tar as Victoria collected various dark coloured oily distillates to transfer to the next section where Maddie mixed it with benzoic acid and lime, beginning a second distillation to produce a steady drip-drip of almost pure benzene. Meanwhile, Belle was carefully mixing and heating various chromium based oxidising compounds in large beakers with sulphuric and nitric acids, taking great care to control the reactions.

Absorbed with their individual tasks, nobody noticed the door open quietly and a figure creep in. "Starting without me? That's not exactly cricket is it?" a voice rang out in a highly accented tone, but with a familiarity sufficient to make a startled Victoria turn … and then glare.

"Good Lord! Hey everyone, never mind the prodigal son, the Angel Gabriela is back early from her wanton ways. Got bored with shagging half of London have we?"

Abby, not amused by Victoria and especially her tone, stood calmly, her hands on her hips, seeing instantly that she had not endeared herself to her best friend and was very unwelcome.

"Vikki, you and me can have one mother of a slanging match if you want outside, but such language, in front of Mauveine, Maddie and Belle is out of order and inappropriate."

Victoria put down her beaker. "I'm sure the three of them know what shagging is. We're all big girls now," she shouted.

Maddie and Belle remained silent. They hadn't seen their mother and Abby so angry with each other. Belle continued draining out a retort full of reagents, whilst Maddie helped.

Mauveine suddenly walked between them. "Victoria, just hang on one minute. I suggest we all take a very deep breath, become civilised and that we listen to what Abigail has got to say. And we are at a critical point in this experiment."

"Okay, but I've got work to do, Mauveine," Victoria barked. "If Abby wants to speak, she can speak, but Maddie, Belle and I need to continue regardless. I agree this is critical, the final oxidation process is just beginning." Victoria and Mauveine walked back to the second bench and adjusted some of the reagent mixtures.

Abby debated instantly whether to storm off and return to London for good, but she drew breath, thought hard and spoke, as the others continued pressing on with the next stage of the production of xanthene.

"I had a letter from Morag which went from Mr Faraday to Mr Babbage and then finally to John Ruskin which detailed how sick James had become. On receipt I immediately caught the train back. I had no idea, until then, that there was anything amiss, so I'm really, really sorry that I wasn't here to do more."

Victoria stopped fiddling with test tubes and looked over severely. "But why Abby? Why just disappear like that? Have you given up all hope?"

Maddie and Belle also stopped but Mauveine continued, swishing and stirring in a variety of reagents into the final retort which she started to gently heat.

Tears rolled down Abby's cheeks. She felt desperate to want to cry badly but was holding her emotions in check as hard as she could. "This whole experience … everything happening was beginning to be just too much and yes, I admit it, and I know it was wrong, but I was beginning to give up, feeling increasingly resigned to staying in 1841 for the rest of my days. I just couldn't see any progress and now James. It was that fucking bastard Lynton that finally drove me onto the dark side. His blatant and continual flaunting behaviour with those rich, aristocratic women with time on their hands and nothing else to do but steal husbands, and now he's decided to shack up with one, an actress, in Covent Garden. God knows how his daughter is coping. That was it, well and truly and finally it." She sobbed hard before pulling out a silk handkerchief and wiped her nose and eyes. "I needed comfort, fun, some reason for living again, my art, paintings, dresses, status, all those things which make me who I am … and above all I wanted love and to be wanted. I found it all with John Ruskin. He's besotted, amazing, and has asked me to marry him. So that's it … I'm a complete mess and no value whatsoever to any of you." She sobbed quietly.

Victoria fell silent. Maddie, upset, was torn desperately inside, with her own deep love for Abby versus her loyalty and affection for her mother. But it was Belle who spoke up in her usual dispassionate way.

"But Abby, we all understand how you've been feeling, but you also have to be logical. Lynton is not your husband here, neither is Julian my dad or Mum's husband either. They may look like them and share characteristics and I agree they *are* fucking bastards including Ned and Zac too, sorry for the language. But that's the way the space-time rupture dice fell. And whilst the grass may seem greener on the other side, it isn't and we're not giving up yet. Our priority is to make James well, then go from there. We've all got options if we can't get back to our own time. I'm going to the Crimea with Mauveine to join Florence Nightingale, whoopee."

"And I'm going to marry Disraeli," Maddie joined in. "A great, radical mind with a truly liberal compassion."

Everyone laughed including Abby who stopped sobbing and wiped her eyes as Victoria walked over with her arms wide to give her a hug. "For fuck's sake Abby, come here will you, we've really missed you, me especially and we have made progress. Be careful; don't touch my gloves … sulphuric acid."

Mauveine called out. "We definitely have now. Look at this … exactly as I did it in 1864."

They all turned to see Mauveine holding a large beaker under a condenser outlet as an orange-red liquid dripped rapidly inside.

"Okay and thanks all, reality check truly taken on board," Abby said softly, a smile emerging from her face. "Perhaps it's time I started making my contribution. Morag explained what you're all doing in here, preparing something to administer to James. I assume that red liquid has antibiotic properties. The science is way beyond me but have you thought how you're going to get it inside him? And he's been vomiting. I haven't seen sight of a hypodermic syringe anywhere."

Maddie took over from Mauveine who was frowning hard. "Abigail is quite correct. In the excitement we never thought and hypodermic needles were only invented when I was a little girl, another ten years on yet so there are none anywhere."

Belle walked over holding the first flask of pure dye. "Is xanthene soluble in a saline solution, Mum?"

"Yes, why?"

"Because during the 1830s, when the first cholera epidemics in Europe started, a cholera specialist in England, I think his name was Stephens, launched a controversial saline fluid replacement treatment in the north. It worked, many people survived who would have died, and he was a hundred years ahead of his time but he was ignored and ridiculed then by many of his jealous contemporaries. He used a special syringe to deliver the solution rectally, for fast ingestion. I know it's not very nice, but better than leeches or being bled."

"And much better than dying," Victoria replied. "The delectable Dr Kirkby said he was a cholera specialist and is keen on new methods. I would bet he has such a syringe."

"I'll go and fetch Agnes," Abby interjected, desperate to start doing something. "Oh and Morag is coming down any minute. And she is likely to have something to say about Julian and Ada too."

"Like what?"

"I'd better leave that to her," Abby replied and disappeared out of the door.

*

"Thank you all so much, what a beautiful colour. But it looks very much like a dye?" Morag cried, holding up the first beaker to the light. "Why is the second beaker bright yellow?"

"Err … same family, so I was told," Victoria murmured, taking the beaker off her. "We mix them for maximum effect."

"Mmm … interesting … excellent. Now, I'm going to ride into town in two minutes and find Dr Kirkby personally and bring him back. All this medical activity has made me realise that his surgery would benefit from relocation into much larger premises … and the estate verily owns a perfect venue. I shall offer to donate to him free of rent, the whole of Cinderblack Cottages, once we have cleaned it all up."

Victoria looked up startled. "But isn't that where Mr Fazackerley lives with his family and makes his living from?"

Morag grimaced, disdainfully. "Not for much longer. You will never believe what that invidious man has done or rather I should say what Ada has concocted up this time."

Abby walked back in. "I'm just going to relieve Esther shortly, she hasn't eaten all day and is feeling weak. Agnes also has to do the cooking for dinner. Mrs Williams has pulled her back again lugging sacks of potatoes, and must rest."

"Thank you dearest cousin," Morag replied. "We are all so pleased to see you back in the fold once more, not least of all me. Now where was I? Oh yes … Ada informs me in her most brisk and precise written prose, that she is 'buying my blacksmith' and will be moving Mr Fazackerley and those dreadful boys and dogs, down to another of her houses in Embankment, where he will work exclusively for her and her growing properties around England and Scotland. William, her husband, is apparently very enthusiastic, the poor fool. Little does he know or maybe doesn't care about her insatiable need for hordes of undesirable men around her. Mr Fazackerley, as one would expect, agreed on the spot and the family will be gone in a week."

Victoria became very quiet, sullen even, then glanced at Abby and remembered what Belle had said earlier. Get over it, the 1841 Julian is irrelevant. She forced a smile. "He must have made some indelible impression on Ada, Morag? But from what you said, Ada and Mr Fazackerly's sister are great friends too?"

"Yes, I'm sure," Morag replied waspishly. "Ada is welcome to the ménage, all very cosy family. Good riddance I say unequivocally. And, would you also believe, Ada is indeed up in Lancashire today, cavorting with Mr Fazackerley at the Aintree races for the second year of the Grand Liverpool Steeplechase. You already know her excessive predilection for card games and betting. Caitriona confirmed to me that he was a heavy gambler one time and Ada wants to put into practice her so called mathematical system she has been developing which guarantees the odds to win. Two gamblers together. They make a well-suited pair, destined to lose their entire fortunes. She will be arriving later to say hello to everyone and enquire how James is progressing. Now, I must fetch Manny and that special syringe. I assume, Victoria, when we return you will have sufficient of your infusion to give to the patient?"

"Yes, we will be ready for Dr Kirkby to administer the treatment."

In a second, Morag had dashed out of the back door. They watched her through the window, galloping off down the drive.

"Cousin Morag seems to have suddenly developed a strong interest in our handsome young Dr Kirkby, or should I say, Manny," Abby said, smirking. "Julian is forgotten already but what about Faraday?"

"She never mentioned him coming back on the train. Call it instinct but I have a horrible feeling she knows. He's probably confessed in a long, religious diatribe," Victoria grumbled.

"Knows what, Mum?" Maddie asked, very curious.

Victoria reddened and Belle grinned.

"Your mother and Mr Faraday became good friends down in London, err … isn't that your option sorted, Vikki?" Abby replied, deadpan.

"Possibly," Victoria replied, changing the subject. "More importantly, can we prepare those beakers of xanthene in a saline solution please? I have no idea about concentrations or how much to give. We'll have to leave that to Manny's judgement but I suppose we could try and treat him as if he was on a course of strong antibiotics. Insertion every three hours? James is going to howl."

"I suggest Victoria that you watch how Dr Kirkby administers the first insertion and then take over. It should be no different to treating horses for constipation," Mauveine added, matter of fact. "I think I'd better return to the rectory. Isi will want his dinner. An excellent afternoon of science work together, now let us pray that this endeavour works."

*

It took the combined efforts of Abby, Esther and Mr Williams to hold James down along with the requisite towels, bowls and lint plugs. The howling was indeed intense but after the first dose was administered, the second, three hours later, which Victoria skilfully undertook under the watchful eye of Dr Kirkby, went much better. James said he almost enjoyed the feeling, especially after Victoria had worked out that the addition of some butter around the syringe tube would have no deleterious chemical effect on their proto-Prontosil solution. He was also given a plant sedative which eased him into a long needed sleep, under the watchful eye of Mr Williams, doing the evening shift.

Dr Kirkby and Morag retired for a drink and a private chat in her study, whilst Victoria, Abby, Maddie and Belle took a well deserved rest in the drawing room with some pre-dinner champagne to celebrate, an unusually fine tasting drink, imported from France which Agnes uncorked with gusto. The well known reputation of the Orsbrick Hall wine cellar had a heritage going back a long way.

"Given that Morag may be pregnant, hitching up with the doctor may not be such a bad thing. He is apparently the youngest son of a wealthy Duke and they are probably of a similar age," Abby said, swirling her champagne and admiring the splendid cut glass.

"Pregnant?" Maddie whispered looking quite horrified as Belle sat up in her chair. "But who is the father?"

Victoria sighed. "A long story, both of you. It may be Mr Faraday or it may even be Julian Fazackerley. Or it may be a phantom. She doesn't want to talk about it anymore."

"Oh my God," Maddie retorted, her mind racing with all kinds of permutations and combinations of future off-spring.

"My word, what on earth is that racket outside?" Abby cried, as they turned and put down their glasses. "Someone is coming in and doing a lot of shouting."

The door was flung open and Ada breezed in with style, dressed in a magnificent black, swirling cloak, white gloves, her luxuriant long, brown curls topped with an enormous matching bonnet bedecked with purple flowers and her personal maid alongside, whilst her driver unloaded numerous cases and bags down the corridor. "Good evening everyone, guess what happened to me today? I won fifty pounds on the races after Julian persuaded me to make a mad accumulator bet with only one shilling, so I have presents for everyone. Now I must go and see poor James, how is he doing? Where is Morag?"

"Ada, what a pleasant surprise," Victoria uttered with a smile through gritted teeth. "Morag is in private discussion with the doctor. May I be allowed to take you, but we most walk quietly as he is probably asleep. He's been very poorly. We are treating him with a new remedy." She took Ada by the arm and led her gently outside, Maddie and Belle staring open-mouthed.

"Gosh, the princess of parallelograms," Belle whispered, in total awe.

"No, that was her mother. I think you mean the enchantress of numbers ... so Charles Babbage once remarked," Maddie replied. "I think a little more champagne is required. I do like her crazy outfits though, fashion par excellence."

Abby topped up their glasses. "Yes, grand entrances are an Ada speciality, goes with the Countess territory, and being a deadly poker player ... I lost a fiver at her house in no time and do you know what? I found it under my pillow when I went to bed with a book on probabilities. She is a character."

"So Victoria, have you considered my generous offer, yet?" Ada purred, as Williams sauntered off for a beer break. They stared down at James, sleeping peacefully. "Julian adores you, and you could take rooms in his spacious new house, a lovely location, becoming very fashionable and near some marvellous restaurants. Is that not irresistible?"

"Does he? I never quite had that impression, last time he was here," Victoria replied, reaching for lint to wipe the sweat off James's brow.

"Of course he does, don't be silly. Morag flaunting herself over him was a temporary distraction. He immediately recognised your desirable intellectual superiority and intriguing beauty, an uncanny resemblance to earlier McKenzie women, especially Fiona, Malcolm's grandmother, a formidable and shrewd woman. I liked her, very lively, quite unlike Morag. But he's mine now, all mine, so no designs, agreed?" Ada giggled softly.

"My priority has solely been James, Ada," Victoria replied in a whisper, feeling his head. "I'm still considering your proposition and have not yet had the time to speak to my daughters."

She continued to look closely at his neck. Not only was James sleeping better but his temperature had dropped from raging to high and she was certain his swelling was less. Perhaps the xanthene infusion was already having some effect. She smiled, watching Ada who was gazing out of the window also deep in concentration.

"I feel so much better, Victoria, even the gastritis has stopped. Julian is good for me, I feel alive again."

Victoria breathed in hard … this strange situation was very hard to bear.

"James is more rested, we should go downstairs now. Let me shut the door. Are you staying for dinner?"

"Of course."

They stepped into the corridor and Ada grabbed her arm.

"Wait. I have a paper with me I finished this morning on refining the method of differences that I want your opinion on, and something else very, very radical. You must tell absolutely no one until I have worked further on the concept. I believe we could apply such iteration with the Engine way beyond numbers to non-numerical variables. Can you not imagine say the ordered, musical tones of scales and arpeggios being produced by instruction? And a machine then produces a symphony to rival Beethoven? The impact on society will be unbelievable. My mind is alight with such crazy thoughts and inspiration right now. Some days, Charles believes I should be placed inside a madhouse and the door shut tightly. He ran out of the house last time, tearing his hands through his hair!"

Victoria laughed softly. "You're not crazy, Ada. You have the most formidable foresight for a future world that I have ever seen. I know such things will happen. Men will fly through the air on machines, travel by rocket to the moon, speak through the air without wires and process your non-numerical data faster than the human brain using electrically driven Engines and …"

She stopped. Shit, she knew it; she was getting carried away again. Ada's never-ending enthusiasm and thirst for knowledge was incredibly infectious.

Ada smiled. She stared hard into Victoria's eyes, penetrating and intense. "I know you know. What I want to find out is why and how you know it."

"Mrs Hammelaar, are you there?" A voice, weak but clear sounded from the bedroom. James was awake.

Victoria ran alarmed back into his room with Ada behind, but to see him sitting up in bed and smiling. "James, you should be asleep, rest is important. I'm sorry I woke you."

"Can I have some water please," he croaked. "No, I want to tell you, it is very important. I'm feeling so much better already and that terrible pain in my belly is going down. Thank you for taking care of me, I believe you've saved my life and I will forever be grateful."

Victoria grinned and felt his temperature again as Ada passed him a glass of boiled water. "You are certainly less feverish but we must continue the treatment exactly the same tomorrow to make sure. You've been a brave young man so far, I know the experience is not pleasant at all."

"This boiled water is becoming an acquired taste, but I do still prefer beer," he whispered. "I am resolute for the treatment, no matter how painful. I am determined to stay alive Mrs Hammelaar and when I'm recovered a new dawn in my life will start. You have shown me better than anything the real power of science and I am resolved from now on to use my abilities, study hard and devote my life and my future wealth to such pursuits, because science is the key to a better future for mankind. I want you and my mother to teach me all you know, so that I can embrace my responsibilities as a man and as the McKenzie heir just as my father did."

Victoria tucked him back in. "Of course, I promise. Now you must rest. Mr Williams is here now to look after you and no beer together yet!"

Victoria and Ada left quietly and walked slowly down the long corridor.

"Morag will be pleased to hear that news, Victoria, a real turnaround. You have acquired a special bond already with the boy and as I always said to her, he is indeed very astute and clever with a prestigious future ahead of him. It is as if you and James were kith and kin, like being his true mother. You should adopt him, a remarkable meeting up. But then, as I said earlier, you are a remarkable woman. And an excellent scientist."

"I'm just being no more than a good governess," Victoria replied carefully. "Anyway, he's not out of the woods yet, but I feel more hopeful than any time since I diagnosed him."

"Let's head for the dining room," Ada said, walking faster. "I can smell Agnes's special beef stew. She always used to cook such a meal regularly for my mother and very nutritious and tasty it is too. And I promise, no card games this evening. Abigail becomes over-excited and rather carried away and I don't want to fleece her again, it was like taking candy sweets from a tiny baby."

Victoria laughed and linked Ada's arm. "Good, we don't want Morag's cousin falling onto hard times. Now I would like to know who makes your beautiful dresses, especially the one you're wearing. Such an unusual pale green and those huge puffy sleeves, I haven't seen anything like it."

Ada grinned. "You won't because the Queen's designer has only just made it. I am convinced the style will become a new fashion trend … I persuaded him quietly to let me have the first one. Privilege has its advantages Victoria as I hope to show you in the future."

*

As ever in Ada's company, the dinner party was a lively affair with one after the other of hilarious stories about amusing misdemeanours of a déshabillé kind, taking place inside Buckingham Palace, including a well known but naked Earl, left on a high balcony all morning for the amusement of the many voyeurs after being locked out by his mistress. Victoria managed to have a word with Morag about James's improved progress, but gave no mention of his declaration to dedicate himself to science. Morag excused herself immediately to see him but of course James was fast asleep. However, she readily saw how improved he appeared. Ada was especially interested in the lives and loves of Maddie and Belle and quizzed them relentlessly about their science interests and background although she was disparaging about their fashion sense, indicating that they should spend a week at St James's Square and attend some balls at Court to meet eligible rich men. Abby felt extremely nervous as the probing continued and was relieved when Maddie fended off a difficult interrogation about their supposed father with a brilliant exposition of life as the child of a successful wool merchant. What true historic inspiration she had drawn on was as compelling as her vivid imagination for storytelling.

Morag arrived back and whispered a 'thank you and well done' to Victoria, before returning to the conversation. Victoria sat quietly, watching the dynamic carefully as the discussion veered into politics and liberalism. Abby stepped rapidly into a great stride with her firebrand socialist opinions, vehemently espousing the Whig point of view. Ada appeared to favour the Tory perspective but more likely argued for the sake of opposing Abby; Belle and Maddie also joined in on opposite sides. Victoria decided that any opportunity to be contentious was always a game for Ada and she played it cleverly to suit her whim of the moment.

Victoria watched Morag carefully. Despite her earlier thank you for saving James, she remained sullen and noticeably indifferent, and her whole body language dictated something was seriously wrong. The sourness was equally directed to Ada. Victoria ran through a multiplicity of reasons. Was Morag definitely pregnant? Was she jealous of her attention to James? Was she jealous of her breadth of science expertise? Was she upset about Ada's connivances with Julian and dropping in unannounced? Did she know of Faraday's fling? Also Victoria overheard Morag instructing Agnes to leave all the chemicals and related equipment in the laboratory … Was she conflicted again about her science direction? And perhaps, after seeing the industrious and successful chemistry team effort, was thinking about discontinuing the electrical work for Faraday? Maybe it was aspects of all of those things. But Victoria pondered that whilst a favourable momentum continued that she should show Morag how the dye which was curing James was made.

Once Esther was clearing the dinner table, Ada suddenly announced she would retire to Morag's study as she had two papers to finish and needed to do some extensive reading in the library. She insisted Maddie and Belle go with her to learn some proper mathematics despite complaining bitterly that Morag's study library was excessively filled with literature and lacked sufficient high-level science. Victoria was very tired. The day had been stressful and exhausting. Abby looked equally worse for wear and also decided to go to her room. An early night beckoned. Agnes ran upstairs to prepare warm baths as Mrs Williams hobbled downstairs to make bedtime hot chocolate.

Morag was sat quietly and alone, staring into space, absorbed with something deep in her mind.

Victoria got up and walked over. "It has been an arduous day, Morag, you look tired. Early night for all of us I think, but I'm glad you're pleased that James has turned a corner and is on the mend … I couldn't wish for more either."

Morag looked up. "Yes, I'm sure you couldn't. I'm fine, but there is something I need to do."

Instantly, Morag shot up out of her chair and without a word brushed past Victoria and strode over to Williams. She stood in the doorway, to whisper a few words in his ear and the two of them walked off towards the porter's lodge, as Victoria watched, puzzled. A minute later she heard a clip-clop of hooves and through the window in the haze of the gaslight saw Morag gallop off in the moonlight towards the town.

# Chapter Fifteen

A slight drizzle permeated the windless air. At the same time, the clutter of piled up trunks and bags was loaded back onto Ada's carriage. It was early morning and Ada was departing again, but apart from Agnes running back and forth only Victoria stood patiently outside under a large umbrella to see her off. Abby was still fast asleep as were Maddie and Belle. Since Morag's peculiar departure off into the night, Victoria had seen no sign of her and Williams remained, as ever, tight-lipped and almost surly.

Checking on James first thing, she and the night nurse had successfully managed to give James another enema, which he bore without a whimper. Four more left to go. His progress had continued well during the night, the feverish temperature stabilising right down and he was eager, for the first time, to have a proper breakfast of scrambled eggs and toast. The effect of the crude antibiotic had been remarkable on his throat pain and neck swelling; both had subsided considerably along with his difficulty swallowing. Only the intestinal pain seemed to remain but much less than the day before. Barring some unexplained reversal, Victoria was confident he was going to live, but where was Morag? Even Agnes had no idea, suspecting she had gone out late and left early as a piece of her favourite brown bread had been cut and buttered in the kitchen.

Ada came skittering down the steps holding a large pink umbrella and wearing a dazzling all-white outfit with black boots, her hair tied back into a severe bun, showing off that impressive forehead, undoubtedly seething inside with more scheming. She joined Victoria whilst the last of the luggage was thrown on and covered over.

"Thank you so much for seeing me off. The abode is quite dead this morning but I do see James's coefficient of friskiness is increasing admirably. I like to see a man tucking into his breakfast in bed, don't you? Mind you, Michael Faraday refuses to ever eat any, such a silly fool when it comes to being a normal individual," she said pointedly. "I have some business in Liverpool for the next couple of days, after which I shall return with Medora to see you all again and then she and I will spend some time with the children and my beloved husband, who are now at my Ockham country seat in Sussex. You will like William, the Earl of Lovelace, he is decidedly your type. I forgot how invigorating fresh air in the country is so I intend to indulge again in a few rural pursuits, but travel regularly into London of course. I have Mr Julian Fazackerley to house." She grinned at Victoria who nodded back blandly.

Victoria was convinced that in reality Ada would be picking up Julian for some cavorting first. The implied idea of being palmed off into becoming an occasional diversionary mistress of Lord William Noel-King, Ada's husband, was not at all appealing.

"It has been a pleasure seeing you again Ada, and the girls haven't stopped talking about you."

"Likewise. Madeleine and Annabelle are each intriguingly entertaining. I hope my children grow up as mature and worldly-wise. At their age I was a naive baby, molly-coddled by an oppressive mother, lonely and excluded from normal company and then married off immediately … at nineteen. How ridiculous really but William is handsomely wealthy. We must get them a first-rate mathematics tutor. As Morag reluctantly intimated, they know of imaginary numbers far better than her. I drummed the new theory of quaternions, invented by my friend William Hamilton, into their heads last night and they became very excited with the notion of working in four dimensions, including time. Actually so am I, the merging of mathematics and poetry harmoniously together. Mary Somerville will do it; she was an excellent tutor to me, or my other friend, Augustus de Morgan. Such a logician you will never better. I expect a decision, Victoria, when I return … you will know why then."

Victoria glanced back uneasily but Ada was staring at a piece of paper scrawled with algebra. "I'm sorry that Morag isn't here to say goodbye. I have no idea where she is."

"I do," Ada replied, still staring at her equations. "You know, whilst I was at the races who should I bump into? Such a small world, but the Duke of Kirkby is a distinguished man of considerable means and a great philanthropist to the poor of Liverpool. He's looking forward to his new grandchild. Goodness me, we're ready. I must go, see you in a few days Victoria, bye-bye."

Victoria looked back puzzled, watching Ada hop nimbly into the carriage which immediately shot off down the drive. Suddenly, thinking of all people her Aunt Eveline who would have loved to have been here, she decided to walk to the pond and ponder awhile, the drizzle abating. She pulled down the umbrella and continued slowly. There were many more trees around the wooded area which went back as far as the eye could see, fields being tended on either side. She spotted a couple of nice wooden log-seats under the large oak tree still there, and sat down to stare at the clear water, a few large white fish circling into the reeds.

Then it struck her. The Duke of Kirkby was Dr Kirkby's father. Morag had casually mentioned it but she was only half listening, her mind very absorbed on James's condition. Fuck, Morag *was* pregnant and the father must be Dr Kirkby or Manny as he preferred to be called. Cunning Ada never missed a trick, how did she know all that? Morag obviously had no intention of telling anyone. That's where Morag must have gone, and perhaps why she was so indifferent the previous evening. She may be intending to marry Manny, certainly they appeared well suited in many ways, but that wasn't the point. What difference would it make to James's future and destiny? She had to go and wake Abby.

*

By day four, James's condition had improved encouragingly. Without any doubt, the nascent antibiotic properties of the yellow dye, introduced to a virginal-bacterial recipient, had accelerated his recovery dramatically. Victoria, however, remained convinced that the prompt action taken to get him home had caught the vicious typhoid cycle in its early stages. Nevertheless, as Belle pointed out, the initial public trials of penicillin in the mid 1940s had the same dramatic effect on infections until gradual bacterial resistance crept in. Most importantly, James's energy was returning and he was even eating almost normally. The nurses were discharged. Dr Kirkby was enthusiastically impressed and keen to know more about the reagent, but Victoria continued to obfuscate, watching him and Morag with amusement, as they continually disappeared into her study for private chats. He must have visited at least six times, which even Agnes started to comment on. But Morag maintained her contradictory behaviour towards Victoria, on the one hand being effusively grateful and complimentary about saving James's life and on the other displaying an air of distant and increased formality in their conversations, which had become significantly fewer. Victoria already was taking short periods of time with James alone to begin, on his request, his journey into chemistry. Alternating with Abby, she also tutored Ellen again who was now joyful her brother wasn't going to die. James's attitude towards his mother changed. He appeared to dramatically mature overnight since his illness, talking enthusiastically to Morag about taking the Bluecoat School scholarship examination in three months time, the old sullenness and antagonism gone. All talk of Rocket, Edward and Zackary stopped. Everyone was pleased with that situation.

James finally told his mother of his commitment, to become a scientist like her, not an engineer following his father. But to Victoria, Morag seemed surprisingly lacking in enthusiasm, almost as if she neither believed him nor cared about that goal any more. But *he* certainly did, as Victoria discovered each day, taking care not to overtax him Already, he was showing astonishing capability to grasp chemical concepts and ask demanding questions for a near thirteen year old. Perhaps, Victoria mused, Morag had other pressing personal concerns around her own pregnancy which was not raised or hinted at again. It was agreed that James would remain in bed for at least another week to get his strength back.

Victoria, Maddie and Belle with Abby found time together to ride over to the rectory and report back to Mauveine and Isi. Mauveine was smiling again but insisted that Victoria show Morag how xanthene was made as quickly as possible and try and nudge her back into chemistry. It seemed to everyone that the time was opportune.

During the afternoon of day five, Victoria plucked up courage and asked Morag if she would like to see how the xanthene dye had been produced. Agnes continued to transfer the rest of the contents of the storeroom, including all the chemicals and the rest of the equipment, back into the laboratory and had moved out all the electrical equipment. She was surprised that Morag immediately answered yes and they walked silently into the laboratory.

Morag was especially intrigued with the mock glass fractionating tower and impressed with the methodology which Maddie had undertaken, of making the base benzene, producing a far purer product than what she had originally used. Victoria noticed that a new shelf of bottles of natural indigo and red madder dyes had been put up, and on a separate shelf stood a small bottle with a purplish-mauve liquid in it.

Morag picked the bottle up. "This reagent is what I was last working on, from controlled oxidation reactions using Mr Faraday's benzene with indigo and madder dye and sulphuric acid. I can't work out how to test it yet but I'm sure the compound is a new dye, similar to indigo. But whether it works on fabrics such as silk or calico, I never unfortunately got that far."

"I'll show you how to test it," Victoria said. "I see you have a folder of fabrics in the corner there. You've got most of the right chemicals here, although some haven't been invented yet, sorry I mean utilised."

"I heard you the first time, Victoria … again, you say the strangest way of things. What exactly are you looking for?"

"Do you have any hydroxide of sodium?"

"Yes, in that sealed container but be careful, it will burn your hand off."

"I know, thank you, I've used it many times. We may need a mordant for the wool. Aahh … I can see some tannic acid, an excellent alternative, we don't need to make any."

"A mordant? What is that?"

"A fixative. It does for dyes what sodium thiosulphate does for silver plate photographs, integral to the whole dyeing industry and processes. Most plant dyes don't need mordants but will often benefit from using them, and they depend on the fabric itself.

Morag went silent. She was concentrating hard as Victoria went, one by one, through the processes to produce xanthene, many of which were not dissimilar to what Morag had been attempting with her own early dye experiments. Then she lit the burner and commenced a practical demonstration, handing beakers to Morag to participate, writing down the steps in understandable language.

"I must apologise for what Alice did to Mr Faraday's burner but you can see the flame is much improved with increased oxygen to the gas."

"Yes, amazing and so simple. I'm not interested whatsoever in Mr Faraday's crude workmanship," Morag exclaimed, holding the first beaker under the final condenser as drops of yellow tinged with streaks of red xanthene dye dripped rapidly into the beaker she was holding.

Victoria could see that for the first time for days Morag was beginning to relax with her and even smile. It was time to query. "I must ask you the obvious question," she began. "Seeing that Agnes has moved in all the chemical contents in the store and moved out all the electrical apparatus, you may need the batteries incidentally, I can show you why later. Well? Are you returning to your dye work now?"

"Yes. That is, as you say, an obvious deduction. I have concluded that my strengths are as an innovator in chemistry and a follower in electrics and I don't follow anyone, or indeed any man. And I want to create an environment for James, to work with his newly found enthusiasm," she replied clinically.

"But your strong commitment to Mr Faraday? Is that over?"

"I never want to see Faraday or hear his claptrap about electrical theories again."

"But why Morag? Mr Faraday is an experimenter of genius capabilities and ..."

Morag cut her short instantly. "You know why, Victoria, and I don't wish to talk about it."

Victoria felt her face redden. Shit ... Maybe Morag had found out and Ada was correct. She said nothing.

"Now, I think we've done enough for today," Morag said, restless to go.

"Let me show you something Morag, one final thing, this will amaze you. Something else you can do with xanthene. Before I forget, I have kept some other distillates from the coal tar and labelled them carefully. They will be useful for you in your future work as a base, alongside your benzene. Pass me the chloride of zinc and the chromic acid, oh ... and the dichromate of potassium. What I'll do is not the most brilliant way but it will work with this specific preparation of xanthene."

Victoria carefully assembled a separate oxidation chamber with some of Mauveine's spare tubing and added the reagents together to the xanthene, carefully mixing in some additional ferric chloride and heated it gently. Within a few minutes the red dye had changed colour into a strange, greenish-yellow cloudy mix, shimmering a bright fluorescence in the sunlight streaming through the windows. She had repeated a simplified version of the experiment she had last done in her laboratory, and created fluorescein using Mauveine's methodology.

"My goodness," Morag exclaimed, her eyes wide and scared by what she was experiencing. "What in the Lord and Heaven's name is that liquid? I have seen nothing remotely like it. Victoria, you have knowledge and capabilities of science way beyond anything I have ever experienced. You are frightening and I don't understand …we must go please. Shut it down."

"Alright Morag, I just wanted you to see … well, what can be achieved if you and James continue with your dye experiments."

Victoria shut everything down carefully and switched off the gas. They walked out silently back towards the study, when Morag stopped and turned. "Ada is returning tonight with Medora. I wish, in fact it is essential, for all of us to meet before dinner, including you, Abigail, Madeleine and Annabelle. I have something I want to say to you all."

Victoria felt a cold chill running up and down her spine. Morag looked extremely ill at ease, something was seriously amiss. Her tone said it all. What was going on? "Certainly Morag, but pray, what is troubling you so much? Do you wish to share anything before we all meet first?"

"No, I'm sorry Victoria, really, really sorry," Morag replied stiffly, her face drawn into despair. "But I have no choice. I will see you later in the drawing room, once Ada and Medora have arrived. Please alert Abigail and your daughters for me."

Victoria watched as Morag disappeared hastily without a further word up to her bedroom. A crisis was building up that was plain. Was Morag going to fire her and tell her to leave? Or worse? But why would Ada and Medora need to be present too? She had to find Abby, Maddie and Belle immediately and desperately wished Mauveine was there again.

# Chapter Sixteen

Flustered and behind schedule, the moment Agnes changed her bed, Maddie sat cross-legged on it in her bell dress. She was missing her skinny jeans badly and browsing through more of Morag's magazines containing excerpts from the latest Charles Dickens novel, 'The Old Curiosity Shop'. Ada had insisted she should read it to understand life in 1820s England and had giggled that even Queen Victoria had found the novel an interesting piece of work. Belle was sat quietly in the small armchair overlooking the window, absorbed with Ada's present to her mother the geometry book by Legendre, concentrating on the quaint French writing. She was finding the translation a real challenge, but more intellectually satisfying than playing Minecraft on her mobile phone, the object she still missed the most. Ada had promised to take them to Charles Dickens's town house for a literary soiree when they came to London as he was a close personal friend, an awesome offer.

Both were conflicted with where they found themselves. In many ways they wanted the 'Mauveine Paradox' as they jokingly referred to their predicament, to end and be back in their own era, but as Belle suggested, having Ada as a mentor, which she was keen to become, would provide them with unique opportunities in the top echelons of 1841 society they could only have dreamt of experiencing. Maddie agreed. At least their options held out some prospect of a future but when would they know and how? Too many unknowns remained and that glass sand timer on the shelf, which they had reset, was steadily running down as Mauveine's deadline of the end of the week loomed large. They took some comfort that Mauveine's prediction was a guestimate and at least life in Orsbrick Hall was proving comfortable, especially now relations with Mr and Mrs Williams had been repaired.

A loud knock made Belle jerk out of her seat as the door opened and Victoria and Abby entered their faces glum.

"What is the matter with both of you?" Maddie whispered, closing the door behind. "I thought we would be celebrating James's recovery when Ada arrives. I'm rather getting used to this champagne and four-course dinner lifestyle."

"Make the most of the happy memories, because things may be coming to a shuddering halt," Victoria said ominously. "Sit down both of you; I need to explain something that's been happening."

Belle poured out glasses of Agnes's lemonade each and Victoria repeated what she had just explained to Abby, focussing on the increasingly distanced behaviour of Morag, possible reasons, and the summons to the drawing room when Ada does arrive.

"You'd better be quick, Mum," Maddie cried, looking out of the window, "because I can see Ada's carriage coming down the drive now. She's early, probably left Dad at the racecourse."

Nobody laughed.

"I have a bad feeling about this," Abby added. "Morag has also stopped confiding in me too … I suspect she knows more than we thought and her pregnancy has brought things to a confused and anxious head."

Maddie cut in sharply. "But do we know who the father is now? Oh my God, it isn't really Dad is it?"

"Julian Fazackerley isn't Dad, Maddie, nor am I married to him," Victoria replied sternly. "Let's be clear about him, but we can't rule that possibility out, or Michael Faraday, and maybe there are others we don't know about, although Ada believes the father is actually the captivating, young Dr Kirkby."

"Who has been fancying you rotten, Belle," Maddie said. "Eyeing you up and down and admiring your glasses."

Belle squirmed in her seat. "Gosh, I must admit he is very dishy, it feels gross now somehow and Morag is so demure and proper … but puts it about a bit doesn't she?"

"Sign of the times," Abby replied, feeling herself blush. "But, the good thing is we have succeeded in ensuring James doesn't depart this mortal coil so quickly, and both he and now his mother are turned on by chemistry and dyes. But this entire psychic-return, I can't think of a better word, is more complex than any of us imagined. Even Mauveine still has no idea how to reverse it, yet. I can sense your termination of contract is on the cards Vikki. In which case we need a mitigating story. Everyone start thinking."

"All is not totally lost," Victoria muttered quietly. "It's time, I suppose, I confessed. Ada has offered me, Maddie and Belle a relocation contract to London and work with her if this goes pear-shaped tonight. We need to bring you with us Abby."

"I'm not surprised," Maddie added. "The way she was going on to me and Belle about being in London … all makes sense. But isn't Dad, sorry Mr Fazackerley, being headhunted down to London?"

"Yes, we would live in the same house that Ada is providing for him, Ned and Zac."

"Gosh, how bizarre," Maddie said and sighed. "Perhaps this is the next stage of the time-rupture. Abby, you don't have to tell, but what did you reply to John Ruskin when he asked you to marry him?"

"I said I would think about it and give him an answer next week," Abby replied, "Based on the rationale that if Mauveine is right we're all here to stay if nothing shifts."

"Okay," Victoria whispered, as they drew closer together. "At least we have a Plan B which makes me feel marginally better. What on earth is that? All the racket outside, I do believe Ada's here."

On cue there was a loud knocking at the door and Ada immediately breezed in, followed by Medora who shut the door quietly behind her. "I thought you would all be in here. Why in the Lord's name, the second I walk in the door, has Morag invited us all down for a revelatory inquisition to the drawing room?" Ada said in a loud voice. "Actually, reserve that thought, I suspect I probably know why. And I want you all to understand that whatever Morag has to say, I will back you unreservedly, and that includes you Abby. I would have thought she would be over the moon now given James's remarkable recovery and all of it, Victoria, down to you. But I can see clouds of hysteria developing. She's behaving exactly like when Malcolm died. Medora, you're Morag's best friend. Do you have an opinion?"

"We all know she's expecting, she's just over a month and a half gone. I think she may have a form of bad depression just as some women do after birth, except Morag is experiencing it before birth. Remember, Ada, it happened to you last time."

"Having three in three years would make anyone depressed," Ada replied with a grin. "You may be right … I'm not convinced. I suggest we all go down now and get this over with. I'll keep the champagne on hold until after the hanging."

They all laughed stupidly, therapy to relieve the growing tension. Ada, as ever, could lighten the mood in a second, exactly like her father had been known for his mastery of, years before.

"And thank you Ada. I really appreciate all you've said," Victoria added as they stood up and filed out of the door.

"Medora and I, we'll chat afterwards with you Victoria, when everyone has gone to bed. You too Abigail."

*

Inside the drawing room, a small fire had been lit to take off the chill and the armchairs and sofas already rearranged so they could sit in a circle with the large coffee table in the middle. It was obvious which one would be Morag's chosen seat. Ada chatted about her visits to numerous antique furniture and book shops in Liverpool, where she had indulged in all kinds of purchases to be shipped down to her new townhouse in Embankment, although no mention whatsoever was made of Julian.

Williams came in and fussed with the drinks cabinet until in the end they agreed on a glass of Burgundy red wine. Agnes followed, carrying a large plate of very enticing pastries.

"I've made these especially Countess, they're your favourites that I used to do for your mother, Lady Byron."

"Why Agnes, how very thoughtful of you," Ada replied delighted, gazing closely at the selections. "Thank you. They are very moreish everyone, but avert your eyes if you're watching your delicate waistlines. I assume you want one Morag?"

They all looked up surprised, to see Morag approaching quietly carrying a large glass of lemonade. How Ada sensed she was there nobody could see.

"No thank you Ada, I don't feel hungry," Morag replied before sitting down on her allotted chair gracefully.

There was a long hush as they shuffled in their seats, making themselves comfortable. Abby had already drunk her wine almost in one go and Williams promptly walked over and topped it up.

Ada broke the silence. "Morag, we're all intelligent and mature women of the world in this room, and I count Madeleine and Annabelle in that. So, pray, can you get on with what you have to say, succinctly please, and then we can all go and enjoy dinner."

"Thank you Williams and Agnes, you may leave now," Morag said formally.

"As you wish, milady," Williams replied, pushing Agnes onwards and out through the door, closing it quietly behind him.

Another silence ensued. Morag finally took a deep breath. "Yes, I will be succinct, accurate and scientifically precise, as Victoria, you are always telling me I should. First, I wish to publically thank Victoria for everything she, her daughters and Mrs Langton did to prepare a special medication which has unequivocally saved James's life. For that I will always be grateful. However, for your gross betrayal of my affections and you know precisely what I am talking about Victoria, I cannot and will not forgive you, ever."

"Just hang on one minute Morag," Ada cried. "I assume you're talking about the genius in mind but pygmy in emotion Mr Faraday. You and I know, or you should have known, that his deep convictions towards his wife and his staid religion would forever be unbreakable. He enticed you with a scientific nirvana and you took the bait, but he would never have augmented that with true love and union … that was never why

I brought you and him together. I wanted you to broaden your science and have fun, now I bitterly regret it. You can't blame his failings on Victoria who just happened to put on a good show, so Mr Babbage reported, at the Academy lectures."

Morag stood up. "Please, speak no more Ada, don't ruin our friendship, I beg you. This is my house. I insist." She sat down again, her face flushed and emotional. "No, you don't know it all, you have absolutely no idea how Mr Faraday felt towards me or why but Victoria ruined it all, didn't you Victoria for your own wicked ends. Lord above, please give me the strength to say what I must."

Victoria sat, immobile but calm, saying nothing as Belle reached over and held her hand tightly. Abby was feeling increasingly restless and uncomfortable as was Maddie. They glanced at one another.

Morag continued, her voice wavering. "Do you all really want to know? Do you Ada? Michael confessed. He broke down and sobbed bitterly in my arms, asking for my total forgiveness or his God would strike him down dead with a thunderbolt and his mind would dissolve into swill of pigs. He told me everything Victoria. How you went back and seduced him, completely, carnal and base, with a physical passion like I have never heard before in my life. You acted like a common and obscene whore in the East End of London. He provided me with every little detail, nothing whatsoever was missed out. Your daughters need to hear this Victoria, to cleanse their souls. But that isn't all. He announced you were the devil incarnate he had always been expecting and Hell was the source of all your mysterious scientific knowledge, and why you speak in forked tongues and incomprehensible tones, because you are Satan in disguise."

Medora raised herself up and rushed forward to comfort Morag. "Please, you are overwrought with child, my dear friend. Please stop all this; it leads only to sorrow ..."

But Morag brushed her aside. "Please let me be. I must finish, please ... sit."

Medora returned to her chair, her face grave with concern as Morag clasped both hands forward. "I have forgiven him unconditionally, but we must never see one another again. That was the condition his God gave him for his soul to be saved and not to burn in Hell."

"Yes, all very convenient. He can now return to his wife with his conscience cleared and embarrassment spared with you out of his life," Ada intervened. "I've never heard so much nonsense, Morag. I thought you were an unbeliever. For heaven's sake, you're a scientist, think clearly and rationally will you. He never wanted you so he had a quick fling with Victoria, so what. We all do it ... get over it ... and as Medora pointed out, you have far more important things now to consider and make right."

"I'm not listening to you Ada, you're in league with that malevolent harlot, I just sense it. So, Victoria, I hereby pronounce that your contract in this house is terminated forthwith. You will leave immediately, back to Holland, I don't care. You will receive a month's wages and your things are already packed and in the carriage. Williams has seen to it. And as for you dearest cousin, I know ... I heard things about you too. I want you to leave and never come back to this house again. I cannot have either of you polluting and corrupting the minds and souls of my dear children. Be gone ye foul excrements of the Devil. I have asked the Reverend Thomas Langton to come later and exorcise this house and remove any shadow of your evil left."

Victoria had uncharacteristically remained calm and composed, as she listened to this bizarre and rambling diatribe, disappointed and dismayed by Morag. But inside, her mind and body were boiling over with anger and rage and her face reddened as she rubbed her hands together. She felt like a pressure cooker that was about to explode.

Abby and Maddie looked across at each other. They had no need to say anything; their heads were pounding like crazy. They each knew the signs; a psychic crisis was building up fast. Abby looked at Victoria, and realised instantly; she had seen that look once before and it wasn't pretty. "No, Victoria, stop, for fuck's sake don't say anything."

It was too late. Victoria stood up, hands on hips, swaying, her face blazing. "How dare you Lady fucking Morag McKenzie, speak in that disgusting and disparaging manner to me. Who do you think you are? Yes, I fucked him, but as Ada said, so what? You've not exactly been whiter than white yourself, have you? What was it you said? We widows must stick together? You've got yourself pregnant and unmarried, Morag, and by the sound of it you don't even know who the father is either. If I'm Satan, heaven knows what you are. I really, really have cared for you, and James and Ellen. You don't know the half you ungrateful bitch ..."

"No, Victoria. No, don't, stop," Abby shouted, leaping from her chair, but Maddie knew it was impossible to curtail her mother now and jumped up and took Abby's arm, forcing her back into her seat. Medora stared, alarmed at what was unravelling across the room. Belle glanced across at Ada. She remained serene, a smile cutting slowly across her face. Belle got up and sat beside her on the floor, also remaining quiet, and held Ada's arm.

"No, Morag. And I'm not moving out of this house," Victoria continued, raging. "This is my house, don't you dare order me out of my own house."

Morag sat down, her face ashen. Never had anybody ever spoken to her in such a way. "What do you mean Victoria? Your house? What nonsense is that? You're a whore from Holland and that's where you're going back or more likely to the Gates of Hades."

Abby held her head in her hands, the pounding was getting worse as Maddie comforted her, feeling just as bad.

"Orsbrick Hall, Lady McKenzie, *is* my house. And, as for my incomprehensible science, spoken in riddles, tongues and strange tones, I'm sorry to disappoint you," Victoria raged. "I've been living it all, it's happened already, not devil-speak, my words are reality, Morag. The electric trains, the aeroplanes that fly across the sky, the computing machines which work a trillion times faster than Mr Babbage's Engine, the medicines which have eliminated cholera, smallpox and polio from the world, the horseless carriages that transport you wherever you want to go, the rockets to the Moon and Mars, the hundreds of artificial dyes, do you want me to go on …? She drew breath for a few seconds. "I live it, you stupid silly woman!" she screamed at the top of her voice.

Morag stared, her eyes wide, totally baffled. What was the meaning of all this? "I don't understand you Victoria. What in the Lord God Almighty's name are you talking about? Nothing makes any sense to me," she croaked, tears streaming down her face, already regretting what she had said, to unleash such unexpected venom from the governess she had trusted and almost loved as her own sister.

Medora meanwhile, standing in front of the window, watched with amazement as the weather started to change and the blue sky, almost in a moment, blackened over and dark clouds, tinged with strange yellow edges bunched together, the wind getting up. Lightning could be seen in the distance but no thunder.

"I know exactly what Victoria is talking about," Ada suddenly announced, as the room went quiet and everyone turned to see her face, calm with a large and mischievous smile. "I think I should get the champagne, because at last Victoria, you have confirmed what I had already worked out a while back because there was no other logical explanation … and I pride myself Morag in keeping an open, rational mind … not reverting to ranting medieval nonsense about devils. From the moment I met you, Victoria, I knew you were special and exciting. What intrigues me most is how you finally did it? Crossing space and time multiverses, all finally decoded. I want to find out. There is so much to learn and I am so hungry to learn, very hungry."

"Oh Lord save my soul," Morag cried. "Ada, what have you found out?"

"The future may learn from the past, but the past may never learn from the future. Another of Mr Faraday's unwise sayings and a falsehood now. Do you agree Victoria?" she replied, rubbing Belle's arm at the same time.

"Yes," Victoria said firmly. Abby looked up horrified, then followed Medora's anxious gaze out of the window … shit.

"What year?" Ada asked, nonchalantly.

"2026."

"That is so remarkable, a whole century and a half bypassed. I knew, I just knew, especially after our last discussion and my little night time chat with the beautiful and clever Madeleine and Annabelle. It was your computer programming sketch Annabelle that finally convinced me … sorry I know I shouldn't have plied you and Madeleine with more wine to loosen the tongue. Neither of you were speaking of this time whatsoever. My mind was ablaze all that night and I've been madly excited ever since."

"Ada ... what heresy are you speaking? You mean Victoria, Madeleine and Annabelle are from the future?"

"Yes, of course they are ... for God's sake Morag, look at Victoria and do some science will you. She's a McKenzie right down to the bone features, eyes and hair, my physiognomy analysis has never been wrong. She's a descendent ... the image of Fiona, Malcolm's grandmother. Lady Victoria McKenzie undoubtedly. This is the scientific find of the century and I want to own it, know so much more and learn. Morag, just think of the progress we could make with our society and accelerate needed applications, a daunting task but achievable. But Victoria, one little thing I must ask. I expect you know don't you. I need to plan every day now in minute detail. How long have I got? Do you know when I will die?"

Victoria paused. What on earth had she done? ... The situation had become irreversible. She couldn't say it, especially as Ada only had a short life left of increasingly painful illness and personal misery.

"Oh Ada ... dear Ada ... I can't, yes I know, but I can't, please don't ..."

But Medora interrupted sharply. "My God, what is that thing?"

A great clap of thunder echoed across the room and a strange, yellow light was lighting up the grey sky, piercing and blinding. They all turned to look out towards the pond and the fields beyond to see a huge orange ball, at least fifty feet high, rolling rapidly over the fields towards the house, red and yellow flames firing off from the spherical circumference setting everything alight in its path. Abby jumped forward, grabbing Maddie. "Vikki, Belle, come together, now, now now," she shouted at the top of her voice as they ran together and huddled each other closely.

The last thing Victoria heard was Medora and Morag petrified and screaming hysterically and saw Ada, still sitting serenely, a glass of champagne now in her hand, watching and wearing the broadest grin she had ever seen. The next moment the blinding light enveloped the entire room accompanied by a massive, deafening explosion. They were thrown together high in the air and floated upwards, trapped inside the giant orange ball, slowly, no sounds and no speaking, up and away towards the stars, twinkling in a hazy silhouette through the semi-transparent surface ...

# Chapter Seventeen

A skylark, rare at the best of times, sang and chirped merrily in the bright, warm sunshine, high up over the fields where the genetically modified spring wheat was shooting up for an early harvest. Victoria rubbed her eyes and gazed around. She was stood, wearing tight purple and yellow cycling gear with her back against a very large elm tree, looking from the towpath across the Leeds and Liverpool canal towards the fields. Everywhere was deathly quiet, not even a discernible faint hum of traffic. The sky was beautiful, blue and cloudless, the prelude to a hot summer. An unfamiliar but expensive graphene-fibre racing bicycle was propped against a bench.

One thing was absolutely and totally crystal clear; her memory of the last seven days. She took in large gulps of breath to orientate herself back to a semblance of reality, whatever reality could ever be again. Was she back in the normal world and the time she knew, so loved and desperately missed? She fished around inside her zipped pocket to find a wallet full of credit cards and her new Blackberry Frakis smartphone, and punched her arm into the air with a yell but then realised she needed to pull the flip lid open and check the date. She couldn't afford to take anything for granted after that experience, burned into her brain.

Behind her, a screeching of brakes and a shout made her turn violently, still scared witless with whatever massive implosion had just taken place. The subconscious memory of the former Ahrendolie refinery blowing up, virulent from all those years back, had never gone away.

"Check the date, it's rather interesting," the figure uttered, panting hard, pulling off a safety hat, dark glasses and shaking out her orange curls. "For an oldie you look pretty good in that figure-hugging lycra. Your racer looks even more expensive than mine. Unauthorised large dents on the credit card seem to have become the order of the day."

"Jesus Christ, Abby? Oh, my goodness, thank the Lord above, you're safe—we're both safe." Victoria rushed forward to hug her friend hard.

"Steady on, let me put my bike down, you'd better watch the expletives, you sound a bit 1840ish," Abby replied, laughing as they hugged each other hard, Victoria uncharacteristically emotional as tears ran down her cheeks. "No kissing on the lips … I haven't turned turtle yet, despite the rollercoaster love lives of the last week."

Victoria stepped back. The relief could not have been more palpable in her eyes. "Where have these bicycles come from? Although I do like the matching apparel, perhaps this is Mauveine's hint that both of us are out of condition."

Abby grinned. "Look at the date first."

Victoria flipped open the lip, pressed the screen page and peered at the date and time at the bottom, thinking hard as her brain was still befuddled with the time frame she had departed from. "Crikey … this is two days before we boarded the Queen Lusitania, so we haven't actually gone on the ship journey yet. So what does that mean?"

She fiddled with the settings, spotting that all connections were off and pressed the wireless tab back on. Instantly, the 5G mobile signal triggered a slew of emails and text messages, as if she had been on a plane and switched her phone back on.

"I'm used to this, remember," Abby said as Victoria looked quickly at the messages. "I've come back twice before but you have no idea what awaits when you open your eyes. But these things we're seeing are for a reason, because assuming the rupture in the space-time has been healed, then the chances are that the distorted and missing history between the late eighteen hundreds and 1860 is back to where it should be. Well something must have worked or we wouldn't be here. I'd be marrying John Ruskin. How is your memory?"

Victoria looked up. "Frightening and stunningly accurate. I remember absolutely everything. Listen, before we talk about that, I've had a text from Kessler, apologising for the sudden cancellation of the Queen Lusitania launch. They had a serious engine failure testing it up the River Mersey ... so everyone will be refunded and a fifty percent discount if they rebook for a month's time. So we haven't gone yet to the US. I want to go by plane now. But where are Maddie and Belle?"

Abby pulled out her iPhone. "I've had a text from Maddie."

"Show me. Where are they? Are they both safe?"

"Yes, yes, no panic. Maddie phoned me. I think they 'landed' marginally before us. They found themselves together on a train heading for Southport. Then Maddie got a call from Judy. They're on their way to meet her, Jarvis and all the children apparently, for a day treat and fish and chips at the amusement park. It's Saturday of course. I really can't get used to Judy being Mrs Cockle. They'll see us tonight, the whole tribe are returning for dinner at Orsbrick Hall and Claire is busy organising everything. Maddie and Belle are both fine, happy to be out of those bell dresses and back into jeans and looking forward to a day of silly trash and fun with the kids. But like us they remain totally and wondrously crystal clear. The whole experience has been so momentous we'll need some quiet time together shortly, once we've all digested things. But Maddie said that she and Belle were really sad and sorry to have left the remarkable and funny Ada behind ... but that's non McKenzie family history, unfortunately."

"Yes ... I agree. I'm not sorry though to see the back of Morag. Lady McKenzie had a lot more issues than I realised."

"But gosh, Vicky, you went ape-bonkers then. I've never seen you so mad. That was the most bizarre drinks party I could ever imagine, Morag was totally fucked up. But, Mauveine was right in one sense. What you said in anger triggered a reverse rupture, quite possibly we could still have been there."

"And in deep shit. Despite all of Ada's stellar praises, the thought of Belle tramping her way through the mud fields of the Crimean war to become medically recognised isn't a big turn on, is it. But what about Mauveine and Isi? I expect we'll bump into them back at Orsbrick Hall."

"Yes, I assume so but it seems strange them reverting back to being ghosts, like a major come-down almost. I know that sounds silly."

"Mmm ... I can see what you mean, but as you said, that's the history of the space-time family pathway. All we've done is straighten out a potentially fatal kink. Where are we? I don't recognise this part of the canal. We're nowhere near Orsbrick Hall, that's for sure. This is very rural and there are mountains behind us." Victoria screwed her eyes up.

"We're beyond Parbold," Abby replied, waving up the towpath. A few more miles on and we'd come to Appley Bridge."

"How strange. I don't know of any connection between here and Orsbrick. Oh gosh, I almost forgot. Julian, Lynton and the boys? What on earth has happened to them? I'm just going to look through this mass of texts and emails."

"I've got nothing from either ... although the way they were carrying on, it's not surprising they feature low down the list. You know, I would have liked to have married Ruskin."

Victoria looked up. "No you wouldn't and we're in 2026 again."

Abby sighed. "I suppose so, but a girl can dream ..."

"Hey, Julian has sent me a WhatsApp message. Hang on, the bloody app is updating first ... fuck ... okay. Oh my God. I'll read it out."

*Hi both - if you've heard no need to be alarmed. Lynton and I just returned on time to help Ned and Zac put out a fire in the barn. Jeb and Kai raised the alarm. Almost a catastrophe but Sabrina connected the fire-hose and went inside and doused the flames as we got the horses out. Cause unknown. Some damage to the back wall and the hay needs replacing but very lucky. Found Ned in bed with Nancy, and Zac and Dottie naked in the pool. All four are very sheepish. Lynton just laughed but can you have a word with them? See you later. Enjoy the cycling. Lots of love XX*

Abby pondered quietly as Victoria looked through more messages still coming in. "Mmm ... they're back and the fire was put out," she replied. "Or maybe they never even left and what we thought were Julian, Lynton, Ned and Zac were some sort of contrived manifests to counterbalance our presence and provide foils to lubricate the passage of events. Remember, they never recognised us."

"That sounds very deep Abby. Note my reformed character though these days. I didn't say psychic mumbo-jumbo? Well I can't exactly now can I. But you may be right; actually I hope you are right. We'd better contact Maddie and Belle and tell them. I'll phone them shortly. Hey Julian has sent a postscript." *Forgot to mention, I have to do some surgery on Sabrina, her right hand melted and the microchips are damaged. A replacement is on its way. She says she had an out-of-body experience which didn't compute saying she saw a strange man with a moustache and unrecognisable clothes waving matches who walked through the wall. I think some of her electronic brain may have frazzled too! Love you xx*

"Gosh ... Sabrina, I forgot about her," Abby whispered. "Not so out of body, methinks. She did see Isi but whatever's transpired it never happened so they definitely won't remember anything. Jeb and Kai, when I visited the Cinderblack cottages they definitely knew me, Julian couldn't work out why they were so friendly. Not everything is perfectly transformative, obviously."

"Or linear either. Anyway, seeing that we've suddenly acquired these super-bikes why don't we cycle back to Parbold and have a pub lunch on me in the Windmill and work out what we should do next. I hope they've improved the privies since I was last in there and that Lynton doesn't turn up again on a horse!"

"Not much chance of that these days," Abby replied grudgingly, replacing her helmet. "Although the exercise might get some of that wine-belly off him."

They shot off down the towpath with Victoria in the lead and Abby panting to keep up.

*

The relief was palpable once they were back at Orsbrick Hall. It was incredibly good to all be home again. Having chatted together on group-Skype before arriving, they agreed to act as normal as possible, which wouldn't be that difficult because the

427

previous timelines up to the fire would be the same. Victoria and Abby had worked out an ingenious plan to explain the bicycles, if necessary, once they realised the machines were Dutch made, having decided that the psychic linkage was some subconscious inversion for both, back to their early shared flat years in Rotterdam, when they cycled everywhere together. They were looking forward to dinner and genuine normality again, eager to quietly contrast Claire's four-course special with that prepared by Agnes and Mrs Williams. In the Windmill, Victoria had already rebooked them all onto flights to Boston after Maddie had explained the delay to her US friend, Janine, at Harvard. Picking up again with their US trip and where they were supposed to be was still going to be fun.

Walking up the drive together to the house, the four immediately saw the charred remains of the back of the barn. The smell of burning and a faint persistence of smoke permeated the air, but the horses with fresh hay were already safely re-housed in the other outbuilding, albeit a little more cramped.

A deep barking made them turn as Jeb and Kai bolted from their kennels at the side and rushed towards them happily, the welcome being noticeably effusive, both wanting to be fussed, exactly as if they had been separated. Abby was correct. Fortunately they couldn't speak but the two looked perfectly fine.

Approaching the front door, it was immediately flung open and Julian strode out, holding a large piece of wood to which reins were attached that he was shaping in his workshop.

"You lot back already? My God, the way those dogs fuss, you'd think you'd all been gone a month," he boomed, with a smile. "Missed all the fun earlier, but we got it under control. Lynton and I are just going into town to get some more wood cladding from Perkins, and tomorrow we and the boys will replace the back wall whilst the weather's good. The quicker we bring the horses back into their normal stable the better. Lynton?" he shouted back. "Where are you?"

Lynton finally appeared, moving in a semi-trot and precariously holding a large flagon of beer which he had almost consumed. His shirt was hanging out of his tight trousers, accentuating the wine-belly even more than usual as Abby and Victoria stared at it and burst out laughing.

"What's so funny?" he uttered, grinning. "Okay, Abby, I get it, but I promise, tomorrow I'm going to buy a bike like yours then race you along the canal and get fit again."

"Some hope, I think your energy level will need to rise somewhat first," Abby replied, feeling very odd seeing Lynton again and acting normal, but already liking the familiar feeling coming back. She did still love him after all … perhaps the spicing up effect of a paranormal affair with John Ruskin could bring some renewed dividends to their relationship.

Julian had sidled up to Victoria. "Mmm … I like your new sexy cycling gear. You're just as slim and sylph-like as when we first met, when we did up this place. Remember the boiler incident? Time I replaced the old one, don't you think?"

"Yes, I remember the boiler incident, as do a thousand others including a few ghostly voyeurs … not in front of the children please," she replied, giggling. Julian still looked as desirable as ever and she had soon lost interest in Faraday, although it was rather good for the ethereal moment. A historic style spice-up, which had done no harm, was already forcing her to think about what she should be doing with her life and not be working seven days a week making dyes.

Julian continued. "Actually, it's my turn for announcements tonight, over dinner. I want you and me to spend more time together. I hope though you're going to read the riot act to Ned and Zac, I didn't know where to look."

"Mmm ... interesting darling and yes, I have thought about them," Victoria replied coyly. "It's time you and I accepted that those boys are pretty well grown men now and if they want to sleep with their girlfriends in their own bedrooms and the four of them are responsible, as I believe they are, that is entirely up to them. You and I don't need to be judgemental in 2026."

"I don't know ... but well what if in fairness, like the girls here also wanted to ... you know?

Maddie screwed up her face. "Dad, it's really time you came out of the nineteenth century. You don't have to live out of your novels. Anyway," she whispered coquettishly. "Belle and I are not gross in your face like Ned and Zac. *We* are refined and genteel upper class ladies, who conduct their affairs with discretion and sophistication ... in other words you'll never know!"

Abby and Belle snorted with laugher as Victoria and Lynton followed suit, all highly amused to see Julian's puzzled face. Job nicely done. They could finally get on with their lives. Normality reigned already.

Victoria, Abby and the girls began to walk in, seeing the welcoming faces of Claire and Danielle, alongside Sabrina minus hand at the front door and immediately smelt a delicious waft of roast beef percolating through. Julian suddenly turned and shouted back.

"Oh, before I forget, take a look at today's parish magazine. I've left it on the table. They've finally repaired the nave roof on the church with that new polymer you recommended which looks and feels exactly like lead. The photos would fool the best inspector in English Heritage. They are very pleased on the Parish Council and you get a special mention of thanks. And at long last the church authorities have found a replacement for poor old Welly. Gosh it's taken long enough, so unsatisfactory with all those temp vicars."

"Why would you care, you never go in there," Victoria replied, jauntily.

"They start properly next week, The Reverend Thomas Langton and Mrs Alice Langton, the regulars will be pleased. See you later."

Victoria continued to stare, as her mouth dropped. Julian and Lynton jumped into the pickup truck and shot off up the drive. Maddie and Belle were speechless.

"Shit … hell and damnation as Morag would have said," Abby cried. "We can't possibly be hearing what we have just been hearing? Surely to God, I don't believe it. It must be a mistake. A psychic joke thrown in to amuse us, if there is such a thing."

"Mum, you said it on the phone earlier. Not everything transfers linearly," Maddie said. "But if it is Mauveine and Isi we are going to need a very good storyline between us all … and what will they look like?"

"Like us but in reverse for them," Belle suggested. "I propose tomorrow morning we meet in the library and have an archive and shelf inspection to see what's changed, if anything, and then we head on our bikes over to the rectory in the afternoon. We're all intelligent women of the world, Ada said. Got to get practical, this may be the new normal."

"All I can think is … Lord have mercy on our tortured souls," Victoria uttered with a long sigh. "Mauveine did say Isi fancied a career as a vicar. Well at least we can indulge in a relaxing dinner and tease Ned and Zac again. Judy should be here soon with the tribe as well as Dottie and Nancy, a full house, but … it's nice isn't it? Christ, whatever you do, nobody laugh at Sabrina."

They giggled and linked arms, hollering nonsense to Claire, with Jeb and Kai yapping playfully beside them.

*

Shelf by shelf was scoured forensically, Maddie and Abby concentrating on the books and Belle and Victoria the papers and diaries, including the section of old local newspapers starting at 1835. Breakfast had been hurried, with poached eggs and kippers, Belle still nibbling a piece of toast. In the distance they could hear hammering and banging and a circular saw whining intermittently. Julian, Lynton and the boys were already working inside the barn, also keen to get on as Ned and Zac were playing in a snooker match in the afternoon. It was much quieter once Judy decided not to stay overnight and she, husband Jarvis and the seven children departed home in their new mini-bus. The eighth and ninth were also announced at dinner, with twins due next Christmas. Judy was hugely delighted and Abby grinned inanely. She and Lynton had no idea until then. This almost overshadowed Julian's announcement to quit writing. He had purchased an option to buy a large adjacent farm, cottages and land which would triple the size of the Orsbrick estate, taking it right down to the border with the town with the intention of building low cost housing and workshops, providing opportunities for rural craft artisan employment and to start proper arable farming again. He said he had a new personal mission to become an active twenty-first century version of the former nineteenth century gentleman squire of Orsbrick, and hoped Victoria might like to join him and delegate more of her dye work in the factory to the new graduates she was employing. Lynton was coming alongside too, having announced he had had his fill of buying

432

endless art and wanted to move on to something nearer the earth and get back on a horse which set Abby off with roars of laughter again.

Copies of engineering and science books were turning up from the missing period of time, together with papers and letters of Malcolm McKenzie, factory invoices for railway manufacture and inventories of machined parts for steam engines, much of the work having been subcontracted in Manchester to a Willet & Sons Ltd.

Morag's original papers on dye work were also found, more than Victoria had seen, patently not having been privy to much of Morag's original chemistry researches. Nothing was found on the electrical practical investigations. True to expectation that must have been destroyed as Morag implied.

The huge archival void, missing up to 1841, was being filled and explained, with the general picture they had surmised and worked out over the week. But what happened after 1841? They continued quietly going through all they could, to discern what was new or uncatalogued previously. Nothing was said exactly, it didn't need to be. But they all knew what they were looking for. What happened to Morag's baby? And who did he or she become? Was that event linked to Mauveine and Isi perhaps displaced from their allotted time in the McKenzie family history? They could only really get to the bottom of that conundrum when they went to the rectory later. It could still feasibly be, as Abby put it succinctly, all a psychic hoax.

Perched on a high ladder, Belle was examining one of the furthermost shelves and became suspicious of the slightly irregular layout of the books, a row of novels of Charles Dickens, published in Mauveine's time. She pulled a few out and spotted some old, tatty newspapers shoved at the back, hidden for many, many decades, if not from when they were dated. Glancing at the title, Belle saw she had an old, yellowed copy of the then weekly Orsbrick and Burscough Gazette, a very early version with a difficult to read typeface on cheap paper. Taking care, she turned the first few pages then caught the date, as the paper had been folded away from the cover, and read the inside leader article.

Holding it carefully, Belle steadied herself back and trod carefully down the ladder. "I think you'd all better come and see this; I'll read it to you."

Victoria brought four chairs around the small table. They sat, sipping Agnes style lemonade, intrigued, as Belle carefully opened the paper and started to read out:

*Orsbrick and Burscough Gazette*

*Date: January 8th 1842*

SHOCK DEATH ANNOUNCED

*It is with deep felt sorrow that we report the sudden passing, from complications of childbirth, of the respected Lady Morag McKenzie, age 26, of Orsbrick Hall, yesterday at 10.00am. Sadly the baby girl was stillborn and has not been named. A private family burial has been requested to take place at an unnamed London cemetery but a memorial service at St John the Baptist Church will be held on the morning of Sunday the 21st January when all will be welcome. Donations may be offered towards the society for typhoid and cholera relief. The McKenzie family wish for privacy in their deepest grief and sorrow but it is understood that thirteen year old James Callum McKenzie, eldest son of the late Sir Malcolm and Lady Morag McKenzie will immediately inherit the vast wealth and land title of the Orsbrick estate. He has made a short statement to confirm that his priority will be to fully maintain and expand the estate commitment of jobs and security to all tenants and workers and continue the social and economic support of the town. He also pledges to further the scientific work which his mother had started.*

The reaction was an induced and guilty shock. Somehow they had all expected a happier ending for Morag, each staring rigidly into their glass.

Victoria broke the silence. "I know it's illogical and would have had no bearing on what happened, but I feel really bad letting rip in the way I did."

Nobody responded for half a minute then Abby piped up. "One has to look at it this way. The incidence of death in those times from childbirth was sadly very high, with few standards of medical hygiene as we know it. And for any birthing complication occurring, they had neither the knowledge nor the expertise to deal with it … many women bled to death. And, Vikki, most importantly, if you hadn't said what you did we wouldn't be sat here now."

Victoria nodded and breathed in and out hard. "Yes you're right. What else is in that paper Maddie?"

Both had glanced at the other newspaper, which Maddie took and looked through. "Gosh, there was more … listen."

*Orsbrick and Burscough Gazette*

*Date: January 29th 1842*

*LOCAL DOCTOR FOUND DEAD*

*On the morning of the 25th January, following reports by neighbours of a strong leakage of coal gas, Sergeant Henry Hargreaves and two constables broke into the surgery of Doctor Emmanuel Kirkby to find him dead in the kitchen. A piece of tubing had been used to connect the gas supply into the range oven where he had crawled in and closed the door, leaving the gas running. He asphyxiated from the toxic odour. The premises have since been made safe and neighbours returned to their homes. A suicide note was found in which Dr Kirkby declared he* had nothing to live for, following the death two weeks ago of *Lady McKenzie and blaming himself for her death. It has now been revealed that Dr Kirkby was present at the delivery and that he and Lady McKenzie had become secretly engaged the previous Christmas Day. Speculation is that he was the father of the child.*

*The body has now been returned to the family home of the Duke of Kirkby, where a private chapel funeral and burial will take place tomorrow. In the short time he had been resident at the practice, Dr Kirkby had become a very popular and respected figure with local townspeople, being diligent and caring in his treatment of maladies. The Town Council have expressed their shock and sorrow and a special memorial service will be held at St John the Baptist Church at 11.00am on the evening of February 1st.*

"Goodness me," Abby said softly. "How very, very tragic. James must have been thrown completely in at the deep end. What we do know is between Morag's death and by the time he became twenty-one, he successfully completed studies at Cambridge University, married his wife Susannah and extramaritally conceived Mauveine as well as rapidly becoming an acknowledged expert in the growing industry of textile dyes. He also had built a factory producing new coal tar products. His philanthropic work too was already embedded deeply into the local community. He grew up and matured with phenomenal speed. Morag, and I'm sure his father, would have been very proud of him … It was what she always wanted."

Victoria sighed loudly. "Yes, you're right. I think we've done enough for today, but I do wonder what became of Ellen. There's nothing in these records and she's not buried in the family graves."

"I know the answer to that, I think." Maddie replied, pulling a book out of the pile behind her. "When I was rooting amongst the personal belongings of Great-Uncle William, ages ago, I found this tatty 1925 Yearly Almanac. Inside, a page was bookmarked on a chapter of deceased artists and an Ellen Newcomen was ringed. I thought no more of it, assuming she was someone linked to his active social network of painters and musicians at the time. Having perused countless books on engineering and steam engines, when Belle and I started to organise Morag's library, I learned a huge amount and something in my head linked the two names last night. A Thomas Newcomen, in 1712, invented the first atmospheric steam engine used to pump water out of coal mines, a major catalyst of the industrial revolution. Eventually they evolved and improved, mainly by James Watt, over the next hundred years into the locomotive engines designed by Stephenson and also Morag's husband, Malcolm McKenzie. These artisan inventor families continued their work, driven by patent acquisitions, from generation to generation, often as rivals and but equally as collaborators. Here Abby, you read it."

Abby grabbed the Almanac and read the article out at speed. "Gosh, this is quite amazing. Ellen Newcomen, nee McKenzie, born in 1832 at Orsbrick Hall in Lancashire, married Joseph Newcomen in 1850 and after her husband died became a student in Paris in the mid 1860s with Camille Corot to become a landscape painter. Influenced by Manet, she went on in later years to perfect her own individualistic approach to figure painting, using techniques of cubism she learned directly from Picasso. She had no children and died in obscurity in Sarajevo, having migrated from France to the Kingdom of Serbs, Croats and Slovenes in 1918."

Victoria smiled. "She led an interesting and richly artistic life, right to the end of her ninety-three years, so you did make a lasting art impression after all, Abby."

Abby laughed. "Who would have guessed? But why did Eveline never mention her?"

"I guess Aunt Eveline never knew," Victoria replied. But obviously Uncle William had some connection. Ellen appears to have been quite reclusive by then, perhaps he had even been in touch when she was in her final years in Sarajevo … Some of our McKenzie history will forever remain cloaked in secrecy, and that's how it should be I think."

"Talking about secrets? What are we going to say when we arrive at the rectory after lunch?" Belle asked.

Victoria grimaced. "Heaven knows. Just when you thought it was all over it isn't. To be honest I could do with a stiff drink, even though it is only midday. Join me in the drawing room Abby?"

"Yes, why not," Abby replied, her face lighting up.

Maddie stood up and stretched hard. "I'm going to get a shower and change, I feel worn out."

"Me too," Belle said. "We'll see you both at lunch. Wonder how the building fraternity are doing? That electric saw has been going all morning. I don't think Ned has worked so hard in his entire life."

Victoria groaned. "I can sense the next obsession is already working up. I still can't quite get my head around Mr Julian Endersby-Finnis, gentleman squire of Orsbrick, although I can quite see him strutting around. Tripling the size of the estate is interesting though, a good investment while we can afford it. The landholding will become larger even than it was in 1841. Hey, let's go, I've really had enough."

Sat quietly in the drawing room, after long and welcoming warm showers, Victoria and Abby swirled the old French brandy, using the exact same blue balloon glasses that Morag had served them with last time.

"These heirlooms have lasted well. How do you feel Abby, I mean like psychically, thinking of the jaunt out later to the church?"

"Absolutely fine, totally normal as I believe is Maddie. That is what is so odd, I would have thought quite the opposite. No sign of Mauveine or Isi either since we arrived back. I don't know what to think, but we managed to play it well in 1841, so if necessary we'll have to try and do it again … But what do we tell the males in the vicinity who know, see or speak no evil?"

Victoria laughed nonchalantly. "I'm actually beginning not to care. Bloody hell, who at this time of the day is banging on the door like that? What a racket. I'd better see who it is." She was interrupted as a mini-skirted Sabrina waltzed into the room, sporting a silvery metal hand.

"Temporary fix until the new one arrives. I just made it in Julian's workshop, no problem, very easy machining. Victoria, enjoy your drink. I shall go and find out the cause of the disturbance."

The loud banging continued until they heard the door open, then all went quiet, bar a series of continuous muffled voices, with Sabrina questioning the person knocking. A second silence ensued.

Abby looked across at Victoria. "You know, something like this happened once before when you were in hospital, but at the back door. That was when Ned got abducted by those crazy priory monks and then Lynton went and came back as white as a sheet, followed in by Mauveine and Isi."

"Really? I missed all the excitement then didn't I. Sabrina, who is it?"

Sabrina stood there, her forehead furrowed, as the electronic brain chips struggled to create her normal clear and rational response. "I am sorry Victoria but this experience has no programming parameters in my circuitry which I can draw upon."

"You mean you don't know?" Victoria replied bemused.

"A very strange woman is standing at the door dressed in the most peculiar clothing, agitated and begging to be let in because she is frightened and doesn't understand where she is. I ordered her to wait or there would be consequences, I am trained in six martial arts," Sabrina growled, her metal hand rotating aggressively at a fast speed.

Abby stood up, a sinking feeling churning in her stomach. "Is it Mauveine? Did she say her name?"

"Oh yes … ah … sorry, no, I forgot to ask when my visionary receptors struggled with the image recognition."

Victoria shot up from her seat. "Come on Abby, I don't have a very good feeling about this."

"No me neither."

They walked quickly to the door with Sabrina right behind and stopped dead, to be met by a tall, pretty woman, perhaps in her early twenties, with long, black hair parted in the middle and braided into a pony tail of tight ringlets, swept around her left cheek and held together by small pink ribbons. She was wearing a long and yellow billowed out full skirt to the floor, looking like some type of evening dress but made of muslin with a crossed front corsage and gathered tightly at the waist, the corsage decorated with deep flounces. The unusual short sleeves consisted of five puffs of linen, separated by grey ribbons.

Abby's fashion brain, taking in the intricate and unusual design, was back in high speed mode, noting everything. They both realised she wore Victorian clothing but the style and fabrication was more sophisticated than what they had just experienced in 1841.

The woman was petrified, her face white as she stared open mouthed, first at Victoria and then at Abby looking hard at their skinny jeans and tight tee-shirts. Maddie and Belle had also appeared, standing quietly at the back.

"Help me, please. Who are you? I don't know where I am or what I'm doing here. Everything around me is so strange and peculiar. Am I in Hell? Please don't tell me I'm in Hell. Oh Lord above, save and absolve me from this ghastly torment."

Her clear and rich voice had an unexpected strong Irish lilt to the accent, tinged with the familiar local south Lancashire, a combination none had heard before. She looked up as a jet fighter plane on a training rendezvous from the local air force base suddenly shot across the sky, the thunderous sound filling the air, and screamed loudly, covering her face with her hands.

Victoria rushed forward and put her arms around the violently shaking woman. "No, I can assure you you're not in Hell, definitely not. Don't worry, whatever it is you're running from you're safe now. Come in and sit down."

Abby and the others parted to allow Victoria to take the woman by the arm and gently lead her through the hall towards the drawing room. She gazed, wide-eyed and incredulous at the furniture and the entire ambience, touching the wall as she walked. In a moment she was seated in one of the armchairs, still shaking, but stared hesitatingly again all around. Total incomprehension spread across her face as she watched the muted international tennis on the wall television screen, ducking her head backwards and forwards as the balls were served.

Maddie immediately switched it off. "Mum, she's familiar with this room ... but in another period," she whispered. "You can see it in her face. Take care with what you say."

Abby half-filled a glass with brandy and handed it to her. "Just take a few sips and a deep breath. You'll be fine now. Tell us. What do you remember last?"

The woman gulped down the brandy and smiled for the first time, wiping her face with a silk handkerchief. "I had not long stepped out of my carriage. It was a beautiful, sunny morning and I was enjoying standing by the canal staring at the barges, awaiting my grandfather, when I felt dizzy and could feel myself fainting. I sat down on the grass and must have passed out ... When I opened my eyes, everything had changed into a strange and unknown kaleidoscope, like the novel Alice in Wonderland I am reading. I was frightened and panicked and ran to your door. I can see this is Orsbrick Hall but not my Orsbrick Hall, or what should be mine." She handed the empty glass, wide-eyed, to Sabrina, whose metal fingers creaked loudly grasping the stem as she walked off muttering she had to oil them straight away.

"Who is she?" the woman gasped, turning again to Victoria, who at least seemed to her to be the sanest person in charge of this crazy-house.

"Err ... a robot," Victoria answered, having decided that the explanation of least resistance seemed the most sensible.

"Robot? Do you mean rabbit? Please. Who are you and what do you want?"

Victoria glanced at Abby before returning to the woman. "Before I answer that, what date is it?"

442

"The twentieth day of April, 1865 of course. It was my grandmother's birthday. Why?"

Abby let out an audible sigh as Victoria smiled and continued. "And your name is?"

"Fenella."

"Oh my God, but which one?" Abby blurted out before realising. She caught a sideways expression of deep alarm from Victoria, shaking her head. Neither could scarcely believe what they had heard.

Maddie decided to cut in and try and make immediate sense. Something unexpected had obviously occurred when the space-time rupture sealed up. "Fenella," she asked softly. "My name is Madeleine. Now, would you like to tell us your surname please?"

Fenella looked up, her eyes running over Maddie from top to bottom and gently nodded her head a couple of times. "Madeleine ... what a lovely name, the same as my sister ..."

"Hi everyone, we've finished at long last. Shall we all go down to the George for lunch and celebrate? The others have already gone. Kebabs are on me."

A familiar voice rang out from the hall as Julian strode in unaware, holding a bottle of beer. He stopped dead in his tracks at the sight of the oddly dressed stranger sat there demurely. "My word. Who is this? Are you a friend of Abby's? On your way to a fancy dress party, I assume. I must say, your Victorian outfit is very good, the crinoline is accurately authentic." He continued wiping his glasses aimlessly and looking for a glass in the drinks cabinet.

Fenella stared at him, eyeing his clothes and mannerism, confused and disorientated again. "Reverend?" she whispered despairingly.

"Pardon?" he replied, shoving his glasses back on and squinting back hard at her.

Meeting his eyes with her ferocious and determined stare, Victoria spoke softly. "Julian, will you take your beer and leave us please. We'll see you all down at the George later."

He glanced at the woman then back again at Victoria whose intention could not have been plainer. "Sure thing darling, we'll keep the best seats for you. Bye everyone," he replied, sidling out quickly before laughing quietly to himself having met another of Abby's weird, arty associates, as usual with issues.

Victoria returned to the interrogation. "I'm so sorry Fenella but, well that was my husband. Now where were we? Yes, so are you Fenella McKenzie?"

The woman's mouth dropped as she jerked back her head, puzzled. "Husband? No, no, not McKenzie, Kirkby. I'm Lady Fenella Kirkby."

A pin dropping would have sounded like a bomb going off, although to Abby a bomb had just mightily exploded. "This is not possible," she muttered, shaking her head. "It just cannot be possible whatsoever …"

"I think by now, Abby, we can discount the notion of anything being impossible, don't you?" Victoria replied, in a determined whisper, concerned that her best friend was becoming distinctly overwhelmed.

Belle interrupted. She was twiddling with her iPhone, having caught the renewed and fascinated gaze again of Fenella who continued to remain wholly mystified with her Alice in Wonderland environment. "I suggest we change our arrangements for this afternoon to the evening. I've just had a tweet from a certain @missdyehead?"

Victoria nodded. Whatever was about to unfold, she had to take charge, thinking nostalgically way back to 1990 when the rumbustious Sergeant George Hargreaves rescued her that late evening, a naive fifteen year old on the towpath, from the purple pig floating in the Leeds and Liverpool canal. She would be resolute. Plain speaking from now on was the most logical, rational and scientific way to proceed.

"Fenella, I'm Victoria McKenzie. You are indeed sat in Orsbrick Hall … But not, I'm afraid in 1865, but on the date of the twentieth of April, 2026. Welcome to the family."

**To be continued in Book Four.**

# About the Author

Roy Baldwin was born in South Lancashire and has lived and worked around the UK in various mathematical and scientific guises as an educationalist, civil servant and management consultant. Morag is his eighth novel and the third book in the Mauveine Series, a collection of historic fantasy stories based around the former aristocratic family of Victoria McKenzie, a modern day polymer scientist. His last novel, Rhapsody of Moon, is the latest book in the Rhapsody Series, which follows the adventures and life challenges of nuclear scientist and company CEO, Professor Lauren Hind.

He is a full time writer and book designer and regularly commentates on books and indie publishing through twitter. In between writing and digital publishing, Roy tries to enjoy the fabulous beauty of the Norfolk countryside and seashore where he now lives. All Roy Baldwin's novels can be bought in both eBook and print versions from online bookstores worldwide.

Further information can be obtained from the author's writer site:

http://www.creativepubtalk.com

Here, you can subscribe to an email newsletter keeping you in touch with further writer releases and developments.

If you have enjoyed this book, please support the author by providing a personal review on Amazon, Goodreads, Twitter or any other favourite online book site or social media.

Author Twitter: http://www.twitter.com/creativepubtalk

Also from Roy Baldwin:

Mauveine
Prism of Purpurine
Rhapsody of Restraint
Rhapsody of Power
Rhapsody of Fate
Rhapsody of Succession
Rhapsody of Moon

# Have you read Mauveine and Prism of Purpurine?

MAUVEINE: Aged sixteen, wayward Victoria McKenzie flees desperate and confused from home in West Lancashire to a commune in Amsterdam and never speaks to her parents again. Now aged thirty five, single and fancy free, she is settled as a senior polymer chemist working in the ailing Ahrendolie refinery in Rotterdam. Following a serious and unsettling plant incident, she is forced into a long recovery break and plans to take off on holiday with Abby, her best friend and designer flatmate, always up for a new challenge. But Victoria is startled to suddenly learn of an unusual inheritance, Orsbrick Hall, taking her mind back to childhood events and places alongside the Leeds and Liverpool canal she never hoped to experience again. Intrigued by her news, she is summoned to a strange meeting with a Liverpool solicitor and bumps into the quaint Julian, an introverted steampunk writer, all grey hair and flying scarves. But what is it about the creepy Orsbrick Hall that nobody wants to talk about? Why does her past now unravel into an unexpected explosion of crazy scientific revelations and discoveries a hundred and fifty years before, which she would never have believed possible or credible? With Abby and Julian she must track down the source of past family secrecies and find out who the terrifying woman in the purple shawl really is. But will this unleash evil and powerful forces hell bent on her eternal destruction and damnation? And is Julian all he makes out to be?

### An excerpt from Mauveine:

... She knocked on the pale green door and Victoria heard a firm but certainly elderly voice, in a very posh accent, reply. "Do please come in."

Mrs Grable held the door wide and Victoria walked into a large and very high ceilinged room, papered with a striped design she had never seen anywhere before and the walls finished off with a marbled Georgian coving. All around the walls were adorned with wonderful hanging pieces of fabrics, again like nothing she had seen, intricately designed and colourful, where she could make out themes of an outdoor nature, trees, water lilies, meadow flowers, orchids. She immediately thought of Abby, wondering why she was taking so long.

A high rear window, from floor to ceiling, which could be opened out, and letting in lots of daylight, especially noticeable with the sun shining in brightly, took her gaze. Standing in front, staring motionless at the view and holding onto two sticks stood a small elderly lady in a mauve cardigan and chocolate brown skirt, her hair white but thick. She turned around slowly, her soft complexion, highlighted with a bright red lipstick and smiled. "Victoria, how wonderful to see you at last."

But Victoria, ready to move forward and kiss her cheek, stopped dead, frozen in her tracks as she looked into the beneficent face and her face dropped. The likeness was so uncanny, she couldn't believe it, it was like looking at herself in the mirror, admittedly a much older face, but Eveline had remarkably few lines, great skin and her thick white hair, cut in a fashionable bob, just a little shorter than her own blonde style. But the eyes and the intense look were identical.

Eveline looked quite amused and didn't seem in the least bit surprised. "Well, my dear, I must admit you have inherited the family likeness and are quite beautiful"

Victoria stared perplexed, who was this woman …?

**PRISM OF PURPURINE:** Scientist Victoria McKenzie and her best friend, fine artist Abby, are looking forward to organising their double wedding and leading new lives in West Lancashire now that the restless spirit of Mauveine is finally content. But a clearing out of historic family junk triggers unexpected events, alerting Abby to question whether all in Orsbrick Hall has returned to the state of normality assumed. A strange artifact of pagan origin is discovered, exhibiting unusual characteristics which Victoria can't scientifically explain, but her mind is forced to focus on more pressing and personal matters. Fifteen years on and Victoria's life has evolved. Her dye business is flourishing, Abby runs her international art gallery and both families are nicely settled. However sixteen year old twins Maddie and Bel and their twin brothers Ned and Zac, out on a canal cycling trip, find a key to a local murder which sets off a train of peculiar happenings and confessions. Have the horrific, seventeenth century demons, over whom Mauveine had no influence, gone away or are they back for revenge? Abby quickly realises that the responsibility to confront the McKenzie curse lies with her and now Maddie. But have they the capabilities to overcome the myriad of ghostly, hideous challenges waiting, once the true and disarming nature of their friends and family comes to light?

**An excerpt from Prism of Purpurine:**

…Victoria strode into her school laboratory. The atmosphere almost felt like being back in Ahrendolie again, except in here it was a lot less sophisticated. She peered inside the ancient fume cupboard and noted the materials prepared for her class at nine o' clock, with lab coats on the wall hooks and the apparatus for her ten scholarship students already laid out on the benches. She hoped she wasn't going to get into another argument with Danielle again about pinning her waist-long hair up; she was as feisty as Abby.

Christine was in her prep room, early as usual pottering about. She worked extraordinarily long hours, sheer unblemished dedication over many years to the job.

"Hi Victoria, come in here and take a look at this. Your father was quite obsessive about it. He brought the thing out of its box every day and polished it, like a sort of ritual. Warding off the evil spirits no doubt, particularly Dr Edith Marples, who ran the school with an iron rod in those days!"

Victoria stared at the object lying on the bench. Shit, it was a twin of the same weird glass artefact that she and Abby had found in the telescope room. Yet another large glass prism, but a more startling blood red in colour. She touched it, and it felt oddly warm. "Good heavens, I've got a twin of this prism that we found before Christmas, also when we had a clear out. Actually, apart from a slight variation of colour, this one is the same, slightly rough on one edge. I wonder whether they are pieces of the same original. Have you any idea what it is or what it means?"

"None whatsoever. Your father refused to discuss 'crimmy' as he called it, although I did gather the prism was some kind of long-standing family heirloom. Rather than cluttering the place up, you may as well have it, or I'll put the thing in the skip."

"No, no. I'll take it home. Maybe I'll get to the bottom of the puzzle sometime. I reckon there's a third piece too, from the shape."

She put the prism segment carefully back into its blue, velvet-lined, wooden box and placed it into her bag.

"Well if I find that as well, I'll keep it for you. Now, we've just got time. How do you want your demonstration set up at the front? And if that silly girl, Danielle creates again about her lab coat being too unfashionable, I shall personally strangle her, especially as this experiment will be under test conditions."

Victoria laughed. "Don't worry. After my one-to one with her last time, I think she will be quite chastened this morning. I was used to some unruly male graduates in my lab at the refinery. Danielle received the same treatment, works a dream. I can be quite severe when I want."

"Take after your father, Victoria. Jack was the same, never did his pupils any harm. I still miss him … finding that glass thing brought him all back."

"Really?" Victoria said, as she watched Christine go atypically quiet, into a slight dream and a little flushed. She pondered, and pondered again and smiled. There was a lot about her father she simply never knew. Maybe he and Uncle William were not so different after all …